QUEENS
of the
ABYSS

QUEENS
of the
ABYSS

Lost Stories from the
Women of the Weird

edited by
MIKE ASHLEY

This collection first published in 2020 by
The British Library
96 Euston Road
London NW1 2DB

Cataloguing in Publication Data

A catalogue record for this publication is
available from the British Library

ISBN 978 0 7123 5391 5
e-ISBN 978 0 7123 6775 2

Frontispiece illustration by Sandra Gómez

Cover design by Mauricio Villamayor with illustration by Sandra Gómez

Text design and typesetting by Tetragon, London
Printed in England by CPI Group (UK) Ltd, Croydon, CR0 4YY

CONTENTS

INTRODUCTION

We should never underestimate the power of women writers in shaping and popularizing the weird tale. Although the history of the ghost story often emphasizes the role of male writers, from Joseph Sheridan Le Fanu through Lord Bulwer Lytton, Arthur Machen, M. R. James, H. P. Lovecraft and so on to Stephen King and others today, it is all too easily overlooked that the development of the field, helping the weird tale to progress, was as much the territory of women. And that was true from the very start.

When Horace Walpole introduced the gothic novel with *The Castle of Otranto* in 1764 he established a popular vogue for stories, usually with a historical setting, often European, where ancient castles are haunted by apparent (or even genuine) supernatural manifestations, often enacting some family curse or legend. Clara Reeve, the daughter of a Suffolk rector, whilst enjoying the atmosphere of *Otranto*, thought that the effects Walpole had produced were too extreme and therefore less believable. In *The Old English Baron* (1777) she openly criticized him saying that the atmosphere was so heightened that the end result was deflating, leaving her "vexed" and feeling cheated. In her novel she modified the effects and produced a more acceptable if less atmospheric form of the gothic novel.

The author who managed to sustain the atmosphere of Walpole but keep the supernatural at a believable (albeit rationalized) level was Ann Radcliffe. In a succession of novels, peaking with *The Mysteries of Udolpho* (1794), Radcliffe developed an exciting adventure, redolent with atmosphere and hints of the supernatural, but an acceptable conclusion that left the reader wanting more. *Udolpho* is regarded as the pre-eminent gothic novel, complete with a beautiful heroine and a handsome lover. It was one of the most popular novels of its day and made Radcliffe wealthy. Though Jane Austen parodied the novel in *Northanger Abbey* (1817 but completed by 1803), her portrayal of an easily influenced young girl passionately attracted to *Udolpho* almost certainly reflected the reality of many readers of the day.

So it began.

Between them Clara Reeve and Ann Radcliffe had laid down a simple ground rule which helped establish the weird tale. Do not over embellish. Keep it simple. Heighten the atmosphere by all means, but in a subtle and believable way, and thereby the ghost story becomes all the more effective.

It was a ground rule that the Victorian women writers further developed. While Edgar Allan Poe, Joseph Sheridan Le Fanu and Lord Bulwer Lytton, amongst others, were heightening the dramatic atmosphere, at least in their early stories, the women were creating effective and memorable stories. Catherine Crowe, Elizabeth Gaskell, Amelia Edwards, Rhoda Broughton, Margaret Oliphant, Charlotte Riddell, Mary Molesworth—it's a long list which I could easily double, even treble—are just a few of the Victorian women who wrote some of the best ghost stories of the Victorian age.

But rather than concentrate on them, because their stories have frequently been reprinted, and quite rightly so, I wanted to explore other writers, some well known—either for their weird tales or something else—but many less well known, who took the supernatural tale from the late Victorian period into the twentieth century. Amongst the well known names are those whose careers or lifestyles somewhat shocked Victorian society—Mary Braddon, Marie Corelli and Edith Nesbit—which in turn gave their fiction a degree of notoriety. Amongst the less well known are those who dared enter the male stronghold of the pulp magazine and established their own reputation for the modern weird tale— Greye La Spina, G. G. Pendarves, Margaret St Clair and Mary Counselman. And there are others who became highly regarded for their strange tales but are too easily forgotten today—Marie Belloc Lowndes, May Sinclair, Lady Eleanor Smith and the sur-realist Leonora Carrington.

There is another factor common to many of these authors. In addition to their visions of looking into the abyss of horror, most of them also had to rise from the abyss of poverty or other adversity in their childhood or married lives. It is possible to see how they channelled the anguish of their disadvantaged lives into their fiction, making it all the more real. Many of these stories deal with loss or despair.

I have deliberately chosen lesser known stories, even by the better known writers, but all of them show how women writers continued to experiment and develop the weird tale from its gothic beginnings and its thriving Victorian heyday into the twentieth century. These are not simple stories of ghostly manifestations. You will find a psychological element in Marie Lowndes's story, a religious allegory in Marie Corelli's, a historical drama in Marjorie Bowen's, and a risqué phantom love in May Sinclair's.

By pushing the boundaries these queens of the abyss kept the weird tale alive, fresh and invigorated for the new century.

MIKE ASHLEY

A REVELATION

Mary E. Braddon

Mary Elizabeth Braddon (1835–1915) was the bestselling woman novelist of the Victorian period. Like some of her heroines, who can survive everything that life throws at them, she also overrode scandal and prejudice to become a revered and respected grand dame. Mary was raised by her mother, Fanny, after she left Mary's duplicitous father. Her mother became a capable accountant and taught young Mary. But finances were always tight, and when she was twenty-one, Mary became an actress touring the provinces. It was while she was at Beverley in Yorkshire that she began writing, contributing poems to the local newspaper and placing a serial with the local printer which appeared in 1860 as Three Times Dead, or the Secret of the Heath, *soon issued in a book edition as* The Trail of the Serpent. *It was this type of sensational novel, much in the vein of Wilkie Collins, in which Braddon excelled, but she refined it through her next few novels and serials until she perfected her style in* Lady Audley's Secret *(1862). This tale of bigamy and attempted murder became one of the most successful novels of the Victorian era. By this time Mary had met publisher John Maxwell and moved in with him, feigning marriage, even though his wife was still alive and incarcerated in an Irish asylum. Maxwell was a rather incompetent businessman and it was Mary's money that kept him solvent and eventually successful. Maxwell already had five children by his first marriage and Mary bore him six more, one dying in infancy. Motherhood and her exhausting schedule of writing and editing led to Mary having a* breakdown in 1868 but she recovered. She and Maxwell married in 1874 after his wife died.

   Mary's output of novels and stories was huge. Her novels included Aurora Floyd (1863), John Marchmont's Legacy (1863), Joshua Haggard's Daughter (1876) and one of interest to fans of the macabre, Gerard, or the World, the Flesh and the Devil (1891) a reworking of the Faust legend. But although she published several collections of short stories she never assembled a volume solely of weird tales. It was not until Richard Dalby compiled The Cold Embrace (2000) that the majority of her supernatural stories were brought together. The British Library has since published its own volume, The Face in the Glass (2014, reissued in this series in 2019). Since almost all her short fiction was published anonymously, and sometimes pseudonymously, it's entirely possible there are more Braddon tales to discover—perhaps some reprinted as simply by 'Anon'. The following story, first published in 1888, has all the Braddon hallmarks, including bigamy and the occult.

"I S NOT YOUR DETERMINATION OF GOING TO ENGLAND A sudden one?"

"Yes," answered Colonel Desborough. "And I have been so many years in India that perhaps it feels more like my home than my own country will. But a sea voyage will do me good, the doctors say. I have been far from well lately."

"You have looked ill, certainly, and you have seemed very depressed. Is there anything wrong? Excuse the question."

"My dear Breakspear, our friendship justifies a very natural inquiry. Yes; something is wrong, very wrong indeed. Except to the two doctors, I have not mentioned the cause of my bad health and spirits to anyone; but, as the *Jumna* sails next week, and we may never meet again, I will confide it to you."

"There you are with the blues again. We *shall* meet again, and I hope you will have a wife by that time. You ought to marry, Desborough; you have lived too long alone."

"No," replied the Colonel. "I am nearly forty, and my opinion is that by that time one gets fixed in habits and ideas. A wife of a suitable age would be the same—we should clash. A young wife would bother me. But the matrimonial question isn't worth discussing."

"Well, then, let us return to the cause of your illness."

"You remember our expedition to the hills, and the tiger-hunt?"

"Yes, of course, just five months ago; you were quite well then—in tip-top spirits, I remember."

"For the last time," replied Desborough, sadly. "You know, we pursued our game far into the jungle, killing him there. On returning, the moon was up, making everything light as day. I was in the front as we filed down the narrow pathway. Ahead all was clear—a solitude, in fact. Suddenly I saw standing a few feet from me the figure of an early friend, whom I had neither seen nor thought of for many years; but there he was, in the middle of the path. He raised his arm and beckoned me."

"It must have been a shadow," observed Major Breakspear, remarking how pale and nervous Desborough became while speaking.

"So thought I at the time, believing the vision to be a freak of memory. Well, I dismissed the subject from my mind; but," lowering his voice, "a night or two afterwards, while looking in my toilet-glass, I saw him immediately behind me, standing in the centre of the room. He motioned to me again, inviting me to follow him. The strange part of it is, that, though I recognized him perfectly, he was not a young man, as when we parted, but his hair and beard were iron grey, and he looked as doubtless he would look after the lapse of fifteen years."

"All imagination," said the Major. "Have you had any recurrence of this—this phenomenon?"

"Any recurrence! I wish I could say no. I see him frequently at most unexpected times—and not always at night, but generally standing in a deep shadow, in that alcove, for instance;" he glanced towards it nervously as he spoke. "I am not superstitious, and have never believed in spiritual demonstrations. I have been through battles, and have seen the horrors of a prolonged siege; but I confess I have never felt so thoroughly shaken as by this appearance."

"It is very strange, certainly; you said your mind had not dwelt upon your friend lately," observed Major Breakspear.

"Not in the least. He is three years my senior; we were together at Rugby and Sandhurst. On his father's death he succeeded to the baronetcy, and married. I came out to India at eighteen, and only went home on leave at four-and-twenty. I found my old schoolfellow a widower with one little girl. That was fifteen years ago. We exchanged a few letters; but I have not heard from him, or thought of him, these ten years. Yes; I read his second marriage in *The Times* two or three years ago. Now he seems to possess me; when I sleep I dream of him, and wake to see him standing in the middle of the room. Breakspear, the question is—Am I mad?"

Major Breakspear, noting his friend's extreme agitation, laid his hand kindly upon his shoulder: "No, no," said he; "you must not think that for a moment; system out of order—nothing more."

"There is an account in Sir Walter Scott's *Demonology and Witchcraft* of a gentleman, high in the law, who was pertinaciously haunted by an imaginary presence, actually wasting away and dying under the ordeal. That may ultimately be my case. My reason is inadequate to combat the effects of what is either reality or a morbid state of the brain."

Major Breakspear looked at him attentively, noting how much the powerful form had wasted, and how haggard the fine frank face had grown. Desborough had been celebrated as one of the finest men in the army, standing over six feet in height, of splendid physique, lithe and active, with an elegant erect carriage, and head well poised and thrown back; a fine Saxon face, classical features, fair complexion (much bronzed by the sun), blue eyes, and thatch-coloured hair. He was eight-and-thirty—far handsomer than many of his juniors.

"A sea voyage will brace your nerves, and set you up," said Breakspear. "I advise you to get away as fast as you can."

After the Major's departure, Colonel Desborough paced the room, lost in thought. "No," said he to himself, "I am not mad; but I will probe the mystery. I will see Henry Chalvington. It is not for my health alone I go to England." Then he summoned his soldier servant. "Have you made up your mind whether or not you will accompany me, Blencoe?"

Blencoe, a good-looking man of about thirty years of age, saluted.

"I would go with you to the ends of the earth, Colonel, only—not to England."

"I suppose, like myself, you have no ties there."

"On the contrary, sir, I have one too many—a wife!"

The Colonel could not help laughing.

"You surprise me!" he said; "I had no idea you were a married man."

"No one knows it here, Colonel; in fact, I entered the army to hide myself, and get away from her. Blencoe is not my real name. I have been here for six years—not long enough to alter me much in personal appearance. If I were to meet my wife she would recognize me."

"Then I shall take no servant with me, but engage one in London. Had you consented to go, I would have made it worth your while. Your education has been superior"—Blencoe, in fact, assisted in the paymaster's office. "You could read to me, and write from dictation on the voyage, for I am far from well."

The man eyed the Colonel wistfully.

"If I could be sure of not meeting her. Listen, sir. I was clerk in a lawyer's office, but in an evil hour married that woman. My father was a hard man—a Methodist; he turned me out of doors. I kept late hours, and my master turned me out of his office. I went on the stage, but found I could not act. I draw a veil over my precious wife's goings on. I bolted—and here I am."

"A graphic and succinct account. I see that there is no inducement for you to go to England."

"There are two very strong inducements, Colonel. One is to be with you, sir, for you are a gentleman; you have been kind to me, and more than once have been good enough to mention my education; it might have been better had I not been a wild lad. The other inducement"—continued Blencoe, looking down to hide his glistening eyes—"is to take a look at my mother's face—if she is alive. I think I'll risk it, sir, and go."

There was not a braver man in Her Majesty's service than Colonel Desborough. He was clever, and so devoted to military life that, although possessed of an ample fortune, which had come to him through the death of an elder brother, he had remained in India, and had, up to the present moment, lived as inexpensively as a man of very modest means could have done. Whether he had remained in a hot climate too long, or was otherwise out of health, he could not determine; ghost stories he had always ridiculed as unworthy of a practical man's consideration, much less belief. The frequent and unexpected appearance of his early friend he set down to diseased imagination. Yet so profound was the impression that appearance had made upon him that he was going to England in order to sift this strange affair to the bottom.

"It is my mind which is affected," he told himself, gloomily; "for a week I have been well occupied in preparations for departure and saying farewell to my friends: my spirits have risen, my thoughts have been diverted into other channels, therefore this incubus on my imagination has ceased—change of scene will cure it."

In direct contradiction to this theory, at a time when his mood was gayest, for he had just returned from a supper with a few friends the night before sailing, as he opened his bedroom door he distinctly saw Sir Henry Chalvington standing in a ray of moonlight, which penetrated through the verandah. As he entered the room, the figure seemed to recede before him, until it vanished out of the open window. Following, he gained the terrace before his bungalow. A sentry was pacing to and fro.

"Has anyone passed here?" asked the Colonel.

"Not a soul since I've been on duty, sir," replied the soldier, presenting arms.

II

"Who is Colonel Desborough?" said Lady Chalvington, taking the card just sent up to her, and examining it through her gold eyeglass. "I never heard the man's name before?"

"*Non lo so, Excellenza.* First he did ask for the sir, *après pour Madame.*" The man who answered the lady in this gibberish was an important person in the lady's establishment. Sometimes she described him as her *homme d'affaires,* sometimes as her *maggiordomo.* He was an olive-skinned foreign-looking individual, with black shining hair, worn rather long, a black moustache, small restless eyes, an aquiline nose. He was well-dressed in a suit of black, and wore a glittering watch-chain; also many rings on large, bony fingers. He never spoke in any one language properly; expressing himself very ungrammatically with the first words that came to him. As he answered Lady Chalvington, he looked at her straight in the eyes, and she returned his look, but with an expression of inquiry.

"Do you know the name, Mary?" she asked, turning to her step-daughter.

Miss Chalvington raised her head from her embroidery, and considered.

"I think I remember him. I have a dim recollection of a Colonel Desborough staying with us at Methwold, when I was a little girl," she said. "He was very kind to me."

"Shall I see him—or not? Yes; show him up here, Texere."

The attendant bowed low, left the drawing-room, and a minute afterwards ushered in Colonel Desborough. He looked considerably better after his voyage, but still bore an expression of anxiety on his face. Yet he had seen nothing to trouble him during the voyage, and had consequently slept well. Rest, combined with sea air, had set him up. As he entered the room, Lady Chalvington thought she had never seen so handsome a man. For his part he was startled by the brilliant appearance of the lady who advanced to receive him.

She appeared about seven-and-twenty years of age, a handsome woman, of a fierce beauty, if it may be so described; a face in which large black eyes, with long lashes, were accentuated by strongly marked black brows; a complexion of delicate texture and of the palest olive; a nose with round nostrils, of rather African type; a full-lipped mouth of richest carmine. She was about the middle height, with rather a full, but well-proportioned figure. Her costume consisted of crimson velvet trimmed with antique yellow lace; her wavy black hair was piled up on the crown of her head, and diamonds sparkled in her ears.

"Thank you for receiving me, Lady Chalvington," said the Colonel. "I am an early friend of Sir Henry, just arrived from India. I called at your house in Brook Street, and learned you were here at Brighton. I am told that Sir Henry is abroad for his health. Nothing serious, I hope?"

"Ah!" sighed the lady, waving a white richly bejewelled hand towards a settee, and subsiding into a chair beside it, with a studied grace. "His health is delicate to the extreme—he cannot breathe in a cold winter. England is too foggy and damp for him."

"I am sorry to hear it. Will he return in the spring?"

"I fear his absence will be for an indefinite period."

"Indeed!" replied the Colonel surprised. "Excuse the question; but may I ask why you are not with him?"

"He does not wish it, as in that case I should be debarred from taking my place in society."

"Will you give me his address? I wish to write to him."

"I will forward a letter with pleasure. This arrangement is by Sir Henry's express desire."

The Colonel's face showed unqualified surprise. Chancing to glance at the young lady who was seated at the other end of the room, and behind Lady Chalvington, he saw her shaking her head to him in denial. Seeing his eyes suddenly fixed on some object, Lady Chalvington turned sharply round, but only to find her step-daughter diligently engaged with her needlework.

Colonel Desborough was quite equal to the occasion. He arose with outstretched hand, advancing towards his friend's daughter.

"Can this be little Mary?" said he.

"Little no longer," replied Miss Chalvington, with her sweet smile, placing a small thin hand in his. "But she remembers Colonel Desborough—and how he used to crawl upon his hands and knees, and roar, pretending to be a lion, for her amusement."

"That was when I was young—fifteen years ago," said he. "You were a little girl then. About four years old I take it."

"I am nineteen now."

"Shall you be writing to your father soon?" asked he.

The girl raised her serious grey eyes to his. What expression did they bear—was it entreaty, fear, doubt? That looked puzzled him.

"I hope I shall," said she, glancing at her stepmother. He retained her hand in his, gazing intently at a very pale, wan face. A faint blush rose to her cheek. Her eyes filled with tears. The Colonel was distressed; he ventured to press that frail hand which lay so confidingly in his. At this signal of friendship, she suddenly returned to her seat, burying her face in her handkerchief, sobbing sadly.

"Go to your room, directly," exclaimed Lady Chalvington, coming up to them. "You ought to be ashamed of yourself, a great girl behaving like a child!"

Mary rose hurriedly, and left the room without a word, her handkerchief still to her eyes. Desborough looked after her with much interest. He then observed that she was a very tall slight girl, straight as a reed, with fair hair coiled behind a classically formed head. She was dressed in a plain grey dress, simple as a Quaker's, which contrasted strikingly with her stepmother's gorgeous raiment.

"She appears delicate," said he.

"Mary is not delicate. She looks so because she is so white; but she is naturally wiry," replied Lady Chalvington, with evident irritation.

"When you write to Sir Henry, mention my name, and tell him I will see him on the first opportunity."

"I will," answered the lady, advancing to the bell.

Finding he had stayed as long as etiquette permitted, the Colonel withdrew. In the vestibule he found a footman and Texere.

"What is Sir Henry's address?" asked the Colonel abruptly of Texere, who bowed low.

"*Entschuldigen Sie, mein Herr; in verita non posso; je ne sais pas, Monsieur.*"

"How long has Sir Henry been ill?"

"*Depuis quand est il malade*—dree years. He has consumption."

"Who forwards his letters?"

"Mi-lady."

"Who manages his affairs?"

"Mi-lady."

The Colonel departed.

"What have I gained?" he asked himself, as he stood on the pavement outside the house in Eastern Terrace. "Nothing. What is wrong there? Where did he pick up that wife who paints her face and lips, and blackens her bold black eyes. Then the poor girl! How imploringly she looked at me. There is something I cannot understand. Well, my journey to Brighton is fruitless. I will go to the family place in Norfolk, and see the steward."

Colonel Desborough was a man of action. That night he was back again in London; a day or two afterwards he was at Norwich, whence he posted to Sir Henry Chalvington's hereditary seat,

Methwold. Late in November the country looked dreary enough, and the task he had undertaken weighed on his spirits. Where was his friend? In the first instance he drove to the land-steward's house, which he remembered as standing near the entrance to the Park. The steward was, fortunately, at home; but the man whom he sought had been long dead. The present steward was another and a younger man.

"We have letters from Sir Henry from time to time," said he, in answer to the Colonel's inquiries, "always through the medium of my lady—who is a capital woman of business. The cheques come regularly. But where he is nobody knows, there is no address on the letters. He wishes his place of residence to be kept secret."

"Is not that very odd?"

"We think so here; but what can we do?"

"Tell me something about Lady Chalvington," said the Colonel, "who and what is she? I knew the first wife."

"As to who the lady is, I can only say that she was a Comtesse d'Acluna, a widow, a half-foreigner, of South American origin, I believe. Sir Henry married her three or four years ago, in Paris. She is a remarkably fine woman. As to what she is—I can assure you she gives the best parties in London, and is a thorough woman of fashion."

"And people actually go to her balls?"

"They almost beg for invitations. Sir Henry, I know, disliked so much company. Some think that is why he prefers to live in retirement abroad."

"What of Miss Chalvington?" asked Desborough.

"She and my lady do not get on very well together. Miss Chalvington likes living here. My lady hates the country."

Colonel Desborough looked grave.

"How long ago did Sir Henry leave England?"

"Eight months ago. He and my lady went to the Engadine together, and it seems he would not return. Would you like to go over the house, sir?"

"I think I should like a look at the old rooms again. But I remember the short cut across the Park perfectly. I will not trouble you to accompany me."

Methwold was an old Elizabethan house, surrounded by trees, and beyond the park there were woodlands. It was the central feature of an extensive estate. How familiar it looked! The housekeeper received the Colonel with pleasure, and showed him over the mansion. How well he remembered it! yet it appeared darker and smaller than in his younger days. Where were the two thoughtless boys who raced up and down its corridors? Where the two young cadets home from Sandhurst? Ah me! one is a grave man scorched by India's suns—the other—where is he?

Last of all the Colonel entered the picture gallery, which extended the whole length of the building. There hung Sir Henry's portrait when a pretty boy of seven years old, painted by Harlstone. Another of him, as a youth in his uniform, by Richmond. Thinking thus sadly of the past, Desborough turned away. He started! His friend stood a few paces from him. He saw him distinctly, looking gravely and sadly, his hair touched with grey. This time the Colonel gave way; he sunk upon a sofa, utterly overcome.

"You are not well, sir," exclaimed the housekeeper. "Seeing the old place again has been too much for you." She hastened away, returning with water and a decanter of brandy. When he had quite recovered, before leaving Methwold, he put the housekeeper through a course of questioning.

"No, Sir Henry was not strong—something wrong with his heart," she said. "He had given up hunting, and disliked having the house always full of visitors, which my lady delighted in, for she sung beautifully, and acted in private theatricals. Last March they left Miss Chalvington behind, and went on the Continent. My lady returned alone, with the courier gentleman, whom nobody liked—indeed, Mr Groves the butler left directly. How did my master look, sir, when he left home? Well, older than his years, very thin—and oh! he'd turned so grey."

At this, Colonel Desborough took his departure. What could he think? Back again to London. Now for the family solicitor in Bedford Row.

The following morning he called at this gentleman's chambers. Yes—Mr Bruce would see him for five minutes—if he was on particular business.

"My dear sir," said the solicitor, "I know Sir Henry Chalvington's address no more than you do. This curious concealment is a whim of his, I suppose. I take things as they come. I send in the accounts to Lady Chalvington; she, in return, forwards me Sir Henry's drafts and cheques, properly signed by him. It is all right enough; but I wish he would come home, all the same!"

"I must and will have authentic news of him," said the Colonel; "it is a matter of the very greatest importance to me. I shall offer a reward for information as to his present address, or any news of him."

"My dear sir—my dear sir—is that necessary? He will turn up of his own accord if you wait."

"That is what I cannot do. I am going to offer a reward of five hundred pounds."

Before carrying out his intention, he ran down to Brighton in the hope of obtaining another interview with Lady Chalvington; but this time he was denied admittance, Lady Chalvington being particularly engaged.

Could he see Miss Chalvington? No, the young lady did not receive visitors. But the Colonel was persevering. Late in the afternoon he called again in Eastern Terrace. This time Lady Chalvington was out, which was true.

He wrote a few words on his card: "Pray let me see you."

This, accompanied by a sovereign, he placed in the hand of the surprised Thomas, for Texere was out with the carriage.

"I will take up your card, sir," said the footman, "but my lady never allows Miss Chalvington to receive visitors."

"Try, at any rate, my good fellow."

Thomas hesitated, but finally ushered the Colonel into a small room, used as a receptacle of hats, umbrellas, and carriage rugs, shutting him in cautiously.

After a short interval, a light, rapid footstep descended the stairs, and Miss Chalvington entered. She looked frightened and nervous.

"Do not keep me long," said she in a whisper. "Lady Chalvington may return; she will be angry."

"You fear her!"

"She is my gaoler. I am a prisoner in everything but name!"

"And your father?"

"Oh, Colonel Desborough! Find him, I implore you; for the sake your old friendship, find him! He never writes to me—only to her. It is eight months since I saw him! He was a loving father to me!"

"Does she keep back his letters?"

The girl trembled from head to foot, glancing at the door nervously.

"Why should she intercept your letters? Why does she keep you shut up?" asked he.

"Because she hates me. Oh, Colonel Desborough, I am miserable about my father. I know not what to think."

"My dear," said the Colonel, smoothing her fair hair, as he had done when she was a child. "I *will* find your father, I promise it solemnly. But who is this woman?"

Miss Chalvington shivered. "A woman to fear, a woman to shun, a woman without pity—a wolf in sheep's clothing. Now go, for Heaven's sake, go!"

"I will," said the Colonel bitterly, "and come back to release you. This mystery shall be solved!"

III

Five hundred pounds reward is offered to any person giving accurate information as to the present residence of Sir Henry Chalvington, Baronet, of Methwold Park, Norfolk, to his old friend, Colonel Desborough, Morley's Hotel, Charing Cross.

Such was the advertisement which appeared day after day in *The Times*, as well as in the *Galignani* and other foreign newspapers. But time went on, and no answers came. Christmas was approaching, the weather began to be severe, causing anxiety to Colonel Desborough in case of his going abroad, which he had determined to do, being convinced that the baronet was somewhere on the Continent. Since his return to England, Desborough's health had improved, and the conviction that he had been subject to mental delusions gained force; still it was a strange coincidence that Sir Henry remained absent, and although no longer the victim of the appearances which had been so frequent in India, the Colonel was as anxious as ever to probe the mystery, not only for himself, but for the sake of Mary Chalvington.

At last one day he received a foreign letter, written on thin paper, with the postmark of Nice upon it. The letter was a little mysterious, as everything appeared to be connected with his quest. It stated that although the writer could not name the whereabouts of Sir Henry, yet he believed he could give a clue that would find him. The Colonel was to go in person to the "Albergo Aggradevole", Scarena, near Nice, and inquire for "Carlo".

Overjoyed at the chance of obtaining definite information, the Colonel gladly quitted the cold and damp of England for a more genial climate. Scarena, he ascertained, was a village in the Maritime Alps, a few miles from Nice, on the road to Turin. Desborough allowed himself no rest until he reached the inn to which he was directed, and put up there for the night. It was a decent little hotel, principally supported by the tourists on their way to visit the magnificent scenery of Sospello.

From the avidity and obsequiousness of the *albergatore*, his wife, and servants, it was evident that he (the Colonel) was expected. It was not, however, until he had dined that he inquired for "Carlo", which personage proved to be, as he anticipated, mine host himself.

"*Si*, Signor, I am Carlo, at your service. Seldom is it that I see *Galignani*, but what is to be will be. One day a copy was given to me when I was at Nice, and on my return home I read it to my wife; then I came to your advertisement. 'I have heard that name,' said I, 'but when, remember I cannot.'

"'Stay,' said she, 'it was in the notebook dropped by the English milor, who stayed here with the lady his wife, two days, see'—Maria opened the *scrittoriello* and produced the book—which now I have great pleasure in offering to you, Signor."

So saying, the innkeeper handed Desborough an ordinary notebook. On the fly-leaf was written in the well-remembered hand of his former friend: "Henry Chalvington, Brook Street, Grosvenor Square."

The book contained several entries, such as the time for trains or packets. One item actually brought a tear to the Colonel's eye. It was only a line or two hurriedly pencilled—"Saw Jack Desborough's name mentioned in news from Simla, must write to him."

That was all—yet, under the circumstances, how affecting!

The *albergatore* watched him with visible satisfaction.

"Now tell me of the lady and gentleman who stayed with you. When were they here?"

"Last April, Signor," answered mine host, settling himself comfortably in his chair. "They drove up in a travelling carriage. The gentleman was very pale and thin, leaning on the arm of the courier or servant, I know not which. He seemed ill, and wore a fur-lined coat, although the weather was not cold. As for the lady—no words can described her beauty—she was superb! They stayed here two days, Signor, and were on their way to La Chiandola to see the waterfalls; but from what the domestic said, I think they were seeking a house in which to remain a few months for the milor's health. At any rate they departed, and left this notebook behind. Is it of use to you, Signor? If it belonged to the friend you seek, I will assist you to the utmost of my power in your search. We must go over the mountains by Scarena, Sospello, La Chiandola, Saorgio, Tenda, Simone, Savigliano, and so on to Turin, making inquiries right and left of the road," said mine host, as he glibly named the towns, checking them off on his fingers.

The man seemed intelligent, and acted in good faith; the liberal reward offered would to him be a fortune.

The following day hurried preparations were made, and with good horses and a light calèche, the search commenced. It is unnecessary to follow their footsteps through the places enumerated by the *albergatore*, and where their inquiries met with more or less success. Tourists are so numerous in the season, that unless it had been from the facts that the gentleman wore a fur-lined coat, and the lady was handsome, with magnificent eyes, the Chalvingtons would scarcely have been remarked. However, at the town of Saorgio, all traces ceased—no one remembered them at the hotels in that place.

"We must turn back, Signor. Your friends never reached so far," said the *albergatore*.

Instead of following the road superbly constructed by Victor Amadeus, King of Sardinia, and completed in seventeen years, the highway from Nice over the Maritime Alps to Turin, they branched off towards the country, visiting the villages which lay on the banks of those streams which fertilize this part of Piedmont. Still no success.

Disheartened at repeated failures, they drove up once more to the post-house at Simone. The Carrozza di Viaggio, a kind of stagecoach, was drawn up, changing horses.

Suddenly Carlo Rigo uttered an exclamation, hurriedly descending from the calèche.

"There! there!" cried the innkeeper, in extreme excitement. "The coat—milor's fur coat!" And he ran to the side of the vehicle, which was the diligence plying between Tenda and Sospello.

The driver, who wore the coat in question, was seated with a long whip in his hand, awaiting the fresh horses. He was unmistakably Italian, and was not a little surprised when the *albergatore* exclaimed:

"*Cospetto!* where did you get that coat?"

An animated dialogue took place between the two. Desborough waited until the innkeeper returned, his face radiant with delight.

"Signor," cried he, "it is an affair finished. Nicolo is a most respectable man; he has driven the *carrozza* these ten years. He tells me he bought that coat a month ago, to protect him against the searching winds we have here in springtime and winter. It was hanging at the door of Isacco the Jew, at Sospello."

"Then to Isacco we must go," said the Colonel.

Once more they drove into the little town. Isacco was an old man with fine aquiline features and a venerable white beard, who would have been a good model for one of the Patriarchs. He willingly gave the desired information. The coat had been brought to his shop eight months previously by the servant of the English gentleman who had bought the Villa Cipresso. His master and mistress were going to Naples, and the coat would not be required.

And where was the Villa Cipresso? Some miles away in the chestnut woods, he understood.

When once the address was gained, progress was easy. A postilion knowing the locality was engaged to drive the Colonel and his companion to the Villa the following morning, it being too late that day to proceed further. It lay at about eleven miles distant, so embedded in trees as to be undiscernible until you came upon it. A lovely spot, but the house was solitary and neglected. Weeds and brambles overgrew the paths and flower-beds; the windows were boarded up. The noise of the carriage wheels brought an old woman to the door, who appeared overcome with astonishment at their arrival. She was tall, dark, wrinkled, and clad in miserable garments, and she stood as if transfixed in the doorway, staring wildly at the visitors.

"Is this the Villa Cipresso?" asked Carlo Rigo.

"*Si*," answered the old woman.

"Is Sir Henry Chalvington here?" demanded the Colonel.

The effect caused by this question was most unexpected. She threw up her arms, groaned aloud, and, rushing down a stone passage, entered a room and locked herself in.

"She is alarmed," said Desborough. "Can she be living here alone?—the house appears empty."

The innkeeper went to her door, knocked, and spoke to her kindly to reassure her, but she did not reply. The moaning noise continued as if she were in great sorrow.

The Colonel and his companion went over the building. It was not large, the furniture was very simple, and the house was evidently without occupants. There was not a book, or a scrap of paper to give a clue as to who the last inhabitants of those rooms had been.

The postilion took out the horses, and led them to the stables, empty and neglected, the only living things being a few half-starved fowls straying about the yard. Colonel Desborough walked round the grounds, which were overgrown with great sprawling cacti and untidy-looking pepper trees. There were ornamental fountains that played no longer, there were myrtles and other shrubs thickly planted, and tall dark cypresses which gave a sombre, melancholy appearance to the grounds. Outside was almost a forest of cork trees, and beyond this wooded screen the magnificent Alps shut in the view, and seemed to say, "Thou shalt proceed no further."

In the meantime the old woman's curiosity appeared to have got the better of her alarm, and after a conversation through the door with Carlo Rigo, she was prevailed upon to open it, and prepare a meal with the refreshments they carried with them, which she did with avidity, for she was starving. But to all their questions she shook her head, refusing to give any information.

"We will remain here tonight," said the Colonel grimly. "I *will* learn more before I leave."

In the evening he and the *albergatore* strolled forth once more in the garden. The sun had gone down behind the mountains, and the whole atmosphere was of that beautiful violet tint, known as the after-glow. What a solitude! The shadows of evening deepened when they entered upon a glade of cypresses.

"Look—look, Signor!" cried Carlo suddenly. "There is the English milor!"

Desborough raised his head, thrilled at those words. There, a few paces before him, stood the form of his friend, more distinct than ever; pale, grey, motionless, the outline of his figure clearly defined against the dark background of green trees.

"Why is he motioning to us?—why is he pointing to the earth? Ah! he is gone!" cried the affrighted Italian.

The Colonel tried to speak, but could find no words. He leant against a tree for support, wiping his brow in extreme agitation.

"You saw him then?" said he at length to Rigo; "saw him plainly?"

"The English milor? *Si*, Signor."

"I thank heaven," cried Desborough, raising his hat reverently. "I am not mad!"

"I do not understand it, Signor," said the bewildered innkeeper.

"No," replied the Colonel, "you cannot; for he whom we have seen is no inhabitant of this world. Let us obtain picks and shovels—it is my belief that under that sod Sir Henry Chalvington lies buried!"

What a strange revelation! What a chain of seemingly natural incidents had guided Colonel Desborough to that spot, where he was destined to unravel a mystery, and rectify a great wrong; for in the grey light of dawn what remained of Henry Chalvington was unearthed. Was it murder?

"No no," cried the old woman, flinging herself at his feet. "Do not suppose it—do not think it—the Englishman died a natural death. He had bought this Villa, he and his lady came to see what furniture it required. They had driven from Nice—he seemed ill and weak. On the third day after his arrival while at the dinner table he fell back suddenly—dead! It is true, I swear it. The lady was in terror, so was the servant they had with them. 'Listen,' she said to me, 'if known to be a widow I shall be a poor woman. While my husband is supposed to live I am rich! We will keep it secret—we will bury him under the cypress trees, and I will provide for you. Continue to live here; you shall have money as long as you do not talk.' Then Signor Texere, the domestic, dug the grave, and we laid him there, the poor Inglese!

"Miladi and her servant departed. At first they sent me money, not much, but sufficient for my wants. Recently it has ceased. I am near starving. Why should I keep the secret longer? The compact is broken; I tell all. But, Signor, I swear it was no murder. I was in the room helping to wait upon them at dinner when he fell back in his chair, dead. It was his heart that was affected. I had seen the same look in his face that there was in one of my kindred who died in the same way."

Once again the scene changes to Eastern Terrace, Brighton. Lady Chalvington, richly attired in gold-coloured brocade, was about to depart to the theatre when she was informed that Colonel Desborough and Mr Bruce desired to see her. It was indeed those two gentlemen, accompanied by Blencoe and a constable in plain clothes, who waited in the vestibule.

Lady Chalvington entered the library where these unwelcome visitors awaited her.

"I am at a loss to imagine the purpose of this visit, gentlemen," she exclaimed haughtily, as she entered the room. "Morning is the time for business, Mr Bruce."

"Ours is far more than a business visit, madam," answered the Colonel. "We come to inform you that the remains of your late husband have been found, and brought to England for Christian burial."

For one instant the guilty woman stood transfixed; then she rushed to the door and was crossing the hall, when she suddenly stopped, her eyes glaring, her breath gasping. She was confronted by Blencoe.

"Stop her—stop Lady Chalvington," shouted the Colonel.

"Lady Chalvington!" cried Blencoe, seizing her by the arm. "There is no Lady Chalvington here. I own with shame and disgust that this woman is my wife, Harriet Lemoine, and that man," pointing to Texere, who had appeared upon the scene, "is her brother, who lived in my house, the forger, the gambler, the swindler; turning day into night, night into day. It was to escape from such a wife, and to sever myself from her hateful brood, that I went to India. That woman was no wife of Sir Henry's. I can prove her identity with the girl I married at St Pancras Church eight years ago."

Six weeks after this sudden *dénouement* Colonel Desborough entered the drawing-room of the house in Brook Street, looking stronger and better than he had done for nearly a twelvemonth before, although greatly shaken by the strain upon his nerves. The incubus once removed, his spirits improved, and his customary good health returned; although, possibly, a deeper and graver tone would remain with him during life, from the knowledge that he had held communication with the spirit world; a world he had hitherto scarcely thought of, but now believed in with reverence, concluding that, under some circumstances, such revelations are permitted.

Mary Chalvington, attired in deep mourning, advanced to receive him, looking fair and fragile as a lily.

"Yes," he said, "I have come to say goodbye. The *Crocodile* sails from Southampton tomorrow."

"Oh!" cried Mary. "What shall I do when you are gone, my best, my only friend? What is to become of the orphan whom you have rescued from a thraldom that was worse than death? Why will you not stay in England?"

"Because I have no ties here. I am a solitary man."

"Need you be so?" said the girl softly, in a low voice.

The Colonel looked at her, then began to walk up and down the room in an agitated manner.

"If I thought—" said he, and then stopped. "If I dared—but I am nearly twice your age, my darling; how could I ask for such a sacrifice?"

"It would be no sacrifice," murmured Mary, "it would be happiness!"

Colonel Desborough *never* went back to India.

THE SCULPTOR'S ANGEL

Marie Corelli

Marie Corelli (1855–1924) was regarded by many as Braddon's successor as Britain's bestselling female novelist, but with a more extreme form of sensationalism. Braddon kept her novels within the human realm, but Corelli ventured far into the spiritual. She had success with her first novel A Romance of Two Worlds *(1886) in which a young woman, trying to recover from a breakdown, meets a guiding spirit in a dream and is taken on a tour of the solar system to expand her consciousness. Corelli had a deep belief in the occult and reincarnation and her books attracted a devoted readership.* The Soul of Lilith *(1892),* The Sorrows of Satan *(1895),* Ziska *(1897) and especially* Barabbas *(1893) increased her popularity amongst the general public whilst incensing the literary critics who regarded her work as deplorable. Most of her novels are unreadable today, and they have overshadowed her shorter works which include several stories of genuine atmosphere and ability, such as the following, which appeared in her collection* The Love of Long Ago *(1920).*

Corelli was the illegitimate child of the Scottish poet Charles Mackay and his servant, Elizabeth Mills, though they did later marry. Corelli was an accomplished pianist and gave performances early in her career, which was when she adopted the Corelli alias. Her novels attracted a divided readership but it is claimed she was Queen Victoria's favourite writer. She was good at keeping her name in the public eye, and it was Corelli who spread the word of the "curse of the pharaohs" with the discovery of Tutankhamun's tomb. In her final years Corelli donated some of her fortune to preserving and restoring the antiquarian buildings in Stratford-upon-Avon. She even claimed she was the reincarnation of Shakespeare!

"YOU ARE A GREAT ARTIST, MY SON," SAID THE ABBOT, with a favouring smile, "and, what is far better, you are noble and pure-hearted. And to you we entrust the high task of filling the vacant niche in our church with an Angel of Peace and Blessing. We will give you all possible freedom and leisure for the work, so that you may complete it before Christmas. On the Feast of the Nativity of our Blessed Lord we shall hope, God willing, to see your Angel in the chancel."

He, the renowned and well-nigh saintly Head of one of the most famous among England's early monasteries, spoke with an authoritative dignity which gave his words, though gently uttered, the weight of a command, and the monk Anselmus whom he addressed heard him in submissive silence. They were standing together in one of the side chapels of a magnificent Abbey Church—the creation of devout and prayerful men who gave their highest thought and most fervent toil to the service and praise of their Maker, and the days were those when implicit belief in a Divine Power, strong to guard and to defend the right, was the chief saving grace of the nation. The blind and unruly passions of that age were held in salutary check by the spiritual force and sanctity of the Church—and neither priest nor layman then foresaw the coming time of terror when desecrating hands should violate and pillage the holy shrines so patiently upbuilt to the honour and glory of God, leaving of them nothing but the ruins of their grandeur—the melancholy emblems of a faith more ruined even than they.

"You will," continued the Abbot, "have your time to yourself—that is, of course, such time as is not occupied by the holy services, and we will take good care that nothing shall disturb the flow of what must be a truly divine inspiration. Yes, my son, all labour is divine, and our best thoughts come from God alone, so that we of ourselves dare claim no merit. In the making of an Angel's likeness, angels must surely guide the sculptor's hand, and bring his work to ultimate perfection! Is this not so? You hear me? You understand?"

Anselmus had remained mute, but now he raised his bent head. He was not a young man—youth seemed to have passed him by in haste and left him old before his time. His face was worn and thin, and showed deep furrows of pain and sorrow—only his eyes, sunken, yet bright and almost feverish in their lustre, flashed with the smouldering fires of suppressed and dying energy.

"I hear—and I understand," he answered, slowly. "But why not choose a better man—a better sculptor? I am not worthy."

The Abbot laid a kindly hand upon his arm.

"Who among us is more worthy!" he said. "Have you not bestowed upon us the treasures of your genius, and do we not owe much of the greatest beauty of our Abbey Church to your designs? Good son, humility is becoming in you as in us all—each one of us is indeed unworthy so far as he himself is concerned—but your gift of art is from God, and therefore of its worthiness neither you nor I must presume to doubt! It is a gift that you are bound to use for highest purpose. Need I say more? You accept the task?"

"Father, when you command I must obey," replied the monk. "Nevertheless, I say I am not worthy of so much as the passing dream of an Angel!—but to satisfy you and our brethren I will do my best."

"That best will be sufficient for us," said the Abbot. "And while you work, you must relax a little in the rigorous discipline to which you so constantly submit yourself by your own choice. You fast too long and sleep too lightly—take more food and rest, Anselmus! —or the spirit will chafe the flesh with so much sharpness that the end will be disaster to both brain and body. Ease and freedom are as air and light to the artist—we give you both, my son, as far as may be given without trespass against our rules. Work at your own time and pleasure, and we will make it a sacred charge to ourselves and our brethren not to break in upon the solitude of your studio—we will leave you alone with your Angel!"

He nodded, smiling graciously, and, making the sign of the cross in air, paced slowly out of the chapel into the nave, and out of the nave again into the cloisters beyond, where among the many arches his tall and stately figure in its flowing robes disappeared.

The monk Anselmus stood for a few moments gazing after him, then with a deep sigh that was almost a groan, turned back into the deeper and more shadowed seclusion of the chapel, where, with a movement of utter abandonment and despair, he threw himself on his knees before the great Crucifix which had lately been sent as a gift to the monastery from the Holy Father in Rome.

"O God, God!" he prayed, under his breath. "Have mercy upon me, Thy wicked and treacherous servant! Lift from my soul the heavy burden of its secret sin! Teach me the way to win Thy pardon and recover the peace that I have lost! Lighten my darkness, for the shadow of my crime is ever black before my eyes! Spare me, O Redeemer of souls! for my remorse is greater than I can bear!"

He covered his face with his hands, and crouched rather than knelt before the sculptured figure of the crucified Christ, shuddering with the suppressed agony which seemed to rack his body with positive physical pain. His own thoughts whipped him as with a million lashes—they drove him through every memory of the past, sparing no detail, as they had driven him remorselessly over and over again till at times he had felt himself almost on the verge of madness. He looked back to his early days of boyhood and manhood in Rome, when as a young and ardent student of art, working under one of the master sculptors of that period, he had hewn life out of senseless marble with a power and perfection which had astonished his fellows in the school; he remembered how just when the wreath of fame seemed his to win and to hold he had suddenly become possessed and inspired by an enthusiastic faith and exaltation toward the highest things—a faith and exaltation which had moved him to consecrate his life and genius to the Church—and how, convinced of his vocation, he had voluntarily severed all ties of natural affection, leaving father, mother, and home to take the monastic vows and devote himself to the service of God, and how, when this was done, he had gladly joined a band of earnest and devoted brethren who were sent from Rome to England to assist by their labours the completion and perfecting of one of the greatest abbeys ever founded in Britain. And then he recalled the almost passionate love of his work which had filled his brain and strengthened his hands when he first saw the splendid church and monastery, a vision of architectural magnificence and purity, lifting its towers heavenward in the midst of a landscape so peaceful and fair, so set about with noble trees and broad green fields and crystal streams that it seemed like an earthly realization of the dream of Paradise. And he had laboured so lovingly and patiently, and done so much to adorn and beautify the sacred shrine that he had endeared himself greatly to the Abbot, who knew that in Anselmus he had a sculptor of rare genius—one who, if he had chosen to follow a worldly career rather than embrace the religious life, would have made a name not easily forgotten. As it was, however, he seemed entirely content—he was as careful in his religious rule as in his art labours—and the wonderful chancel screen which he, alone and unaided, had wrought out of the native stone of which the monastery itself was built, was not more perfect than the discipline and obedience to which he had submitted himself for many peaceful years. Then, all suddenly, the great test presented itself—the fiery trial from which he did not come out unscathed. And thus it happened:

Among his many duties he was sent out from the monastery twice every week among the scattered villages lying about the church lands to inquire into the needs of the sick and the poor, and on one of these occasions he met the fate that befalls all men sooner or later—love. A mere glance, a touch of hands, and the whole bulwark of a life can be swept away by the storm of a sudden, irresistible passion—and so, unhappily, it chanced to the monk Anselmus. And yet it was only a very loving, foolish, trusting little maid who had in all ignorance and innocence beguiled him from his monastic vows—a little peasant, with cheeks like the wild rose and eyes blue as the summer sea, whom he had found tending, unaided, upon an aged and sick woman, her grandmother, working for her uncomplainingly, and keeping the poor cottage in which they lived clean and sweet as a lady's bower though there was hardly any food to share between them. Touched to the heart by the sight of so young and fair a creature bearing her daily lot of hard privation with such gentle patience and content, Anselmus brought much-needed relief from the monastery—medicines and wine for the aged sufferer, and supplies of bread and new milk and eggs and fowls for the better help and sustenance of the girl, who, however, asked for no assistance, and could hardly be induced to accept it even from the bounty of Mother Church. And Anselmus saw her again and yet again—together they talked of many things, and often at the monk's request she would walk with him from her cottage door through the long, deeply shaded avenue of thickly branched trees that led to the gates of the monastery—till at last one fateful evening, when she had accompanied him thus and was about to turn back alone, his long-suppressed man's heart arose within him, and yielding to a reckless impulse, he caught her in his arms. Their lips met, and as he felt the tender, clinging warmth of that first kiss of love he suddenly experienced a sense of happiness he had never yet known, an ecstasy so intense that it seemed to lift him to a heaven far beyond even that of which he had dreamed in long nightly vigils of prayer.

This was the beginning of many secret meetings—meetings fraught with fear and joy. He, the ascetic monk, scholar, and rigid disciplinarian in all the duties of an exacting religious Order became an ardent, passionate, and selfish lover—while she, poor child, overcome and carried away by the burning warmth of his eager caresses and words of endearment, asked nothing better than to be loved by him, and in return loved him herself with all the strength and devotion of her fond little heart and soul. Their dream-like idyll of forbidden love was brief; Anselmus, like the rest of his sex, soon tired of what he had too easily obtained, and in order to escape from the tender tie he had so willingly fastened upon himself began, somewhat late in the day, to consider the dangers he ran by his unlawful conduct. His own safety and convenience now seemed to him of far greater importance than the peace or the happiness of the loving soul he had set himself to conquer and contaminate, and the more he dwelt upon his position the more irksome and unbearable it proved. One day, goaded beyond endurance by her gentle solicitude and wonderment at his altered manner, he harshly told her that they must meet no more.

"I have," he said, "committed an unpardonable sin in allowing myself to be entangled by your company. I must do penance for it with many years of fasting and of prayer. You tempted me!—it was not I—*you*, with your appealing eyes and smile—*you* led me from the path of purity and honour; surely God knows it was more your fault than mine! I am sorry for you, poor child!"—here his accents were softer and almost paternal—"Forgive me for any wrong I have done you, and forget me! You are young—you will be happy yet!"

And then, having spoken as he thought reasonably and sensibly, and being too hardened to realize that his words were as death-blows dealt brutally on the tender heart of the girl who loved him, he waited for tears, reproaches, the bitter abandonment of grief and despair. But she gave him no trouble or pain of this kind. All she did was to raise her pretty sea-blue eyes to his face with a look in them which he never forgot—a look of sorrow, pity, and pardon, then she caught his hand, kissed it, and turned away.

"Stay! Are you going?" he called. "Without one word?"

She made no reply. On she went, steadily—a little figure, glimmering whitely through the shadows of the bending trees, and without giving him so much as a backward glance, she disappeared.

He never saw her again. But that same week, when he went on his usual rounds of charity through the district, he learned that she had been found drowned among the reeds of the slowly flowing river that wound its clear ribbon of liquid light through the monastery lands. And the old grandmother she had so loyally cared for, and to whom she was more than the sunshine itself, hearing she was dead, would not believe it, and sat chattering stupidly all day about the hour when she would return to prepare the food for supper —and even when the small, frail corpse was brought into the cottage dripping with its weight of water and clinging weed, she would not look at it nor accept it as the body of her grandchild, but merely said—"No, no! It is not she—God gave her to me and He is good!—He would not rob me of her in my age—He would remember how much I need her!"

And the monk Anselmus, proffering spiritual consolation, trembled within himself, knowing the guilt of his own conscience which branded him as the murderer of the dead girl. But he kept his secret and betrayed no sign of his inward torment. And so, like all things sad or pleasant, humorous or pathetic, the little tragedy of a lost life was soon forgotten. No one ever knew that the poor drowned child had had a lover, and certainly no one in their wildest conjectures would have suspected that a monk could be that lover—a monk of austere reputation, who was sometimes called by his brethren "our heavenly sculptor, Anselmus."

Years passed—and his sin had never found him out, save in secret hours when the remembrance of his little dead love's last look haunted him with a kind of ghostly terror, and he could feel her last kiss upon his hand like a scorching coal of fire. Just in these latter days the thought of her had been so prominent in his brain as to leave him no peace. There was no especial reason why he should perpetually dwell upon the recollection of her sea-blue eyes and child's smile, yet somehow he could not shut her memory from his mind. And it was because of this constant, remorseful impression and the knowledge of the irreparable wrong he had wrought upon her that he had almost involuntarily told the Abbot that he was unworthy to perform the task for which he was commissioned, namely, to fill the last remaining empty niche in the chancel with the statue of an Angel. Burdened with the hidden weight of his sin, and feeling that even in his most rigorous fastings and penances he was nothing more than a hypocrite in the sight of the All-Knowing God, he wrestled with himself in prayer, and with tears, but all in vain. And even now, abased in supplication before the crucifix, he felt no answering thrill of hope or consolation, so that when he rose from his knees it was with a kind of desperate resignation to the inevitable—a resolve to do the work he was set to do, not with pride or gladness, but by way of punishment. In this spirit—so far removed from the joyous elation of an artist who knows that his hand can accomplish what his brain conceives—he began his labours. Carefully taking the exact measurement of the niche to be filled, he made a similarly sized one of rough wood and set it up in his own workshop or studio, so that he might study its height and breadth and try to realize within his mind the attitude and appearance the "Angel" should assume. Sitting opposite to it, and looking attentively at its interior vacancy, he saw that the figure would have to be life-size, and he presently began to draw on paper in charcoal the suggestion of a form and face, but without success or satisfaction in any actual conception.

"It is not for me to see divine things!" he said, bitterly. "Such inspiration as I once had is killed at its very source by sin! Shame on my weak soul that it should be trapped by a woman's eyes! If she had not looked at me—if her smile had not been so sweet! —if she had resisted my passion she might have saved herself and me!"

So he argued—as Adam argued before him—"The woman tempted me." So will men, in their pitiless egotism, argue in their own defence till time shall be no more.

All that first afternoon of attempted "work" he sat, weary and puzzled, alternately gazing at the empty niche and at the paper on his drawing-board, where as yet he had only traced a few unmeaning lines. The sun began to sink, and through the broad mullioned windows of his monastic studio he saw the western sky glowing like melted rubies in a belt of sapphire blue. The bright glow flared dazzlingly upon his eyes and made them ache—he covered them with one hand for a minute's space. Then, uncovering them again, he looked away from the sunset light toward the niche he had been studying all day, and—looking—uttered a smothered cry of mingled terror and rapture and fell on his knees! For the niche was no longer empty—an Angel stood within it!—a Figure delicate, brilliant, and surpassingly beautiful, with folded wings like rays of light on either side, and a Face fair, radiant, and full of an exquisite tenderness such as is never seen on any features of mere mortality. Awed and overwhelmed beyond all power of speech, Anselmus, kneeling, gazed upward at the ravishing Vision which bent its star-like eyes upon him with a look of divine and affectionate compassion. The red glow of the sunset deepened, and within the studio all the lights of heaven seemed transfused, circling gloriously around the one white uplifted Wonder that shone forth from the niche like a lily illumined with some pale hidden fire—then, almost mechanically, Anselmus groped for his pencil and his drawing-board, and trembling with fear, essayed to make a hasty similitude of the gracious Loveliness which, like a beautiful dream, confronted him. But, gradually as the sunset light faded into grey shadow, the vision faded also, and by the time darkness began to steal slowly over all visible things, it had vanished! In a kind of mingled ecstasy and anguish, Anselmus rose slowly from his kneeling attitude—the Angelus was ringing—it was time for him to leave his work for the day and betake himself to prayer and vigil. Like a man too suddenly awakened from deep sleep he walked slowly, absorbed in thought, and the brethren who watched him enter his choir-stall to join them in the singing of the vespers glanced at each other with meaning in their looks, one or two murmuring to each other, "Our Anselmus is at work! He has the air of one inspired by Heaven!"

The next morning dawned fair and bright, and as soon as the light had fully come Anselmus hastened to his studio. Full of an almost feverish haste and eagerness he caught up the drawing he had attempted—the picture of the visionary Angel—but alas! there was nothing suggestive enough for any attempt at further elaboration or completion, and he flung it aside with a sigh of bitter disappointment. The sun peeped sparkling through the windows, shooting rays of light along the stone floor—and Anselmus, seating himself in his accustomed working place, slowly and half-fearfully raised his eyes toward the niche which on the previous night had held, as he now thought, a dream of his own brain. Then he caught his breath and remained still, not daring to move—for there again— there stood the Angel! In full daylight, and whiter than the whitest cloud tipped by the sun—there, with folded wings and divine, inscrutable smile it waited, as though it sought to be commanded, its delicate hands outstretched in an attitude of mingled protection and blessing! And now Anselmus did not kneel, for, more than ever convinced that this miraculous sight was the chimera of his own mind, he resolved to turn it to use.

"It is my own creation!" he said. "A vision evoked from my own thoughts, and from my desire to fulfil the task our father Abbot has set upon me. Let me, therefore, work while it is day—" And he did not finish the sentence, "For the night cometh when no man can work."

He began to draw, and everything came to him easily as in the former days of his early skill and power —with light and facile touch he soon completed a rough outline of the form and luminous drapery of his heavenly visitant, and then—then, when he attempted to get some idea of the divinely fair face and features his hand trembled—he looked again and again and his heart suddenly failed him! For surely he had seen those eyes before!—that wistful child's smile! Shuddering as with icy cold he murmured:

"God have mercy upon me! Spare me my brain, O Lord! Let me not go mad until my work is done! Is this Thy punishment?—and can the dead arise before Thy Judgment Day? It is not yet the time!—not yet!"

His eyes smarted with the pain of unshed tears as he lifted them to the Angel in the niche—a Vision silent as the light itself, but expressive of all sweetness, all patience. Seeing that it did not move, but remained quite still as though it were in very truth a model, posed for his study and treatment, he fell to work again with a sort of passion that consumed his energies as though with a devouring fire.

Day after day he toiled unceasingly, giving himself scarcely any leisure for food or sleep, and for the first time in his life almost grudging the hours he was compelled to pass in the duties of his religious Order. Day after day, with miraculous fidelity, the Angel stood in the niche confronting him, and never stirred! Treating the vision as a delusion or imaginary creation of his own brain, he worked from it steadily, knowing that it was a perfect presentment of the ideal "Angel" he sought to create—and very soon after his drawings were made he began to mould the figure in clay. Slowly, but surely, it grew up in his hands toward a beautiful completeness, and still the Angel stayed with him, apparently watching with steadfast, sweet eyes the modelling of its own likeness.

More than a month passed in this way, and the Angel in the niche became so much a part of the life and work of Anselmus that he could not imagine himself able to accomplish any good thing without the influence of its shining presence. The autumn deepened into winter—the withered leaves fell in rustling heaps on the gravel-paths and disfigured the smooth green grass-walks round the monastery, and bitter winds blew from the northeast, bringing sudden gusts of sleet and snow. The bare room or studio where Anselmus worked became very cold—sometimes he felt a chill as of death upon him while modelling the figure of his "Angel" in the damp clay. Yet from the niche, where the heavenly Vision faithfully remained, streamed an unearthly light that was almost warmth, and Anselmus would have died rather than have left the spot for a better room in the monastery, which the Abbot had offered him in kindly solicitude for his health.

"We do not seek to know what you are doing," he said, "nor would we look upon your work till you yourself summon us to see it finished. But you appear to suffer—you are worn to the merest shadow of a man! Let me entreat you, my son, to take more care and rest—or cease work for a while—"

"No, no!" interrupted Anselmus, excitedly. "I cannot cease work, or I must cease to live! I am well —quite well! Have no trouble concerning me—let me finish my task, or else the Angel"—here he smiled a strange, bewildered smile—"Yes, the Angel may leave me!"

The Abbot was puzzled by his manner, but forbore to press any further advice upon him, though both he and all the brethren of the Abbey noticed with deep and regretful concern that their "heavenly sculptor" seemed stricken with some strange mortal illness which, though he did not complain of any ailment, was visibly breaking him down.

Things went better for him, and he appeared to suffer less, when, having finished his model in the clay, he began to hew out his "Angel" in stone. He was an adept at this kind of hard work, and the physical exertion needed for it did him good and restored to him something of his old vigour and elasticity. From dawn to dusk every day he worked steadily and ardently, and from dawn to dusk every day the radiant Vision filled the niche and adorned it with rays of light more brilliant than the sunbeams. From dawn to dusk the sweet, mysterious Angel-eyes watched him as he hammered and carved the rigid stone, forming it into an apparently pliable grace and beauty, till at last the day came when, having spent all his thought and energy on the last few fine perfecting touches—looking every moment at the delicate features, the eyes, and divine smile of his visionary model, and making sure that he had rendered them as faithfully as only a great artist can, he realized that his task was done. Throwing down his tools, he fell on his knees, stretching out his hands in an agony of appeal. For there was now no longer any need to try and deceive himself, or to feign to his own accusing conscience that he had not recognized the face he had sculptured, the sweet lips he had so tenderly chiselled, the dimple in the soft cheek, the drooping eyelids—he knew it well!—it was the face of an Angel truly or the face of a Vision—but more than all it was the face of the little dead girl who had loved him and given him all her life.

"Angel of my soul!" he murmured. "Angel of my dreams! Spirit of my work! Speak to me! Oh, speak, and tell me why you are here!—why you have stayed so patiently and long!—you, who are the heavenly likeness of one whom I wronged!—why have you come to me?"

There followed a moment's silence—a silence so tense and deep as to be fraught with ineffable torment to the mind of the suffering man. Then the answer came—in a voice sweeter than the sound of a crystal bell:

"Because I love you!"

Thrilled by these words, and gazing upward, he met the sea-blue radiance of those angelic eyes in mingled fear and rapture.

"Because I love you!" repeated the Voice. "Because I have always loved you!"

He heard—incredulous.

"I am mad!—or dreaming!" he whispered, tremulously. "This Miracle speaks as She would have spoken!"

"Love is the only miracle!" went on the Voice. "It cannot die—it is immortal! Oh, my Beloved! Your sin before God was not the breaking of a religious vow but the breaking of a human heart— the ruin of a human life!—a heart that trusted you!—a life that gave itself to you!"

The unhappy monk wrung his hands in despair.

"Punish me!" he cried. "Wreak lightning vengeance now upon me, O Angel of the Most High! Slay me with one look of those sweet eyes, O spirit of my murdered love! Let me not live to lose the memory of this day!"

The figure of the Angel stirred—its folded wings quivered and began to expand slowly like great fans of light on either side.

"Love has no vengeance in its hands!" said the Voice, in accents surpassingly tender. "All is pardoned, my Beloved!—all is finished save the story of our joy which no mortal shall ever know!—a joy beginning but never ending! Out of my death I give you life, and for the wrong you wrought upon my soul, I bring you, in the Name of God, pardon and peace! Beloved, your work is done!"

And now the radiant Form rose slowly, like a fine mist coloured through by the rays of the sun—it floated out of the niche where it had stood so long and patiently, and soaring upward, upward, melted away on a flashing stream of light into vaporous air.

Late that evening, as Anselmus did not appear in his place at vespers, some of the brethren sought the Abbot's permission to go to his studio and see if anything ailed him. The Abbot himself readily accompanied them, and by the light of a pale moon they found their "heavenly sculptor" lying unconscious before the empty niche, while standing on a rough pedestal was the completed statue of an angel, more angelic in form and feature than any they had ever yet seen. Full of wonder and compassion, they raised the sculptor's senseless body and bore him to his cell, where after some hours he revived sufficiently to recognize his surroundings and to express with pathetic humility his gratitude for the Abbot's fatherly solicitude and the brethren's anxious care. He was too feeble and ill to suffer much converse, therefore they humoured him in his evident desire to be spared all praise for the noble work of art he had achieved. All he would say when the Abbot expressed his admiration and reverence for what he justly considered the most perfect statue of an angel that had ever adorned any church was:

"God made it—not I!"

And he lay quiet for many days, without the strength to move— till at last the hours wore peacefully on to the blessed time of Christ's Nativity. Anselmus, brooding on this, began to rouse himself from his painful torpor and feebleness—nothing should prevent him, he said, with gentle, smiling earnestness, from standing in the choir with his "Angel" on Christmas Day!

So when the glorious morning came he went to Mass, supported by two of the brethren, one on each side to guide his faltering steps, and took his own place, his stall being immediately opposite the niche where his sculptured Angel was now set up in all its glory— a beauteous figure so instinct with genius as to be almost living, stretching out its hands in Peace and Blessing. White, worn, and weary, Anselmus was the centre of sorrowful interest among all the brethren who looked upon him—his thin, intellectual face and great burning eyes suggested some haunting tragedy in his brain—and they watched him in a kind of fear, feeling that he had about him the sense of something supernatural and strange.

The music surged around him, and the chanting voices of the monks made a deep, rhythmic wave of melody upon the air; the light through the stained-glass windows glittered and glowed, throwing long rays of purple and emerald, rose and blue across the steps of the altar, and Anselmus listened, looking at all things vaguely as one far off may look from some great height at the little plots of land and houses spread below—wondering within himself at the curious impression he had of unreality in all these sights and sounds, and more conscious of the statue of his Angel opposite to him than of anything else. The stately ritual went on till it reached the supreme moment of the oblation of the Host, when all were seated with heads bent in profound meditation and prayer. The bell rang, and the resonant voices of the brethren chanted solemnly— "*Sanctus, Sanctus, Sanctus! Dominus Deus Sabaoth! Plein sunt cœli et terra gloria tua!*"—when Anselmus, suddenly looking up, was struck across the eyes, as it were, by lightning. Thrilled by the shock, he sprang to his feet. There, on a shaft of dazzling luminance far brighter than the day, and poised on radiant wings between him and the statue he had wrought, was the Angel of his vision!—the Angel with the face of the little maiden he had wronged—the Angel of his inspiration—the Angel of his finished work! Ah, what tenderness now in the sea-blue eyes!—what sweetness in the divine smile!—what heavenly welcome in the outstretched arms and beckoning white hands!

"Beloved!—Beloved!" he cried, then with a choking sound in his throat he staggered and fell forward. The chanting ceased—the Abbot at the altar paused, with the sacred chalice in his hand—the brethren gathered hastily round the prone figure in consternation and sorrow—but all was over. Anselmus was dead.

A cloud swept across the sun, and for a moment the chancel was darkened, then, while two of the monks knelt by the fallen man and gently covered his face, the Abbot, with tears rising thickly in his eyes, again lifted the chalice. The sun came out anew, shining brilliantly through the chancel and lighting up the Angel-statue with a sudden whiteness as of snow, and with trembling voices the brethren resumed the interrupted service, making the arches of the noble Abbey resound and respond to a mystic Truth which the world is slow to recognize—

Benedictus qui venit in nomine Domini!

FROM THE DEAD

Edith Nesbit

When we think of Edith Nesbit (1858–1924) we think of her books for children, most famously The Railway Children *(1906) but also* The Story of the Treasure Seekers *(1899),* Five Children and It *(1902) and* The Phoenix and the Carpet *(1904). It comes as a surprise to many—indeed, it did when she was alive—to discover that she also wrote stories of the macabre and supernatural. One of her earliest books was* Grim Tales *(1893), which included her best-known stories, "Man-Size in Marble" and "John Charrington's Wedding", and the following story.*

Nesbit's private life was turbulent. She married Hubert Bland, a bank clerk, in 1880, when she was twenty-one and seven months pregnant. She soon discovered that Bland, a notorious philanderer, had previously been engaged and had a child by that girl, whilst a friend of Nesbit's, Alice Hoatson, was also pregnant by Bland. Alice came to live with the Blands as housekeeper and Edith raised her child (and a later child) as her own, later adopting them. Edith had three children with Bland, Paul, Mary and Fabian. The last was named after the Fabian Society, a socialist organization out of which the Labour Party emerged. It had been founded in 1884 with the Blands as two of the founding members. Edith was a noted lecturer and writer on socialism until her time became absorbed with her children's books. Over the years her books for adults have been forgotten. Amongst them is a romantic tale of possible immortality, Dormant *(1911).*

Some of Nesbit's turbulent life is reflected in the following story along with her personal phobias of the dark and of premature burial.

"**B**UT TRUE OR NOT TRUE, YOUR BROTHER IS A SCOUNDREL. No man—no decent man—tells such things."

"He did not tell me. How dare you suppose it? I found the letter in his desk; and since she was my friend and your sweetheart, I never thought there could be any harm in my reading anything she might write to my brother. Give me back the letter. I was a fool to tell you."

Ida Helmont held out her hand for the letter.

"Not yet," I said, and I went to the window. The dull red of a London sunset burned on the paper, as I read in the pretty hand-writing I knew so well, and had kissed so often:

DEAR: I do—I do love you; but it's impossible. I must marry Arthur. My honour is engaged. If he would only set me free—but he never will. He loves me foolishly.

But as for me—it is you I love—body, soul, and spirit.

There is no one in my heart but you. I think of you all day, and dream of you all night. And we must part. Goodbye—Yours, yours, yours,

ELVIRA

I had seen the handwriting, indeed, often enough. But the passion there was new to me. That I had not seen.

I turned from the window. My sitting-room looked strange to me. There were my books, my reading-lamp, my untasted dinner still on the table, as I had left it when I rose to dissemble my surprise at Ida Helmont's visit—Ida Helmont, who now sat looking at me quietly.

"Well—do you give me no thanks?"

"You put a knife in my heart, and then ask for thanks?"

"Pardon me," she said, throwing up her chin. "I have done nothing but show you the truth. For that one should expect no gratitude—may I ask, out of pure curiosity, what you intend to do?"

"Your brother will tell you—"

She rose suddenly, very pale, and her eyes haggard.

"You will not tell my brother?"

She came towards me—her gold hair flaming in the sunset light.

"Why are you so angry with me?" she said. "Be reasonable. What else could I do?"

"I don't know."

"Would it have been right not to tell you?"

"I don't know. I only know that you've put the sun out, and I haven't got used to the dark yet."

"Believe me," she said, coming still nearer to me, and laying her hands in the lightest touch on my shoulders, "believe me, she never loved you."

There was a softness in her tone that irritated and stimulated me. I moved gently back, and her hands fell by her sides.

"I beg your pardon," I said. "I have behaved very badly. You were quite right to come, and I am not ungrateful. Will you post a letter for me?"

I sat down and wrote:

I give you back your freedom. The only gift of mine that can please you now.—

ARTHUR

I held the sheet out to Miss Helmont, but she would not look at it. I folded, sealed, stamped, and addressed it.

"Goodbye," I said then, and gave her the letter. As the door closed behind her, I sank into my chair, and cried like a child, or a fool, over my lost play-thing—the little, dark-haired woman who loved someone else with "body, soul, and spirit".

I did not hear the door open or any foot on the floor, and therefore I started when a voice behind me said:

"Are you so very unhappy? Oh, Arthur, don't think I am not sorry for you!"

"I don't want anyone to be sorry for me, Miss Helmont," I said.

She was silent a moment. Then, with a quick, sudden, gentle movement she leaned down and kissed my forehead—and I heard the door softly close. Then I knew that the beautiful Miss Helmont loved me.

At first that thought only fleeted by—a light cloud against a grey sky—but the next day reason woke, and said:

"Was Miss Helmont speaking the truth? Was it possible that—"

I determined to see Elvira, to know from her own lips whether by happy fortune this blow came, not from her, but from a woman in whom love might have killed honesty.

I walked from Hampstead to Gower Street. As I trod its long length, I saw a figure in pink come out of one of the houses. It was Elvira. She walked in front of me to the corner of Store Street. There she met Oscar Helmont. They turned and met me face to face, and I saw all I needed to see. They loved each other. Ida Helmont had spoken the truth. I bowed and passed on. Before six months were gone, they were married, and before a year was over, I had married Ida Helmont.

What did it, I don't know. Whether it was remorse for having, even for half a day, dreamed that she could be so base as to forego a lie to gain a lover, or whether it was her beauty, or the sweet flattery of the preference of a woman who had half her acquaintance at her feet, I don't know; anyhow, my thoughts turned to her as to their natural home. My heart, too, took that road, and before very long I loved her as I never loved Elvira. Let no one doubt that I loved her—as I shall never love again—please God!

There never was anyone like her. She was brave and beautiful, witty and wise, and beyond all measure adorable. She was the only woman in the world. There was a frankness—a largeness of heart—about her that made all other women seem small and contemptible. She loved me and I worshipped her. I married her, I stayed with her for three golden weeks, and then I left her. Why?

Because she told me the truth. It was one night—late—we had sat all the evening in the veranda of our sea-side lodging, watching the moonlight on the water, and listening to the soft sound of the sea on the sand. I have never been so happy; I shall never be happy any more, I hope.

"My dear, my dear," she said, leaning her gold head against my shoulder, "how much do you love me?"

"How much?"

"Yes—how much? I want to know what place I hold in your heart. Am I more to you than anyone else?"

"My love!"

"More than yourself?"

"More than my life."

"I believe you," she said. Then she drew a long breath, and took my hands in hers. "It can make no difference. Nothing in heaven or earth can come between us now."

"Nothing," I said. "But, my dear one, what is it?"

For she was trembling, pale.

"I must tell you," she said; "I cannot hide anything now from you, because I am yours—body, soul, and spirit."

The phrase was an echo that stung.

The moonlight shone on her gold hair, her soft, warm, gold hair, and on her pale face.

"Arthur," she said, "you remember my coming to Hampstead with that letter."

"Yes, my sweet, and I remember how you—"

"Arthur!" she spoke fast and low—"Arthur, that letter was a forgery. She never wrote it. I—"

She stopped, for I had risen and flung her hands from me, and stood looking at her. God help me! I thought it was anger at the lie I felt. I know now it was only wounded vanity that smarted in me. That I should have been tricked, that I should have been deceived, that I should have been led on to make a fool of myself. That I should have married the woman who had befooled me. At that moment she was no longer the wife I adored—she was only a woman who had forged a letter and tricked me into marrying her.

I spoke: I denounced her; I said I would never speak to her again. I felt it was rather creditable in me to be so angry. I said I would have no more to do with a liar and a forger.

I don't know whether I expected her to creep to my knees and implore forgiveness. I think I had some vague idea that I could by-and-by consent with dignity to forgive and forget. I did not mean what I said. No, oh no, no; I did not mean a word of it. While I was saying it, I was longing for her to weep and fall at my feet, that I might raise her and hold her in my arms again.

But she did not fall at my feet; she stood quietly looking at me.

"Arthur," she said, as I paused for breath, "let me explain—she—I—"

"There is nothing to explain," I said hotly, still with that foolish sense of there being something rather noble in my indignation, the kind of thing one feels when one calls one's self a miserable sinner. "You are a liar and a forger, that is enough for me. I will never speak to you again. You have wrecked my life—"

"*Do* you mean that?" she said, interrupting me, and leaning forward to look at me. Tears lay on her cheeks, but she was not crying now.

I hesitated. I longed to take her in my arms and say: "What does all that old tale matter now? Lay your head here, my darling, and cry here, and know how I love you."

But instead I said nothing.

"Do you mean it?" she persisted.

Then she put her hand on my arm. I longed to clasp it and draw her to me.

Instead, I shook it off, and said:

"Mean it? Yes—of course I mean it. Don't touch me, please. You have ruined my life."

She turned away without a word, went into our room, and shut the door.

I longed to follow her, to tell her that if there was anything to forgive, I forgave it.

Instead, I went out on the beach, and walked away under the cliffs.

The moonlight and the solitude, however, presently brought me to a better mind. Whatever she had done, had been done for love of me—I knew that. I would go home and tell her so—tell her that whatever she had done, she was my dear life, my heart's one treasure. True, my ideal of her was shattered, at least I felt I ought to think that it was shattered, but, even as she was, what was the whole world of women compared to her? And to be loved like that... was that not sweet food for vanity? To be loved more than faith and fair dealing, and all the traditions of honesty and honour? I hurried back, but in my resentment and evil temper I had walked far, and the way back was very long. I had been parted from her for three hours by the time I opened the door of the little house where we lodged. The house was dark and very still. I slipped off my shoes and crept up the narrow stairs, and opened the door of our room quite softly. Perhaps she would have cried herself to sleep, and I would lean over her and waken her with my kisses, and beg her to forgive me. Yes, it had come to that now.

I went into the room—I went towards the bed. She was not there. She was not in the room, as one glance showed me. She was not in the house, as I knew in two minutes. When I had wasted a precious hour in searching the town for her, I found a note on my pillow:

"Goodbye! Make the best of what is left of your life. I will spoil it no more."

She was gone, utterly gone. I rushed to town by the earliest morning train, only to find that her people knew nothing of her. Advertisement failed. Only a tramp said he had seen a white lady on the cliff, and a fisherman brought me a handkerchief, marked with her name, which he had found on the beach.

I searched the country far and wide, but I had to go back to London at last, and the months went by. I won't say much about those months, because even the memory of that suffering turns me faint and sick at heart. The police and detectives and the Press failed me utterly. Her friends could not help me, and were, moreover, wildly indignant with me, especially her brother, now living very happily with my first love.

I don't know how I got through those long weeks and months. I tried to write; I tried to read; I tried to live the life of a reasonable human being. But it was impossible. I could not endure the companionship of my kind. Day and night I almost saw her face—almost heard her voice. I took long walks in the country, and her figure was always just round the next turn of the road—in the next glade of the wood. But I never quite saw her, never quite heard her. I believe I was not all together sane at that time. At last, one morning, as I was setting out for one of those long walks that had no goal but weariness, I met a telegraph boy, and took the red envelope from his hand.

On the pink paper inside was written:

Come to me at once I am dying you must come IDA Apinshaw Farm Mellor Derbyshire.

There was a train at twelve to Marple, the nearest station. I took it. I tell you there are some things that cannot be written about.

My life for those long months was one of them, that journey was another. What had her life been for those months? That question troubled me, as one is troubled in every nerve by the sight of a surgical operation, or a wound inflicted on a being dear to one. But the overmastering sensation was joy—intense, unspeakable joy. She was alive. I should see her again. I took out the telegram and looked at it: "I am dying." I simply did not believe it. She could not die till she had seen me. And if she had lived all these months without me, she could live now, when I was with her again, when she knew of the hell I had endured apart from her, and the heaven of our meeting. She must live; I could not let her die.

There was a long drive over bleak hills. Dark, jolting, infinitely wearisome. At last we stopped before a long, low building, where one or two lights gleamed faintly. I sprang out.

The door opened. A blaze of light made me blink and draw back. A woman was standing in the doorway.

"Art thee Arthur Marsh?" she said.

"Yes."

"Then th'art ower late. She's dead."

II

I went into the house, walked to the fire, and held out my hands to it mechanically, for though the night was May, I was cold to the bone. There were some folks standing round the fire, and lights flickering. Then an old woman came forward, with the northern instinct of hospitality.

"Thou'rt tired," she said, "and mazed-like. Have a sup o' tea."

I burst out laughing. I had travelled two hundred miles to see *her*. And she was dead, and they offered me tea. They drew back from me as if I had been a wild beast, but I could not stop laughing. Then a hand was laid on my shoulder and someone led me into a dark room, lighted a lamp, set me in a chair, and sat down opposite me. It was a bare parlour, coldly furnished with rush chairs and much-polished tables and presses. I caught my breath, and grew suddenly grave, and looked at the woman who sat opposite me.

"I was Miss Ida's nurse," said she, "and she told me to send for you. Who are you?"

"Her husband—"

The woman looked at me with hard eyes, where intense surprise struggled with resentment.

"Then may God forgive you!" she said. "What you've done I don't know, but it'll be hard work forgivin' *you*, even for *Him*!"

"Tell me," I said, "my wife—"

"Tell you!" The bitter contempt in the woman's tone did not hurt me. What was it to the self-contempt that had gnawed my heart all these months. "Tell you! Yes, I'll tell you. Your wife was that ashamed of you she never so much as told me she was married. She let me think anything I pleased sooner than that. She just come 'ere, an' she said, 'Nurse, take care of me, for I am in mortal trouble. And don't let them know where I am,' says she. An' me being well married to an honest man, and well-to-do here, I was able to do it, by the blessing."

"Why didn't you send for me before?" It was a cry of anguish wrung from me.

"I'd *never* 'a sent for you. It was *her* doin'. Oh, to think as God A'mighty's made men able to measure out such-like pecks o' trouble for us womenfolk! Young man, I don't know what you did to 'er to make 'er leave you; but it muster bin something cruel, for she loved the ground you walked on. She useter sit day after day a-lookin' at your picture, an' talkin' to it, an' kissin' of it, when she thought I wasn't takin' no notice, and cryin' till she made me cry too. She useter cry all night 'most. An' one day, when I tells 'er to pray to God to 'elp 'er through 'er trouble, she outs with *your* putty face on a card, she does, an', says she, with her poor little smile, 'That's my god, Nursey,' she says."

"Don't!" I said feebly, putting out my hands to keep off the torture; "not any more. Not now."

"*Don't!*" she repeated. She had risen, and was walking up and down the room with clasped hands. "Don't, indeed! No, I won't; but I shan't forget you! I tell you, I've had you in my prayers time and again, when I thought you'd made a light-o'-love of my darling. I shan't drop you outer them now, when I know she was your own wedded wife, as you chucked away when you tired of her, and left 'er to eat 'er 'eart out with longin' for you. Oh! I pray to God above us to pay you scot and lot for all you done to 'er. You killed my pretty. The price will be required of you, young man, even to the uttermost farthing. Oh God in Heaven, make him suffer! Make him feel it!"

She stamped her foot as she passed me. I stood quite still. I bit my lip till I tasted the blood hot and salt on my tongue.

"She was nothing to you," cried the woman, walking faster up and down between the rush chairs and the table; "any fool can see that with half an eye. You didn't love her, so you don't feel nothin' now; but some day you'll care for someone, and then you shall know what she felt—if there's any justice in Heaven."

I, too, rose, walked across the room, and leaned against the wall. I heard her words without understanding them.

"Can't you feel *nothin*? Are you mader stone? Come an' look at 'er lyin' there so quiet. She don't fret arter the likes o' you no more now. She won't sit no more a-lookin' outer winder an' sayin' nothin'—only droppin' 'er tears one by one, slow, slow on 'er lap. Come an' see 'er; come an' see what you done to my pretty—an' then you can go. Nobody wants you 'ere. *She* don't want you now. But p'raps you'd like to see 'er safe under ground afore yer go? I'll be bound you'll put a big stone slab on 'er—to make sure she don't rise again."

I turned on her. Her thin face was white with grief and rage. Her claw-like hands were clenched.

"Woman," I said, "have mercy."

She paused and looked at me.

"Eh?" she said.

"Have mercy!" I said again.

"Mercy! You should 'a thought o' that before. You 'adn't no mercy on 'er. She loved you—she died loving you. An' if I wasn't a Christian woman, I'd kill you for it—like the rat you are! That I would, though I 'ad to swing for it afterwards."

I caught the woman's hands and held them fast, though she writhed and resisted.

"Don't you understand?" I said savagely. "We loved each other. She died loving me. I have to live loving her. And it's *her* you pity. I tell you it was all a mistake—a stupid, stupid mistake. Take me to her, and for pity's sake, let me be left alone with her."

She hesitated; then said, in a voice only a shade less hard: "Well, come along, then."

We moved towards the door. As she opened it, a faint, weak cry fell on my ear. My heart stood still.

"What's that?" I asked, stopping on the threshold.

"Your child," she said shortly.

That too! Oh, my love! oh, my poor love! All these long months!

"She allus said she'd send for you when she'd got over 'er trouble," the woman said, as we climbed the stairs. "'I'd like him to see his little baby, nurse,' she says; 'our little baby. It'll be all right when the baby's born,' she says. 'I know he'll come to me then. You'll see.' And I never said nothin', not thinkin' you'd come if she was your leavin's' and not dreamin' you could be 'er 'usband an' could stay away from 'er a hour—'er bein' as she was. Hush!"

She drew a key from her pocket and fitted it to a lock. She opened the door, and I followed her in. It was a large, dark room, full of old-fashioned furniture and a smell of lavender, camphor, and narcissus.

The big four-post bed was covered with white.

"My lamb—my poor, pretty lamb!" said the woman, beginning to cry for the first time as she drew back the sheet. "Don't she look beautiful?"

I stood by the bedstead. I looked down on my wife's face. Just so I had seen it lie on the pillow beside me in the early morning, when the wind and the dawn came up from beyond the sea. She did not look like one dead. Her lips were still red, and it seemed to me that a tinge of colour lay on her cheek. It seemed to me, too, that if I kissed her she would awaken, and put her slight hand on my neck, and lay her cheek against mine—and that we should tell each other everything, and weep together, and understand, and be comforted.

So I stooped and laid my lips to hers as the old nurse stole from the room.

But the red lips were like marble, and she did not waken. She will not waken now ever any more.

I tell you again there are some things that cannot be written.

III

I lay that night in a big room, filled with heavy dark furniture, in a great four-poster hung with heavy, dark curtains—a bed, the counterpart of that other bed from whose side they had dragged me at last.

They fed me, I believe, and the old nurse was kind to me. I think she saw now that it is not the dead who are to be pitied most.

I lay at last in the big, roomy bed, and heard the household noises grow fewer and die out, the little wail of my child sounding latest. They had brought the child to me, and I had held it in my arms, and bowed my head over its tiny face and frail fingers. I did not love it then. I told myself it had cost me her life. But my heart told me it was I who had done that. The tall clock at the stairhead sounded the hours—eleven, twelve, one, and still I could not sleep. The room was dark and very still.

I had not yet been able to look at my life quietly. I had been full of the intoxication of grief—a real drunkenness, more merciful than the sober calm that comes afterwards.

Now I lay still as the dead woman in the next room, and looked at what was left of my life. I lay still, and thought, and thought, and thought. And in those hours I tasted the bitterness of death. It must

have been about three when I first became aware of a slight sound
that was not the ticking of a clock. I say I first became aware, and
yet I knew perfectly that I had heard that sound more than once
before, and had yet determined not to hear it, *because it came from
the next room*—the room where the corpse lay.

And I did not wish to hear that sound, because I knew it meant
that I was nervous—miserably nervous—a coward, and a brute. It
meant that I, having killed my wife as surely as though I had put
a knife in her breast, had now sunk so low as to be afraid of her
dead body—the dead body that lay in the next room to mine. The
heads of the beds were placed against the same wall: and from
that wall I had fancied that I heard slight, slight, almost inaudible
sounds. So that when I say I became aware of them, I mean that
I, at last, heard a sound so definite as to leave no room for doubt
or question. It brought me to a sitting position in the bed, and the
drops of sweat gathered heavily on my forehead and fell on my
cold hands, as I held my breath and listened.

I don't know how long I sat there—there was no further
sound—and at last my tense muscles relaxed, and I fell back on
the pillow.

"You fool!" I said to myself; "dead or alive, is she not your
darling, your heart's heart? Would you not go near to die of joy,
if she came back to you? Pray God to let her spirit come back and
tell you she forgives you!"

"I wish she would come," myself answered in words, while
every fibre of my body and mind shrank and quivered in denial.

I struck a match, lighted a candle, and breathed more freely
as I looked at the polished furniture—the commonplace details
of an ordinary room. Then I thought of her, lying alone so near

me, so quiet under the white sheet. She was dead; she would not wake or move. But suppose she did move? Suppose she turned back the sheet and got up and walked across the floor, and turned the door-handle?

As I thought it, I heard—plainly, unmistakably heard—the door of the chamber of death open slowly. I heard slow steps in the passage, slow, heavy steps. I heard the touch of hands on my door outside, uncertain hands that felt for the latch.

Sick with terror, I lay clenching the sheet in my hands.

I knew well enough what would come in when that door opened—that door on which my eyes were fixed. I dreaded to look, yet dared not turn away my eyes. The door opened slowly, slowly, slowly, and the figure of my dead wife came in. It came straight towards the bed, and stood at the bed foot in its white grave-clothes, with the white bandage under its chin. There was a scent of lavender and camphor and white narcissus. Its eyes were wide open, and looked at me with love unspeakable.

I could have shrieked aloud.

My wife spoke. It was the same dear voice that I had loved so to hear, but it was very weak and faint now; and now I trembled as it listened.

"You aren't afraid of me, darling, are you, though I am dead? I heard all you said to me when you came, but I couldn't answer. But now I've come back from the dead to tell you. I wasn't really so bad as you thought me. Elvira had told me she loved Oscar. I only wrote the letter to make it easier for you. I was too proud to tell you when you were so angry, but I am not proud any more now. You'll love again now, won't you, now I am dead. One always forgives dead people."

The poor ghost's voice was hollow and faint. Abject terror paralysed me. I could answer nothing.

"Say you forgive me," the thin, monotonous voice went on, "say you love me again."

I had to speak. Coward as I was, I did manage to stammer:

"Yes; I love you. I have always loved you, God help me."

The sound of my own voice reassured me, and I ended more firmly than I began. The figure by the bed swayed a little, unsteadily.

"I suppose," she said wearily, "you would be afraid, now I am dead, if I came round to you and kissed you?"

She made a movement as though she would have come to me.

Then I did shriek aloud, again and again, and covered my face with all my force. There was a moment's silence. Then I heard my door close, and then a sound of feet and of voices, and I heard something heavy fall. I disentangled my head from the sheet. My room was empty. Then reason came back to me. I leaped from the bed.

"Ida, my darling, come back! I am not afraid! I love you. Come back! Come back!"

I sprang to my door and flung it open. Someone was bringing a light along the passage. On the floor, outside the door of the death chamber, was a huddled heap—the corpse, in its grave-clothes. Dead, dead, dead.

She is buried in Mellor churchyard, and there is no stone over her.

Now, whether it was catalepsy, as the doctor said, or whether my love came back, even from the dead, to me who loved her, I shall never know; but this I know, that if I had held out my arms to her as she stood at my bed-foot—if I had said, "Yes, even from the grave, my darling—from hell itself, come back, come back to me!"—if I had had room in my coward's heart for anything but the unreasoning terror that killed love in that hour, I should not now be here alone. I shrank from her—I feared her—I would not take her to my heart. And now she will not come to me anymore.

Why do I go on living?

You see, there is the child. It is four years old now, and it has never spoken and never smiled.

THE CHRISTMAS IN THE FOG

Frances Hodgson Burnett

Like Edith Nesbit, Frances Hodgson Burnett (1849–1924) is best remembered—perhaps only remembered—for her two children's books, Little Lord Fauntleroy *(1886) and the perennial favourite,* The Secret Garden *(1911), but she wrote much more besides, over forty books, from* That Lass o' Lowrie's *(1877) to the posthumously published* In the Garden *(1925). Because she lived for so long in the United States and became a US citizen in 1905, it's easy to forget she was born in England, at Cheetham, Manchester. Alas her father died when she was only three. The family survived but finances became increasingly tight and in 1865 Frances's mother took up the offer of the family moving to Tennessee to join her brother. Frances was already a voracious reader and once settled in the United States she determined to become a writer, selling her first story in 1868, when only eighteen. In fact, she sold two in quick succession, because the magazine editor wanted proof of her abilities. Stories tumbled out of Frances, enabling her to support the family until her mother died in 1870, and her siblings married. Frances married twice, neither marriage being happy, and she had two children. She frequently returned to England, and for ten years (1898–1907) lived at Great Maytham Hall in Kent, where a lost garden became the inspiration for* The Secret Garden. *She returned to the United States in 1907, living the rest of her life at a home she had specially built at Plandome Manor, near New York.*

Starting in 1914 Frances wrote an occasional series of sketches which were part autobiographical and part story. They were memories from her youth which sparked thoughts on those little things in life which stir the imagination. She looked back on these episodes as if she were two persons, the one writing about them and the one experiencing them, whom she called the Romantick Lady. Whilst not overtly supernatural, they are all strange tales, as the following—the first of them—reveals.

T HE LEAST IMAGINATIVE OF PERSONS, BEING IMPRESSED EVEN to the verge of stimulation by long reiterated quotation, will admit, though it may be with reluctance, that Truth is Stranger than Fiction. There is to such individuals a suggestion of bold flight and daring in the statement, made with whatsoever of conservativeness of mental reservation. The suggestion, however, that Truth is as a rule more *entertaining*, more delightfully coloured, more varied than Fiction, not having as yet been generally accepted as a point of view assuming the aspect of a proverb, might, by the inelastic mind, be regarded with distrust. Yet this is the suggestion which I have the courage to offer.

I was about to say that I offer it quite unreservedly, but for a moment I pause to reflect. Do incidents marked by all the picturesqueness, the colour and character-revealing quality, usually regarded as being the attributes of mere fiction, occur continually to every human being? That is what I ask myself. After the pause for reflection I decide that it is more than probable that they do. Because they are things which merely *happen* as part of the day's work, and are not incidents recorded on a printed page, they are passed by comparatively little noticed, except by the born romancer—of whom there are many who have written no line of fiction in their lives.

This aspect of affairs renders the Book of Life enthralling. It is crowded with the fantastic, the unexpected, the pathetic, the alluring. Each individual hour is "To be continued in our next." There is a certain exhilaration in realizing that if one sat down today to read a realistic history—thoroughly well done with actual atmosphere and feeling—of all that oneself would do and think and see during the next week, or all that one's nextdoor neighbour thought and felt and saw two weeks ago, one would read entranced until the story was finished, and rise enchanted, murmuring, "How delightful! How human!" With a stimulating recognition of this fact in view I have been lured by a fancy for telling little stories—or rather making sketches of Things which Happened.

When I say they "happened" I mean literally what I write. They are not invented, they are not elaborated, they are simply recorded as they occurred. Mere episodes they are, not stories with a beginning, a middle, and an end; not even adventures—mere episodes whose chief interest may perhaps lie in the fact that they are, as I have said, Things which Happened.

The fact is that when even comparatively trivial incidents taking place in the everyday life of a person who has the mental trick of seeing things as stories—dramas—pictures, if he or she has also the constitutional story-teller's habit of presenting them vividly in casual conversation to friends, when these incidents are narrated, audiences have also a trick of exclaiming—after laughter, derision, or temporary emotion are at an end—"Why don't you make that into a story?" "Why doesn't somebody write that?" And after these things have been said persistently enough, and the reply, "Oh! There isn't enough in it," has been sufficiently often protested against, somebody almost inevitably does end by writing them. And there you are!—to quote Henry James.

It was, in fact, after this manner that these odds and ends of records came into written existence.

To begin with. They occurred in the ordinary day's work of a person known ironically to herself and to me as "The Romantick Lady"—a name which the bearer of it owns she privately bestowed upon herself after having studied her own case for half a lifetime. She found it, she says, useful when arguing with herself on the subject of her own peculiarities.

"It seems rather to excuse and modify them a little," was her explanation. "A discerning friend—or enemy—might have chosen the name of The Slightly Mad Lady—The Fantastic Lady—The Fools-Rush-in Lady—or The Sentimental Lady, and far be it from me to say that there might not have been fittingness in any one of them. That is what I myself don't know. But 'The Romantick Lady' is more palliative. And you may be sure that if I choose a name for myself I shall choose one which cheers if it does not inebriate. But you must always spell it with a ' k ' at the end, as it is spelled in those nice old worn leather-bound books with yellowed pages and f's for s's—The Romantick Lady."

I have known her for some twenty years, and during that time have each year recognized more fully the entire fitness of the name it pleased her to decide upon. It is used between us only when she makes a little sketch for me of some of the occasions on which she has suddenly found herself irresistibly impelled to do a thing which at the moment seems the one and only right thing in the world to be done, but of whose ultimate results she finds herself entirely uncertain when the flaring glow of the impelling moment has died down, and leaves her gazing with wistful curiosity at her work and wondering—wondering.

"Perhaps I am really an interfering person. I have told myself that sometimes." She said this speculatively, in one of her analytical moods, superinduced by an occasion on which she felt it probable that she had made a frightful though well-meaning idiot of herself, and probably wrecked dynasties, so to speak. "I do interfere. I see something which I feel *must* be helped—some trouble, some awful lack—and I dash in—because it seems the Law of the Jungle. It may be right, it may be wrong, but suppose it is *interfering!* who knows!"

Some time ago she made me a confession.

"Once," she said, "I think I committed a crime. I can never be sure whether it was one or not, but I can never forget it. Perhaps I was mistaken. Perhaps it was only a little thing—but perhaps it was immense. No number of years makes any difference in the anguish of fear and doubt which fills me each time the memory comes back to me.

"This was what happened. One morning I was walking in a crowded street in London. You know what that means, and how people hurry by. Suddenly I looked ahead of me and saw a little boy of about seven or eight hurrying with the rest. He was only a few yards away, and he did not see me—he did not see any one—he saw only the cruel, the hopelessly cruel or heartbreaking or terrifying thing he was thinking of—facing—possibly going to meet and suffer. At least that was the thought which suddenly gripped at my heart. He was a shabby little boy, carrying a small bundle, and sobbing low and breathlessly as he went. His face was white, and his eyes had that horribly bewept, almost blinded look one shudders before when one sees it in an older person. That a child's face and eyes should look so was inhuman—unnatural."

"You spoke to him?" I suggested.

"That was my crime. I didn't." She answered. "The first moment there seemed only one thing to do—to stop him—to kneel down before him if need be so that he would know one was *close* to him—to put both hands on his poor little shoulders and say: 'Look here! Tell me! Tell me what it is. I can help you. I *can!* If any one has hurt you or frightened you they shall not *dare* to do it again! I can prevent them. I can make them afraid.' At times like that something leaps up in me which makes me *know* I could make lions and tigers afraid. I don't know what it is. I had an appalling vision of some brute and devil who had either hideously beaten or ill-treated him—or had sworn to do it, when he reached his destination with his little bundle. I saw it all, and knew his heart-broken, abject, child terror and helplessness before his fate. What can a child do?—And yet, with that in my mind I found myself suddenly overwhelmed with a sort of shyness. Even as he came nearer I realized certain things I know about boys—how they hate being made conspicuous, how they shrink from public emotions, how they abhor being meddled with when they do not want to own that they are crying. I thought a thousand things in one minute. It might make a sort of scene for him—"

"If you had knelt on the pavement to put your hands on his shoulders and pour out your soul," I interposed, with firmness and logic, "that entire hurrying crowd would have stopped, and formed a mob in five seconds. You would have impeded traffic, and a policeman would have ordered you to move on or taken you and your boy in charge."

"In that one minute I saw all that," she made swift, uneasy answer. "But it ought not to have mattered. Nothing ought to have mattered. I said to myself: 'I must stop him! I *will*. I can't let him pass! I dare not.' And because I was a hesitating coward—it was all over in two minutes I suppose—I let the crowd sweep him past me and swallow him up—his little awful, bewept face and eyes, his breathless sobs and tiny bundle, were gone! Yes, I did that. I, your friend, did that! And I shall never know *what* I allowed to pass me by, and to what woe it went its piteous helpless little way, when *I* might have stepped in between. Being the kind of person I am—whatsoever kind that may be—my brain has a trick of making absolutely real pictures for me. I wish it hadn't. I shall not tell you all the things it showed me which might have happened that day to that one small sobbing boy. I made a new prayer that night—something like this: 'Whatsoever You let me do, never—*never* let me *pass any one by.*'"

I, for one, realized fully that the unforgettable memory of this possible crime had formed a background for many things. It had made her afraid.

"It may seem rather insane to do it," I have heard her say half to herself, "but suppose it was a thing one ought not to pass by? Suppose it *was!*"

Her being is the screen upon which the cinematograph of Life throws human pictures. They leap unbidden into existence before her and will not be denied. She *sees* the Story. To her, not so much the "stranger than fiction," but the "more entertaining than fiction," occurs with delightful continuity.

"The interestingness of things—the absorbingness, the picturesqueness," she exclaims, "of things which really happen in the most casual and everyday way! As if they were nothing, you know!"

Her Romantick mistakes assume naturally now and then the proportions of her Romantick visions. It is, of course, a mere trivial detail that she gives of her substance to dramatic beggars in defiance of all laws of political economy; it is also a detail, though perhaps less trivial, that she also gives of it to persons not beggars who do not in the least deserve it. But for a certain grim little sense of humour she would probably die of grief at times, but she fortunately sees in herself quite as much reason for ironic laughter as others do, and finds in her own entity an object for impersonal analysis and detachedly logical contemplation. In each experience she saw her Vision and obeyed it.

"And sometimes things come right," she says, totally without prejudice. "Everything is a sort of experiment. To live is an experiment—though one did not undertake it deliberately."

This slight summing up may explain her, and in a measure make clear such brief episodes as I may record.

"You may tell them if you like," she says. "None of them matters to any one. And I shall only be the shadow of a Romantick Lady. And I might also be either a sort of warning—or a sort of encouragement."

There is no warning in the incident of The Christmas in the Fog; there is, in fact, little in it but the lights and shades of a curious picture.

After a year or so of wandering in various countries she took passage for New York in one of the huge liners which was to sail two days before Christmas. The day before she left London a great fog had descended and enfolded the city in a yellow blanket so thick that traffic had gradually become dangerous and at last almost impossible. It was a fog to be remembered. People lost themselves and wandered helplessly about for hours, garnering material for thrilling anecdote which enlivened many dull evenings during the remainder of the winter. It was a fog which lasted for several days.

A fog in London, however, does not always presuppose a fog in the country. One may leave the Strand groping in the darkness of the Last Day, take a train at Charing Cross or Waterloo, and after a few miles of uncertain and slow journeying through various degrees of eerie yellowness, gradually emerge through thinning veils of mist into clear air—sometimes into sunshine.

This is what the Romantick Lady anticipated when she settled herself into the corner of her railway carriage lighted by a lamp the fog dimmed, and peered out of the window trying to follow the shadowy figures whose outlines were lost in the gloom at a yard's distance and less.

"We shall be out of it in half an hour at most," she thought. "We may sail out of the Mersey in a glittering sun."

But there was a character of pertinacity about the thing. The train moved slowly, explosions of fog-signals were heard along the line, the platforms of stations were mere dull orange glimmers of light in an orange-brown darkness through which muffled voices shouted, and uncertain ghosts of would-be passengers were bundled into first-, second,- or third-class carriages by assisting ghosts of porters who banged doors or said hoarsely, "Than 'y, Sir," for tips. All the world seemed muffled and mysterious and hoarse. Ordinary existence was temporarily suspended, or performed its functions after the manner of a sort of Blind Man's Buff. That it was weird and interesting could not be denied—neither could it be denied that it was dangerous.

The yellow blanket spread its heavy folds farther beyond London than was usual; even when it began to attenuate itself a little, its thinning to a semi-obscurity took a long time. Even after that had happened it trailed along, and here and there seemed to thicken in certain places. It hung over towns which were not accustomed to it, and it lay heavily in hollows and fields. The Romantick Lady began to watch it, looking backward, as the train pushed ahead.

"It is an eerie thing to look at. It is like an unescapable Giant Wraith who is following us," she thought. "I hope it will not be able to keep up."

To face the prospect of steaming out into the Mersey crowded with craft of all sizes, from huge ocean-liners to tugs and fishing-boats, all blinded in the swathing of this enfolding, light-and-sound-deadening yellow gloom, was not cheering.

Just before reaching Liverpool the Wraith seemed to have failed to keep up speed. There was a dimness in the air, but one could see where one was going. There were no actual difficulties in the way of descending from the train, of securing porters and one's belongings, of making way through the steamer-bound crowd, and of climbing the gangway and getting on board in the old familiar fashion with which half the world has become so intimate during the last twenty years. It was just as always, but that few people had come to see their friends "off." The weather had been too dire. The boarding crowd, however, was in rather good spirits, congratulating itself that the Wraith had been left behind. A breath of fresh sea air would be good to inhale, people said, after those last two suffocating, throat-stinging days in London.

The gang-plank was withdrawn, the last good-byes were shouted across the widening gap between the steamer and the wharf, the great liner swung out slowly, while the band played something joyous and promising. The usual people went up and down the stairways to look at the saloon, the library, the drawing-room; the rest either wandered about passages searching for their staterooms or stewards, or, having found their special apartments, occupied themselves with the arrangement of their belongings and the opening of packages and letters.

The Romantick Lady was never able to tell me how many letters and packages she opened, and how many of her steamer books she dipped into—how long it was, in fact, before she became conscious that she could not see clearly—that she could scarcely see at all—that she was actually in need of a light. She dropped her book and looked about her stateroom. Even the gay chintz of the hangings of her berth had faded into indistinctness; a thick yellow curtain had been drawn across the window.

"What has happened?" she said. "We sailed at three o'clock. I have not been here more than an hour, surely."

She had been so absorbed that she knew she could not be sure of her own estimate of time; also she had not been conscious that the steamer had been moving very slowly. She became aware now that it was scarcely moving at all—and there broke forth in the dimness a wild and hollow booming roar such as a Megatherium, as it rooted up and trampled down great trees in a primeval forest in darkest ages, might have bellowed in his lonely rage. She knew it well. What ocean traveller does not? It was the fog-horn!

"Woo—oo—oo—ooh!"

"It has followed us," she said, sitting down among her belongings. "It has got us. It has shut us in."

Then the steamer shuddered a little, went more slowly—more slowly still—stopped!

"And here we are," thought the Romantick Lady. "A thousand or so of us. I wonder how many are in the steerage?"

That was the opening of the little episode. The Giant Wraith had fallen behind merely to gather strength and volume. Upon the river crowded with shipping—with great and small craft, most of them making their way toward its mouth, either to pass in or out of the open sea—it had dropped its heaviest mantle, and shut out all chance of safety in movement. To move was almost certain disaster. Who would be mad enough to do it? Not the guider of a giant liner with the lives of more than a thousand souls in the hollow of his hand.

"The fact that it is rather awesome does not make it any less one of the most weird and nerve-thrilling of adventures." This was the mental attitude of the Romantick Lady. "An adventure it is. I must go out and inquire into detail."

Others had left their staterooms for the same purpose. In the corridors several somewhat anxious-looking women were standing at doors, or were just emerging from them. There were excitedly curious faces and some excitedly alarmed ones. Male relatives were being questioned or were being dispatched to investigate. "We've stopped! What is the matter? How dark it is! It is the fog. It came on all at once. I rang for the steward. It is like the Day of Judgment!" Several people had rung for steward or stewardess, who presented themselves with uncertain but determinedly reassuring aspects. On the stairs and in the companionway were groups of talking passengers. It was not difficult to hear the facts of the situation. There was no reason for concealment. The captain had hoped to be able to steam out of the pursuing fog, but it had descended upon and surrounded its prey with extraordinary suddenness, thickening as it closed in. There was no possibility of safe movement, however slow. The obviously discreet course was to light warning lights, blow warning fog-horns, and wait until the fog lifted—which might happen at any time.

Other craft had decided upon the same action, it became evident. Out of the muffling yellowness were to be heard at intervals from one point and another hollow roars, hollow toots, shrill terrified little whistles, and big demoniac warning ones. One immense incoming liner was due at the very time of peril. It was somewhere not far away. Its awful fog-horn bellowed forth the fact from the fog's thickest enclosing. But it had also ceased moving. No doubt its lights of warning were in proportion to its size, but only those near enough could suspect their presence. "They say everything has stopped. You can't see a yard ahead. It is quite awful. Nothing dare stir. It can't last long. It may lift in about half an hour. We are hanging in a thick murk. It's like the Inferno."

Those exclamatory remarks the Romantick Lady heard with many others from the different groups. She also gathered much doubtless wholly incorrect information connected with fogs and captains and disasters. The general opinion was that the fog would lift in an hour at most—in half an hour, perhaps. It was not possible for people who had just begun a journey to regard it as credible that they were to be absurdly stopped at its outset. A touch of wind would blow the yellow curtain aside, and the way would be clear. If *nothing* moved—incoming or outgoing steamers or sailing vessels large and small, safety was at least secured, and those who wished might occupy themselves and settle down as they chose, endeavouring to possess their souls in patience. So the groups gradually melted away to staterooms, or the smoking-room, or to the library, where letters might be begun depicting dramatically the singular situation. There would be a satisfactory amount of colour in any first letter from a voyager which was headed, "In a Fog in the Middle of the Mersey."

In half an hour the gloom had not disappeared, in an hour it had become even heavier and deeper, and the steamer did not move. To the Romantick Lady there presented itself the alluring idea that to mount to the deck might be to make a mental record of a unique order of picture.

It was unique enough. When she found herself outside she stood still to make the most—for her own peculiar pleasure—of the mysterious unearthliness of it. The great ship hung enclosed as though in opaque yellow walls. The fog of which they were built covered the decks, as it covered land and sea. But for the dimmed orange glow of numerous lamps it would have been impossible to guess where one was moving. And but for the ship's rail an explorer might easily have walked overboard.

The Romantick Lady began to make her way slowly. At intervals the booming roar of the fog-horn prolonged itself in the midst of the stillness, and the incoming liner who had also lost her way seemed to respond, while smaller hollow or shrill sounds added their protesting warning.

"Don't move! Don't move! It's death to stir. Here I stand motion-less—here—here!" the Leviathans bellowed as the Romantick Lady translated them. And the smaller craft shrieked in terror: "And here am I—here-here—here! If you move you may sweep me to the sea's bottom!"

No one seemed to be on deck. To the Romantick Lady the deck appeared her sole demesne. The remoteness, the sense of being at once shut in and shut out from the world, from life itself, was an uncanny and spectral thing. A new-born ghost wandering in ghostly spaces as yet unknown, might have felt it. When, as she made her second round of the deck, there loomed up out of the mystery a few feet ahead of her a tramping male passenger. He was but another disembodied creature, who silently drew near and passed through the non-obstructing wall which closed behind him. He made her feel more ghost-like than before. Round the deck he went apparently as she was going, but in the opposite direction. As they went round they passed each other again—emerging from the veil, nearing, silently passing, and swallowed up in its swathing folds. Again and again they passed each other, but always as shadows and ghosts. Neither really saw the other, and throughout the voyage which followed neither recognized in the body the disembodied thing which had touched its sphere in its ghostly wanderings.

At length the Romantick Lady paused at the rail at one end of the deck, and leaned against it to look down. It was not that she anticipated seeing anything, but a Romantick thought had suddenly appeared upon her mental horizon. She began to think of the steerage passengers. How many were there? Of what nationalities were they? How many men—how many women—how many children? They would most of them be uneducated peasants. How many of them would know anything about a London fog— particularly a London fog which, escaping its lawful boundaries, had journeyed to Liverpool and settled upon the shipping in the Mersey.

She began to see pictures, and deplore that first-class passengers were forbidden to go down into the steerage. It was a rule hygienically sound, no doubt, and highly creditable to the sagacity of the

Health Officers, but it placed an obstacle in the way of Adventurous Romance. What might not a Romantick Lady find among Goths and Huns and Russian Jews journeying in the steerage of a great steamer to a new land and life and fortune?

There was a deadened sound of footsteps which came to a stop in the pit of dimness just below her. There was the shuffling sound of more than one man making himself comfortable, sitting down on something—a coil of rope perhaps. There were evidently two of them, and their voices came up to her rather mumblingly at first. Whosoever they were, they had come to look at the fog as she had—or had braved it because a foggy deck was more desirable than the depths of a foggy steerage. And out of the indistinctness of the mumbling she heard this:

"A bit thick, ain't it?" in a hoarse Cockney voice. "No wonder they're frightened 'arf out of their senses. Lot of Russian Jews and Italians and Poles. Eight hundred of 'em got to be kept quiet."

The Vision rose before her, and she leaned farther over the rail and dropped a question down into the pit, forgetting that a disembodied voice might seem a startling thing. She thought only of what she wanted to know.

"How many children are there?"

The detached voice plainly was sufficiently startling. She heard quick movement, and there was a pause in which there was evident listening.

"How many children?" she dropped down again. Something like suppressed laughter, and then a disembodied voice came up to her.

"I can't see yer, laidy!"

"I can't see you either, but we can hear each other. How many children are there?"

More suppressed chuckling and a mumbled interchange of words. Then the answer ascended, "About a hundred and fifty—laidy—most of 'em squealin'."

"Thank you."

That was all. She went away and resumed her walk, and while she walked she saw pictures of the fog which had crept down into the steerage, of the Poles and Italians and Russian Jews, and the hundred and fifty children on their way to America to begin again—to begin differently. They gave her plenty to think of, and from this visionary figure and that branched stories of all shades.

Several times in her talk with me of this incident she has wondered curiously how many of the passengers have remembered it, how many of them felt the three days of fog to be weird enchantment, how many felt them merely draggingly dull.

For three days it actually lasted—for three days they were held motionless by the soft but impenetrable gloom. There must have been deep sleeping through the silence of that first night. In many cases there was late waking after it, because the night and the morning were as one, and there were no sounds of working engines when consciousness came back.

The most mysteriously interesting of human characteristics is human adaptability to circumstances, which, indeed, seems almost automatic in its action. After the first hours of amazement, nervousness, and talk, the entire passenger-list began to adapt itself to lamplight and yellow mist in staterooms, corridors, and saloons, and more or less resignedly settled down. Men began to play cards and talk over their cigars in the smoking-room, women began to read, and write letters, and chat in the library and sitting-room.

Gradually people appeared on deck, and made themselves comfortable with furs and rugs in steamer-chairs under the dulled yellow glow of the many lights.

Lying in her berth before she breakfasted, the Romantick Lady had entertained herself by evolving a seasonable little plan. She had asked questions of her stewardess, who was an intelligent person. She had verified the statements of the detached male voice which had answered her out of the pit. There were eight hundred Russians, Poles, Italians, etc., in the steerage. They carried among their bags and bundles a hundred and fifty children of all shapes and sizes. They were all going to make their fortunes in America. There was also another interesting detail. The Romantick Lady evolved therefrom her little seasonable plan.

"Tomorrow is Christmas Day." She thought it out with her usual joy in the small drama. "One hundred and fifty little pairs of hands are going empty—quite empty—into America. How nice—how *cheerful*—to put something into every one of them—just *something*, even if it is not much—so that they will not go in *quite* empty. And why not do it on Christmas Day?"

After this she thought further, and through the depths of a fog a point of light gleamed.

"I am not a good beggar," she mentally proceeded. "I am too conceited and too cowardly. But *any one* would give you a penny—if you asked for no more. I shall therefore get up and dress myself, take my bag in my hand, and go over this entire ship—except of course the steerage—and ask *everybody* for a penny. A steward could give you a penny, so could a stewardess (out of the sovereigns you tip them with)—a sailor could give you one—but I shall not ask sailors, because they won't have purses in their pockets."

Later in the day, at an hour when no one could be remaining in bed, and therefore every one was to be found in one quarter or another, the passenger in the first chair of the first row on deck—a large, businesslike, middled-aged man folded comfortably in a most desirable travelling-rug—was roused from a dozing reverie on fogs by the sound of a voice speaking at his side.

"If you please, will you give me a penny?" it said.

He roused himself with a start and pushed back his cap, which had been pulled down over his eyes.

"Eh! What? Beg pardon!" he stammered.

It is not an infrequent experience of the Romantick Lady's, she tells me, that she is conscious that there are occasions when the first impression she produces upon really intelligent persons is that she is slightly mad—not very mad really, but the harmless victim of hallucinations. That a practically minded first-class passenger on a voyage across the Atlantic should find himself suddenly addressed by a comfortably clothed and furred woman who rises out of the fog to hold out her hand and ask him for a penny, might be regarded as an incident a trifle startling and unexplainable.

"Would you mind giving me a penny?" she said again.

And again he stammered, "I beg—I beg your pardon. I don't quite understand!"

"Tomorrow is Christmas Day," explained the Romantick Lady. "I want it for the children in the steerage. There are a hundred and fifty of them. I am going to ask every one for a penny. Any one will give a penny. And it will mount up. If it is not enough I shall add something myself. I want *every* child to have *something* in its hand when it lands in America."

The end passenger probably still held—in the back of his mind— the idea of harmless hallucinations, but he was a lenient and gener- ous person. He fumbled in his pocket, murmuring something civil as he searched for his pocketbook. When he found it he handed her a five-dollar bill.

"That is two hundred and fifty pennies, I believe," said the Romantick Lady. "Oh, I *am* grateful to you!"

"Not at all! Not at all!" answered the end passenger, replacing his pocketbook.

By this time the next passenger was awake, and the next, and the next, until as the Romantick Lady passed slowly on her way, a mendicant ghost in the orange-brown mist, one by one the whole row of chairs was aroused, and asked questions as she approached, and dived into pockets or opened bags and made ready for her.

"Will you give me a penny?" she asked—never for any more, and she could not easily have asked for less. "Will you give me a penny?"

But nobody gave her a penny. Some gave her sovereigns, some half-sovereigns, some dollars or two dollars, or even again sumptu- ous five-dollar bills, some gave half-crowns or florins, and children proudly forced upon her sixpences or shillings. She asked stewards, she asked officers, she let nobody escape, and it was apparent that nobody wished to elude her. Everybody was interested as well as amused, and every one was kind. People who were beginning to feel apathetic and bored were not in the mood to refuse, find- ing themselves provided with an incident to talk over. Between ourselves we have often since then laughed at the odd humour of the scene—the fog-enveloped decks, the bundled ghosts of passengers in their steamer chairs under the luridly smoky lights, and the Mendicant Shadow looming out of the mist, extending a hand, and uttering her mysterious appeal, "Please, will you give me a penny?"

She had not gone far on her round before there sprang out of a dark corner chair a tall and cheerful boyish young man who had sat near her at table the night before.

"Let me go with you and carry the bag," he said. "I can take you into the smoking-room. Most of the men are there. May I come?"

With her he went, and when they had made their tour of the decks they invaded the smoking-room. It was more than usually well filled, and the smoke of cigars and cigarettes added to the floating fog made greater mystery. Men were playing cards, men were smoking, with whiskey and sodas before them, some were dozing on chairs, and some were talking. Enter a Mendicant with extended hand and attended by a squire of dames. All who were near enough to see her turned quickly round. Had she mistaken her way? What was going to happen?

"Please, will you give me a penny?" she said. "Tomorrow will be Christmas Day, and there are a hundred and fifty emigrant children in the steerage, etc., etc."

That most of them stared, is not to be denied; that the theory of the harmless hallucination occurred to several, the Romantick Lady was quite aware. They had not lain in their berths and thought out the picturesque emotional features of the case. There were those who for a few moments looked rather stupefied, and as if they could not quite understand. To these she endeavoured in a few words to make clear the picture of the small empty hands. Her hearers no doubt did not see the thing quite as she did, most of them being hard-driven business men for whom emigrants created no particular

Vision. But they were all good natured and generous. The little bag gradually filled itself, and she began to stuff bills and pieces of gold and silver into the pocket of her fur coat. The number of pennies bestowed by the Smoking-Room made an appreciable addition to the fortunes of the one hundred and fifty.

When she returned to her stateroom and poured out her garnerings on the couch, there lay before her a most respectable pile.

Here perhaps it would be illuminating to pause and make a certain note—illuminating as to the characteristics of the Romantick Lady.

"How much had they given you?" I not unnaturally asked when I first heard the story.

She was in the midst of the glow of it, laughing here and there at herself, and touched and warmed by the humanness of the bundled-up passenger wraiths. She stopped and reflected, she looked down at the carpet and thought deeply, then she looked up with a puzzled expression.

"It was quite a *lot*," she said slowly, "but I can't remember how much. I actually can't remember."

"You wouldn't, you Romantick thing," I answered resignedly. "One needn't expect it of you."

"But what does it matter? The children *got* it," she triumphed. "It was distributed the next day after their Christmas dinner. Of course they did not understand where it came from. They probably thought it was an agreeable American custom to serve money as one of the courses. My stewardess told me all about it. She also said that after some of the children had been given their share, their fathers shuffled them to the front again, and pretended that they had been overlooked and had had nothing."

In the afternoon of Christmas Day the fog lifted, and the ship went on its way.

"But," said the Romantick Lady, "as we swung past the Statue of Liberty in the harbour, and I went to lean over the rail again and looked down at the crowd standing about or sitting huddled among its bundles on the steerage deck, I was suddenly beset by the usual question. Perhaps my Romantic moment had really resulted in one of my fell deeds. Perhaps I had firmly imbedded in the minds of the hundred and fifty the seed of pauperism, and they would sail in with their hands held out for charity and not for work. How can one know?"

THE HAUNTED FLAT

Marie Belloc Lowndes

Marie Adelaide Belloc (1868–1947) was the sister of the author Hilaire Belloc but established a solid reputation for herself. She wrote under both her maiden name and, after her marriage to journalist and sub-editor on The Times, *Frederick Lowndes, as Marie Belloc Lowndes. Her writing ran the full range as journalist, novelist and short-story writer. She was known for her interviews in the 1890s—indeed she interviewed Frances Hodgson Burnett in 1896. She is best known for her novel* The Lodger *(1913), which drew upon the Jack-the-Ripper murders. It was memorably filmed by Alfred Hitchcock in 1927, starring Ivor Novello. It earned Lowndes a reputation for exploring the psychology of crime. Less well-known today is that she also explored the psychology of the supernatural. One of her stories, "The Unbolted Door" (1929), dealt with how the spirit of a dead son helped mend a rift between his distraught parents, and was highly regarded in its day. What's less known is that Lowndes had developed that story from an earlier one, "The Haunted Flat", which was the last in a sequence of stories called "The Ivory Gate" published in* The Grand Magazine *in 1920. The series, as the original introduction reveals, dealt with different aspects of spiritualism and how a longing for knowledge of what lies beyond can affect us all.*

"The Ivory Gate" is what remains to many the gateless barrier which separates the seen from the unseen. In this series of stories which have been written by Mrs Belloc Lowndes under that general title, she deals with six different examples of what old-fashioned folk call "the night side of Nature," and which the modern world has elected to style "Occultism." History, from the remotest ages down to, and through, the whole of the Christian dispensation, contains innumerable accounts of the appearance to human beings of both good and evil spirits. Mrs Belloc Lowndes is convinced that the dead are sometimes permitted to return to comfort, to console, to warn those they loved on this earth. And she is one of the many to whom the Angels of Mons were a reality long before Mr Arthur Machen wrote his famous story.

INTRODUCTION FROM *GRAND MAGAZINE*, AUGUST 1920

I

"THE ONLY THING AGAINST THE HOUSE—PERHAPS I OUGHT to say against the flat—is that the last people who had it thought that it was haunted."

The speaker, Ivy Brent, said the words lightly and yet firmly. "I don't believe in concealing anything," she went on, "especially as the house does, after all, belong to my aunt."

May Murchison answered eagerly: "I don't mind how haunted it is! You can't imagine what a joy and delight it is to feel that at last I have a chance of getting something nice—something clean—something cheap—in which to live by myself. I'm sure I've worn two pairs of shoes quite out, tramping about looking for rooms. Your aunt is a true philanthropist!"

"My aunt," said the other girl slowly, "is a good woman of business. When she found it impossible to let that enormous house in South Place Gardens, she divided it up in a rough kind of way into flats—and had a hundred applications in one morning! That's why I've hurried round, dear, to tell you of this top floor being empty. Would you like to come and see it now? I'm afraid you'll have to decide at once; but she's promised to say nothing about it to anyone until tomorrow morning."

As the two girls walked quickly through the empty Kensington streets, for it was a Sunday afternoon, "I've a sort of feeling," said May Murchison, "that I've heard the name of South Place Gardens before—not lately, but a long time ago. I've been puzzling over it ever since I got your note last night."

May Murchison's father had been one of those men of business who, while apparently very prosperous, yet make but very slender provision for their wife and daughter. Now, May, motherless as well as fatherless, at five-and-twenty, was confidential secretary to the head of a big city firm.

South Place Gardens runs round two sides of a pleasant green enclosure. The houses are large and imposing, with big porticos, each house consisting of a huge basement, and of four high stories connected by a steep stone staircase.

The two friends stopped at No. 6, and Ivy Brent rang the bell. A pleasant-faced woman opened the door.

"This is Mrs Clarke, May," observed Ivy pleasantly. "She and her daughter look after the tenants."

"Most of the people who live here are out all day and only want breakfast and supper," said the housekeeper.

"*I* should only want breakfast and supper," said May Murchison eagerly, "for I'm out all day, working in the city."

"We'll go along upstairs and see the top-floor flat," said Ivy. "You needn't bother about us, Mrs Clarke. I know the way."

"Several friends of the tenants have been to see the flat already, miss," said Mrs Clarke; "but I know that Mrs Brent means to keep it till this young lady has seen it."

The two girls started walking up the staircase, and May Murchison told herself that there was something curiously quiet and eerie about the big house, perhaps because it was a fine summer Sunday, and most of the people living there were out.

Up and up they went, till they reached the top floor of all. There, what is sometimes called a "nursery gate" barred the way.

"This gate was here when uncle bought the house, twenty-three years ago. The people had evidently used this top floor for their nurseries, but as aunt and uncle had no children, they didn't use this floor, so the gate was never taken away."

May Murchison walked across the landing into the first big room with quickened interest, asking herself if this was to be her future home.

It was a large, square, pleasant apartment. Off it, to the left, was a much smaller room, with a door on to the staircase lobby; a bathroom with a small gas-stove also opened out of the big front room.

It was not a flat in the ordinary sense of the word, but the rooms offered good points to any intelligent, good-humoured, and healthy solitary seeker after a London home. This top floor was airy and bright, and both the front windows and the big bathroom window commanded a wide expanse of sky and green tree-tops. "I think it simply perfect," exclaimed May. "I never saw a place that looked less haunted! And oh! how glad I shall be to get away from that stuffy boarding-house!"

May Murchison's case was a common one, but none the less painful and disagreeable for that. She had gradually formed a close friendship with a man named Roger Byng, and, on both sides, "friendship" had soon become something much warmer. But perhaps the touch of rather hard, and yet sensitive, common-sense which made her different from her girl friends, had caused it gradually to become quite clear to her that, though he sometimes behaved as if he could not bear life without her company for more than a few hours at a time, yet Roger Byng with his aristocratic name and "good connections," did not intend to marry her. He had first come to the boarding-house where May lived, while he was looking for new rooms, and he had stayed on and on, as she knew very well, because of his attraction to herself. In the peopled solitude of a boarding-house, a young man and a young woman can become far more really intimate than is possible in a watchful home, or even office, atmosphere.

When the girl had gradually discovered that her friend Roger was, to use an old-fashioned phrase, "only amusing himself," her pride and her heart both suffered more than she cared to admit, even to herself.

She made up her mind to make a complete break, with the boarding-house, with her work, and with—him. There should be no harrowing and humiliating farewell. Like most prosperous bachelors, Roger Byng had a large acquaintance; he was often away for the weekend, paying country-house visits. She would choose her time to leave the boarding-house and also to effect a change of work, during one of his absences.

II

And now had come May Murchison's first evening in what, by way of courtesy, was called her "flat." It had taken her far longer to settle in than she had expected it to do, but she had stayed with Ivy Brent after leaving the boarding-house, and each day she had been at No. 6, South Place Gardens for hours; staining the floor of what was to be her sitting-room, putting up and painting her own bookshelves, and superintending the work she could not manage herself in the bathroom-kitchen.

In a sense, she had been glad of all the worries, big and little, which now attend any kind of "flitting," however humble, for it banished painful thoughts. But all the same, there were times, especially at night, when she wondered, wondered, *wondered* whether Roger Byng was really missing her, and what he had thought on reading the cool little note which told him that she had suddenly had the good fortune to find exactly the kind of place she had been looking for, and that she had arranged to take up some new work which would practically absorb all her time. It had been quite a good letter, cheerful and matter-of-fact, and it had ended with the words: "As I expect to be dreadfully busy, I don't suppose there is any chance of our meeting until after your summer holiday,"—in other words, for three or four months ahead!

She had been proudly, steadfastly determined that her letter should in no sense convey an undignified, melodramatic note of farewell. But now that everything had gone exactly as she had meant it to, May Murchison went through some sad hours of self-questioning, in which her future seemed both drab and lonely, and she had felt very depressed when leaving Mrs Smithson to take up her solitary life.

Now, at last, with everything more or less shipshape, and the cold meal she had brought in daintily laid out on the low but solid, well-made little table which was associated in her mind with her dead mother, she stood at one of the windows of her new sitting-room and gazed over the green tree tops.

Suddenly she experienced the curious sensation that someone was looking at her, with a long, eager, steady look. So vivid was the impression that she actually blushed all over.

May Murchison had no claim to beauty. Her upper lip was too long, her forehead too high, but she had a pair of fine grey eyes, swept by long, dark eyelashes; in fact her eyes were her best feature and gave a rather uncommon look of distinction to her pale face.

She turned her head slightly, fully expecting to see the house-keeper standing at the door, and then with a little shock of surprise, she realized that if there had indeed been someone there, that person had noiselessly withdrawn. Withdrawn? But where? Every footfall on the stone staircase could be heard echoing through the house. That was one of the disadvantages of 6, South Place Gardens. She walked across the room and went through into the quaintly shaped apartment which was at once her kitchen, scullery and bathroom. But there was no one there.

After waiting a moment, she went into the third room, that which completed the flat. May had turned it into a pleasant little bedroom, though the furniture she had had stored was all too large for it. Still, it was a comfort to feel that her few clothes would hang henceforth in a well-made, dust-proof wardrobe, and that every drawer would run in and out easily, and not stick, perpetually, as had done those in the boarding-house.

There was a door leading from the bedroom on to the landing, but she had made up her mind to keep it always locked, and to go in and out through the sitting-room. She now noticed, with some surprise and annoyance, that it was ajar. Mrs Clarke must have unlocked it. May shut it, and ran the bolt in. Then she went back into her sitting-room and ate her supper. After she had finished, following an arrangement she had made with the housekeeper, she pressed the bell three times.

She waited a while, and then rang again, but nothing happened. It was clear that Mrs Clarke and her daughter must be out.

May did a little more unpacking in the now deepening twilight, and then she was just about to go to bed, for she felt very tired, when she heard the sound of heavy footsteps coming slowly up the staircase, and Mrs Clarke appeared at the door.

"I wasn't quite sure if you was in yet, Miss," she said dubiously, "or I'd have been up before."

May hesitated; she didn't want to begin her tenancy by being disagreeable, but after all, she *had* rung twice. "I had understood," she said quite pleasantly, "that you wanted me to ring as soon as I had finished supper."

The woman hesitated oddly. "We *did* hear you ring, Miss, in fact we heard two rings, but the bells from this top floor have a way of ringing when there's no one up here."

"I wish you'd told me that while I had the workmen here," May exclaimed, "for whatever's wrong ought to be put right. It will be so very awkward indeed if you never know if it's I who am ringing or not!"

"It isn't the kind of thing that a workman can put right," said Mrs Clarke positively.

"Then we must have an electrician in." May spoke very decidedly.

"That was one of the reasons the last people left," said Mrs Clarke slowly, "that—and other things they couldn't do with—"

"Couldn't do with?" echoed May. "Oh, I remember now. This flat is supposed to be haunted, isn't it? Were the last people afraid? Did they think they saw anything?"

The housekeeper remained silent, but in the gathering twilight, the new tenant saw that the woman looked very uncomfortable.

May felt a thrill of interest and excitement run through her. "I wish you'd tell me," she asked eagerly, "what it is that is supposed to haunt this top floor? For my part, I should like to see a ghost." The girl spoke very gravely.

Mrs Clarke took a few steps nearer. "I don't know as what it's likely you'll ever see a spirit," she observed in a low voice, and looking rather fearfully into the gathering gloom, "but I don't think you'll be here many days before you'll *feel as if someone is looking for something.* That's what it's like—it's as if whatever's here was looking, looking, *looking*—and never finding—" She spoke in a very matter-of-fact voice.

"But how do you know that the ghost, or spirit, is looking for anything, and what could there be to look for in these three rooms?" asked May, puzzled.

"It's looking for someone that it's been expecting for a long time, and who don't come—that's what anyone who comes up here by themselves soon gets to feel. Yesterday it was *dreadful*: my daughter, she wouldn't stay up here by herself; she came and fetched me, and we both felt quite scared, that we did!"

May got up from her low chair. She went across to the door and switched on the electric light. She hadn't got any electric fittings yet, and there was just a plain suspension in the middle of the room. She felt a strange, eerie sensation come over her; she felt rather sorry she had asked these questions—

"I suppose," said Mrs Clarke dubiously, "*you* haven't felt anything yet, miss?"

"I've certainly felt nothing of the kind you describe," said May frankly, "but soon after I first arrived, when I was standing by the window over there, I had the feeling that someone was watching me rather intently, in fact I thought, Mrs Clarke, that you had come upstairs without my hearing you."

"Did the door open after you'd shut it?" asked Mrs Clark in an odd tone.

May shook her head, and then she said: "By the way, Mrs Clarke, I do want that door of *my* bedroom kept locked. I locked it after the workmen had gone yesterday. I suppose you or your daughter opened it today?"

"I never opened it," said Mrs Clarke in a rather offended tone, "I haven't got a key that *would* open it, Miss. But there—you'll soon find out how queer things are up here!"

She took up the tray. May had made an arrangement that the mother and daughter should do her washing up.

After Mrs Clarke had gone, May went into her bedroom and slowly undressed. Her mind went over and over again the odd things that the housekeeper had told her. But with regard to the locked door, Mrs Clarke had reddened when it was mentioned. If she were not the culprit, then her daughter must be. They both were aware that all her small personal belongings had been moved in the day before, and May knew by certain unpleasant happenings at the boarding-house, how extraordinarily inquisitive and curious a certain type of young woman can be.

For the first time since she had made the break with Roger Byng, she went to sleep without thinking of him, and perhaps because of that, she slept really well—a good omen, so she thought, when she woke up, for her new work.

As she went off that morning, she saw for the first time one of her fellow tenants. He was a nice looking man, and as he looked at her he smiled pleasantly. She knew that his name was James Dowson, for his card was up on a board in the hall.

When she came back, late that afternoon, her mind full of her new work and her new employer, she did experience one very curious sensation. She felt, that is, as she passed into her sitting-room, that there was someone there waiting to welcome her—so vivid was the impression that she uttered joyfully the name of the good, faithful girl-friend whom she felt sure must be in one of the two other rooms. "Ivy!" she called out, opening the bathroom door—but there was no Ivy Brent there. And then quickly she went across to her bedroom—it too was empty.

There are times in life when nothing seems to happen and yet which are, in a spiritual sense, constructive. Such a time followed for May Murchison the coming to 6, South Place Gardens. Her stormy heart grew calmer; the new work she was doing began really to absorb her, and she gradually acquired a jealously-guarded secret belief that her new home was indeed—could it be called *haunted*? No, rather *pervaded*—by some gentle, beneficent influence which wished her well. She kept this belief to herself, but it was strange that the more *she* became convinced that there was about her constantly some other-worldly influence, the more the housekeeper and the housekeeper's daughter asserted that the new tenant had *banished* the ghost which had so disturbed her predecessors in the flat. They both declared that *now* they could feel nothing.

The weeks went by quickly. May could not take a holiday that autumn, for moving in had taken all her ready money; but she felt well, extraordinarily fit, and she had soon formed a slight, pleasant acquaintance with the man who lived downstairs. Once when Ivy Brent was to be there, she asked him up to tea… It comforted her sore, lonely heart to feel that this stranger was beginning to feel keenly interested in her… But there came a day when he too went off for his holiday, and when there was no one left in the big house but May herself.

It was then, on a Saturday afternoon in September, that she bethought herself of her only remaining social link with her long-dead mother. This was an old lady named Mrs Smithson, who lived in a tiny house close to South Kensington station. May made a point of going to see her perhaps two or three times a year. Mrs Smithson never altered: she was always the same, placid, kindly soul, interested in all that her dead friend's daughter had to tell her, and yet never disagreeably inquisitive about May's concerns.

But this time, when the girl explained that she had at last found pleasant quarters which had induced her to leave the boarding-house where she had lived so long, Mrs Smithson showed unwonted excitement.

"6, South Place Gardens? My dear, what an extraordinary thing! Unless I'm mistaken, it's the very house which your poor mother made your father give up after your poor little sister Sally's death."

"Do you mean that my parents lived at 6, South Place Gardens?" exclaimed May. "I understand now why the name seemed vaguely familiar."

"They were only there a year," answered old Mrs Smithson. "Your father bought the lease cheap, but all the same, I think they weren't sorry to give it up. It was too large a house for them. And then there came the tragedy of little Sally's illness and death. I can remember as if it were yesterday, your mother taking me up to the top of that big house, into a large, airy room (people didn't have day nurseries in those days). The child was lying close up to the window in a kind of big cot. She was four years old; you, my dear, were only two, and they had sent you away to the country, to some friends."

"What was Sally like?" asked May. She felt moved and inter-ested, although the little sister who had died when she, May, had been little more than a baby, was but a name to her. Still, she had always been slightly jealous of her mother's ever-enduring grief for the long dead child.

"Sally was a strange little thing," answered Mrs Smithson slowly. "She was like a child out of one of those curious little goody-goody books that people used to give me when I was a child, sixty years ago. She was so intelligent, and so unselfish, poor little mite, bearing her pitiful disease—a most unusual one for a child to suffer from—with extraordinary resignation and patience. Your mother, my dear, never really got over her death."

"No," said May sadly, "I don't think she ever did."

When the girl at last got up to go, her old friend exclaimed. "I can make quite sure as to whether No. 6 *was* the house. I expect you'd like to know?"

It was on the tip of May's tongue to say, "Oh, don't trouble, I don't really mind one way or the other—" or, as a fact she would have preferred to think that No. 6 had *not* been associated with that long-ago tragedy. But Mrs Smithson was already unlocking one of the bottom drawers of an old-fashioned upright desk. Out of it she extracted a fat bundle of letters. "Yes," she exclaimed, "here they are! I was a good deal in the country then, keeping house for my widowed brother, and your mother wrote to me constantly. Look, my dear—?"

May came across the small room almost reluctantly. From one of the peculiar-looking, small, highly-glazed envelopes she took out a sheet of note-paper. On it, written in her mother's delicate, clear handwriting was the address, "6, South Place Gardens," the date, "May 29th, 1898," and the words: "My dearest Laura; don't think I am ungrateful for your sympathy, but my little child is dying, and my heart is breaking…"

May did not read any more. She handed Mrs Smithson back the letter…

That evening May Murchison found that she could not banish the thought of little Sally from her mind and heart. She would shut her eyes and try and think what the room had looked like as a nursery. She wondered near which window the sick child's cot had been placed. As it grew darker and darker, she began to cry, softly. That strange, tragic mysterious thing, human life, suddenly overwhelmed her with a sense of infinite sadness. She felt she would give years of this finite life to know that there is a happier beyond.

III

Roger Byng stepped hesitatingly into the large, square room which had been transformed by its present occupant into such a delightful sitting-room study. He felt at once triumphant, anxious, ill at ease, and, yes, extraordinarily happy! He had spent such nightmare days and weeks trying to track her down, and now he could hardly believe in his own good fortune!

The woman who had opened the door had not seemed surprised at his nervous question—"Does Miss Murchison live here?" At once she had invited him to go upstairs and wait, adding that Miss Murchison would be sure to be in very soon. Walking through the hall, he had noticed the names of the tenants written up on a board. There were four sets of names—all women's names, with one exception, "Mr James Dowson." Roger Byng had felt acutely, ridiculously jealous of May Murchison's fellow-occupier of this big, bare-looking house! But he had gone up the steep stone staircase, torn with an extraordinary mixture of feelings in which joy, a simple human emotion, seldom experienced in Roger Byng's conventional, self-centred life, certainly predominated.

After a few minutes, he began moving about the room. What a different setting for this girl he now knew he loved, and wished ardently would be his wife, to the rather dingy boarding-house where he and she had first become acquainted! He looked about him with an almost painful interest, and spent what seemed to him a long time examining her books, some of them old friends he and she had often discussed, others which had evidently belonged to her father, obviously a man of cultivation and taste.

How different was this room—how different the woman he was waiting for, to the room and to the lady on whom he had paid an early call on this Saturday afternoon! The lady was a novelist, and Roger Byng had stood by smiling, while in answer to some question as to how she composed her stories, she had said: "I seem to hear the people in my stories talking to one another; it is as if I were eavesdropping—"

He had thought to himself, "How silly and affected!"

And then, quite suddenly there came to Roger Byng the experience which in his heart he had utterly disbelieved to be possible when he had heard it described by his late hostess. He seemed to sense, that is, a voice speaking quite close to him, almost into his ear. The voice seemed to belong—if one could so express it—to a being from another sphere, and to a different dimension. "Roger Byng! Roger Byng!" came the whispering voice. "You have entered into an enchanted hour, into that hour in which a man may be happy all his life—can he but find it." And his heart thrilled a wordless "Yes" in answer.

And the tiny stuffless voice went on: "Give up being the manner of man you have been. Be no longer a cautious, self-seeking, timorous, and snobbish, if in a sense, worthy example of the great nation to which you belong. You won the Military Cross for an act which in any other war would have won you the Victoria Cross, but this War did not give you the finest courage of all, *moral* courage. Forget yourself, and think henceforth only of the girl who, as even you realize, has made a man of you. You do not deserve the wife that she will make." "Most true," he whispered back.

"You are only just in time, Roger Byng! In a very little time a better man than you would have won her..." And then it was as if he saw before his shrinking eyes the card on which was written the name "James Dowson"—that card which had attracted his unwilling, inimical attention as he had walked through the empty hall downstairs.

The voice stopped suddenly, and as Roger Byng moved uneasily in his chair he heard a curious fluttering sound. It was as if a bird, prisoned for a moment between the four walls of the room, had flown out of one of the widely opened windows. Had he unconsciously fallen asleep on this hot autumn afternoon? Of late, especially during the last few days, he had experienced the disconcerting sensation that youth was slipping fast away from him. And then all at once he felt a curious, violent physical commotion! There fell on his ears the sound of May Murchison's footsteps on the stone steps of the staircase outside.

Roger Byng jumped up from his chair and stood at attention. Then came the click of the latch of the little nursery gate, and May Murchison opened the door.

For a moment they stood looking at each other. Then, very, very humbly he said; "I've been looking for you so long! And now that I've found you at last I never want to lose you again—" And, as May remained silent, he asked, and she felt the pain in his level voice, "Are you sorry I've found you, darling?" And as he took her in his arms, she whispered, "Not exactly sorry... *glad*. Though I was trying, Roger, to forget you, and I'd very nearly succeeded!"

A MODERN CIRCE

Alicia Ramsey

Alicia Ramsey (1864–1933) is remembered today only by devotees of the pulp magazine Weird Tales, *where she appeared in just one issue, January 1926, with a gruesome story, "The Black Crusader", about the fate of a man who desecrates a tomb. But she should be remembered for much else. In her day she was best known as a writer of stage plays, several with her future husband Rudolph de Cordova. When the movie business began, some of her plays were adapted for the screen, and she turned to writing scenarios, but until then she had a profitable career as a short-story writer and novelist. Most of her stories were light romances, sometimes with a twist, but she could turn on the strange and bizarre when she chose. Her best book is* The Adventures of Mortimer Dixon *(1913) which began as a series of magazine stories in 1908. Dixon is a journalist struggling to make his name when, in the first story, "No. 13", he stumbles upon an assassin's club. In the next story, "The Mysterious Airship", he stumbles again upon what he thinks is a planned invasion of England, and finds himself alone in flight on a new form of airship which is out of control. These stories show a different side to Alicia Ramsey, full of pluck, mystery and adventure. On occasions this led her into the realms of the supernatural, as evidenced by the following, hitherto unreprinted story, from the pages of the rare* Novel Magazine *for December 1919.*

I T HAPPENED IN A LITTLE COUNTRY VILLAGE IN THE SOUTH OF Italy. I know it's true, because I was there when it happened. I had been ill, and was spending the winter there to try and regain my health.

The first day I was there I noticed him. He was the kind of person you couldn't help noticing if you tried. He was tall and broad, with a magnificent pair of dark eyes and a mop of thick black curls. With his red shirt and his white teeth and his swaggering walk, he was like one of Franz Hals roistering cavaliers stepped out of its gold frame and come to life.

My little maid who used to bring me my coffee told me about him. He was a stone-mason by trade, but, like his father before him, he had run away to sea. When his father died he had come back. He had sold his father's vineyard. His name was Ferdinando. All women loved him, and his wicked ways had broken his poor old mother's heart. Not the only heart he had broken, I gathered from the passion that throbbed, during the recital of his sins, in my little maid's soft voice.

I don't know whether it's because I'm fond of pretty voices, or because I've a fellow-feeling for sinners—being something of a sinner myself—but my interest in Ferdinando was instant and profound. The handsome rogue was not slow to perceive it and turn it to his own advantage. Before a week was out he had established proprietary rights in me. The rest of the community, agape for "soldi," had vanished into the background, where they stayed.

I was well contented it should be so, for a better guide or a more amusing companion it would be hard to find. In his wanderings across the seas, Ferdinando had foregathered with many men and many nations. He was full of queer fancies and strange histories. A natural instinct for beauty combined with his southern temperament stood him in place of refinement and education. Most potent of all attraction, he shared with me a passion for strange, out-of-the-way things. Many and many a queer story he told me of lawless loves and fierce hates and undying feuds, but never a queerer one than the one which he himself lived while I was with him, and the truth of which I can vouch for as witnessed with my own ears and eyes.

We were coming back late one afternoon from an excursion we had made together; I, riding my mule, he, walking by my side. The day was close; the air was sultry. A blazing sun was going to its rest in a fury of scarlet and gold. Ferdinando, a bunch of red berries tucked over his left ear and the eternal cigarette in the corner of his mouth, was joyously carolling to me the legend of the hearts he had broken, ending up with Marguerita, my little maid. "A dove with silver feet is little Marguerita! The voice of a nightingale which has pierced the heart of a white rose. The worn beads round her white throat are not more pure than her soul; and the kisses of her lips behind the door, when the old witch, her grandmother, isn't looking, are sweeter than Appenine honey!" He snatched a branch of eglantine from a bush as he passed and flung it round his neck, where it shone in the luminous light like a necklace of stars.

"When the old witch, her grandmother, is dead and I have made yet one more journey, I will return and marry the little Marguerita. She will have five cows and ten pigs, and she can take in the strangers' washing. I, Ferdinando, will lie in the sun and tell my rosary for the dear women who have loved me and when my turn comes to die, the prayers of the little Marguerita will ascend to Heaven, and the good God will forgive me my transgressions for the sake of my tender and faithful wife."

"Why wait for her grandmother to die?" I asked him. "Why not marry her at once?"

"I am my father's son," said Ferdinando proudly. "I broke his heart, but he loved me. He would arise from his tomb, the good old man, if his Ferdinando married a girl without a suitable dowry."

I don't know whether it was the buoyant air, or the red berries, or Ferdinando's dark eyes, luminous as the stars, profound as night, looking up at me out of the twilight—perhaps I'd fallen a victim to the handsome vagabond too!—but the fancy seized me to play the god-in-the-machine to the little Marguerita. As delicately as I could, I asked the breaker of hearts to name his price.

There was delicacy about Ferdinando when it came to money.

"One hundred pounds," said he.

His eyes betrayed him. Not much stars or night about them at that moment. Nothing but sheer greed. I divided the sum by two.

"I'll give Marguerita fifty pounds the day you marry her," I told him promptly.

Nothing doing on Ferdinando when it came to promptness. He swept me a bow that would have graced a duke. "Signora, in the name of that dead saint, my father, and the old witch, her grandmother, I invite you to grace with your presence the betrothal *jesta* of the gallant Ferdinando and the little Marguerita tonight."

He seized my hand and kissed it. He smote himself on the breast and called on Heaven to witness his unworthiness. He embraced his mule with such fervour as to cause that admirable animal to nearly buck me out of my saddle. Pulling his amulet out of his breast, he registered an oath to Heaven that from henceforth he would lead the blameless life of an honourable citizen, a faithful husband, and a good father, and be a shining example to all his fellow-men.

"The blessed Madonna be my witness!" he cried. "I have done with women from this hour." He raised the little silver crucifix hanging on the little chain round his neck to his lips, when the sound of a woman's laughter filled the air. Soft yet penetrating, gay yet full of suggestion, pregnant with a thousand strange emotions. I had never heard such laughter. Woman as I am, it thrilled me through and through. I could see it affected Ferdinando no less than it did me. His face went white under its sunburn. His black eyes, cunning no longer, widened and deepened with an extraordinary apprehension.

"It is the Mad Virgin of the hills," he whispered.

I pricked up my ears.

"Who is the Mad Virgin of the hills, Ferdinando?"

"She is the great heart-breaker, Signora. She lives in the solitary places. She has a dog who is an evil spirit. Those who hear her laugh are the ones she chooses. She lures them to her, and they love her and she turns them into dogs."

A modern Circe! I asked him if he seriously believed such stuff.

"But, yes, I believe it, Signora! How should I not believe it? It is true." He clutched at his little crucifix and crossed himself rapidly. *"Madonna mia!"* he whispered. "There she is."

I turned my head and looked in the direction of his trembling hand. On the slope of the hill where the ground was broken into a little plateau, sat a woman on a stone. She had a staff in her hand crowned with scarlet roses and a wreath of scarlet roses in her red-gold hair. A bright blue veil powdered with little gold stars was wrapped round her shoulders and half concealed her face. Its gay ends fluttering in the evening breeze, floated behind her like a cloud. At her feet, in a semicircle around her, lay six huge dogs.

The depth of colouring, the bizarre pose, the whole thing had about it something so fantastic and old-world seen through the glamour of that golden light; it stamped itself upon my memory with an indelible impression that will last as long as I live.

As I looked, enthralled, she laughed again. Again the sound, so inhuman, affected me with the same strange sense of unreality as before. As though it were a whip laid across their backs, the dogs rose to their feet and fawned upon her. Then they sat down on their haunches, three on either side of her.

The woman got up and threw back her veil. I gasped as I caught sight of her. So fair, so scornful, so weary, so white, with a mouth of blood and eyes like blue flames! I thrilled to her face, as I had to her laughter. Behind me, I heard Ferdinando catch his breath like a sob.

She stood there leaning both hands on her staff, looking down on us. The setting sun fell like a glory around her, turning her scarlet roses to unearthly flowers of fire. She stood there and looked at Ferdinando. She took no notice of me.

"Oho! So it's you, Breaker of Hearts, is it?" said she. Her voice was another surprise. Clear and low-pitched, one of those voices that irresistibly arrest the ear. "Why don't you come and break mine?"

Ferdinando said nothing. He stood there with his crucifix in his hand, his black eyes fixed on her face, as if he couldn't tear them away.

Then she laughed again, turned her back on him, called to her dogs and went her way.

The two of us stood stock still in the roadway watching her until the bright ends of her blue scarf passed out of sight.

Then, and then only, did Ferdinando—that bold braggart beloved of women—find his voice.

"I'm a lost man," he whispered. *"Dio mio*, I'm a lost man!"

Not another word could I get out of him. He kept on muttering the same words over and over again all the way down to the village, like a man talking to himself in a dream.

When I told the little Marguerita and her grandmother what had happened, they were as bad as he. "The saints preserve him!" they cried in a breath. "He's lost!"

The sight of the pair of them crossing themselves and clinging together, restored me to my good, sober senses. I summoned Ferdinando and produced my purse.

"No man's lost who has a hundred pounds," I said, rising to Ferdinando's first price on the spur of the moment. "Call the priest and set the table. We celebrate the betrothal *festa* tonight."

The Italian peasant has yet to be born who can resist money. The sight of the little fortune spread out in tangible notes before them speedily cured their supernatural fears. Before they'd well finished counting it, they were fighting and scrambling as to what should be done with it. I went to my siesta well satisfied. The sight of the little Marguerita's face beholding Heaven at the expense of a couple of evening gowns, was good enough value to me.

Later that evening, however, chancing upon the old priest, benevolently watching the innocent rejoicings of his favourite parishioner, I related to him what had happened, and asked him what it meant. To my surprise, instead of laughing, as I expected, the old man looked very grave.

"*Dio mio!*" exclaimed he, clutching at his crucifix like Ferdinando before him. "Miserable Marguerita! Her beloved is a lost man!"

In reply to my questions he told me a strange story.

"She whom they call 'The Mad Virgin' is a mystery. No one knows whence she came. No one knows who she is. She lives alone like the beasts of the fields among the hills. Woe be to the one whom she beckons with laughter. No man can resist her. She has the evil eye." The old man's voice dropped to a whisper. In the soft moonlight his ascetic face, with its saintly halo of snow-white hair, reminded me in some extraordinary way of Ferdinando's. The expression was the same. "Four of our best men have been lost to her—honest husbands, good fathers all four of them, but they could not help themselves. She called and they went to her." He stopped short and looked at me, as though he had more to tell but were afraid to go on.

I was consumed with curiosity to hear the rest.

"And those four, Padre, what happened when they came back?"

"They never came back, my daughter. Those whom she calls never return. They are lost."

"But what does she do with them? They must go somewhere. Where do they go?"

"They stay with her," he said solemnly.

"Do you mean she kills them?"

"She turns them into dogs."

I couldn't help myself. I laughed outright.

"What an absurd idea!"

"Why absurd, my daughter?"

"The thing's impossible."

The old man looked at me.

"It's impossible to speak together when you are absent, yet men talk with each other from all ends of the earth. It's impossible to see through a solid substance, yet men see through brick walls. It's impossible to have warmth and light without fire, yet the night is turned into day by electric light. It is impossible to live beneath the sea, yet men dive and live in submarines. It's impossible to fly without wings, yet men mount into the clouds like birds."

"But all those things are natural science, Father. This would be witchcraft, if it were true."

"We read of witches in the Bible, my daughter."

"Surely *you* don't believe it?"

"My whole life is passed in believing things I do not see, why should I not believe then the things that I do see? I have lived seventy years and I have learnt one lesson—nothing is impossible. There is no limit to the power of Satan or of God." He raised his hand in kindly benediction and left me standing open-mouthed.

I sat in my little balcony watching the impossible miracle of the setting moon renew itself over the enraptured hills. The priest was right. In that magic light, nothing was impossible. Phantoms from the archaic past, psychic emanations from the garish present, white ladies, pale Heinrichs. *Belles dames sans merci*, vaporous Undines passed in ghostly procession before me, filling the luminous void.

From below, the gay sounds of laughter and the mad thrumming of the mandolins floated up to me. The dancers, like painted shadows, flitted to and fro, their feet making no sound on the soft green grass. In the far distance sparkled the sea—a line of undulating fire. The heavy scent of the jasmine, the soft cries of the nightbirds, were borne to me on the still, hot air. In the sky above, glittered a riot of golden stars, jewelled pendants of the waning moon. A fitting setting for a miracle! I found myself wishing that the Mad Virgin and her attendant spirits might appear.

As though my thought had the power of evocation, at that instant she appeared, rose up out of the darkness and come towards me, placidly walking down the white and winding road. Against the ridge of the hills, I could see her slender figure and the forms of the six huge dogs sharply outlined by the moonlight as distinctly as if it were day. At the sight, an extraordinary feeling of expectation ran through me. I am ashamed to say that no thought of what her coming might mean to the happy folks below, disturbed me. I was simply consumed with curiosity to see what she would do.

Nearer she came and nearer, until, at last, I could discern her blue scarf floating behind her and the wreath of roses on her head. In the light of the moon, the blood-red mouth in its setting of shining pallor took on a strange unearthly look. For the first time I appreciated the meaning of the terror of beauty. Even so must the mouths of the vampires, mystic destroyers of men, have looked.

Down below, the music still went on merrily. The mandolins now soft, now loud, now fierce, now tender, yet always charged with a passionate ardour, rose and fell as if they were one. Suddenly they stopped. So suddenly, indeed, it was less like the cessation of sound than the snapping of a string. The painted shadows fluttered, wavered, stood still. They had seen her!

I tiptoed softly to the edge of my balcony and looked down. They stood, the on-lookers, huddled together, the musicians with instruments suspended, the dancers still interlaced, smitten into immobility as if a spell had been cast upon them, their terror-stricken faces turned in one direction, their dark eyes fixed on the slender figure slowly advancing up the moonlit road.

She leant on her staff, and she looked at Ferdinando standing before her. In the moonlight the scarlet roses looked like blood. "Oho, thou Breaker of Hearts! so thou dost dance at thy *festa*! Loose thou that child who is nothing to thee, and come and dance at mine."

As if impelled by some unknown force, Ferdinando's arm fell from his little *fiancée*. Slowly, as if his feet were made of lead, he came forward. They stood and they looked at each other in the moonlight. What secret history of passion and sin lay between the two of them, who shall say?

Then she laughed softly.

"Did I not tell thee when I called thee, thou wouldst come?"

"I'll see thee damned for a witch before I come!"

I caught the glitter of a knife flashing through the air. As Ferdinando hurled himself across the grass, the big dog standing beside her, rose and launched himself at Ferdinando's throat and pinned him to the ground. Not a soul stirred to help him. We all stood there breathless watching him. It was like a scene in a play.

"Thou Breaker of Hearts, that wast to be my master, come thou and be my dog!" She stood for a moment looking down at him and laughing. Then she called to her dogs and went her way.

As the darkness took her, Ferdinando dropped to his hands and knees and crawled up the white roadway on all fours after her with a hideous and incredible swiftness, barking like a dog.

The young English doctor whom I sent for from Naples was a psycho-neuropath of advanced standing. He was wild with joy at the opportunity of investigating such an unusual case first hand. He walked up and down my little sitting-room asking me details of the story over and over again.

"A clear case of suggestion! The man has every symptom of hydrophobia in its most acute form, but the beast never touched him. There's not the sign of a scratch on him from head to foot."

"But what will happen?"

"As long as the influence holds good and his strength holds out, he'll remain to all intents and purposes a dog."

"And when his strength gives out?"

The young doctor shrugged his shoulders.

"He'll die, unless the influence is removed. Then, if it isn't too late, he'll get well."

Oddly enough, he and the old priest were quite at one in their view of the matter. It was strange to see the two of them, the one so young, the other so old; the one a man of science, the other a man of faith; the one a teacher of all things supernatural, and the other a frank disbeliever, whose life was founded on fact, joining issue in this way.

On the third morning as I was sitting with the young doctor and the old priest, the door opened softly and the little Marguerita came in. She put her hand inside her chemisette and drew out a blood-stained knife.

"She'll not laugh any more and turn men into dogs. I found her sleeping and I killed her. Let them take me to prison and do as they will with me. Ferdinando is free." She fell forward.

The old priest looked down very tenderly at the pure oval of the child-like face lying against his arm.

"My good friends," the old man said slowly, "there are rooms which have no ears, though they are not confessionals, and there are good friends who have not tongues, though they are not priests."

He carried the little Marguerita away to her grandmother, and the doctor hurried away to his patient. I stood alone and looked at the knife lying on the table. The scarlet of its shining reminded me of the roses in her hair.

That same day Ferdinando recovered his senses, and in the course of a few days was restored to his normal health. Later, when the gossip had ceased and the red roses were all gone, he married the little Marguerita. I gave the bride away and I danced at their *festa*. I hear Ferdinando makes a model husband. They have ten cows and twenty pigs and Marguerita puts out her own washing. So I gather they are very prosperous and divinely happy. Their eldest little girl is named for me, and Ferdinando invariably ends his letters by anxious inquiries as to my views about her future dowry.

I suppose if you come down to hard plain facts, I really connived at a murder, for Marguerita was never punished. But that fact lies no more heavily on her conscience apparently than it does on mine. Imagine if it had been in England! The police, the jury, the judge, the whole paraphernalia of the law put into motion to avenge outraged civilization! But, southern Italy is not England, fortunately for the little Marguerita. The taking and giving of life is a different thing among the primitive races from what it is with us.

No one will believe this story, but it is true all the same. If you don't believe me, go to Forenzza, that little village tucked away in the hills in the south of Italy, and ask the sacristan of the little church in the square to show you the new statue of the Virgin with the marble dog lying at her feet. Ferdinando carved it as a thank-offering. It is said to be a modern masterpiece.

That all happened more years ago than I care to remember, but I have forgotten nothing. The light and the hills and Ferdinando's eyes looking up at me out of the darkness; and the cry of the mandolins sobbing out their passion in the night to the pure Italian sky. No, I have forgotten nothing! Even as I write these words, I can see the Mad Virgin's white face framed in moonlight and the red roses on her golden head turned to fire. Across the silence of the years, I thrill again as I hear her laugh.

THE NATURE OF THE EVIDENCE

May Sinclair

May Sinclair (1863–1946) was regarded by some as a timid, rather demure woman, unlikely to write ghost stories. In fact, Sinclair, or Amelia St Clair to give her full name, was far from timid. An active feminist and suffragette, Sinclair was strong-willed and determined. She needed to be. Their family had fallen on hard times during her childhood and her father had become an alcoholic. Both her mother and brothers had congenital heart diseases leaving May as the main breadwinner. She managed to support herself by her writing for over forty years. She was fascinated with the theories of Sigmund Freud and explored the psychological aspect of love and death in many of her works. She had joined the Society for Psychical Research to better explore and understand spiritualism and the psychology of paranormal belief. Her weird tales are often daring for their day, considering personal and sexual relationships, as is evident in the following story. She collected most of her weird tales in two volumes, Uncanny Stories *in 1923 and* The Intercessor *in 1931. In 2008 Rebecca Kinnamon Neff assembled a volume of all of Sinclair's weird tales as* The Villa Désirée, *a book which is already becoming rare.*

THIS IS THE STORY MARSTON TOLD ME. HE DIDN'T WANT TO tell it. I had to tear it from him bit by bit. I've pieced the bits together in their time order, and explained things here and there, but the facts are the facts he gave me. There's nothing that I didn't get out of him somehow.

Out of *him*—you'll admit my source is unimpeachable. Edward Marston, the great K.C., and the author of an admirable work on "The Logic of Evidence." You should have read the chapters on "What Evidence Is and What It Is Not." You may say he lied; but if you knew Marston you'd know he wouldn't lie, for the simple reason that he's incapable of inventing anything. So that, if you ask me whether I believe this tale, all I can say is, I believe the things happened, because he said they happened and because they happened to him. As for what they *were*—well, I don't pretend to explain it, neither would he.

You know he was married twice. He adored his first wife, Rosamund, and Rosamund adored him. I suppose they were completely happy. She was fifteen years younger than he, and beautiful. I wish I could make you see how beautiful. Her eyes and mouth had the same sort of bow, full and wide-sweeping, and they stared out of her face with the same grave, contemplative innocence. Her mouth was finished off at each corner with the loveliest little moulding, rounded like the pistil of a flower. She wore her hair in a solid gold fringe over her forehead, like a child's, and a big coil at the back. When it was let down it hung in a heavy cable to her waist. Marston used to tease her about it. She had a trick of tossing back the rope in the night when it was hot under her, and it would fall smack across his face and hurt him.

There was a pathos about her that I can't describe—a curious, pure, sweet beauty, like a child's; perfect, and perfectly immature; so immature that you couldn't conceive its lasting—like that—any more than childhood lasts. Marston used to say it made him nervous. He was afraid of waking up in the morning and finding that it had changed in the night. And her beauty was so much a part of herself that you couldn't think of her without it. Somehow you felt that if it went she must go too.

Well, she went first.

For a year afterwards Marston existed dangerously, always on the edge of a breakdown. If he didn't go over altogether it was because his work saved him. He had no consoling theories. He was one of those bigoted materialists of the nineteenth century type who believe that consciousness is a purely physiological function, and that when your body's dead, *you're* dead. He saw no reason to suppose the contrary. "When you consider," he used to say, "the nature of the evidence!"

It's as well to bear this in mind, so as to realize that he hadn't any bias or anticipation. Rosamund survived for him only in his memory. And in his memory he was still in love with her. At the same time he used to discuss quite cynically the chances of his marrying again.

It seems that in their honeymoon they had gone into that. Rosamund said she hated to think of his being lonely and miserable, supposing she died before he did. She would like him to marry again. If, she stipulated, he married the right woman.

He had put it to her: "And if I marry the wrong one?" And she had said, That would be different. She couldn't bear that.

He remembered all this afterwards; but there was nothing in it to make him suppose, at the time, that she would take action.

We talked it over, he and I, one night.

"I suppose," he said, "I shall have to marry again. It's a physical necessity. But it won't be anything more. I shan't marry the sort of woman who'll expect anything more. I won't put another woman in Rosamund's place. There'll be no unfaithfulness about it."

And there wasn't. Soon after that first year he married Pauline Silver.

She was a daughter of old Justice Parker, who was a friend of Marston's people. He hadn't seen the girl till she came home from India after her divorce.

Yes, there'd been a divorce. Silver had behaved very decently. He'd let her bring it against *him*, to save her. But there were some queer stories going about. They didn't get round to Marston, because he was so mixed up with her people; and if they had he wouldn't have believed them. He'd made up his mind he'd marry Pauline the first minute he'd seen her. She was handsome; the hard, black, white and vermilion kind, with a little aristocratic nose and a lascivious mouth.

It was, as he had meant it to be, nothing but physical infatuation on both sides. No question of Pauline's taking Rosamund's place.

Marston had a big case on at the time.

They were in such a hurry that they couldn't wait till it was over; and as it kept him in London they agreed to put off their honeymoon till the autumn, and he took her straight to his own house in Curzon Street.

This, he admitted afterwards, was the part he hated. The Curzon Street house was associated with Rosamund; especially their bedroom—Rosamund's bedroom—and his library. The library was the room Rosamund liked best, because it was his room. She had her place in the corner by the hearth, and they were always alone there together in the evenings when his work was done, and when it wasn't done she would still sit with him, keeping quiet in her corner with a book.

Luckily for Marston, at the first sight of the library Pauline took a dislike to it.

I can hear her. "Br-rr-rh! There's something beastly about this room, Edward. I can't think how you can sit in it."

And Edward, a little caustic:

"*You* needn't, if you don't like it."

"I certainly shan't."

She stood there—I can see her—on the hearthrug by Rosamund's chair, looking uncommonly handsome and lascivious. He was going to take her in his arms and kiss her vermilion mouth, when, he said, something stopped him. Stopped him clean, as if it had risen up and stepped between them. He supposed it was the memory of Rosamund, vivid in the place that had been hers.

You see it was just that place, of silent, intimate communion, that Pauline would never take. And the rich, coarse, contented creature didn't even want to take it. He saw that he would be left alone there, all right, with his memory.

But the bedroom was another matter. That, Pauline had made it understood from the beginning, she would have to have. Indeed, there was no other he could well have offered her. The drawing-room covered the whole of the first floor. The bedrooms above were cramped, and this one had been formed by throwing the two front rooms into one. It looked south, and the bathroom opened out of it at the back. Marston's small northern room had a door on the narrow landing at right angles to his wife's door. He could hardly expect her to sleep there, still less in any of the tight boxes on the top floor. He said he wished he had sold the Curzon Street house.

But Pauline was enchanted with the wide, three-windowed piece that was to be hers. It had been exquisitely furnished for poor little Rosamund; all seventeenth century walnut wood, Bokhara rugs, thick silk curtains, deep blue with purple linings, and a big, rich bed covered with a purple counterpane embroidered in blue.

One thing Marston insisted on: that *he* should sleep on Rosamund's side of the bed, and Pauline in his own old place. He didn't want to see Pauline's body where Rosamund's had been. Of course he had to lie about it and pretend he had always slept on the side next the window.

I can see Pauline going about in that room, looking at everything; looking at herself, her black, white and vermilion, in the glass that had held Rosamund's pure rose and gold; opening the wardrobe where Rosamund's dresses used to hang, sniffing up the delicate, flower scent of Rosamund, not caring, covering it with her own thick trail. And Marston (who cared abominably)—I can see him getting more miserable and at the same time more excited as the wedding evening went on. He took her to the play to fill up the time, or perhaps to get her out of Rosamund's rooms; God knows. I can see them sitting in the stalls, bored and restless, starting up and going out before the thing was half over, and coming back to that house in Curzon Street before eleven o'clock.

*

It wasn't much past eleven when he went to her room.

I told you her door was at right angles to his, and the landing was narrow, so that anybody standing by Pauline's door must have been seen the minute he opened his. He hadn't even to cross the landing to get to her.

Well, Marston swears that there was nothing there when he opened his own door; but when he came to Pauline's he saw Rosamund standing up before it; and, he said, *"She wouldn't let me in."*

Her arms were stretched out, barring the passage. Oh yes, he saw her face, Rosamund's face; I gathered that it was utterly sweet, and utterly inexorable. He couldn't pass her.

So he turned into his own room, backing, he says, so that he could keep looking at her. And when he stood on the threshold of his own door she wasn't there.

No, he wasn't frightened. He couldn't tell me what he felt; but he left his door open all night because he couldn't bear to shut it on her. And he made no other attempt to go in to Pauline; he was so convinced that the phantasm of Rosamund would come again and stop him.

I don't know what sort of excuse he made to Pauline the next morning. He said she was very stiff and sulky all day; and no wonder. He was still infatuated with her, and I don't think that the phantasm of Rosamund had put him off Pauline in the least. In fact, he persuaded himself that the thing was nothing but a hallucination, due, no doubt, to his excitement.

Anyhow, he didn't expect to see it at the door again the next night.

Yes. It was there. Only, this time, he said, it drew aside to let him pass. It smiled at him, as if it were saying, "Go in, if you must; you'll see what'll happen."

He had no sense that it had followed him into the room; he felt certain that, this time, it would let him be.

It was when he approached Pauline's bed, which had been Rosamund's bed, that she appeared again, standing between it and him, and stretching out her arms to keep him back.

All that Pauline could see was her bridegroom backing and backing, then standing there, fixed, and the look on his face. That in itself was enough to frighten her.

She said, "What's the matter with you, Edward?"

He didn't move.

"What are you standing there for? Why don't you come to bed?"

Then Marston seems to have lost his head and blurted it out: "I can't. I can't."

"Can't what?" said Pauline from the bed.

"Can't sleep with you. She won't let me."

"She?"

"Rosamund. My wife. She's there."

"What on earth are you talking about?"

"She's there, I tell you. She won't let me. She's pushing me back."

He says Pauline must have thought he was drunk or something. Remember, she *saw* nothing but Edward, his face, and his mysterious attitude. He must have looked very drunk.

She sat up in bed, with her hard, black eyes blazing away at him, and told him to leave the room that minute. Which he did.

The next day she had it out with him. I gathered that he kept on talking about the "state" he was in.

"You came to my room, Edward, in a *disgraceful* state."

I suppose Marston said he was sorry; but he couldn't help it; he wasn't drunk. He stuck to it that Rosamund was there. He had seen her. And Pauline said, if he wasn't drunk then he must be mad, and he said meekly, "Perhaps I *am* mad."

That set her off, and she broke out in a fury. He was no more mad than she was; but he didn't care for her; he was making ridiculous excuses; shamming, to put her off. There was some other woman.

Marston asked her what on earth she supposed he'd married her for. Then she burst out crying and said she didn't know.

Then he seems to have made it up with Pauline. He managed to make her believe he wasn't lying, that he really had seen something, and between them they arrived at a rational explanation of the appearance. He had been overworking. Rosamund's phantasm was nothing but a hallucination of his exhausted brain.

This theory carried him on till bed-time. Then, he says, he began to wonder what would happen, what Rosamund's phantasm would do next. Each morning his passion for Pauline had come back again, increased by frustration, and it worked itself up crescendo, towards night. Supposing he *had* seen Rosamund. He might see her again. He had become suddenly subject to hallucinations. But as long as you *knew* you were hallucinating you were all right.

So what they agreed to do that night was by way of precaution, in case the thing came again. It might even be sufficient in itself to prevent his seeing anything.

Instead of going in to Pauline he was to get into the room before she did, and she was to come to him there. That, they said, would break the spell. To make him feel even safer he meant to be in bed before Pauline came.

Well, he got into the room all right.

It was when he tried to get into bed that—he saw her (I mean Rosamund).

She was lying there, in his place next the window, her own place, lying in her immature child-like beauty and sleeping, the firm full bow of her mouth softened by sleep. She was perfect in every detail, the lashes of her shut eyelids golden on her white cheeks, the solid gold of her square fringe shining, and the great braided golden rope of her hair flung back on the pillow.

He knelt down by the bed and pressed his forehead into the bedclothes, close to her side. He declared he could feel her breathe.

He stayed there for the twenty minutes Pauline took to undress and come to him. He says the minutes stretched out like hours. Pauline found him still kneeling with his face pressed into the bedclothes. When he got up he staggered.

She asked him what he was doing and why he wasn't in bed. And he said, "It's no use. I can't. I can't."

But somehow he couldn't tell her that Rosamund was there. Rosamund was too sacred; he couldn't talk about her. He only said:

"You'd better sleep in my room tonight."

He was staring down at the place in the bed where he still saw Rosamund. Pauline couldn't have seen anything but the bedclothes, the sheet smoothed above an invisible breast, and the hollow in the pillow. She said she'd do nothing of the sort. She wasn't going to be frightened out of her own room. He could do as he liked.

He couldn't leave them there; he couldn't leave Pauline with Rosamund, and he couldn't leave Rosamund with Pauline. So he sat up in a chair with his back turned to the bed. No. He didn't make any attempt to go back. He says he knew she was still lying there, guarding his place, which was her place. The odd thing is that he wasn't in the least disturbed or frightened or surprised. He took the whole thing as a matter of course. And presently he dozed off into a sleep.

A scream woke him and the sound of a violent body leaping out of the bed and thudding on to its feet. He switched on the light and saw the bedclothes flung back and Pauline standing on the floor with her mouth open.

He went to her and held her. She was cold to the touch and shaking with terror, and her jaws dropped as if she was palsied.

She said, "Edward, there's something in the bed."

He glanced again at the bed. It was empty.

"There isn't," he said. "Look."

He stripped the bed to the foot-rail, so that she could see.

"There *was* something."

"Do you see it?"

"No, I felt it."

She told him. First something had come swinging, smack across her face. A thick, heavy rope of woman's hair. It had waked her. Then she had put out her hands and felt the body. A woman's body, soft and horrible; her fingers had sunk in the shallow breasts. Then she had screamed and jumped.

And she couldn't stay in the room. The room, she said, was "beastly."

She slept in Marston's room, in his small single bed, and he sat up with her all night, on a chair.

She believed now that he had really seen something, and she remembered that the library was beastly, too. Haunted by something. She supposed that was what she had felt. Very well. Two rooms in the house were haunted; their bedroom and the library. They would just have to avoid those two rooms. She had made up her mind, you see, that it was nothing but a case of an ordinary haunted house; the sort of thing you're always hearing about and never believe in till it happens to yourself. Marston didn't like to point out to her that the house hadn't been haunted till she came into it.

The following night, the fourth night, she was to sleep in the spare room on the top floor, next to the servants, and Marston in his own room.

But Marston didn't sleep. He kept on wondering whether he would or would not go up to Pauline's room. That made him horribly restless, and instead of undressing and going to bed, he sat up on a chair with a book. He wasn't nervous; but he had a queer feeling that something was going to happen, and that he must be ready for it, and that he'd better be dressed.

It must have been soon after midnight when he heard the doorknob turning very slowly and softly. The door opened behind him and Pauline came in, moving without a sound, and stood before him. It gave him a shock; for he had been thinking of Rosamund, and when he heard the doorknob turn it was the phantasm of Rosamund that he expected to see coming in. He says, for the first minute, it was this appearance of Pauline that struck him as the uncanny and unnatural thing.

She had nothing, absolutely nothing on but a transparent white chiffony sort of dressing-gown. She was trying to undo it. He could see her hands shaking as her fingers fumbled with the fastenings. He got up suddenly, and they just stood there before each other, saying nothing, staring at each other. He was fascinated by her, by the sheer glamour of her body, gleaming white through the thin stuff, and by the movement of her fingers. I think I've said she was a beautiful woman, and her beauty at that moment was overpowering.

And still he stared at her without saying anything. It sounds as if their silence lasted quite a long time, but in reality it couldn't have been more than some fraction of a second.

Then she began. "Oh, Edward, for God's sake say something. Oughtn't I to have come?"

And she went on without waiting for an answer. "Are you think-ing of *her*? Because, if—if you are, I'm not going to let her drive you away from me… I'm not going to… She'll keep on coming as long as we don't— Can't you see that this is the way to stop it…? When you take me in your arms."

She slipped off the loose sleeves of the chiffon thing and it fell to her feet. Marston says he heard a queer sound, something between a groan and a grunt, and was amazed to find that it came from himself.

He hadn't touched her yet—mind you, it went quicker than it takes to tell, it was still an affair of the fraction of a second—they were holding out their arms to each other, when the door opened again without a sound, and, without visible passage, the phantasm was there. It came incredibly fast, and thin at first, like a shaft of light sliding between them. It didn't do anything; there was no beating of hands, only, as it took on its full form, its perfect likeness of flesh and blood, it made its presence felt like a push, a force, driving them asunder.

Pauline hadn't seen it yet. She thought it was Marston who was beating her back. She cried out: "Oh, don't, don't push me away!"

She stooped below the phantasm's guard and clung to his knees, writhing and crying. For a moment it was a struggle between her moving flesh and that still, supernatural being.

And in that moment Marston realized that he hated Pauline. She was fighting Rosamund with her gross flesh and blood, taking a mean advantage of her embodied state to beat down the heavenly, discarnate thing.

He called to her to let go.

"It's not I," he shouted. "Can't you *see* her?"

Then, suddenly, she saw, and let go, and dropped, crouching on the floor and trying to cover herself. This time she had given no cry.

The phantasm gave way; it moved slowly towards the door, and as it went it looked back over its shoulder at Marston, it trailed a hand, signalling to him to come.

He went out after it, hardly aware of Pauline's naked body that still writhed there, clutching at his feet as they passed, and drew itself after him, like a worm, like a beast, along the floor.

She must have got up at once and followed them out on to the landing; for, as he went down the stairs behind the phantasm, he could see Pauline's face, distorted with lust and terror, peering at them above the stairhead. She saw them descend the last flight, and cross the hall at the bottom and go into the library. The door shut behind them.

Something happened in there. Marston never told me precisely what it was, and I didn't ask him. Anyhow, that finished it.

The next day Pauline ran away to her own people. She couldn't stay in Marston's house because it was haunted by Rosamund, and he wouldn't leave it for the same reason.

And she never came back; for she was not only afraid of Rosamund, she was afraid of Marston. And if she *had* come it wouldn't have been any good. Marston was convinced that, as often as he attempted to get to Pauline, something would stop him. Pauline certainly felt that, if Rosamund were pushed to it, she might show herself in some still more sinister and terrifying form. She knew when she was beaten.

And there was more in it than that. I believe he tried to explain it to her; said he had married her on the assumption that Rosamund was dead, but that now he knew she was alive; she was, as he put it, "there." He tried to make her see that if he had Rosamund he couldn't have *her*. Rosamund's presence in the world annulled their contract.

You see I'm convinced that something *did* happen that night in the library. I say, he never told me precisely what it was, but he once let something out. We were discussing one of Pauline's love-affairs (after the separation she gave him endless grounds for divorce).

"Poor Pauline," he said, "she thinks she's so passionate."

"Well," I said, "wasn't she?"

Then he burst out. "No. She doesn't know what passion is. None of you know. You haven't the faintest conception. You'd have to get rid of your bodies first. *I* didn't know until—"

He stopped himself. I think he was going to say, "until Rosamund came back and showed me." For he leaned forward and whispered: "It isn't a localized affair at all... If you only knew—"

So I don't think it was just faithfulness to a revived memory. I take it there had been, behind that shut door, some experience, some terrible and exquisite contact. More penetrating than sight or touch. More—more extensive: passion at all points of being.

Perhaps the supreme moment of it, the ecstasy, only came when her phantasm had disappeared.

He couldn't go back to Pauline after *that*.

THE BISHOP OF HELL

Marjorie Bowen

Like so many of the authors in this volume, Marjorie Bowen (1885–1952) was born and raised in straitened circumstances. Her birth name was Gabrielle Margaret Campbell—and despite the many pen names she used, and two marriages (in 1912 and 1917—she's sometimes listed as Mrs Long)—she always regarded herself as Margaret Campbell. Born in Hayling Island, Hampshire, the family moved to London, living in poor, bohemian lodgings. Her father abandoned them and drank himself to death. The mother, who had a strict upbringing in the Moravian Brotherhood, doted on her second child but openly despised young Margaret, wishing she had never been born. Her mother strove to earn a living from writing with magazine stories, plays and novels, but only just scraped through. Young Margaret seemed to have a gift for it and her first novel, The Viper of Milan, *though it was rejected by many publishers, eventually appeared in 1906 and was an overnight success. The name Marjorie Bowen was imposed upon her to avoid confusion with her mother's work, even though her mother wrote as Josephine Campbell. Her mother became jealous of Margaret's success. Marjorie wrote partly to support the family but as much to escape from it, though her mother lived till 1921. Her ability to produce work quickly—which she rather regretted because she loved the English language—resulted in an output of around 150 books, most as Bowen, but also as George R. Preedy, Joseph Shearing, Robert Paye, John Winch and, for her autobiography, Margaret Campbell.*

Bowen had a passion for historical fiction and this sometimes combined with her interest in the supernatural—as the following story shows. The combined genres resulted in her most successful novel of the supernatural, blatantly entitled Black Magic: A Tale of the Rise and Fall of the Antichrist *(1909), which tells of the rise of Pope Joan amidst witchcraft and the occult. Other, rather more mild novels of the weird, include* The Haunted Vintage *(1921),* The Presence and the Power *(1924) and* I Dwelt in High Places *(1933), about the Elizabethan sorcerer John Dee. She wrote many supernatural short stories, scattered through collections of other material, and keeping track of her work is a formidable task. There were several weird tales in* Seeing Life! *(1923),* Dark Ann *(1927) and* The Last Bouquet *(1933), but volumes entirely of weird fiction were* The Bishop of Hell *(1949) and* Kecksies *(1976). This last had been assembled in 1950, but it was a quarter of a century before August Derleth found the finances to publish it under his Arkham House imprint. An excellent retrospective of Bowen's short fiction, compiled by Jessica Amanda Salmonson with a very informative introduction, is* Twilight and Other Supernatural Romances *(1998).*

T HIS IS THE MOST AWFUL STORY THAT I KNOW; I FEEL CON-
strained to write down the facts as they ever abide with me,
praying, as I do so, a merciful God to pardon my small share therein.

God have mercy on us all!

In the hope, vain though I feel it to be, that when I have written
down this tale it may cease to haunt me, I here begin.

It was twenty years ago, and never since, day nor night, have
I had any respite from the thought of this story, through which
you can hear the drums of Hell beat loudly and yet which has an
awful beauty.

God have mercy on us all!

*

Hector Greatrix was my friend, yet to say friend is to profane a
noble word; rather was he my counsellor, companion, and prop
in all things evil.

His reputation was hideous even among the rakehelly crowd
who flattered and followed him; he went lengths from which
others shrank, and his excesses, his impiety, his boldness terrified
even those hardened in wicked ways.

And what added a deeper edge of horror to his conduct was
that he had been an ordained clergyman.

Younger son of a younger son, his father had placed him in the
Church in the hope of rapid preferment, for the Greatrix were a
highly placed family and the great Earl of Culvers was the head of

it; but the scandal of young Hector's life was such that even in those days he was unfrocked. His intimates, in the clubs and gambling dens, called him, in bitter derision, "Bishop of Hell".

I write of the year 1770, when this tale begins.

Hector Greatrix was then in the height of his fame and fashion. No-one could deny him certain splendour; he was literally in physical height head and shoulders above his companions, and mentally also; his wit, his invention, his daring knew no bounds, but all these qualities were turned to evil. He was at this time about thirty years of age, of a magnificent figure, so graceful that his strength was hardly noticeable, tawny haired and tawny eyed, with features as yet unblemished from his debaucheries, the most elegant of hands and feet, the most exquisite taste in dress, and the most engaging of manners. There was not one honourable man nor respected woman among his acquaintances and all his intimates were villains; I do not except myself.

There was, however, one exception. Colonel Burgoyne, his cousin on the female side, had helped him by his countenance and by money. Why, I never understood, because William Burgoyne was the most austere, upright, and punctilious of men, of great wealth, of exceptional position, and of the most distinguished career.

I think now, as I thought then, that it was quite impossible for Colonel Burgoyne to realize what Hector Greatrix really was, or the set to which he belonged. The villain could be most plausible, and his cousin must have believed him to be wild, unfortunate, and blameable, but in no way vile or dishonoured.

In sum, Colonel Burgoyne effectually played the mediator between Greatrix and the chief of the family, Lord Culvers, who, no anchorite himself, was not ill-disposed towards his handsome and seductive nephew; but then his lordship, who was much disabled by gout, seldom left Greatrix Park and knew little of London society, so that he was by no means aware of his nephew's reputation.

I, as one of the most reputable of his disreputable friends, being, as I can truly say, more wild and young than vicious, was chosen to go with Hector to Greatrix Park when the old earl asked his company, and so I was able to see at close quarters how this charming knave pulled the wool over the eyes of his two kinsmen.

The end of the comedy was an allowance for Greatrix, a handsome subsidy from the earl most generously supplemented by a few hundreds more from the wealth of Colonel Burgoyne.

Greatrix was to study the law and live in chambers—suitable to his rank; he had no chance of accession to the family honours of the earl, whose heir, a dull, sickly youth enough, had lately married a blooming young woman of robust constitution, who had provided him with a couple of boys. So, Greatrix, thanks to Colonel Burgoyne, had done better than the most sanguine might have hoped. And he seemed more moved thereby than I had thought possible.

"Burgoyne has done me a good turn," he swore, "and damme if I'll ever do him a bad one."

As for his allowance and the study of the law, he laughed at these things; what he really valued was the countenance of these two great, wealthy gentlemen.

"This visit will help my credit in London," he declared. "It is good for a couple of years' debt."

"And what when two years are up and your credit and the patience of your relatives are alike exhausted?"

"Who am I," smiled Greatrix, "to think two years ahead?"

I think it was impossible for him to conceive of disaster or even common misfortune. His object gained, he was impatient to return to town; a woman with red hair was waiting for him. He had a curious and persistent passion for women with that bright shade of auburn, like burnt gold.

Colonel Burgoyne pressed us to stay a night with him on our way to town, and Greatrix, with an inner curse, for he wanted to be free of this formal, austere man, consented with a winning courtesy.

Moil Place was in Kent, quite near London, a commodious and elegant residence presided over by Mrs Burgoyne, who was some several years younger than her husband.

This type of woman was unknown to either Greatrix or myself; I have had no sisters and could not recall the character or the lineaments of my mother. Greatrix had two sisters, but they were town ladies of smirched reputation, and his mother had been a passionate, reckless, uncommon woman.

To both of us Mrs Burgoyne appeared flat, childish, almost imbecile, almost incredible. She had been married direct from a Clapham boarding school and had there received several tokens (as the doting husband let slip) for deportment and good conduct.

It was June, and she wore a muslin gown with a wide blue silk sash and a wide straw hat tied under the chin with another ribbon of the same hue. She lisped a little and her small face was clearly and definitely coloured like a china ornament; she was, in fact, like the puppets children dress up and play with; then, when she had gone into the house and was pouring tea behind the Burgoyne silver—pieces that looked larger than herself—she suddenly took off her hat and showed a head overflowing with auburn curls, long, glossy, almost vermilion, yet soft and like burnt gold, all knotted up on the crown of her head.

With this revelation of her hair you saw her beauty—the golden eyes with blonde lashes, the features of such an exquisite delicacy, the pearly shades on throat and neck, the delicious carmine of faint carnation.

I did not care to look at Greatrix, and yet I felt that I need not have suffered this embarrassment.

Colonel Burgoyne was the one man in the world for whom Greatrix had expressed any respect or consideration and the lady obviously adored her husband. I was both amused and surprised to observe the manifestations of sentimental affection between them. There was a child too, a little doll in white lace just out of the cradle. What fondness Colonel Burgoyne could spare from his wife was devoted to the infant.

I was cloyed and thankful when we had taken our seats for town. Greatrix, after the effort of the last few days, was in a surly mood. "I have never passed a couple of days so tiresome," he said.

And I, always minded to jeer at him when I could, replied: "You have never seen a woman so beyond your reach, Hector. She never looked at you, I do believe."

He laughed indifferently. "Alicia Burgoyne is ready to the hand of any man who likes to reach out for her."

What was yet good in me was shocked by this insult to our hostess, a woman who, commonplace and childish perhaps, had yet seemed to me to convey a sweet purity, a gentle fidelity, and an adoring affection beyond all reproach.

"She is in love with her husband," I declared.

"The more reason she can be in love with another—'tis your passionately attached wives who fall the easiest victims; that little creature is amorous as a lovebird. Take Burgoyne away for a month or so and she'd flutter into any arms held out—"

"By God, Hector," I swore, "if you can't believe in any nobility or decency, don't defame those qualities. Your words stick in my throat. These people have exerted themselves in kindness towards you. Mrs Burgoyne is silly, maybe, but a gentlewoman deserving of respect."

"Since when have you turned Puritan?" he asked coldly.

I was not affected by his sneers; I felt a certain definite repulsion from him, and from that day I saw less of him and applied myself with some diligence to my studies.

We each of us had rooms in Paper Buildings, and the more I heard of Hector Greatrix the more I withdrew myself from his company. Two of his boon companions shot themselves; the daughter of his laundress was found hanged; a married woman of his acquaintance was taken out of a Hampstead pond one winter morning. His name was associated, secretly and sombrely, with all these tragedies.

Some rumours of these matters must have reached the Earl in his lofty retirement, for I heard from the associates of Greatrix who still continued to be mine that there had been a summons to Greatrix Park, quarrels, and the employment once more of Colonel Burgoyne as mediator.

I had seen little of the Burgoynes; their severe and yet sentimental life, the chaste simplicity of their connubial bliss did not greatly attract me. I had been asked again to Moil Place and had needed all my fortitude to control my yawns. Mrs Burgoyne had now another infant at her breast and was more than ever infatu-ated with her husband.

Another six months and this idyllic family was rudely disturbed: Colonel Burgoyne's regiment was ordered to India for three years and he was forced to leave abruptly his wife and children he so tenderly loved.

That winter, to my surprise, I met Mrs Burgoyne in a London ballroom; it was only a few months since her husband had sailed and I imagined her consoling herself with her babies at Moil Place. When I spoke to her she seemed shy and confused; I learned that she had "moped" in the country, that the doctor had ordered a change, and that these insufferable years of waiting would seem shorter amid the distractions of society. She was staying with a married brother at St James's, and I could not doubt that she was well protected both by her own heart, her position, her relatives, her children; yet when I saw her dancing with Hector Greatrix I did not care to watch.

Needless to follow the course of an experienced and heartless seducer; suffice it to say that Greatrix was soon talked of in con-nection with Mrs Burgoyne, and, unattainable as I believed her to be, I could not forbear an appeal to her pursuer.

I found him, by rare luck, in his chambers.

"For God's sake, Hector," I conjured him, "stop your attentions to Mrs Burgoyne; even though it is impossible for you to destroy her peace of mind, you may blight her reputation."

"What is this to me?" he asked coldly. "Did I not tell you she would come at my whistle?"

I urged him to forbear. "Never before have you compromised a woman of her position. Consider what it will mean to you—the fury of your uncle and of her husband, the scandal that will put you out of society—out of England."

"And there," he interrupted, "I am likely to go in any case. I can keep the duns quiet no longer and my lord will be bled no more."

I told him I hoped he would go before Mrs Burgoyne's good name was smirched by his detestable attentions and I reminded him solemnly of his obligations towards Colonel Burgoyne. He had no answer for me, and soon after I observed with relief that Mr Lambert, Alicia Burgoyne's brother, had taken alarm and that she was being kept from any opportunity of meeting Greatrix.

Yet what availed this?

Hector Greatrix, having spun his credit to the utmost and within a few hours of the Fleet Prison for debt, fled to the Continent and Alicia Burgoyne went with him.

Though I was never squeamish in these affairs, I will confess that this completely sickened me—the man was so vile, the woman so infantile, so pure, so attached to her husband.

The scandal was hideous. The Earl cut Hector off with a curse; the Lamberts adopted the abandoned children; and as soon as they had news of Alicia, sent her a small allowance that was probably the main support of the wretched couple. This money was sent care of a bank in Genoa, but no-one knew where Mrs Burgoyne and her lover really were living.

Through the compassion of His Royal Highness, who had the chief command in India, Colonel Burgoyne was allowed to return to England on the receipt of the awful news and arrived in London something less than two years since he had sailed.

He immediately resigned his commission and returned with his children to Moil Place.

Declaring that he had no intention of following the fugitives, he said simply that if Greatrix ever returned to England one of the two would, in a few days, be dead; and Mr Lambert, with his next remittance, reported this message, advising his unfortunate sister and her paramour to keep clear of their native country for fear of further scandal and horror.

I avoided the possible chance of meeting Colonel Burgoyne. I had no desire to see this broken and outraged man, whose career, that had promised so splendidly, was broken in the middle and for whom life seemed to hold nothing but bitterness and humiliation. This, it might seem, should be the end of the story; it indeed appeared that nothing further could happen, either to the outcasts in their exile or to the betrayed husband, to alter the position of either or in any way bring them together again.

But who would have guessed at the turn Fate had in store?

Colonel Burgoyne had not been home much more than another two years when a severe epidemic of smallpox broke out in England; among the first victims were the wife and children of Lord Culvers; the son by his first marriage, always delicate, had lately died of a decline; and the old earl, then over seventy years of age, did not long endure the shock, but sank under the weight of his bereavement a few days after the funeral of his youngest child.

The estates and the money were both entailed, every portion of property having been strictly tied up by a preceding Earl, and Hector Greatrix was now Earl of Culvers and one of the wealthiest noblemen in England. I could have laughed at the irony of the situation.

Lord Culvers was summoned to London by his lawyers, and on the same day Colonel Burgoyne came up from Moil Place and took a house in Dover Street, Mayfair, not far from his lordship's town mansion, Culver House.

Hector came as far as Paris and there stopped. He still had Mrs Burgoyne with him; not, as I supposed, from any remnants of affection, but because of her allowance, which was till now his sole means of support. I shuddered to think what Alicia Burgoyne must be like now.

There had never been any talk of a divorce, but now people began to ask why Colonel Burgoyne did not permit his wife to marry her lover. They were people who did not know Hector.

I received, unexpectedly, a summons from my lord to attend him in Paris. He had not too many reputable acquaintances then, and I had become a respectable enough citizen while he was sliding down to pandemonium. Therefore, I supposed, this dubious honour.

I went, as one will, partly out of curiosity, partly out of complacence, and partly out of a faint pity for Alicia Burgoyne.

He had, of course, handled plenty of money already, and upset as the city still was, I found them elegantly installed in a *hôtel meublé* that had only lately become national property.

Hector was sumptuous to behold and cordial enough in his wild way; he had changed for the worse—the first bloom of his beauty had gone, the first fineness of his manners; but he was handsome enough, God help him.

She was with him.

I learnt afterwards that she had had and lost in the feverish heat of Italy three children, and never had she been without another woman sharing her lover's favours; often these lived under the same roof with her. She had known, I think, most of the humiliations possible to a refined woman who lives with a vile, brutal man; there could have been little of horror and squalor that she had not seen, nay, been in the midst of!

I could hardly keep curiosity from my eyes—this was the doll of Moil Place, with her lisp, her muslin, her babies.

She was, and this is perhaps the most horrible thing, much more beautiful, rich, opulent in line now, with a full bosom and flowing curves of thighs and shoulders, taller (she had been but eighteen), clever at dressing, clever of speech; gay, abandoned, and intolerably wretched. Her tone was one of bravado, but the look in her eyes was that of a whipped dog who creeps away from the lash.

As soon as we were alone, she was down on her knees to me with a movement so passionately sudden that I could in no way prevent it—on her knees, Mrs Burgoyne of Moil Place!

"Tell me," she implored, "will not William divorce me? Surely you have some message from him?"

I told her, none.

She began to weep. "If I were free Hector might marry me before he returned to England—that is my only hope."

"Surely, madam," said I in pity, "a vain one?"

But she was not yet free of the illusion women are so slow to lose—that they have always some power over a man who has once loved them or been their lover, and she cherished the desperate hope that her husband might set her free and she regain something of all she had lost under the name of Lady Culvers.

Never was there a more futile and piteous hope even in the brain of a foolish woman. I could not forbear saying to her, when I had induced her to rise from her knees: "Madam, has not your association with my lord shown you the manner of man he is?"

"Indeed it has," she answered bitterly, "yet surely he could not, in these changed circumstances, abandon me—"

So she clung to the protection of that honour she had herself discarded, and a panic terror showed in her eyes as she added that she had now nothing with which to keep him—it had always been the money that had held him; the money the Lamberts sent, and, Heaven avert its face, other money, presents from Italian lovers of hers whom he had forced on her; she told me, with a wildness that made me fear for her reason, that she had paid for her last child's funeral by such means.

"And yet, madam," I shuddered, "you wish to continue your association with such a monster? Indeed, I wonder that you have not already left him, if only for the protection of another man."

As she was silent, I added: "Is it possible that you love him?"

She replied: "No, I have never loved any but William and my dear, dear children."

But I doubt if she knew what love was, and I think that for months she had known no emotion save fear.

Seeking to abate her misery I asked her what she could dread worse than had yet befallen her.

"There's Hell," she said.

"I should think," I replied, "that Hell is where my lord is."

But no; to her, still at heart a religious, respectable English gentlewoman, anything was preferable to the life of open shame before her if my lord forsook her; she thought, in her narrow, ignorant mind, that if she could marry her lover her fault would be condoned; and I knew that in the eyes of many it would be.

I advised her that she could go into retreat somewhere with the money that the Lamberts allowed her, but she shook her head with a feeble laugh; she knew, she said with a dreadful accent, her own weakness, and she saw herself, once cast off by my lord, sinking to the lowest depths of degradation, till she reached Bridewell or a foreign lazar house.

And I could see this too. I promised to speak to my lord, but naturally with little hope; but the next day when I saw him, sitting over his breakfast playing with his dogs, he gave me no opening, for he plunged into his own affairs.

"Look 'ee here, Jack," he said, "I was too drunk yesterday to talk business and when I came back from the opera you'd gone. But this is the matter I've sent for you for—has Burgoyne seen reason? As I've no news, I take it he has gone to his prayers and his pumpkins at Moil Place and will give no trouble."

"No," I said, "Colonel Burgoyne came up to London as soon as he heard of your fortune, and has taken lodgings in Dover Street—'tis said that he keeps a watch posted by Culver House for your return."

My lord's face turned ashy.

"What for?" he cried.

"That he may challenge you the moment that you set foot in England."

My lord sprang up then; his rage was diabolic, there is no other word for this fury of a fiend outwitted at last; his oaths and blasphemies were detestable, atrocious, as he strode up and down with his dressing-gown flowing open and his locks, damp from last night's debauch, seeming to rise on his head.

"I never heard," I said, wincing, "that you were a coward, Hector, but it seems you are."

"Coward!" he yelled. "When I eloped with Burgoyne's wife I was a ruined man without a prospect in the world—did I think I'd ever want to return to England with the title and the money?"

He had been, in fact, exquisitely caught, but I could feel no spark of compassion for him.

"You'll have to meet the man," I told him, not looking at his distorted face.

"I'll not. Burgoyne is a damned good shot. Do you think I want to go out when I've suddenly got everything to my hand?"

I could guess that he did not; to him the position, the money, meant the opening of Paradise. He would, no doubt, have a good life—fine flatterers, fine women, all that wealth could buy in London would be his; nay, there would be plenty who would receive him in the finest society of the town and not scruple to offer him their daughters in honourable matrimony; the hounded exile would be the great lord and at last able to get full value for his rank, his beauty, his audacity, his fascination.

"I stay in Paris," he cried. "People will come over to me here. I'll cheat the man that way. Paris is as well as London if you have money."

"It were wiser, perhaps," I said with disgust. "But no-one will endure a man who is an avowed coward, my lord; you'll have to keep the company you've been used to lately if you stay out of England. People will know why—they're beginning to say already that you linger. I for one," and I rose, "would turn my back on you."

"Blast your impudence, Jack," he whispered. "What is this tone to me?"

"You're a peer of England. Culvers is a great name; it'll cover much, but not cowardice."

"Damn that word. I don't want to die—that's reasonable."

"Yes; if I were you, my lord, I should not want to die."

"Bah, you're thinking of my bishopric. Hell! As if I believed in Hell. There's nothing, not even Hell, Jack—one goes out like a snuffed candle—just blackness, blackness, nothingness, nothingness."

The look on his face as he said this was one of such awful despair that I thought this was a moment when he might be softened by his own terrors.

"I can see one possible way out. Hector, if you were to let Colonel Burgoyne know that if he divorced his wife you would marry her—perhaps for her sake, he would forgo his revenge."

He laughed in my face.

"The woman's been the harlot of half the rogues in Italy."

I stopped him. "Don't talk of that—even your corroded heart might blench there. Marry her, if you can, for your soul's sake and hers."

His hideous pride was greater than his fear.

"A kept woman," he mocked. "My God, I'm Culvers now."

"Remember it," I recommended him. "What do you mean to do with this poor creature?"

Then, as if he remembered that she was the original cause of his present predicament, he began to curse her, using those abominable names he so freely applied to women, and as for what he meant to do with her, his project was what the miserable wretch had herself guessed—complete abandonment; and his view of her future was her view—the streets and the *maison de Dieu*.

I reminded him of her birth and upbringing, of her relatives, but he only redoubled his blasphemies.

"Am I answerable if these Puritans breed women who run into the gutter?"

I left him; useless to contemplate a spectacle so frightful. And I avoided any further interview with Alicia Burgoyne. When I returned to London, I observed the watcher set by Colonel Burgoyne near the shuttered gloom of Culver House.

In three months' time my lord returned to London; whether urged thereto by the jeers of his enemies, the flatteries of his friends, or his own pride, or whether unable to endure his Tantalus position, or whether his nerve broke at the suspense and the waiting, I know not, but he came to London. I had heard that he had hopes of approaching Burgoyne with offers of apology or even money; of seeking in some way an accommodation. This sounded ridiculous, but from his nature it was possible to conclude that he cherished some such plan. He arrived in London secretly, with a horrid stealth, and slipped into Culver House under cover of a November evening.

Yet the next morning Lord Mildmay called on him with a challenge from Colonel Burgoyne.

That same evening I was summoned to Culver House.

My lord sat with some of his old boon companions in one of the dismantled rooms (for his coming had been sudden and unexpected); the holland covers were yet over the great velvet and gilt chairs, muslin bags enveloped the candelabra, and where the bottles and glasses stood on the ornate table were rings in the dust; candles had been hastily stuck into tarnished sticks, and the only servants were the French rascals my lord had brought with him.

Rosy *amorini* and florid wreaths peeped from the shadows of the imposing walls, and the lordly pomp of this chill magnificence was a strange background for the men drinking by the huge fire on the marble hearth. Everyone was drunk but my lord, but he, this night, could find no oblivion in the wine cup; panic kept his head clear, and I could see by the ferocious anguish of his face that his thoughts were by no means dimmed.

He met me with bravado.

"If I go to Hell tomorrow, I'll pay you a visit to let you know what 'tis like."

"Is Burgoyne so infallible?" asked one of his followers, and another, with tipsy malice: "He's a damn good shot."

"He has on his side justice at least," I said coldly, for I had now come to detest my lord.

He looked at me in agony. "Say I've a chance," he muttered, and I smiled, always having believed him to be of an invincible courage.

For all that I thought his chance good enough; if Burgoyne was a fine marksman, so was my lord.

"Why don't you get to bed? What time is the meeting?" I looked with contempt at his hideous company; not one of them had set foot in Culver House, or any mansion like it, before.

"Seven o'clock tomorrow morning," said one Hilton, the soberest of the wretched band and my lord's second.

It was now past midnight.

"Why have you sent for me?" I asked again.

He was pacing up and down the room in a very climax of terror and rage, while the drunken crew round the table condoled with and mocked him in a breath. He wore an almond-green velvet coat, overlaced, I recall, with silver—for that year the men's clothes began to be very plain—and his hair was long and powdered in the old-fashioned style still favoured in Italy. I think that the beauty of his lineaments rendered his expression the more awful—the despair, the dread, the fury expressed in that pale visage were awful indeed to contemplate.

"I will not go!" he cried. "I'll not stand up to be killed!"

He then asked me to make his will (I was by then a lawyer of some modest standing), for the Culver property was his to dispose of since he was the last male of his family. Yet when it came to asking his wishes he would not reply, and finally refused to consider the matter; and so I left him staring into the huge mirror with a glass of brandy in his hand and cursing the clock for marking the passing of the time.

I had not dared to ask him anything of Alicia Burgoyne but, as I was leaving, I did demand particulars of the lady from one of the servants, a man I had seen in Paris.

She had been left in Paris, quieted, I gathered, by some lie as to my lord's return. This affair and mainly the memory of my lord's face so wrought on my mind that I could not sleep that night and went out early for news of the duel.

I got this from the creature Hilton, the second.

The meeting had taken place in Hyde Park; at the first shot my lord had fallen. "Killed?" asked Colonel Burgoyne.

"Sir," said the surgeon, bending over the writhing man, "death would have been more merciful—he is shot through the jaw."

"He is marked where I aimed to mark him," replied the implacable soldier coldly. "He will never kiss another man's wife again; nor his own; nor even any drab from Whitefriars."

With that remark he left the Park; his austere figure and his sombre countenance had never changed during the course of the encounter.

My lord was carried home in his carriage; he soon became unconscious, for the lower part of his face was shattered, half blown away, and, though he might well live, he would never be anything but a mask of terror.

Alicia Burgoyne, quieted for the moment by my lord's lies, no sooner lost sight of him than she fell into a fierce panic and resolved to follow him by the next packet. With little more than the price of her journey in her pocket and accompanied by a huge handmaid, who was her last attendant, she landed at Dover twenty-four hours after my lord, and took the night coach to London.

Arriving there, the demented creature could think of no asylum but Culver House; and, as she could hardly believe that the man for whom she had sacrificed everything and with whom she had lived for years would refuse her shelter, she directed her steps to the stately mansion of my lord.

The valet who opened to her knew her and was for refusing admission, but the handmaid said cunningly (Mrs Burgoyne being past coherent speech) that my lord had sent for them; and the servant, not knowing if this might be so, reluctantly admitted them. The two shuddering and draggled women had just reached the great doors on the first landing when my lord came home.

He had regained consciousness, and though his pain was fearful he had no tongue to make lament with; he walked between Hilton and the surgeon, who were indeed not well able to carry so large a man, and so slowly came up the wide treads of the stairs to where Mrs Burgoyne, who had heard the steps, cowered against the door, her silk shawl, her fallen hair, her bonnet disarranged, her face like milk, her lips ashy.

As my lord came into view, with his jaw swathed in bloody bandages and his terrible eyes above them, she broke into shriek after shriek; my lord sprang forward with a strength that made nothing of those who held him, took the frail wretch in his quivering hands and hurled her down the stairs. The surgeon tried to catch her, but she was weak and her high heel caught in her dress; she fell to the bottom of the flight and lay in the hall.

Whimpering, the handmaid scuttled after her; Hilton, to please his patron, from whom he still hoped favours, said: "It's Alicia Burgoyne, the cause of the whole damn business—turn her out," he added to the gibbering valet.

The surgeon, who was a fashionable man and fee'd by my lord, made no protest, and as the Earl was led to his chamber, the servant and the handmaid picked up Mrs Burgoyne and carried her into the street. She stirred as they touched her and the black woman clamoured for pity, so that the valet consented to carry her to a pot-house nearby, where the landlady, after marking her rings and watch, took her in and let her lie in a back room, where the customers came and stared at her and the air was thick with the smell of smoke and beer.

She asked for her husband and a clergyman, but the handmaid was too ignorant to know what she meant; and so, about noon, she died, aged not quite twenty-three years.

It was a clear case of murder, but the landlady and her gossip, the slippered doctor, hushed the thing up, robbed her of her rings, watch, silk, and linen garments—and even the burnt gold hair that had first attracted my lord—and buried her in a pauper's grave. The handmaid they turned into the street; and she, distracted with terror, crept back to Culver House and begged for scraps at the kitchen door. There, out of compassion, they gave her my name and where I was to be found, and I discovered her on my stairs when I came home that night and so learnt from her the manner of Alicia Burgoyne's death. I sent the poor wretch to a friend who had a house of servants and debated whether or not I should write these matters to Colonel Burgoyne.

I was not encouraged to do so by the remembrance of his face on the morning of the duel, and while I hesitated I had news of the death of my lord. This was practically suicide, because his life had never been in danger, but he tore off the bandages with a ruthless hand, turned his mutilated face to the wall and furiously died—the day of the burial of Alicia Burgoyne.

Would that this were the end and that I, who believed in neither Heaven nor Hell, could have here finished with Hector Greatrix, seventh Earl of Culvers. I went out that day to a gathering of people who knew nothing of my lord, and stayed late, endeavouring to forget. I drank and danced and gambled, and fled the gossips who must mouth over the Culvers' scandal.

When I returned I found that the light on the stairs, commonly left there by my laundress, had gone out, so must fumble my way up in the dark and silence of the quiet building. When I reached my room I must fumble again in the dark for flint and tinder, feeling from one piece of furniture to another; it was cold, and through the tall window I could see the moon like an icicle in the dark sky. At last, when I had begun to be considerably oppressed by the dark. I found the tinderbox and struck a light.

As I set the flaming tinder to the candle I perceived that I was not alone in the room; someone was seated in the hooded chair that had its back towards me; a man. I could see the white hand hanging down, the skirt of a coat on which some bullion trimming gleamed. I concluded that a friend, minded to pay me a visit, had gone to sleep awaiting my return.

I approached, holding my light, and with I know not what feeling of unfathomable dread.

The figure turned as I neared.

It was my lord.

He wore the almond-green suit with the silver braiding in which I had seen him hold his ghastly vigil of terror and fury. God have mercy on us all!

His face was alight; where the visage should have been was a ripple of flames quivering upwards, and through this crimson veil of fire gleamed his infernal eyes with an expression of unutterable woe. The flames rose above his head, shaped into a peak; he wore a shining mitre glittering with lambent fires of green and blue like hellish jewels.

This fiend had been forced to keep his oath—to discover to another scoffer the truth of Hell.

My eyes could not long support this atrocious spectacle; as he raised his ashy hand in mock benediction, I fell senseless, seeing as I dropped the demoniacal mitre flare from his flaming brows to a man's height above his tortured eyes.

THE ANTIMACASSAR

Greye La Spina

The life of Greye La Spina (1880–1969) was one of bizarre variety. She was born Fanny Greye Bragg when her father, a Methodist clergyman, was seventy. He died two years later, so she barely knew him. She married when she was eighteen. Her first husband was in the shipping business and they travelled throughout Europe. Alas he died in a shipping accident in 1901, leaving Fanny to raise their young daughter. She remarried, and had another child, but that marriage soon failed. Her third husband was Robert La Spina, Baron di Savuto. Alas, money did not come with the title, and he developed a debilitating condition becoming an invalid. Fanny became the primary wage earner, undertaking photography, bookkeeping, typing services for writers and as a master weaver, designing tapestries.

Her first stories were for the legendary The Thrill Book *in 1919, which included the werewolf tale "The Wolf of the Steppes". She sold to several other pulps before her* Weird Tales *debut with "The Tortoise Shell Cat" in 1924, Many of her stories involve shape-changers—werewolves, vampires, were-cats! Her first serial, "Invaders from the Dark" (1925), includes a seductive Russian shape-changer. Arguably her best werewolf tale is the novella "The Devil's Pool" (1932). In the following story, from later in her career, La Spina uses her knowledge of weaving to provide a warning to others.*

"SHE DIDN'T LAST VERY LONG," SAID MRS RENNER'S RESENT-ful voice.

Lucy Butterfield turned her head on the pillow so that she might hear better the whisperings outside her bedroom door. She was not loath to eavesdrop in that house of secret happenings, if by listening she might find some clue to Cora Kent's mysterious disappearance.

"Because she was not a well woman, missus. It was just too much for her. You should've knowed it, if Kathy didn't."

That, Lucy knew, was the voice of Aaron Gross, the ancient pauper whom her landlady explained she had taken from the county poor-farm to do her outdoor chores. It was a high, cackling voice quite in character with the dried-up little man to whom it belonged.

"Sh-sh-sh! Want to wake her up?"

Lucy sat upright in bed, by now keenly attuned to those low voices in the corridor outside her room. The knowledge that she was not supposed to hear what her landlady and the hired man were discussing lent a certain allure—half mischievous, half serious—to her almost involuntary eavesdropping.

"Kathy had to be fed," said Mrs Renner's sharp whisper. "Listen at her now! How'm I going to put her off? Tell me that!"

Lucy, too, listened. From one of the locked rooms along the corridor she heard a soft moaning and knew that what she had been hearing for several nights was not a dream. Twelve-year-old

Kathy Renner, confined to her bed with rheumatic fever and denied the solace of sympathetic company for fear the excitement might bring on a heart attack, was wailing softly.

"Mom! I'm hungry! Mom! I'm hungry!"

Why, the poor kid! Lying there alone all day with no one to talk to, and crying all night with hunger. Lucy's gorge rose against the hard efficiency of Mrs Renner. How could a mother bear hearing that pitiful pleading? As if some relentless intuition pushed her into explanation, Mrs Renner's voice came huskily.

"Listen at her! Oh, my little Kathy! I just can't bear it. I can't get at them tonight but tomorrow I'm going to take out that honeysuckle!"

Lucy's grey eyes roved across the room to rest with puzzlement upon a tall vase of yellow-blossomed honeysuckle dimly seen in the half light on one shelf of the old bureau between the two south windows. She had thought it pleasant that her landlady brought them in fresh daily, for their high perfume was sweet and they seemed part of the country life to which she had given herself for a two-week vacation from her new and responsible buyer's position in the linen department of Munger Brothers in Philadelphia.

"Don't do it, missus. You'll just be sorry if you do. Don't do it!" Sharp protest in old Aaron's querulous voice. "You know what happened with that other gal. You can't keep that up, missus. If this one goes, it won't be like the first one and then you'll have double trouble, missus, mark my words. Don't do it! Accidents are one thing; on purpose is another. Let me get a sharp stake, missus—?"

"Hush! Get back to bed, Aaron. Leave this to me. After all, I'm Kathy's mother. You're not going to stop me. I'm not going to let her go hungry. Get back to bed, I tell you."

"Well, her door's locked and there's honeysuckle inside. You can't do anything tonight," grudgingly acceded Aaron.

Footsteps receded softly down the corridor. The old Pennsylvania Dutch farmhouse out in the Haycock sank into silence, save only for that plaintive moaning from the child's room.

"Mom! I'm hungry! Mom!"

Lucy lay long awake. She could not compose herself to sleep while that unhappy whimper continued. Against its eerie background her thoughts went to the reason for her stay at Mrs Renner's out-of-the-way farmhouse in Bucks County. It had begun with the non-appearance of Cora Kent, Lucy's immediate superior in Munger Brothers's linen department. Cora had not returned to work at the expiration of her vacation period and inquiries only emphasized the fact of her disappearance. She had left for the country in her coupe, taking a small table loom and boxes of coloured thread.

Lucy had liked Miss Kent as a business associate and felt reluctant at taking over her job. Somebody had had to assume the responsibility and Lucy stood next in line. Her vacation had come three weeks after Miss Kent's and she had insisted upon taking it as a partial preparation for taking over the job. In her heart she determined to scout about the country side to find if she could find some clue to Cora Kent's mysterious disappearance. She felt that Cora would not have gone far afield and so she took up her headquarters in Doylestown, county seat of Bucks, while she carried on her self-imposed detective work.

In the Haycock region outside Quaker-town, where many isolated farms were located, she came upon a clue. She had learned at the Doylestown Museum the names of weavers and inquiries had taken her to Mrs Renner's farm. On the third day of her vacation Lucy had come to an agreement with Mrs Renner for a week's board and weaving lessons. In the upstairs front room that was to be hers, Lucy exclaimed with enthusiasm over the coverlet on the old spool bed, at the runners on the washstand and the antique bureau with its tall shelves and drawers on either side of the high mirror. A stuffed chair upholstered in material that Mrs Renner said was woven by herself caught Lucy's attention and the antimacassar pinned on the back caught her eye particularly. Mrs Renner said with a certain uneasiness that she hadn't woven it herself and her eyes evaded Lucy's shiftily. Lucy offered to buy it and Mrs Renner at once unpinned it.

She said shortly: "Take it. I never did like it. Glad to be shut of it."

When Lucy went back to Doylestown to pick up her belongings, she wrote a brief note to Stan's mother and enclosed the weaving. She gave her prospective mother-in-law Mrs Renner's address. Lucy knew that Stan's mother, with whom she was on exceptionally good terms, would be pleased with the odd bit of weaving and was sure it would be shown to Stan when he came home over the weekend from his senior medical course studies.

The antimacassar wasn't as crazy-looking as she had at first imagined. It was a neat piece of work, even if the central design was loosely haphazard. The decorative blocks at corners and centre top and bottom weren't so poorly designed and the irregular markings through the centre were amusing; they looked like some kind of ancient symbols. Mrs Brunner would be charmed to receive an authentic piece of obviously original weaving. Lucy promised herself to find out about the weaver, once she had gained her landlady's confidence.

She had asked Mrs Renner outright if ever a Miss Cora Kent had been at the Renner place and her landlady had eyed her strangely and denied ever having heard the name, even. On Friday morning, her second day on the Renner farm, Aaron Gross brought Lucy a package from the Doylestown laundry, where she had left lingerie. He acted so suspicious and fearful that she was puzzled. When she stripped the covering from the package, he took it and crumpled it as if he were afraid someone would know she had given her address freely before going to the farm. Lucy counted the small pieces; there were eleven instead of ten. There was an extra handkerchief and it was initialled. It was then that Lucy received the first impact of ominous intuition. The handkerchief carried the initials "C. K." Cora Kent must have lived somewhere in the vicinity.

There was a pencilled note from the laundry. The handkerchief had been mistakenly delivered to another customer and was now being returned apologetically to its owner's address. Cora Kent had been to the Renner farm. Mrs Renner had lied deliberately when she said she had never heard the name.

Lucy looked up at the sound of a rustling starched skirt, to find Mrs Renner staring down at Cora's handkerchief, sallow brow furrowed, lips a straight line, black eyes narrowed. Mrs Renner said nothing; she only stared. Then she turned suddenly on her heel and marched into the house. Lucy was disturbed without actually knowing why, yet Mrs Renner's deliberate lie was in itself a puzzle.

This was only one of the small things that began to trouble her, like the locked door that confined Kathy Renner. Mrs Renner had said definitely that she didn't want people barging in on Kathy, perhaps getting her all excited, what with the danger of heart trouble on account of the rheumatic fever. Kathy, it would appear, slept all day for Lucy was asked to be very quiet about the house in daytime. At night noise didn't disturb the little sick girl because then she would be awake anyway.

Lucy sat up in bed now and listened to the child's whining complaint. Why didn't Kathy's mother give the poor child something to eat? Surely starvation was not included in a regimen for rheumatic fever? There was the faint sound of a door opening and the wails subsided. Lucy lay down then and slipped comfortably off to sleep, feeling that Kathy's needs had been met.

Mrs Renner's enigmatic remarks and Aaron's peevish disapproval of his employer's behaviour on some former occasion dimmed as sleep stilled Lucy's active mind. It was not until afternoon of the following day that Lucy, entering her room to get her scissors so that she might use them when weaving, noticed with sudden sharp recollection of her landlady's whispered words of the previous night that the vase of honeysuckle was conspicuous by its absence. She asked herself vainly what connection had honeysuckle to do with Kathy's wailing cry of hunger? Or, for that matter, with herself?

With the vague idea of blocking Mrs Renner's contemplated design hinted to Aaron Friday night, Lucy managed to pluck several sprays of lilac and honeysuckle from her open window, smartly avoiding carrying them through the house. She put them into the heavy stoneware tooth-mug that stood on the washstand. To remove these flowers, Mrs Renner must come out into the open and explain her reason for taking them away, thought Lucy mischievously.

In the big downstairs living-room where Mrs Renner's enormous lofty loom occupied space, the landlady had cleared a table and upon it stood a small loom about fifteen inches wide. Lucy examined this with interest for she recognized it at once as a model carried in the store where she worked. She said nothing of this but eyed Mrs Renner surreptitiously when that lady explained that it was an old machine given her years ago by a former student who had no need for it. There was a white warp threaded in twill, for a plain weave, Mrs Renner explained.

"What kind of weaving can you do on twill?" Lucy queried, thinking of the antimacassar she had sent to Stan's mother, the piece with the queer little hand inlaid figures woven into it.

"All manner of things," Mrs Renner said. "On a twill, you can do almost anything, Miss. Mostly hand work." She manipulated the levers in illustration as she talked. "You'd better stick to plain weaving at first. Hand work isn't so easy and takes a heap more time."

"That antimacassar you let me have is hand work, isn't it?" Lucy probed.

Mrs Renner flung her an oddly veiled look.

"Tomorrow you can weave a white cotton towel with coloured borders," she said abruptly. "No use starting tonight. Hard to work with kerosene lamps."

Lucy opined that she could hardly wait. It seemed incredible that she was actually to manufacture the fabric of a towel with her own hands and within the brief limits of a day. She went up to her room fairly early and, as she had done from the first, locked her door, a habit acquired from living in city boarding houses. From deep sleep she stirred once into half waking at the sound of a cautious turning of the doorknob and retreating footsteps and the moaning plaint of the little sick girl's "Mom, I'm hungry!" which seemed so close that for a moment she could have believed the child to be standing closely without her locked door. She thought she heard the child say, "Mom, I can't get in! I can't get in!"

Mrs Renner was obviously feeling far from well the following morning. Her eyes were ringed by dark circles and she wore a loosely knotted kerchief about her neck, although the sweltering heat would have seemed sufficient to have made her discard rather than wear any superfluous article of clothing. When Lucy was seated at the loom, she showed her how to change the sheds and throw the shuttle for a plain weave, then left her working there while she went upstairs to tidy her guest's room. When she came down a few moments later, she walked up to Lucy, her face dark and grim, her lips a hard uncompromising line.

"Did you put those flowers up in your room?" she demanded.

Lucy stopped weaving and turned her face to Mrs Renner in feigned surprise but her intuition told her that there was more to the inquiry than was apparent on the surface.

"I love flowers so much," she murmured, deprecatorily.

"Not in a room at night," snapped Mrs Renner. "They're unhealthy at night. That's why I took out the others. I don't want flowers in my bedrooms at night."

The tone was that of an order and Lucy's natural resentment, as well as her heightened curiosity, made her rebel.

"I'm not afraid of having flowers in my room at night, Mrs Renner," she persisted stubbornly.

"Well, I won't have it," said her landlady with determined voice and air.

Lucy raised her eyebrows.

"I see no good reason to make an issue of a few flowers, Mrs Renner."

"I've thrown those flowers out, Miss. You needn't bring any more, for I'll just throw them out, too. If you want to stay in my house, you'll have to get along without flowers in your room."

"If you feel so strongly about it, of course I won't bring flowers inside. But I must say frankly that it sounds silly to me, their being unhealthful."

Mrs Renner stalked away. She appeared satisfied at the assertion of her authority as hostess and the balance of Sunday was spent initiating Lucy into the intricacies of decorative twill weaves, to such good effect that by the time evening came Lucy had completed a small towel in white cotton with striped twill borders in colour.

Lucy fell half asleep in the hammock that evening. The fresh country air and the lavish supply of good country food combined to bring early drowsiness to her eyes. She came awake when a small mongrel dog she had seen from time to time in and out of the Renner barn began to dig furiously around the roots of a nearby shrub, unearthing eventually a small blue bottle half filled with white tablets. She pushed the dog away and picked up the bottle. She looked at it curiously. A shiver of apprehension went over her body. She had seen just such a container on Cora Kent's office desk and Cora had said something about garlic being good for tubercular-inclined people. Lucy unscrewed the bottle cap and sniffed at the contents. The odour was unmistakable. She quickly slipped the bottle inside her blouse. She knew now beyond the shadow of a doubt that Cora Kent had preceded her as a guest in the Renner household. She knew now that the small loom must have been Cora's. The initialled handkerchief was yet another silent witness.

Lucy crept up to her room and again locked the door. She slipped the back of a chair under the knob as a further precaution.

For the first time, she began to sense some threat to her own safety. Her thoughts flew to the flowers Mrs Renner had tossed from the window. Why should her landlady take such a stand? Why had she told old Aaron that she was going to "take out the honeysuckle?" What was there about honeysuckle that made Mrs Renner wish to remove it from her guest's room, as if it had something to do with Kathy Renner's plaintive, "Mom, I'm hungry!"

Lucy could not fit the pieces of the puzzle together properly. But the outstanding mention of honeysuckle determined her to pull several more sprays from the vine clambering up the wall outside her window. If Mrs Renner did not want them in the room, then Lucy was determined to have them there. She removed the screen quietly and leaned out. It struck her with a shock. Every spray of flowering honeysuckle within reaching distance had been rudely broken off and dropped to the ground below. Somebody had foreseen her reaction. She replaced the screen and sat down on the edge of her bed, puzzled and disturbed. If Mrs Renner was entertaining nefarious designs that mysteriously involved the absence of honeysuckle, then Lucy knew she would be unable to meet the situation suitably.

It might have been amusing in broad daylight. She could just walk away to the shed where her car was garaged. Even if "they" had done something to it, Lucy figured that she could walk or run until she reached the main road where there ought to be trucks and passenger cars; not the solitude of the secluded Renner farm, hidden behind thickly wooded slopes.

She told herself sharply that she was just being an imaginative goose, just being silly and over-suspicious. What could honeysuckle have to do with her personal security? She got ready for bed, resolutely turned out the kerosene lamp. Drowsiness overcame her and she sank into heavy sleep.

She did not hear Mrs Renner's sibilant whisper: "Sh-sh-sh! Kathy! You can come now, Kathy. She's sound asleep. Mother took out the honeysuckle. You can get in now. Sh-sh-sh!"

She did not hear old Aaron's querulous protest: "You can't do this, missus. Let me get the stake, missus. It'd be better that way. Missus…"

To Lucy, soundly sleeping within her locked room, no sound penetrated. Her dreams were strangely vivid and when she finally wakened Monday morning she lay languidly recalling that final dream wherein a white-clad child had approached her bed timidly, had crept in beside her until her arms had embraced the small, shy intruder. The child had put small warm lips against her throat in what Lucy felt was a kiss, but a kiss such as she had never in her life experienced. It stung cruelly. But when she yielded to the child's caress, a complete relaxation of mind and muscle fell upon her and it was as if all of herself were being drawn up to meet those childish lips that clung close to her neck. It was a disturbing dream and even the memory of it held something of mingled antipathy and allure.

Lucy knew it was time to rise and she sat up, feeling tired, almost weak, and somehow disinclined to make the slightest physical effort. It was as if something had gone out of her, she thought exhaustedly. She lifted one hand involuntarily to her neck. Her fingers sensed a small roughness, like two pin pricks, where the dream child had kissed her so strangely, so poignantly. Lucy got out of bed then and went to the mirror. Clear on her neck were those two marks, as if a great beetle had clipped the soft flesh with sharp mandibles. She cried out softly at the sight of those ruddy punctures.

That there was something wrong, she was now convinced. That it also concerned herself, she felt certain. She was unable to analyse the precise nature of the wrongness but knew that it held something inimical in the very atmosphere of the Renner farmhouse and unreasoning terror mounted within her. Could she get to her car and escape? *Escape...?* She stared at her neck in the mirrored reflection and fingered the red marks gingerly. Her thoughts could not be marshalled into coherence and she found herself thinking of but one thing—flight. She could not have put into words just what it was from which she ought to flee but that she must leave the Renner farmhouse at the earliest possible moment became a stronger conviction with every passing moment. In her mind one ugly, incontrovertible fact stood out only too clearly: Cora Kent had visited the Renner farm and had not been seen since.

Lucy dressed hastily and managed to slip out of the house without encountering her landlady. She found her car under the shed at the rear of the barn, where she had left it. It looked all right but when she got closer, she saw to her dismay that it had two flats. She had, as was usual, but one spare tyre. She did not know how to take off or put on even that one spare tyre, let alone manage to repair the second flat. She would be unable to drive away from the Renner farm in her car. She stood staring in dismay at the useless vehicle.

Aaron Gross's whining voice came softly to her ear. She whirled to confront him accusingly.

"What happened to my car? Who—?"

"You can't be using it right away, miss, with them two tyres flat," Aaron volunteered, whiningly. "Want I should take them down to a service station for you?"

She cried with relief: "That would be splendid, Aaron. But I don't know how to get them off."

"Neither do I, miss. I dunno nothing about machines."

Impatience and apprehension mingled in the girl's voice. She threw open the luggage compartment and began to pull out the tools.

"I think I can jack up the car, Aaron. I've never done it before, but I do want the car so that I can get to town. Shopping," she added quickly, trying to smile carelessly.

Aaron made no comment. He stood at the end of the shed watching her as she managed to get the jack under the rear axle and began to pump the car off the ground.

"I'll need a box to hold this up when I put the jack under that other tyre," she suggested.

Aaron shuffled away.

Lucy managed to pry off the hub cap but with all her feverish attempts at the nuts and bolts, she could stir nothing. She stopped in despair, waiting for Aaron to return with the box. She thought she might get him to have a mechanic come up from town. Panting and dishevelled, she walked out of the shed to look for him. As she emerged, Mrs Renner confronted her, grim-lipped, narrow-eyed.

"Anything wrong?" inquired Mrs Renner, both fat hands smoothing down blue chequered apron over ample hips.

"My car has two flats. I can't understand why," blurted Lucy.

Mrs Renner's face remained impassive. She stated rather than asked. "You don't need to go into town. Aaron can do your errands."

"Oh, but I do want to get to town," insisted Lucy with vehemence.

"You don't need your car until you're leaving here," said Mrs Renner coldly. She regarded Lucy with impassive face, then turned her back and walked toward the house without another word.

Lucy called: "Mrs Renner! Mrs Renner! I'd like to have Aaron take these two wheels into town to be repaired but I can't get them off."

Mrs Renner continued on her way and disappeared into the house without turning or giving the least sign that she had heard a word.

From the interior of the barn Aaron's querulous voice issued cautiously.

"Miss, want I should ask the mechanic to come out here?"

"Oh, Aaron, that would be wonderful! I'd be glad to pay him—and you—well. Tell him I just can't get those tyres off by myself."

That would do it, she told herself. Once the mechanic was there, she would bring down her suitcase and manage to get into town and have him send someone to bring out her car when the tyres were repaired. She would manage to leave before night. While Aaron was away, she would work on the loom that she was convinced had been Cora Kent's property. That might disarm Mrs Renner's suspicions.

She walked slowly back to the house. She was thankful that Mrs Renner was upstairs tidying the bedroom; Lucy could hear her steps as she walked from one side to the other of the big bed. Lucy sat down at the loom and began to experiment with a coloured thread, to see if she would make an ornamental border like that of the antimacassar she had sent to Stan's mother. It was not as difficult as she had thought it might be and went faster than she believed possible; it was almost as if other fingers laid the threads in place for her. She began to build up the border emblems with growing excitement. The corner inserts looked for all the world like curving serpents standing upright on their tails and the centre one was like a snake with its tail in its mouth. Time passed. The weaving grew under what she felt were guided fingers.

"Why," she said aloud, amazed at what she had woven in so short a time. "It looks like S-O-S!"

"So?" hissed Mrs Renner significantly.

She was standing directly behind Lucy, staring at the woven symbols with narrowed eyes and grim mouth. She picked up the scissors lying on the table and slashed across the weaving with deliberate intent. In a moment it had been utterly destroyed.

"So!" she said with dark finality.

Lucy's hands had flown to her mouth to shut off horrified protest. She could not for a moment utter a word. The significance of that action was all too clear. She knew suddenly who had woven the antimacassar. She knew why the adaptable serpents had been chosen for decor. She looked at Mrs Renner, all this knowledge clear on her startled face and met the grim determination with all the opposing courage and strength of purpose she could muster.

"What happened to Cora Kent?" she demanded point blank, her head high, her eyes wide with horror. "She was here. I know she was here. What did you do to her?" As if the words had been thrust upon her, she continued: "Did you take the honeysuckle from *her* room?"

Amazingly, Mrs Renner seemed to be breaking down. She began to wring her hands with futile gestures of despair. Her air of indomitable determination dissipated as she bent her body from one side to the other like an automaton.

"She didn't last long, did she?" Lucy pursued with cruel relentlessness, as the recollection of that overheard conversation pushed to the foreground of her thoughts.

Mrs Renner stumbled backward and fell crumpled shapelessly into a chair.

"How did you know that?" she whispered hoarsely. And then, "I didn't know she was sick. I had to feed Kathy, didn't I? I thought—"

"You thought she'd last longer, missus, didn't you? You didn't really mean to let Kathy kill her, did you?"

Aaron was standing in the kitchen doorway. One gnarled hand held a stout stick, whittled into a sharp point at one end. A heavy wooden mallet weighed down his other hand.

Mrs Renner's eyes fastened on the pointed stick. She cried out weakly.

Aaron shuffled back into the kitchen and Lucy heard his footsteps going up the stairs.

Mrs Renner was sobbing and crying frantically: "No! No!"

She seemed entirely bereft of physical stamina, unable to lift herself from the chair into which her body had sunk weakly. She only continued to cry out pitifully in, protest against something which Lucy's dizzy surmises could not shape into tangibility.

A door opened upstairs. Aaron's footsteps paused. For a long terrible moment silence prevailed. Even Mrs Renner's cries ceased. It was as if the house and all in it were awaiting an irrevocable event.

Then there sailed out upon that sea of silence a long quavering shriek of tormented, protesting agony that died away in spreading ripples of sound, ebbing into the finality of deep stillness as if the silence had absorbed them.

Mrs Renner slipped unconscious to the floor. She said one word only as her body went from chair to floor. "Kathy!" Her lips pushed apart sluggishly to permit the escape of that sound.

Lucy stood without moving beside the loom with its slashed and ruined web. It was as if she were unable to initiate the next scene in the drama and were obliged to await her cue. It came with the sound of wheels and a brake and a voice that repeatedly called her name.

"Lucy! Lucy!"

Why, it was Stan. How was it that Stan had come to her? How was it that his arms were about her shelteringly? She found her own voice then.

"Aaron has killed Kathy with a sharp stick and a mallet," she accused sickly.

Stan's voice was full of quiet reassurance.

"Aaron hasn't killed Kathy. Kathy has been dead for many weeks."

"Impossible," whispered Lucy. "I've heard her calling for food, night after night."

"Food, Lucy? All Kathy wanted was blood. Her mother tried to satisfy her and couldn't, so Kathy took what Cora Kent could give and Cora couldn't stand the drain."

"Mrs Renner said Cora didn't last long—"

Stan held her closer, comfortingly safe within his man's protective strength.

"Lucy, did she—?"

Lucy touched her neck. Incomprehensibly, the red points had smoothed away.

She said uncertainly: "I think she came, once, Stan. But I thought it was a dream. Now the red marks are gone."

"For that you can thank Aaron's action, Lucy. He has put an end to Kathy's vampirism."

He bent over the prostrate woman. "Nothing but a faint," he said briefly.

"Aaron—?"

"He's perfectly sane and he won't hurt anybody, Lucy. What he's done won't be understood by the authorities but I doubt if they do more than call him insane, for an examination will prove that Kathy was long dead before he drove that wooden stake into her heart."

"How did you know about her, Stan?"

"From the antimacassar you sent Mother."

"With the S-O-S worked into the border?" Lucy ventured.

"So you found that, too, Lucy? Did you know that poor girl had woven shorthand symbols all over the piece? As soon as I realized that they stood for 'Vampire, danger, death, Cora Kent', I came for you."

"What will happen to Mrs Renner, Stan?"

"That's hard to say. But she may be charged with murder if they ever find Cora's body."

Lucy shuddered.

"The likelihood is that she is mentally unsound, dear. She probably never realized that Kathy was dead. Her punishment may not be too severe.

"But come on, Lucy, and pack up your things. You're going back to town with me and we'll inform the authorities of what's happened."

WHITE LADY

Sophie Wenzel Ellis

Along with Greye La Spina, Sophie Wenzel Ellis (1893–1984), from Memphis, Tennessee, was one of the few women contributors of weird tales and the fantastic to the early pulp magazines. Her first such story was probably "The Unseen Seventh", a ghost story in The Thrill Book *in 1919 under her maiden name Sophie Louise Wenzel. She married lawyer George E. Ellis in 1922. Most of her fiction was either ghost stories or mysteries, mixed with a few romances, along with a brief foray into science fiction in 1930. Her recorded output barely reached twenty stories and she was soon forgotten, but her contribution to the field of early science fiction and fantasy is at last being recognized.*

B RYNHILD KNEW THAT SOMETHING HAD WAKED HER, SOME-
thing pleasant and exhilarating, which was to be expected
on this strange island in the most remote corner of the warm
Caribbean sea, where André Fournier, her fiancé, experimented
fantastically with tropical plant life.

Presently she heard it again, music so wild and delicate that she
felt its rapturous vibrations in her nerves, rather than heard them.

Below her, from the house to the placid sea in the distance,
spread an unnatural panorama, lighted by the sun's gaudy hood
just coming out of the water. She looked, and was glad that she
had accepted the invitation of Madame Fournier, André's gracious
mother, to visit their lonely Ile-de-Fleur.

In a few minutes she was dressed and on the trail of the puzzling music. When she closed the back door behind her, she was
immediately in a curious maze of floral wonders, unreal as a painting by Doré. The jungles of the sun-warmed lands had given to
André their rarest treasures, which now sucked a richer life from
the black soil of the Ile-de-Fleur. Nature, in her most whimsical
mood, had not been permitted to rule here; everywhere, among
frond and spray and giant runner, bloomed hybrid blossoms whose
weird forms and colours suggested André's tampering with Nature.

Brynhild heard the music clearer now, long notes that had an
eery, half-human sound, like the tuneless music of a demented
savage. It baffled her, teased her into wilder plunges through the
flower thickets, all jewelled with liquid beads.

When she mounted a hillock and saw, just beyond, a tiny cage built of copper screen, she knew that she had reached her goal. The music seemed to come from this little bower, which was puzzling, for the sole occupant was a blooming plant.

A golden gauze seemed to drop suddenly from the sky, which was the tropical sun's first rays shooting from the sea. The stronger light brought a gasp from Brynhild, for now she could see that even in this land of queer vegetation, the imprisoned plant was a monstrous alien.

From a mass of thick frondage, white and fleshy as her own bare arms, reared a flower whose round, pallid petals formed a face like the caricature of a woman. Draped around this eldritch flower-face and flowing down to meet the colourless foliage, was a mass of gauzy matter that had the startling appearance of a bridal veil.

But what brought a cry from Brynhild was not the human look of this fantastic plant, but what it was doing. Just below the head, almost as large as her own, protruded two slender, dagger-pointed white spines, set in sockets in such a manner that they could be moved like arms. These two spines, rubbing together, produced the music that had captivated her.

After the first frightful moment of comprehension, she longed to see the spectacle closer. She pressed her forehead against the copper screen.

Instantly the spines ceased their serenade, the white flower-face turned and fronted her, and she felt eyes watching her, eyes she could not see. For a moment, flower and foliage remained rigid; then a spasm passed through the entire plant, the arms came together again, and hideous discord shrieked out.

Brynhild, sensing that her presence had caused the change from elfin music to the blood-freezing dissonance, dropped behind a concealing thicket and watched.

While she waited, footsteps approached. André was coming. Like a tall young pagan priest he came forward, arms and shoulders naked, sunshine splashing his bronze curls. He had a beautiful, poetic face and a luminous smile that was now turned on the strange plant.

Instantly the flower music commenced again, louder and more seductive than ever, the queer blossom reeling on its stem as though animal excitement quivered through its pallid flesh.

André called out in his soft French:

"*Bon jour*, White Lady. Are you happy this morning, eh?"

The woman-face swayed toward him; the dagger arms caressed each other rapturously.

Brynhild crouched lower behind her hiding-place, each moment more astonished and horrified. André lifted the latch on the door and went inside.

The music sank to a low, plaintive throbbing, tender as a bird's love-song. André came closer to the flower and touched the white foliage with gentle fingers. Down drooped the flower head until the fleshy cheeks brushed his face.

"Ah, *ma petite!*" André whispered. "My own White Lady! If I could but bridge the gap!"

Brynhild could endure no more.

"André!" she shrieked, leaping from her hiding-place.

Instantly the flower-head stiffened, and turned toward her with a gesture so human that the girl sickened. As André called out an impulsive greeting and came toward her, the unnatural foliage quivered violently and the daggers came together with a piercing din.

André laughed. "She's jealous, the White Lady!" His English had the barest accent. "Did you ever imagine such a flower, Brynhild? Should you have believed if someone had told you of this?"

"It is a nightmare!" She covered her eyes with soft, beautifully formed hands.

"No, Brynhild. She is my dream materialized."

"Stop! I can't bear to hear you speak of it as though it were a woman." Her face had blanched until it was as pale as the flower before her.

In the cage, a terrific noise was going on, shocking in its metallic harshness.

André turned around and looked at the flower. "I'd better go to it for a moment, dear. Come! White Lady is like a dog: if you are good to her, she'll respond with love that is almost human."

Hesitant, as though she feared something evil, Brynhild entered the cage behind André. André caressed the leaves and put his face against the humanlike head. The daggers, rubbing together, gave forth a feline purr.

"Come, Brynhild," said André, with his lucent smile, "pet her."

Brynhild shrank back. How could she touch those leprous, fleshy leaves, that flower-face as unnatural as a vampire's? Trembling, she reached out her little hand to the bleached foliage.

Quick as a streak of lightning, the daggers struck at her, viciously, inflicting a long, bleeding scratch on her hand. The girl screamed and fell into André's arms.

"Darling!" groaned the young man, bending over her solicitously. "I never thought—"

Brynhild buried her golden curls against his shoulder.

"André!" she sobbed. "I can't endure it. That monster—it hates me." Her voice rose hysterically. "Why did you create it?"

"Hush!" He spoke sternly. "She never would have scratched you if she hadn't sensed that you are an enemy."

"You're mad!" She broke from his arms and raised her beautiful face angrily. "This vile monster has gone to your head. Now, as always, you prefer your unnatural flowers to me."

Her white skirt flashed through the open door and on out between the flowery tangle beyond. He followed her, calling a contrite apology. When he caught her and again held her fast in his arms, they were both breathless.

"*Pardonne-moi!*" he pleaded, his thin, spiritual face full of penitence. "But, Brynhild, I'd give half my life if you'd love plants as I do."

And with his hand pressing hers, he told her, in his peculiarly quiet voice, of the supreme joy that can be had from a sympathetic understanding of Nature's strange ways.

"Man has a connection with plant life," he said, "which all scientists will some day concede. Naturalists already agree that there is no real dividing line between the lowest forms of plant and animal life. And what is man but the highest animal?"

He had grown excited, as he always did when discussing plants. His sensitive face glowed with earnestness.

"Who can say," he continued, "how close is the kinship between animals and the carnivorous plants that devour meat? White Lady is not the only plant that has voluntary motion; nor is she the only one that senses instantly the presence of the destroyer." He looked at her intently. "Some of our commonest garden plants have eye-cells in the epidermis of leaves and stalks—eyes that have lenses and are sensitive to light. White Lady is the result of careful cross-breedings that have developed the most humanlike traits found throughout plant life. Oh, Brynhild!" He held her hand against his cheek. "If you could only understand, dear! You would not be shocked that my White Lady is more than an animal plant; that the exquisite, lovely thing has intelligence!"

A long shiver ran through the girl's slender body.

"It is wrong to bring such a monstrosity into existence, André!"

"No!" His eyes filmed with tears. "My only sin is that I developed just one. Had I developed two, White Lady would not now be the loneliest living thing in existence." He flushed as he spoke.

Sudden horrible understanding gripped Brynhild, understanding so overwhelming that she swayed dizzily.

"That monster—it loves you, André! It loves you as a dog loves its master."

He stroked the gleaming gold of her hair, all alive under the sunlight.

"Don't go near it again, dear one," he soothed. "There might be real danger for you. Now there! Mother is calling us to breakfast. Be happy and smiling, won't you?" He tilted up her chin and kissed her gently.

At the breakfast table, Madame Fournier was very much disturbed; André took nothing except milk, into which he dissolved a pinkish pellet.

"No coffee this morning, son?" asked the mother, anxiously.

André flushed. "No, mother; just milk."

"Why, André!" protested Brynhild. "You scarcely eat enough to live. I watched you last night. You actually shivered over the lettuce mother made you eat. Don't you feel well?"

"Excellent. Remember that I drink quantities of milk."

After breakfast, Madame Fournier drew Brynhild aside.

"I'm uneasy," she said. "André is becoming fanatical in his love for growing things. Think of it! He says he can hear his lettuce cry out when he cuts into it."

"A year ago," shivered Brynhild, "I'd have called that nerves; but now that I've seen that monstrous White Lady thing—" She put her hands over her eyes.

No more that day did Brynhild go near White Lady. That night, while the island slept, she sat by her window and enjoyed the splendour of the moon-bathed panorama. Dimly, from the enchanted flowery reaches, came stealing the wild music of White Lady. With the first note, Brynhild stiffened, but, as the seductive sounds sent their sorcery through her, she listened with increasing delight, forgetful of her horror of the morning. Within a few moments, she was reaching for her dressing gown.

Following where White Lady's music pulled her, Brynhild stepped lightly through the thick leafage, exalted as though she were blown along by a jubilant wind.

André's strange world of flowers was like the inside of a giant pearl, for the Caribbean moon, riding full and low, had bleached the island to a luminous whiteness. From the pale hypnosis above and from the honeyed breaths that trembled over the flowers, she drew a new kinship with Nature. There was solemn joy in knowing that the same mysterious force called life which animated her own young body also sent the sap flowing through the plants about her.

Every growing thing on the island seemed to respond to the beauty of the night as happily as she. On all sides, flower-faces that seemed delirious with the joy of living lifted to the white radiance above.

The beauty of the world, then, did not exist for man's sole enjoyment.

Perhaps there was truth in André's contention that plants, with their partially developed consciousness, respond with more delicate delight than cultivated man to such elemental joys as the beauty of moonlight and the soft kisses of the night wind.

She was sure of this when she saw White Lady. The mysterious woman-flower was moon-mad. The roof of the bower, built to shade partially, cut off the moon which was directly above, but White Lady had curved her stem so that her face reached the light.

The music that throbbed from the rubbing arms was so rapturous that Brynhild felt her senses reel. She threw herself upon the grassy ground directly in front of the cage.

Instantly the music ceased, and the monstrous blossom withdrew to the shadows, where it stood tall and straight on its rigid stem, spectral in its veil and cadaverous foliage. Brynhild was prepared for the hideous discord that she had heard in the morning, but from the shadows came such low, enticing harmonies, sweet as the breathings of a wind harp, that she drew closer. The nearer she approached, the dimmer came the music, until the horrible thought came to her that White Lady was enticing her within the cage.

Pressing her hands over her ears, she fled, frightened with the paralysing fear of the unknown.

The next morning, when she told André, he caught her in his arms and cried out:

"Keep away from her! As you value your life, keep away. She has intelligence, but no conscience—no pity for what she hates."

"But, André!" She searched his ascetic face closely. "Will you let such a thing live? Shan't you cut it down?"

"Cut down my White Lady, the supreme achievement of my life?" He looked as though he thought her insane.

"Not even though it hates me, André? Not even though it is trying to destroy me?"

"But I warned you to keep away. Wouldn't you—wouldn't any human being have a right to fight an enemy? You are her enemy, and she knows it."

The dispute ended with Brynhild in tears, but with André as firm as ever about not cutting down his unnatural creation.

Brynhild was jealous, jealous of a flower, and her jealousy increased with the passing of time. Whenever she heard the seductive song of White Lady, elemental hate surged in her heart. She wanted to destroy it, to tear apart those thick, white leaves, to crush that singular woman-face under her heel.

She was afraid to go too close to the screen cage, but sometimes she stole near enough for a good glimpse of the flower. Always she was delighted to see the rage of the horrible thing, and, at a safe distance, laughed at the shrieking dissonance that the flower's striking daggers made. At times, when she approached the cage, White Lady merely stiffened, and then Brynhild knew that it watched her as a cat watches a mouse. André had told her that the invisible eyes in the leaves and stem were very highly developed.

It gave Brynhild unholy delight to know that her very presence was torment to this human flower that seemed to adore André. As though the thing could understand, she would stand at a safe distance and tell how André loved her, and of the wedding which was only three weeks distant. Once, after a scene like this, White Lady lunged at her so viciously with her daggers that Brynhild was barely able to escape.

And the girl knew that, sooner or later, one would succumb to the other.

"It shall be that *bête blanche*," vowed Brynhild, quoting the name that Madame Fournier had given the plant.

As the days passed, André grew thinner, whiter, more spiritual. He was absolutely unlike the brown young athlete with whom Brynhild had fallen in love, two years ago, in Bermuda.

"It's the way he eats," moaned his mother. "How can a strong man who works live on little else than milk? What are we to do, Brynhild? He is killing himself. Sometimes I even wonder if his mind is not going." She began to cry softly. "Did you notice him in the rain yesterday?"

"No. Tell me."

"He walked around as in a dream, with his white face held up toward the dripping sky. When I went to him and asked him to come in, he refused. He told me to leave him alone, because he had found the mood in which he could react to the cool rain just as a plant. He's doing something mysterious to make himself as much as possible like things that grow in the ground."

"It's that White Lady!" said Brynhild bitterly. "Constant brood-ing over a monster like that will unhinge anyone's mind. The horrible freak is getting on my nerves, too. I do silly things." She blushed, thinking of her own scenes with the strange plant.

"We'll have to watch him, Brynhild."

Brynhild did watch, and thereby brought greater suffering to herself, for her surveillance revealed that he not only spent much of the day with White Lady, but that he often went to the plant at night.

Much of his passion for herself had died. His love seemed to have ascended to a spiritual plane which was ethereal in its purity and tenderness. He spoke no more of their approaching marriage, seemed almost to have forgotten it.

When the two were alone, he frequently turned the conversa-tion to morbid subjects.

"Death is beautiful in a land of flowers like this," he told her. "Isn't it a happy thought, Brynhild, to know that when you are put into the warm, sweet earth, your body resolves into its chemical elements and again reaches up to the light in leaf and stalk and fragrant bloom?"

One night, when the forgotten wedding was only a week off, André fainted. After he had responded to the frantic ministrations of his mother and Brynhild, he turned his great, dark eyes pleadingly to them and gasped:

"I want you both to make me a promise."

"What, son?" asked the mother.

"That when I'm dead, you'll bury me, not too deep, under my White Lady." His tired lids fluttered down. "Oh, mother! To think of the roots of that sweet creature reaching down, down for me and resurrecting my atoms to a newer and sweeter life."

"André, darling! Don't! You're breaking our hearts!"

"But will you promise?"

"Yes! Oh, God—help me!"

With André restored and quiet in his room, Brynhild and Madame Fournier sought a secluded corner for their frantic grief.

"It can't go on another day, daughter," said the mother. "André will die before the wedding. We must destroy that *bête blanche*."

"But, mother, wouldn't that grieve him too much at this time?"

"Rather a few days' grief than a grave under that monster." Madame Fournier shuddered.

"Where is the axe, mother?" Brynhild's face was as pale as her dress.

"I'll do it, my dear. I'm an old woman and his mother. Perhaps it might be something like murder to kill that human thing, but I have a mother's right."

"No!" Brynhild's voice was almost fierce. "I want to do it. White Lady hates me, and I hate her. Where is the axe?"

"Wait a little. It is early. One of the workers might see you."

And Brynhild waited until the night grew older and blacker, when she crept from the house with an axe and a flashlight. There was no moon tonight to guide her through the flowery mazes. A strong wind, coming from the sea, followed behind her like an animal sniffing her footprints. It pulled her skirts and her long, flowing sleeves and whipped her hair across her face.

She had the furtive feeling of one who plans a deed of blood and violence. In her mind she outlined what she must do. She would place the flashlight so that its light could fall upon White Lady. Then she would quickly unlatch the door and chop.

Never had White Lady been so beautiful. In the glow of the flashlight, she stood straight and silent in her waxy foliage, with the gossamer veil whipping around her airily and her dagger arms folded like a demure bride waiting for her bridegroom. Brynhild never knew what to expect from this unnatural creature, and its silence frightened her more than the wildest noise it had ever produced.

Before lifting the latch. Brynhild stood regarding it, horrified, trembling, pitying. White Lady was watching, too, and waiting.

The moment Brynhild opened the door and went inside, a scream like the piercing voice of a woman tore through the night. Again and again the awful shriek wailed from the scraping dagger arms, and Brynhild knew that it rode on the wind to the ears of listeners in the house beyond.

Her nerveless hands almost dropped the axe. How could she wield her weapon against that fleshy, human face—against a thing that could cry out like a woman?

But Andre's burning eyes haunted her. She must, for his sake.

Grasping and raising the axe, she went forward, with the wind pushing at her body and snatching her hair over her eyes. The axe fell, with poor aim. It merely crashed through part of the foliage, which cracked with a sickening snap as of crushed bones.

One more dreadful shriek rent the night, a shriek of murder and of rapine; but before its shrill echoes died, another and less hideous woman-voice gave an agony cry.

It was Brynhild.

The wind, tampering with her clothes, had blown her long, loose sleeve against White Lady, where it caught or was grasped by one of the dagger arms. The other dagger arm lifted and plunged, lifted and plunged.

The girl was wild with pain and fright. Held fast as she was, she could scarcely use the axe to advantage, especially as she was forced to avoid the stabbing dagger.

The white veil fell from the thing's head. Before Brynhild could again wield the axe, another dagger thrust found her body. Through the flesh of her left shoulder it cut this time, and she crumpled, half fainting.

Even as she fell, she heard running feet. André's voice called out: "Brynhild!"

Instantly White Lady paused in her stabbing and sent forth another shriek of triumph. Then again the dagger plunged, and Brynhild felt the warm blood flow from her arm.

She never completely lost consciousness, and dimly she was aware of chopping blows made by another, and of her left arm coming away from its horrible mooring. She felt herself lifted and carried for several yards. She felt André's rough, unshaved cheek against her own, and heard soft love words fall from the lips that bent to hers.

André laid her down carefully and shouted for help. Poor fellow! There had been a time when he could have carried her all around the island.

With a supreme effort, Brynhild opened her eyes. The flashlight was still where she had placed it, so that its round eye fell upon White Lady, or what was left of her. Now the plant was only a mass of crushed leaves and petals.

"Yes, I did it," came André's stern voice. "The *bête blanche* would have killed you, darling!" He kissed her hungrily. "I've been a beast, myself—and a fool. Forgive me!"

And later after Brynhild's gaping wounds were dressed, she heard André say four simple words that filled her with delight.

"I am hungry, mother."

THE LAUGHING THING

G. G. Pendarves

G. G. Pendarves was really Gladys Gordon Trenery (1885–1938), born in Liverpool of a Cornish family. She spent much time in Cornwall, the setting for several of her stories. She worked as a journalist and turned to writing fiction in 1923 with "The Kabbalist". Her 1924 story, "The Devil's Graveyard" was reprinted in Weird Tales *in 1926, the first of nineteen stories she would sell to the "Unique Magazine". Several of her stories were about possession in one form or another. "The Grave at Goonhilly" (1930) has an evil magician whose power continues after death in a parcel of land. "From the Dark Hills of Hell" (January 1932) has a violinist whose playing summons an evil force which creates a battle between life and death. Perhaps her best-known story, "Thing of Darkness" (August 1937) is a haunted house story set near to where she lived in the Wirral. She made no collections of her stories during her lifetime but two posthumous volumes are* Thing of Darkness *(2005) and* Thirty Pieces of Silver *(2009), the latter collecting together her oriental stories.*

"VERY WELL, MR DREWE! I'LL SIGN THE AGREEMENT, though no one but you would drive such a devil's bargain."

The speaker's tall, emaciated body vibrated with indignation, and his strange light eyes blazed like incandescent lamps. There was something of the brooding menace of the grey sea in the latter, and a note in his voice reminded me of the sullen mutter of the wind before a storm.

A little shiver of apprehension ran through me as I turned from him to my brother-in-law, Jason Drewe. Nothing could have been more utterly and infuriatingly complacent than the latter, who was leaning back in the most comfortable chair my office afforded, with an expensive cigar in his mouth, his big frame clad in the smartest of light tweeds, and an orchid in his buttonhole.

Jason was an extremely wealthy man, young enough to enjoy his money, and with a son to inherit his millions one day. The loss of Mavis, his wife, had been more of an annoyance than a grief to him; he felt that she had died merely to make things awkward for him—in fact, he added her death to the many grievances he treasured up against her.

I knew that if there is such a thing as a broken heart, he broke my sister's, and I hated him for it. I would have cut off all intercourse with him, only that I had promised Mavis to keep an eye on the boy, and counteract his father's influence as far as possible. Jason knew nothing of this; he believed I hung on to him for the sake of his wealth and twitted me with it quite openly, in spite of the fact that I was never indebted to him for a single dime, and would have cleaned the streets, or sold "hot dogs" rather than owe him a penny.

It seemed absurd to pity him, especially at this moment of his triumph, when he had succeeded in getting the land he wanted at the price he wanted, and was sitting there before me as pink and pleased as a prize baby after its bottle.

Eldred Werne, whom Jason had just cornered so successfully, was the one whom most people would have pitied. But I had only admiration for anyone as determined and strong of soul as Werne. Poor and desperately ill though he was, he was not an object for pity.

As junior partner in the firm of Baxter and Baxter, real estate agents, I was present to witness the signatures and conclude the deal between Werne and Jason; and I wished a thousand times that Baxter and Baxter had never had this affair entrusted to them. It was a sordid, despicable business altogether.

"I'll sign," repeated Werne, drawing his chair closer to my desk, and taking up the parchments in his thin, blue-veined hands. "The land shall be yours at your own price—for the present!"

Anger and instant suspicion showed in Jason's small, heavy-lidded eyes.

"What the devil do you mean?" he said. "If you sign these papers the land is mine, and there's no power on earth can make me pay more for it than the sum set down there in black and white."

"I wasn't thinking of money." Werne's voice was strangely quiet and yet so full of menace that again I felt every nerve in my body thrill to it. "I am sure you will never pay more in money."

"You're right—dead right, Werne," Jason's resonant voice echoed through the room.

"And yet—I think you will pay more in the end. Yes, in the end you will pay more, Mr Drewe."

Jason turned to me blustering and furious.

"Aren't these deeds water-tight! What does he mean! If there is any flaw in these agreements I'll stamp you and your fool firm out of existence!"

Before I could reply, Werne began to laugh. He sat there and laughed long and dreadfully, the bright colour staining his thin cheeks, his grey eyes brilliant and malicious. He laughed until the cough seized him, and he leant back at last utterly exhausted, an ominous stain on the handkerchief he pressed to his lips.

"Let me relieve your natural anxiety, Mr Drewe," he said at last, his hoarse voice still shaken with mirth. "You will pay more, but not in money! Not in any material sense at all."

"What in the name of common sense do you mean?" growled Jason.

"There is nothing common at all in the sense of which I speak. It is very uncommon indeed! I refer to payments which have no connection with money—nothing which can be reckoned in dollars and cents."

Jason looked uncertain whether to call police protection or medical aid, and he watched Werne narrowly as the latter signed the documents.

When the signatures were completed, Eldred Werne got to his feet and stood looking down at Jason—a long, strange, deep look, as if he meant to learn the other's every feature off by heart. Behind

Werne's eyes once more a sudden terrifying flame of laughter danced—flickered—and was gone!

"You don't fear any payment that will not reduce your bank account, then?"

"What other payment is there?" asked Jason in genuine surprise.

"You're wonderful!" said Werne. "So complete a product of your age and kind. So logical and limited and—excuse me—so thoroughly stupid!"

Jason's fresh-coloured face turned a deep purple.

"If you were not a sick man—" he began.

"And one, moreover, whom you have thoroughly and satisfactorily fleeced," interpolated Werne.

"I should resent your remarks," continued Jason pompously. "As it is, I see no use in prolonging this conversation."

"Stay!" cried Werne, as Jason put on his fur coat and prepared to depart. "It's only fair to warn you that if I die out there in Denver City, I shall come back again! I shall be in a better position then, without this wretched body of mine. I shall come back—to make you pay—a more satisfactory price for my Tareytown acres."

Jason stared, standing in the doorway with one plump well-manicured hand on the doorknob, looking like a great shaggy ox in his fur coat, and with that air of stupid bewilderment on his broad face.

"Wha-a-a-at?" he stammered. Then, as the other's meaning slowly dawned on him, he leaned up against the door and showed every tooth in his head in a perfect bellow of mirth. "Are you threatening to haunt me?" he choked, the veins on his forehead swelling dangerously. "Well, my good fellow, if it gives you any comfort to imagine that, don't let me discourage your little idea. You'll be welcome at Tareytown any old time! The Tareytown spectre, eh? It'll give quite an air to the place! What kind of payment will you want—moonshine, eh?" Jason almost burst with the humour of this remark. "Moonshine and ghosts! Seems the right sort of mixture!"

With a last fatuous chuckle, Jason opened the door; and, through the window, I saw him get into his new coupé and drive off, his face still creased in enjoyment of his last sally.

"The descent of man," murmured Werne, half to himself. "There's no doubt that Jason Drewe has descended a considerable way from the apes! The fool—the blind, besotted fool!"

II

It was a perfect day in the late autumn of that same year, when, for the first time, I saw the Tareytown estate.

I dismissed my taxi at the huge stone gateway, and walked slowly up through the woods. After the hectic rush and noise of New York, the golden stillness around me was deeply satisfying; and I thought of poor Eldred Werne, who would never know the beauty and healing peace of this place again. I had seen the notice of his death in Denver City, only a month after he had signed away his rights to these lovely Tareytown woods, and I had thought very often since of the lonely bitterness which must have clouded his last days.

Glimpses of the blue, shining Hudson shone between the trees, and beyond, the flaming russet of the Palisades. On all sides the country stretched out to dim, misty horizons for which Werne's dying eyes must have longed in his exile.

Then, quite suddenly, a chill passed over me. I became aware of the ominous and unusual stillness of the brooding woods. Neither bird nor squirrel darted to and fro among the leaves and branches—not even a fly buzzed about in the hazy sunshine.

I looked around in gathering apprehension. What *was* it that began to oppress me more and more? Why did the tall trees seem to be listening?—why did I have the impulse to look over my shoulder?—why did my heart thump and my hands chill suddenly?

With a great effort I restrained myself from breaking into a run, as I continued upward toward the house. The path doubled back on itself across and across the shoulder of the hill on which the house, Red Gables, was built; and it was fully ten minutes before I arrived breathless in sight of its red roof and high old-fashioned chimney-stack.

In a corner of its wide porch, I caught a glimpse of a boy's figure and let out a loud halloo, glad of an excuse to break the queer, unnatural silence.

There was an answering hail, and my nephew, Tony, came running down the path to meet me.

"Hello, Uncle John! I was waiting for you! Did you walk up through the woods—alone?" The boy's voice held an awed note, which was emphasized by the look of fear in his dark eyes.

He was only eight years old, and exactly like his mother. Thank heaven, there was no trace of Jason's complacent materialism in his son... mind and body, Tony was an utterly different type. I loved the boy, and a real friendship had developed between us, despite the disparity of our years. He was curiously sensitive and mature for his age, and it was a great thing for a bachelor like myself to have a child make a little tin god of me, as Tony did.

"And why not walk alone through the woods?" I demanded, looking down at him as he rubbed his head against my arm like some friendly colt.

"I wouldn't," he replied simply.

"Why not, old man? There aren't any wolves or bears or even Indians left here, are there?"

"Don't laugh, Uncle." The boy's voice sank to a whisper. "There isn't time to tell you now, but there's something in those woods. Something you can't see—that—that is waiting!"

I stared at the boy, and once again the cold chill I had experienced during my walk up to the house crept over me.

"Look here, Tony," I began. "You mustn't get—"

"There is—there *is*, I tell you!" He was passionately in earnest. "Something that laughs—something that is waiting!"

"Laughs—waiting!" I echoed feebly.

"You'll hear it yourself," he answered. "Then you'll know. Father won't let me speak about it to him, and says if I'd play games instead of reading books, I'd only hear and see half what I do now."

"About as much as he hears and sees," I murmured to myself.

"I am sure Father hears it too, only he won't say so," continued Tony. "But I've noticed one thing—he won't let anyone knock at the doors. The servants even go into his study without knocking, and he was always so—so—"

"Exactly!" I said dryly; "I understand."

The small hand in mine gave a little warning pressure, and I saw Jason Drewe's big frame and massive head loom up in the comparative dimness of the interior, as Tony and I reached the entrance door of Red Gables.

"Well, John!" boomed my host, as he rose from the depths of

a vast chair and came forward, cigar in hand. "Made your fortune yet?"

It was the form of greeting he invariably gave me; for he was that irritating type of man who uses a limited number of favourite witticisms and sticks to them persistently, in season and out of season.

Today, however, his complacent heartiness was obviously an immense effort to him, and I was quite startled by the change in his appearance. He seemed conscious of it himself, but there was a certain bravado in the sunken eyes he turned on me, which defied me to remark on his ill looks.

I was certainly shocked to notice how much thinner he was, how grey his skin, and how hunted and restless were his eyes, as he kept glancing from side to side with a quick upward jerk of his big head, as though he were listening for some expected and unwelcome summons.

He motioned me to a chair and poured out drinks with a fumbling sort of touch, which further indicated the change in him since I last saw him in the office of Baxter and Baxter.

Tony curled up at my side on the arm of my easy-chair, as quiet as a dormouse, taking no part in the conversation, but his precocious intelligence enabled him to follow the drift of it; that I could swear to. He annoyed his father, this silent observant child, and in the middle of a discussion Jason turned irritably to the boy.

"Why don't you go off and amuse yourself out of doors like any other boy of your age? You sit round the house like a little lap-dog and waste your time with books—always mooning about like someone in a dream! Just like your mother—just like her," he finished in an exasperated mutter.

When we were alone, Jason turned to me with a frown. "More like a girl than a boy!" he commented bitterly. "About as much pep as a soft drink! What's the use of building up a business and making a future for him, when he'll let it all slip through his fingers later on?"

He went on talking rather loudly and quickly on the subject, with no help at all from me, and it struck me he was talking in order to defeat his own clamorous unpleasant thoughts; working himself up into a pretence of anger to make the blood run more hot and swift in his veins.

As far as he was able, within the limited scope of his primitive nature, Jason loved the boy, and every hope and ambition he cherished was centred round Tony, and Tony's future. I just let him run on and speculated with increasing bewilderment on the cause of my brother-in-law's obvious uneasiness of soul. It must be something tremendous to have shaken his colossal egotism, I argued to myself, and moreover it was something he was desperately anxious to hide—some unacknowledged fear which had pricked and wounded him deep beneath his tough skin.

"I'm not satisfied with that school of his—not at all satisfied!" he went on. "I ask you now, what's the use of filling a kid's head with all that imaginary stuff when he's got to live in a world of bankers and politicians and grafters? How's he going to grind his own when his darned school has exchanged it for a silver butter knife? How's he going to—"

He broke off with a queer strangled groan as a sudden clamorous knocking sounded—a loud tattoo like the sound of war-drums through the quiet house.

The big sunshiny room darkened suddenly and a puff of wind from an open window at my side breathed an icy chill on my cheek.

The horror I had recently experienced in the woods swept over me again, and I saw Jason's face set in a mask of fear and loathing.

Silence held us bound for a perceptible moment, and in the quiet a loud, echoing laugh rang out.

It sounded as though someone were standing just outside the house, and I had a vivid mental image of a figure convulsed and rocking with mirth. But this figure of my imagination did not move me to laughter myself, although as a rule nothing is more contagious than laughter—but not this—not this hateful mirth!

I dashed to the window and looked out; then, making for the door in blind haste. I stumbled out on the porch and ran round the house in a queer frenzy of desire to learn who—or *what*—had stood there laughing... laughing... laughing.

I only caught a glimpse of frightened faces in the servants' quarters at the back of the house as I dashed past, and saw windows and doors being hastily slammed.

When I got back to the living-room again Jason was gone, and I sat down breathless, and shaken to the very soul. I had stumbled on to the secret—or part of it—with a vengeance; and I sat with my unlit pipe in my mouth for the better part of an hour, until the first overwhelming horror of the episode had faded a little.

Jason came in just as I was thinking of going up to my room to change for dinner, and any idea I might have entertained of asking him for explanations was foiled by the extraordinary change in him.

He was his old self again. Large, pink, and prosperous, he breezed into the room and stood with his hands in his pockets, grinning down at me from his massive six feet odd. If there was something defiant in the gleam of his blue eye, if his voice was harsh and his grin a trifle too wide, it needed someone who knew him as well as I did to detect it.

I never liked or admired him as much as I did at that moment; and the determination came to me, to stand by him in this trouble of his, to stay and fight it out, and give what help I could to him and the boy.

I am not a superstitious man, nor counted credulous by my friends or enemies. But here was something inexplicably evil which brooded over the lonely woods of Tareytown like some dark-winged genie.

I went slowly and thoughtfully up to my room, my mind heavy with doubt and perplexity, and as the night wore on and darkness closed in about the house, so did my mind grow darker and more fearful.

III

"Well, Soames! Rather a change from your roof-garden in New York—eh? How do you like it here?"

The old gardener folded his gnarled hands one over the other on the handle of his spade, and shook his head slowly from side to side.

"It was an unlucky day for the master when he came to Tareytown, sir—an unlucky day!"

"How's that? Won't your plants grow for you?"

"You know, sir! I see by your face that you know already!"

"I must confess there's something a bit depressing about the place," I answered. "It's just the time of year, no doubt. There's always something melancholy about the fall."

"There's nothing wrong about the time of year," said the old man. He leaned forward and his voice sank to a whisper. "Haven't you *heard* it yet?"

I gave an involuntary start, and he pursed up his mouth and nodded.

"Aye, I see you have!"

He came closer and peered up at me, his brown face with its faded blue eyes a network of anxious wrinkles.

"Sir, if you can help the master, for God's sake do it! He's a rare hard one, I know, but I've served him for thirty-five years, and I don't want to see no harm come to him. He won't own up that he hears anything amiss, nor go away from this accursed place with the boy, before any harm comes to either of them. He's that angry because he don't understand—*won't* understand there's something more than flesh and blood can hurt us sometimes!"

The old man's words came out in a flood, the result of long-suppressed anxiety, and I marvelled that a man of Jason Drewe's type should command such solicitude from anyone.

"I'm all in the dark, Soames," I said slowly. "Who is it that knocks—that laughs?"

The gardener's eyes grew very sombre. "No mortal man—no mortal man, sir."

"Why, Soames, you're as superstitious as they make them," I said, trying to make light of his words.

"See here, sir," he said, pulling me by the sleeve into the deeper shade of the shrubbery behind us. "I'll tell you what I've never spoken a word of yet. I'll tell you what I overheard one night when this—this *thing* first came here. I was pottering about late one evening, tying up bits of creeper against the wall outside the master's study.

I heard the knock—loud and long as if the emperor of the world was a-knocking at the door, and I looks up to see who was there. The door was only three or four feet from where I was standing with bass and scissors in my hand. And there was no one at all on the steps nor anywhere near the house. While I was a-staring and wondering I heard the laugh! My blood went cold, and I just stood there shaking like a poplar tree in a wind. And since then, night after night, that knock and that laugh comes as regular as the sun sets!"

I stared at my companion in incredulous horror.

"And one time," he continued, "I heard the master call out. Terrible loud and fierce his voice was: '*Have you come for your moonshine, Eldred Werne?—take it!*' And with that, a bottle of whisky comes hurtling through the window and fell almost at my feet. I felt a wind blow across my face same as if it blew right off an iceberg; and as I stood there afraid to move hand or foot, I heard the laugh way down among the trees, getting fainter and fainter just as if someone was walking away down the path—and laughing and laughing to himself all the time!"

I listened aghast to the old man, and a vivid picture arose in my mind of Eldred Werne as I last saw him in life—the tall, emaciated figure, the arresting face with its beautifully chiselled features, and above all the strange grey eyes as they had dwelt in that last deep look on Jason, the burning mocking fire which lit them and the fathomless contempt of the strong mouth.

"You will pay—you will pay!" The words rang in my ears as if Werne were standing at my side speaking them at that very moment.

I sat down abruptly on a fallen tree, and lit a cigarette with unsteady fingers.

"Now look here, Soames," I said at last. "We mustn't let this thing get us scared out of all common sense and reason. I admit it's a beastly unpleasant business, but I can't—I won't believe yet that there is no natural explanation of these things. Someone who owes him a grudge may be putting one over on Mr Drewe. It may be a deliberate plot to annoy and frighten him. There was a—er— well, a misunderstanding between your master and Mr Werne over the purchase of this Tareytown estate, and Mr Werne was quite capable of planning a neat little revenge to square his account a little. He was a very sick man, remember—and sick men are apt to be vindictive and unreasonable."

"I guessed as something had happened between the two," murmured Soames, "but I didn't rightly know what it was."

"You and I will watch the house from now on," I said. "We'll arrange to be outside, one or other or both of us, directly after sunset. And if—if we see nothing, if we find no one there—"

"Aye—you won't, sir!"

"Then I shall do my best to persuade Mr Drewe to leave this place and return to the city."

"And that you'll never do. He'll never give in and go away, not if it means his death. The master is terrible obstinate, and he fair blazed up when I kind of suggested he wasn't looking just himself, and that maybe Tareytown didn't agree with him."

And remembering Jason's defiant eyes and the bluff he put up last evening for my benefit, I was inclined to agree with Soames.

"I'll do what I can," I said, getting up and brushing off twigs and leaves.

"I'm thankful to know you're here, sir. There was no one I dared say a word to until you came. The servants are in mortal terror, and never a week passes without one or more of them leaving. Soon we won't be able to get anyone to stay a night in the place!"

"If your master could be persuaded to send the boy away for the rest of his vacation—"

"He won't do that," was the lugubrious reply. "That would be sort of owning up that there *was* something here he was afraid of! He'll never admit that—never!"

IV

Our first vigil took place that night. The boy was safe indoors—he never went over the threshold of the house after dusk fell, I noticed. Jason had established himself with his favourite drink, a stack of newspapers, and a box of cigars, in his library. I left him looking as immovable as the Rock of Gibraltar—and as grey!

Soames and I planted ourselves in strategic positions on either side of the porch, where we could see both the big entrance door, and the whole of the front porch which ran in front of the library, dining-room, and sun-parlour.

A pale moon sailed serenely overhead, and I felt a passionate longing to be as far away from this evil-haunted little piece of earth as was the moon itself. Revolt which was almost nausea seized me, as I looked around at the shadowy woods, and felt the unnameable creeping horror which waited there.

Slow minutes passed. The shadows grew denser, and the silence so profound that the falling leaves rattled like metal things on the dry ground, and the creak of the great trees made my heart thump furiously against my ribs.

I could see Soames' small tense figure bent forward in a listening attitude, his face turned toward the entrance door. He looked like a terrier-dog straining eagerly on a leash.

My eyes roved restlessly to and fro, and fell at last on the long, uncut grass which grew about the tree-trunks. Quite suddenly I saw the reeds and grasses bend and quiver as if before a strong wind. In a long thin line they bent—a line advancing rapidly from the blackness of the trees out toward the open—toward the house—toward the entrance porch, with its broad steps gleaming silver in the moonlight.

My hand flew to my throat to stifle the cry that rose as I saw that sinister trail being blazed before my eyes. It advanced to the extreme edge of the tall grasses in a direct line with the entrance-door.

A moment of unendurable suspense—an agony of terrified expectant waiting! Then it came—loud—thunderous—awful as the stroke of doom! The knocker had been removed from the door, and on the bare wood itself beat that devil's tattoo.

I was paralysed with the shock and thunder of it, and only when I saw Soames stumbling forward, and heard his hoarse cry, did I move—stiff and uncertainly as a man might move after a long illness.

We clutched each other like two terrified children when we arrived at the foot of the steps, and I felt Soames's body shaking against my own.

Then, abruptly, the infernal racket ceased; and in the momentary silence which ensued, a laugh broke out that sent our trembling hands over our ears, but we could not shut out the sound of that demoniac laughter. Uncontrolled and triumphant it rang out again and again, and the vision of someone rocking with mirth rose as before in my imagination.

But nothing was there on the porch in the moonlight!

The whole porch was visible in the clear white light. No one, no thing, could have escaped our staring, straining eyes. There was no one there, and yet almost within touch of our outstretched hands some invisible, intangible Thing stood laughing—laughing—laughing...

V

After that night the horror fell more and more darkly.

Soames, who was out all day working in the gardens and shrub-beries, noticed increasingly sinister signs that our invisible enemy was marshalling his forces, and closing in on the last stages of the siege.

More and more frequently the old man would see the grasses bending and swaying around him in loops and circles, as though the laughing Thing moved to and fro in the mazes of some infernal dance. Often Soames felt the chill of the Thing's passing, and noted the shrivelled, blighted foliage which marked its trail.

The woods grew darker with every passing day, despite the thinning of the leaves. The autumn mists which lay so white and cloudlike in the valleys of the surrounding country, drifted in among the trees on the Tareytown estate like grey, choking smoke, dank and rotten with the breath of decay, shutting out the sunlit earth beyond, and the clear skies above, rolling up around the house with infinite menace and gloom.

Louder and more clamorous grew the nightly summons, and the laughter which followed echoed and echoed about the house throughout the night, sounding at our very windows, then growing faint and ominous from the depths of the brooding woods.

VI

At last, the boy's terror precipitated a crisis.

Jason, who had brought this cursed thing upon himself, it seemed, refused to acknowledge that he had been wrong, to make any amends which lay within his power, or even to move from the place which Eldred Werne had loved so passionately in the flesh, and haunted so persistently in the spirit.

Jason's courage, though I admired it in one way, was not of the highest order. I mean that his conduct was guided by no reason, but only by blind impulse.

I tackled him more than once about Tony, and only succeeded in rousing furious opposition.

"What the devil are you driving at?" he roared at me. "This is my house, isn't it? These are my woods and my lands. I paid for them according to my bond. No one is going to drive me out—no one, d'you hear—neither man nor devil!"

"But Tony!" I protested. "You ought to consider him. He hears the servants talking. He hears whatever it is that comes knocking at your door, Jason—you know best what it is! The boy is almost beside himself with fear. Can't you see he is desperate? He doesn't eat or sleep properly. D'you want to kill him as you did his mother?"

I added bitterly, remembrance of my sister's lonely, unhappy life with Jason goading me to speech.

But Jason was always impervious to anything he wished to ignore, and he brushed aside my last words and returned to Tony.

"The boy has got to learn—he's got to learn, I say! If this house is good enough for me, then it's good enough for him, too. Tony'll stay here with me to the end of his vacation. If I give in about this thing, it will be the thin end of the wedge, He'll expect me to indulge every girl's fad and fancy he has—and the Lord knows he's full of them! Here I stay, and here he stays, and that's all about it. Why on earth do you stay yourself, feeling as you do?" he added roughly. "If you're afraid, I'll excuse you the rest of your visit."

I didn't trouble to deny the fact that I was afraid, and went off cursing myself for interfering, and probably making Tony's relations with his father even more difficult.

VII

That evening Jason seemed absolutely possessed. Whether he had been drinking heavily, or whether his endurance had reached the breaking-point suddenly in the long, silent combat of wills with his invisible enemy, or whether the blind grey figure of Fate had written the last chapter, and he had no choice but to obey, I do not know.

Everything that happened that last fatal night seemed obscured and fogged with the waves of terror and desolation that swept over the house and the surrounding woods.

From early morning the attack on us strengthened perceptibly. Every hour I felt we were fighting a losing battle, and I had no comfort for Soames when he sought me out, and led me off to the potting-sheds after a pretence of breakfasting.

Tony had remained in bed, to his father's unbounded disgust. The boy had spent a sleepless night and I had given him a bromide and persuaded him to stay in his room to rest.

"Making a mollycoddle of him!" growled Jason, his eyes light and dangerous as a wild boar's above his flabby, sallow cheeks. He put down his cup with a rattle on the saucer, and scraping his chair noisily on the polished flooring, he rose and strode heavily out of the room, and I heard the stairs creak under his weight as he went up to the boy.

Throughout the day, his evil mood grew on him, and Tony could do nothing right.

"Mark my words, sir," Soames had said to me as we stood in the potting-sheds that morning. "I've a feeling we've about come to the end! That Laughing Devil will knock for the last time tonight—for the last time! Mark my words!"

And as the day wore on I felt more and more assured that Soames was right.

Every hour the sense of imminent and immense danger grew heavier, and every hour Tony grew more and more nervous and Jason more brutally obstinate; for the sight of the boy's terror goaded his father into senseless anger.

The sun set that night in a bank of heavy dull cloud, which spread and darkened until thick impenetrable dusk closed about us.

With the coming of twilight we waited in fearful anticipation of our usual visitation; but dusk deepened to night and no summons sounded at the door, no mocking horror of laughter was heard at all.

Yet this silence brought no feeling of reprieve. Rather our expectancy grew more and more tense, and Tony sat by the fire with cold shaking hands thrust deep into his pockets, and tried to prevent his father noticing the ague of fear which shook his thin little body.

Jason did not send him to bed at his usual time—we all sat there waiting—just waiting!

The big logs smouldered dully and reluctantly on the hearth-stone. Jason's face was a grey mask; his thick lips sneered; his eyes gleamed between their puffy lids. He was like a cornered animal of some primeval age—a great inert mass of flesh slumped down in his big chair by the dying fire.

Nine—ten—eleven! The torturing hours crept on and still we sat there like people under a spell, just waiting—waiting!

With the deep midnight chime of the clock in the library, the spell was broken with a hideous clamour that made Tony leap up with the shriek of a wild thing caught in a trap.

Jason got to his feet in one surprising movement, and stood with feet apart and lowered head, as if about to do battle.

I sat clutching the arms of my chair, held by a blind terror that was like steel chains about me.

It was the Laughing Thing at last! Long and furiously the knock resounded, sinking to a low mutter and rising to a crescendo of blows that threatened to batter down the heavy door. And over and above the thunderous blows rose the high mocking laughter—triumphant, cruel, satisfied laughter!

I blame myself—I shall always blame myself for what happened then. I might have held the boy back—guarded him more closely when he was too frenzied with fear to guard himself. But

I did not dream what he was about until it was too late! When he ran from the shelter of my arms, I thought he meant to seek another refuge!

But no—the boy was crazed beyond all reason and control, and ran desperately to the very horror which had driven him mad.

I heard his quick, light steps along the hall, and I thought he was making for the staircase, not the door—my God, not the door!

There was the quick rattle of a heavy chain, the groan of a bolt withdrawn—then a long, wailing shriek of terror!

With one accord Jason and I dashed out into the hall—Soames came rushing from the kitchen-quarters—and there stood the door flung wide, and from the porch without came a long exultant peal of laughter.

We flung ourselves forward and out into the night. In the distance among the trees we heard the dying echoes of that infernal laughter—then nothing more.

VIII

Until dawn we searched the woods of Tareytown, and as the first grey glimmer of light broke in the east we found him.

Have you ever seen anyone dead of a sudden violent poison—such as prussic acid—with teeth showing in a terrible grin—the muscles of the face stiffened in inhuman laughter? It is the most dreadful of all masks which death can fix on human lineaments.

So we found Tony!

His eyes—awful contrast to his grinning mouth—mirrored a terror too profound for any words to convey. Eyes which had looked on the unnameable—the unthinkable; spawn of that outermost darkness which no human sight may endure.

That night was the end of my youth and happiness. Jason packed up and went for a prolonged tour of Europe with his fears and his memories, and I have never seen him since.

For myself, I live, and will always live, on the Tareytown estate, where perhaps Tony's spirit may wander lost and lonely, still possessed by that evil which caught him in its net.

I must remain at Red Gables, and perhaps here or hereafter I may atone for the selfish fear which made me fail Tony in that desperate crisis.

Somewhere—somehow, beyond the curtain of this life, I may meet the Thing which laughed—the evil, bitter Thing which once was Eldred Werne—the Thing which may still possess the boy and hold him earthbound and accurst.

I failed Tony once, but I will not do so a second time. I will offer my own soul to set him free—and perhaps the high gods will hear me and accept the sacrifice.

CANDLELIGHT

Lady Eleanor Smith

Lady Eleanor Smith (1902–1945) was the daughter of the barrister and politician Frederick Edwin Smith who was made Earl of Birkenhead in 1919 when he became Lord Chancellor. Father and daughter shared an immense zest for life, even though both died tragically young, the father of cirrhosis of the liver and the daughter of heart failure. Lady Eleanor believed she had inherited gipsy blood and researched the Romani culture for her book Tzigare *(1935). By association, she became fascinated with circus life and was the first president of the Circus Fans Association in 1934. She even performed in a circus, on horseback. She threw herself with great vigour into everything that interested her and when she turned to writing she produced a book or two a year for the last half of her life. The majority of her weird tales will be found in* Satan's Circus *(1932).*

IT WAS DURING DINNER ON SATURDAY NIGHT THAT MRS Marriage first admitted to herself that her weekend party could not possibly be described as going with a swing. The party was small and select. It consisted of a married couple, Mr and Mrs Lethbridge, and of a young man, an ex-Guardsman, named Roderick Noakes. There was also Mr Marriage, but somehow he really did not seem to count.

Briefly, the position of these five people was as follows: Mrs Marriage understood Mr Lethbridge to be strongly attracted towards her, and Mr Lethbridge wasn't at all sure that she was not right. Mrs Lethbridge, on the other hand, had no objection to her husband amusing himself with Mrs Marriage provided he did not interfere between herself and Mr Roderick Noakes, whom she had brought with her to the party because she really could not bear to be separated from him. Mr Noakes frequently told Mrs Lethbridge that she was a living reincarnation of La Belle Dame Sans Merci, and he much enjoyed shutting her wild eyes with kisses. Mr Marriage was in love with no one, but he ignored his wife and idolized his garden.

Mr Marriage, a retired stock-broker, was a short, thick-set man of about forty with a face like an intelligent mastiff, and discreet, short-sighted eyes. Mrs Marriage, who was fond of hunting, was tall and willowy, with long legs, like a boy's, ash-gold hair, and swimming, greenish, sentimental eyes. She frequently focused these eyes, with a certain amount of effect, upon Mr Lethbridge, who was by profession a sculptor, a tall, burly man of florid good looks. Mrs Lethbridge, lovely, untidy, and rather slovenly, allowed her bronze hair to cluster in masses upon a broad white forehead, talked in a husky voice, like a sigh, and honestly imagined that her eyes were violet. Mr Roderick Noakes, who stared at her pensively from time to time, was a sturdy, sunburnt youth with white teeth and a toothbrush moustache. Before meeting Mrs Lethbridge he had devoted himself exclusively to hunting and polo. He had not been on a horse for some time.

The dinner-party had begun to be a failure for the simple reason that Mr Marriage was so indisputably the odd man out. He was inoffensive, certainly, but at the same time it was really impossible to ignore him completely, and unfortunately, although he seemed unaware of it, he had the effect of making his wife feel self-conscious when she would rather have been listening undisturbed to the ardent conversation of Mr Lethbridge. Mrs Lethbridge, seated on the right hand of Mr Marriage, was singularly untroubled by any such nonsense as good manners, and devoted herself exclusively to Mr Noakes; he, on the other hand, at times felt slightly uncomfortable and insisted upon addressing occasional remarks to Mr Marriage, who replied in polite but vague monosyllables, conscious, no doubt, of being a bore. Mr Lethbridge, on the left of his host, turned right round in his chair to face Mrs Marriage, and appeared to find her husband's face distasteful. Anyway, he did not bother to look at it.

They were dining on the veranda, for the June night was soft and radiant. A slip of young moon drifted through a film of racing clouds; but there were not many clouds, and the dark vivid sky was brilliant with banks of stars. The lawns below were grey and dewy; in the distance a waterfall splashed with a tinkling sound, and here and there, above the eaves of the veranda, wheeling bats whistled faintly from time to time. The dinner-table, illuminated only by a cluster of winking candles, resembled a little gay and brightly lighted island in the dusky vastness of the night. It was unreal, like a scene at the theatre. A perfect setting for romance, and yet somehow everything was going wrong.

Mrs Marriage, bending her face close to the face of Mr Lethbridge, became suddenly irritable. Really Amos was intolerable, sitting there like a deaf mute, glum, impassive, a skeleton at the feast! She should have invited another woman, but women bored him, unless they knew all about rock gardens; and anyhow, everything was spoiled. She wanted to be out there in the dark quiet garden with Ian Lethbridge, and she wanted Ian Lethbridge to kiss her. Damn Amos, ruining her weekend party! Mr Lethbridge, on the other hand, was wondering whether or not she was cold. He was prepared to bet she wasn't. He, too, wanted to go into the garden. Mrs Lethbridge, half-closing her eyes, fixed Mr Noakes with a swooning siren glance and wondered vaguely if La Belle Dame Sans Merci had had bronze hair with gold shades in it. Perhaps she was the only one of the five who was honestly enjoying the dinner-party, although, of course, nobody could possibly diagnose the mental state of the silent Mr Marriage. Roderick Noakes, wrenching away his gaze from the heavy-lidded eyes of Mrs Lethbridge, addressed one more desperate remark to his host.

"Your garden must be attractive in the daytime, sir. Unfortunately, I arrived too late to see it."

The word garden had at once the effect of a stimulus upon Mr Marriage. He roused himself immediately.

"Well, of course," he said, almost cordially, "it's not looking its best at the moment—not enough rain—but the herbaceous border and the rock garden are well worth a visit. You really ought to get up before breakfast tomorrow and—" He paused, for somehow he didn't really think that Mr Noakes would be up for breakfast next morning.

The ex-Guardsman persevered.

"What's that dark mass of trees at the end of the lawns?"

"That's the forest," answered Mr Marriage in a melancholy tone of voice.

"The forest?"

"Yes. The oaks and beeches are supposed to be very fine. In the old days it was said to be a haunt of witches and evil spirits. Nowadays it's infested with tramps." And he sighed gustily, as though he regretted the witches and deplored the tramps. Once more he relapsed into silence, but conversation having languished round the table, every one had heard his last remark.

"Witches!" whispered Mrs Lethbridge, and she thought again of La Belle Dame. Perhaps she, too, had been a witch.

"Such nonsense!" said Mrs Marriage, and looked indulgently at Mr Lethbridge. But he, for the first time condescending to notice that there were others at the table, observed to the world in general, in a drawling tone of voice:

"Such superstitions die slowly. Even now in many remote villages no doubt children throw stones at harmless old women who profess to cure ailments with herbs."

"Must witches always be old?" inquired Mrs Lethbridge in a petulant tone of voice.

"Probably not," replied Mr Lethbridge indifferently. He added, in a lower voice: "Personally, I've always imagined them to be young, with long limbs, and yellow hair. That's your true sorceress—irresistible."

"If only Amos would go to bed!" sighed Mrs Marriage to herself.

Mr Marriage then surprised her; his hearing must have been more acute than she had hitherto supposed. He said, in a conversational voice:

"Not at all, Lethbridge. Your true witch is, on the contrary, invariably dark. A fair witch indeed!" He tittered and relapsed once more into silence.

Mrs Marriage felt that she loathed the sight of him. She turned once more to Ian Lethbridge.

Port was handed round, and brandy. The party drank, and in ten minutes or so every one except Mr Marriage became a little more friendly towards one another. Even Mrs Marriage, fascinated, repelled, and thrilled by a whispered remark made to her by the audacious Mr Lethbridge as he lighted his cigar, felt suddenly less irritated by her silent and embarrassing husband.

"Poor Amos!" she observed at length, in a high unnatural tone. "It's too sad for him; he makes the odd man tonight at dinner. Really, I should have asked another woman to make the party complete. Will you forgive me, Amos?"

Mr Marriage nodded his head politely.

Oh, he's impossible, she thought, once more exasperated; was there ever such a wet blanket? Why can't he warm up like every one else? She decided to be bold; soon, when he had finished his brandy, she would ask Ian Lethbridge to stroll in the garden with her.

And then Mr Roderick Noakes proceeded to startle them.

"What's that?" he cried suddenly, and sprang to his feet, peering forth into the garden as though by staring he would pierce the darkest shadows, those that lay thickest upon the lawns beneath the trees.

"What's what?" asked Mrs Marriage sharply, and Mr Lethbridge wanted to know what the hell was the matter with him and his blasted nerves. Mrs Lethbridge looked beautifully apprehensive, and even Mr Marriage put down his cigar. But Mr Noakes remained firm.

"Over there," he said obstinately, pointing to a rosebed near the fountain, "there's something moving. I saw it distinctly. Look, now… can't you see?"

They gazed, but the shadows were impenetrable, and they laughed incredulously.

"Come and see, then," proposed Mr Noakes defiantly.

"Oh, yes," said Mrs Marriage eagerly, thinking of the garden, "let's hunt the ghost, all of us! Come on, Ian."

Like shadows themselves, they stole forth from the brilliant veranda into the secretive gloom of the garden, the men's cigars like glowing fireflies, the women sprites, one white, one silver.

"We must spread out," said Roderick Noakes excitedly, "and surround the rosebed. Then we'll catch it."

"Ian," whispered Mrs Marriage beneath her breath.

"The dew's thick; I shall get my feet wet," protested Mrs Lethbridge peevishly.

Slowly, warily, they stalked their prey, creeping nearer and nearer to the low bed of the rose-trees. Mr Noakes was first; he reached the ambush before them and his shout of triumph echoed over the sleeping garden as he bent, seeming to seize hold of something that wriggled; but the moon was behind a cloud, and they could not see very clearly.

"What did I tell you?" he cried aloud. "Wasn't I right? Look, I've caught it; a nymph or a ghost or some dam'fool thing, but here it is, and kicking me, blast it!"

They stole nearer, forgetting for a moment their own personal preoccupations, and perceived on closer inspection that Mr Noakes grasped the arm of a young girl, or woman, who was wrapped in a long cloak. Mr Marriage lighted a match.

"Gipsy," he said in a disapproving voice; and then the match went out, but not before Mrs Marriage had a brilliant idea.

"Oh, listen!" she said excitedly, pinching Mr Lethbridge's arm— "we've found exactly what we wanted, the extra woman for Amos! Could anything be better, I ask you? Roddy, she's got to come back to the veranda and have a drink—tell her she makes the party complete."

"Fool," muttered Mr Lethbridge disgustedly, "just as we'd got out into the garden."

"Nonsense," she retorted; "there's plenty of time, and this is fun. Now we'll tease Amos."

And the party returned to the veranda, headed by the triumphant Mr Noakes, who still grasped the arm of the unknown, and by Mrs Lethbridge, who did not seem very pleased with him.

They reached the little glittering island of the dinner-table rather like shipwrecked mariners, flung ashore from the dark ocean of the garden. In the candlelight Mr Noakes, still clutching his captive, turned eagerly to examine her, while the others, drawing close, stared with a sort of bantering curiosity at this creature found crawling in the blackness of the night.

The gipsy was young, a wisp of a woman, wrapped in a patched cloak of poppy-red; her thin legs were bare; her head, too, was bare, a mane of coal-black waving hair; her face might have been beautiful had it not been wilder, more savage, than that of an animal; her great eyes smouldered, unafraid, and her skin was burned to the brown tint of bracken. She wore necklaces of red berries, like ropes of coral about her throat; bits of fern and grass adhered to her black snaky locks; her feet were naked save for rough sandals that looked as though she had fashioned them herself.

She had ceased to struggle, finding such efforts useless, and stood calmly there, eyeing them with that air of cunning defiance common to her race. Perhaps because she was as fierce as a young wolf, she made the other women, both better-looking than herself, seem temporarily uninteresting, commonplace, like a pair of wax dolls. Mrs Marriage, in spite of white satin, assumed rather the air of a hobbledehoy, altogether too angular for her graceful and feminine draperies; Mrs Lethbridge, who had seemed wild before, now appeared, by the side of this tigress, rather tamer than a plump tabby-cat on a hearthrug.

The silence, hilarious to begin with, had become slightly hostile when it was suddenly broken by Mr Lethbridge.

"And might we ask," he demanded, thrusting his hands into his pockets, "what you were doing creeping about this garden spying on us?"

The gipsy asked, in a curious, gruff little voice: "Is this your garden?"

Mr Marriage, hovering in the background, now intervened.

"The garden is mine," he announced, stirred to the core of his being. "What were you doing, trespassing here at this time of night? You weren't"—he almost choked—"you weren't trying to steal my—my rock plants?"

The gipsy slid her eyes towards him, eyeing him speculatively, shifting one foot.

"Stealing? I wasn't stealing. I come in from the forest, seeing your lights. I hid there, back in the bushes, watchin' you eat. I meant no harm. I was goin' in a minute."

Mr Marriage asked suddenly: "Are you hungry?"

"Hungry?" She gave an odd husky laugh. "I'm more'n that—fair clemmed, I am, for sure."

Mrs Marriage clapped her hands.

"Oh, this is marvellous! Amos shall feed her! Let's sit down again. And ring the bell, Roddy—the gipsy must have something to eat. Get a chair, Amos, for your lady friend."

And once more they sank into their seats, lighting cigarettes, passing round the liqueurs, while the gipsy sat, with great self-possession at Mr Marriage's left hand, waiting for the butler to bring her food. It came at last, a plate of cold duck, with salad and potatoes, followed by gooseberry tart and Devonshire cream. (The butler was damned if he was going to resurrect the fish for a dirty tramp!)

The gipsy was really astonishing; she bolted her food in two or three gulps, as a dog does, and drank some wine, wrinkling her nose as though it was medicine. Once more they all stared at her, as though she were something behind bars; and she returned their gaze with a defiant and brazen scrutiny.

"Well," said Mr Noakes, at length, pouring himself out some more port, "surely, now that she's eaten, the lady ought to do something to amuse us? Don't gipsies dance, or sing, or tell the future? What are your parlour tricks, madam?"

Mrs Marriage interrupted. She had, oddly enough, been watching her husband, and she was struck by the docility with which he had accepted the intrusion of the gipsy into their ill-assorted party. She could have sworn that he would have protested, he who was always so drearily conventional; but he hadn't. He had raised no objection, and he had actually, during the last ten minutes, made two or even three brief remarks. She said gaily, and let Mr Lethbridge give her a glass of Grand Marnier:

"Of course she'll amuse us, like a good girl, won't you, gipsy? Why, only just now we were talking of witches, and here we've got one, dropped from the skies at our feet; for every one knows that all gipsy women meddle in witchcraft. Can you tell fortunes?"

The gipsy nodded. "Fortunes? To be sure I can, by the palms or by the crystal, any way you please, lady. You want I should tell yours?"

"Mine and every one else's," commanded Mrs Marriage imperiously.

From some secret fold of her shabby cloak the gipsy now produced a shining ball of glass, that glowed like white fire in the moonlight and caught, too, reddish glints from the dwindling candles on the table. Pushing away her plate, she laid the crystal before her and waited patiently. She had had her supper; she must pay for it; this, she seemed to think, was fair.

"Me first," said Mrs Marriage eagerly.

The gipsy cast an eye round the dinner-table.

"They goin', the other folk?"

"Not us," said Ian Lethbridge.

"Of course not; it's half the fun to listen to other people's fortunes," Mrs Lethbridge declared in her husky voice.

Mrs Marriage, emboldened by Grand Marnier, shrugged her shoulders.

"Oh, well, I don't care! Let's be brave. Go on, gipsy."

But the gipsy fixed her with eyes that were like dark pools.

"I canna say what I see with all of them listening. Secret, fortunes should be. That's what my granny taught me years ago, up on the heath near Norwich."

"Nonsense," said Mrs Marriage. "If I don't mind, it's not your business, is it? But"—and she addressed her guests—"if I do it in public, then so must you. Is that understood?" And as they nodded agreement, she turned once more to the gipsy: "Come on, then. And the truth, mind—tell me all you see."

The gipsy shrugged her shoulders. Let them all go to hell, she seemed to say. Bending over the crystal, cradling it with her long tawny hands, she mused for a minute, then looked up, great eyes blazing with some demon's light that made her seem indeed a sorceress, burning, perhaps, with fire and brimstone straight from hell, or from Satan, her master.

"She gives me the creeps," whispered Mrs Lethbridge, and shuddered.

The gipsy began to speak, in her low, rather hoarse voice.

"You're for runnin' off with that gentleman over there," and she jerked her head towards the galvanized Mr Lethbridge. "You should—you'd be well mated. You've got gold, and he ain't. He likes you fine, for the moment, and he'd be faithful for as long as he could; that's two, maybe three years. After that, you'd leave him; but you're one as tires soon of any man. You wasn't that way once, but you had a kid, and it died, and you was funny ever after. You don't know yet if you'll run off or not, and I can't tell you, for the clouds come when I try to see. Maybe you will, for you're terrible weak where this gentleman's concerned. If you do, you'll cross the seas… Now show me your palm: I might see more."

During the terrible and frozen silence which succeeded this prophecy, Mrs Marriage snatched away her hand as though she feared being bitten by a scorpion, her face blanched save for its spots of rouge, her heart beating wildly. She cast one glance of panic towards the shadows where Mr Marriage sat quietly, so quietly that she prayed God he might be asleep, or dreaming of his garden. Mr Lethbridge, pulling himself together with an effort, laughed loudly and rather unnaturally.

"You damn little liar!" he said to the gipsy. "Who's been stuffing you with that pack of nonsense, eh?"

The gipsy, glancing at him contemptuously, remained silent. Mr Lethbridge, anxious to divert attention from himself, hastily pointed an unsteady finger in the direction of his wife.

"You now, Chloe. Come on, my angel, listen to the oracle. Let's hear some of your charming secrets for a change."

"Not I," said Mrs Lethbridge, not at all in her society voice. "What I've heard of yours—you cad—is quite enough to last me for tonight… and for God's sake don't let that gipsy come near me… she makes my flesh creep, like a snake… Roddy, give me another liqueur."

But Mr Noakes had left his chair and was approaching the oracle. Slightly drunk, he still maintained a gentlemanly demeanour.

"Me now," he said firmly. "Come on, you little devil. And make it snappy—see?"

"Don't you dare, Roddy, you fool!" protested Mrs Lethbridge hysterically. "Not with that brute Ian about the place…"

"Oh, shut up, Chloe! Now then, gipsy, step on it!"

The gipsy once more bent her black head low over the crystal. When she raised her eyes again they smouldered, like the eyes of a great cat, within a few inches of Mr Noakes's heated face. They held him for a moment, those eyes, seeming to pierce like searchlights to the very core of his being. Then she began to speak.

"That fancy-lady of yours, the lady over there, she likes you plenty better than you likes her. At the moment you don't think so, but just you wait a bit… six months today you'll meet another lady, one you wants to splice up with this time, and then your fancy-lady's goin' to make trouble…"

A short smothered exclamation from Mrs Lethbridge. The gipsy turned, glanced at her briefly, and resumed:

"Letters, that's what's goin' to cause the trouble. Letters of yours. It's no good… you've written 'em already, and she's got 'em. It's black ahead for you, my gentleman, and more'n once you'll be tempted to do away with yourself, but don't you… Have patience, an' you'll get the young lady in the end. Cards isn't lucky for you either… Why, only the other night…"

Mr Noakes's face had grown curiously mottled. With a sudden abrupt movement he flung out his hand and sent the crystal ball rolling heavily off the table on to the floor. Then he laughed, an ugly defiant laugh.

"That's about enough from you, you little liar! Damn your

eyes! Who's been putting you up to this, eh? I've got a pretty good mind to wring your neck."

The gipsy said listlessly, sullenly, all the fire dying out of her face:

"You asked me for the future. I told you. I don't make up. It's all there."

And she dived beneath the table to find her crystal, while Mrs Marriage, under cover of all this disorder and confusion, slipped like a swift ghost into the garden.

Amos had heard nothing—he hadn't even awakened when Roddy knocked the crystal off the table! It was too wonderful; never again would she scold him for falling asleep after dinner. And so she fled, and Mr Lethbridge, after one last scowl at the gipsy, ignored his wife and glided away in unobtrusive pursuit. Mrs Lethbridge was too agitated to notice his departure; pale and tearful, she walked away to the French-windows and stood there motionless, staring unhappily into the drawing-room. Here Mr Noakes joined her, considerably ruffled.

"Chloe! For God's sake don't make a scene! You surely don't believe that gibberish?"

Mrs Lethbridge muttered: "She knew all about us. She was right about that, wasn't she?"

"Oh, that!" He stuffed his hands into his pockets. "She made a lucky guess, that was all. They're wonderfully sharp, gipsies. But, Chloe…"

"She knew about that money you lost. That money you can't pay. She knew about Ian and Phyllis. Was that guessing?"

"Oh, drop it, Chloe! You know I only like you—that there's no one else. Can't you be reasonable?"

"I'm going to bed," she said petulantly, and swept away through the drawing-room. Mr Noakes paused, swearing beneath his breath. He shook his fist at the gipsy, hesitated once more, and then hurried into the house after Mrs Lethbridge.

The veranda was now very silent. The gipsy had retrieved her crystal; still on her knees, she rubbed it gently with her cloak and was about to return it to her pocket when it occurred to her to examine the dark aloof figure of Mr Marriage, bowed in his chair. She considered him for a moment in silence, then addressed him.

"Don't you want your future told, too?"

Mr Marriage roused himself.

"No, thank you," he said, and his voice was weary; "you'd better go home now, hadn't you?"

She ignored this remark.

"Was you asleep just now?"

"No, I was awake."

"What I said was true, wasn't it?"

"I fancy it must have been," agreed Mr Marriage.

"The one with yaller hair's married to you, ain't she?"

"Yes."

The gipsy said, in a caressing tone of voice: "You should have been asleep, my gentleman."

And she rose, swiftly, wrapping herself in her cloak.

"Wait a minute," he said, and walking across to the table, he brought a candle and held it close to her face, where it struck with a flickering light upon her tawny skin, her white teeth, and her black snaky locks. "You're a strange girl. I wonder what you think of all this, of these people. Have you ever seen anything like them before?"

"Ah," she said reflectively, "many a time! At the races."

And a curious smile curled her lips.

"Do your own people ever behave like—like that?" inquired Mr Marriage, who felt that he must talk to some one or go mad.

"My folk? No, not as I knows on. Only swells goes on that way."

"Are you married?"

"No."

"And what," next asked Mr Marriage unhappily, "would a gipsy husband do if he found that his wife was unfaithful to him?"

"I dunno. Out with his knife, I suppose."

Her impersonal indifference, her complete lack of interest in these domestic problems, coming so soon after her diabolical performance as a prophetess, interested him not a little. Was she really filled with some witch's fire when she gazed into the crystal, or was she merely a superb actress?

He observed, after a pause: "If I took a knife to that fellow Lethbridge, I should be tried for wilful murder."

"Go off, yourself, then," suggested the gipsy casually.

"I haven't got anywhere to go," he confided, after appearing to consider this proposal. "That's the best of being a gipsy like you. You have no roots—one place is as good as another."

But the gipsy would have none of this.

"No," she said firmly, "that it ain't. Some is much better'n others."

"Where are you going tonight?" he asked.

"Me?" She sank down cross-legged on the veranda, playing with her crystal, holding it up so that the moonbeams caught it like silver spears. "Me? I'm off at dawn to the crossroads beyond the forest. There'll be a swift horse waitin' for me, held by a lad of our race, and I'll be off an' away before the sun is up, carrying a bag of something that doesn't concern you, my gentleman."

"Where will you go?"

"To a heath fifty miles away from here. There, where the gorse grows thick, I'll find my nest an' hide what I'm carryin'. I'll water my horse, sleep there in the heather, and be off again by dawn."

"And where to?"

"To find my tribe, that'll be campin' in a green lane the other end of nowhere."

"It all seems very vague," commented Mr Marriage. "Suppose you don't find them?"

"Oh," she answered, "I'll find 'em for certain sure, even if they lie like foxes in the earth. I'll trace 'em along the roads by the *patrin* they leaves behind, handfuls of grass, crosses made of sticks, knots of fern. Those'll point the way."

"And will your tribe be pleased to see you?"

"That they will. There'll be a feasting off stolen meat, and singing, too, I shouldn't wonder, and fiddles. All for me."

She sighed, and he guessed that she was homesick for all this gaiety and music; she who had crept, starving in the night, to watch them feed in their bright circle of candlelight.

"Then where will you go?" he asked rather wistfully.

"Over the border."

"What border?"

"Wales. Among the mountains. There we'll run wild till summer's over. I'll be weaving baskets, and out all day tellin' fortunes to servant girls, and then at sundown, I'll be back like a pigeon to the thickets where we live hid away. None can find us there, only the conies and the swallows. Our homes is always secret."

She paused, and he was sorry, for her voice had become deep music, and she had smiled, showing a gleam of white teeth.

"I'll be off now," she said.

"No, wait a minute," said Mr Marriage, again. "When you're out, earning money, what do the men of your tribe do?"

"Them?" she considered, and smiled again. "They has a fine time. They trade horses, an' gossip, and smokes pipes, and play the fiddle a bit, or they fish for trout in the stream, or box with the gloves—they're handy men with their fists."

"Idyllic," said Mr Marriage, and sighed. "But when winter comes, what do you do? That's a very different matter, isn't it, now?"

She shook her head.

"It's all right. We camps in barns, or in the shelter of haystacks, an' builds up roaring fires. We don't feel cold, like you folk, an' we can smell spring a mile away. Oh, winter's not bad!"

She got up, put her crystal away, and stood looking out at the garden. The young moon seemed paler, the stars were less brilliant.

"It'll be dawn in an hour," she said, "and I must start for the crossroads."

Mr Marriage came across to her and plucked at her cloak.

"Look here," he said, "take me with you."

"You?"

"Yes. I—I want to get away. I'm sick of all this. Let me come with you."

She turned her eyes towards him.

"In them fancy togs?"

"No, of course not. I could change—I wouldn't be a minute. But, please—won't you let me come?"

"And what about all them others as is kissin' in the garden? The yaller-haired one?"

Mr Marriage repeated obstinately: "I want to get away. I'm tired of them, all of them."

She shrugged her shoulders.

"Well, you know best. I'll take you—I don't care one way or t'other. And we can ride turn about on the horse. But you must be quick."

"I won't be ten minutes. But please wait."

And he went inside the house.

The gipsy waited, while the stars grew fainter, and a streak of rose appeared in the sky. She realized that she was unobserved, and being one who seldom neglected opportunities, she presently crept through the French-windows into the drawing-room, where she filched several antique jewelled snuff-boxes, which she concealed beneath her cloak. She then returned to the veranda.

Mr Marriage meanwhile changed into his gardening-sweater and a pair of flannel trousers. He slipped some loose change into his pockets, tied up some handkerchiefs and a pair of socks into an untidy package, and tiptoed away from his bedroom like a conspirator. In the passage he almost collided with Mr Roderick Noakes, who seemed somewhat disconcerted by the encounter, and who stammered out something about having been sent to procure aspirin from Mrs Lethbridge.

"I have always noticed," said Mr Marriage pleasantly, "that the amount of headaches contracted by people at country-house parties is out of all proportion to the amount of wine previously drunk at dinner. However, I mustn't detain you. Goodbye, Noakes," and he held out his hand.

"Goodbye?"

"Yes. I'm going off with the gipsy, and we've got to be at the crossroads by dawn. After that our movements are uncertain. But you must get my wife to ask you again."

And he hummed as he ran downstairs.

The gipsy was still waiting, wrapped in her cloak.

"Ready?" asked Mr Marriage.

She nodded.

"Come on, then."

Together they walked across the lawn, past the rose-beds, and beyond where the waterfall splashed. Suddenly, near a grove of yew-trees in the midst of which stood a marble seat, there was a startled exclamation as Mrs Marriage brushed past them like a wraith. Behind her a glowing cigar-end indicated the whereabouts of Mr Lethbridge.

"Well, Phyllis," said Mr Marriage.

She gasped, and put her hand to her side.

"I thought," she said, "that you'd gone to bed, Amos. I couldn't sleep—it's stifling, and I came across Ian here. It must be very late."

"It is," said Mr Marriage. "In fact, you mustn't detain us. We've got to be at the crossroads by dawn."

"What are you talking about?"

"I am running away with the gipsy," explained Mr Marriage contentedly. "First of all, we're going to a heath, then to a green lane, then, I think, over the border. Isn't that right?" he inquired of the girl, who nodded her head in silence.

"I don't understand a word of what you're saying," said Mrs Marriage vaguely.

"Do try to pull yourself together. Aren't I speaking plainly enough? The gipsy and I are going away together, possibly for good. Is that clear?"

She recovered her wits with an effort.

"Not a very funny joke," she said angrily.

"It isn't a joke," Mr Marriage explained patiently. "I swear it's true. I'm sick of you and of Lethbridge, and of this house, and of my life, and even of my garden. So I'm going to start a new life, and the gipsy's coming with me. I'm sorry, Phyllis, but I really can't stand it any longer."

"Oh, I see!" she said furiously, "you're trying to humiliate me with that tramp girl, so as to make me give up Ian! Well, let me tell you you couldn't have done anything more tactless, more idiotic. I won't…"

Mr Marriage interrupted her.

"You misunderstand the whole thing," he said warmly. "Why, even if you never saw Lethbridge again it wouldn't have the slightest effect on my plans. I've made up my mind. Phyllis, don't you see I'm serious?"

Mr Lethbridge now stepped forward.

"Look here, Marriage…"

"Shut up," said Mr Marriage rudely. "I've had quite enough of you. I suppose if you were sculpting me you'd stick a pair of horns on my head—well, the worm's turned, and I wish you joy of Phyllis with all my heart."

The gipsy, who had been standing motionless during this conversation, now addressed Mr Marriage over her shoulder.

"Come on," she said indifferently.

"I'm coming," he answered. "Goodbye, Phyllis, I hope you won't have any more trouble with the servants. Goodbye, Lethbridge. Tell Noakes I hope his headache will be better tomorrow."

The gipsy, without casting another glance behind her, set off at once towards the gate that led into the forest. He caught her up with one stride, barely conscious of the fact that on the lawn Mrs Marriage was laughing hysterically, only partly calmed by the encircling arm of Mr Lethbridge. They walked together in silence until they reached the road. Then he spoke to her.

"It's odd, you know," he said, "I've waited nearly forty years for this sort of adventure."

"The crossroads is a mile away," observed the gipsy, who was plainly a woman of one idea.

They quickened their pace.

In ten minutes or so they were passing down a ride, tunnelled over by arching beech-trees. The night was silent; their footsteps fell softly on the sward.

"This is fine, isn't it?" asked the gipsy suddenly, and she smiled at him like a comrade.

Mr Marriage, retired stock-broker, drew a deep breath.

"Yes," he agreed, "fine is precisely the word I should have chosen."

Then they passed like dark shadows among the darker trees and were gone, leaving no trace behind them.

THE WONDERFUL TUNE

Jessie Douglas Kerruish

Jessie Douglas Kerruish (1884–1949), descended from an ancient Manx family, ensured her immortality, at least amongst devotees of weird fiction, with The Undying Monster *(1922), a tale of lycanthropy and a family curse. Surprisingly, though this book proved popular, and was filmed in 1942, it was initially rejected by several publishers. Jessie had been deaf from childhood and though her widowed mother had sufficient private means, and her elder sister worked as a dressmaker, Jessie looked after the house. Little is known about her writing life, but she seems to have started around the time of the First World War, probably when her mother died in August 1914. She was a frequent contributor to* The Weekly Tale-Teller, *where her series of Arabian tales,* Babylonian Nights' Entertainment, *ran in 1915 and appeared in book form in 1934. Kerruish won the first prize of £750 (around £50,000 today) in a competition in 1917 for her adventure novel* Miss Haroun al-Raschid. *She followed this with* A Girl from Kurdistan *(1918), set in Persia (modern Iran). She was a friend of Christine Campbell Thomson and contributed to several of her* Not at Night *series of anthologies in the 1930s. Alas, in later years, her sight and health also failed and her writing days were over.*

I T SEEMED SUCH AN INNOCENT LITTLE THING WHEN LARSSEN
rehearsed the details. Besides, it was Magic; ergo, Bosh.

"What is the Huldra King's Tune?" asked Iris.

"It is the crowning piece of Huldra music; and there is a spell
attached to it," said Larssen.

"As long as it is played in its entirety all present must dance to
it," he further informed her. "Also the player cannot stop playing
it—however he wishes to…"

Heaven knows he himself wished to stop playing it that night!
I'd like to forget it myself—get that tune out of my head, and
the sound of the beastly thuds, the disgusting pad, padding! If I
set it out in words perhaps they may not come into my reluctant
memory so often.

*

This happened a good while ago, when it meant rough travelling if you wanted to get from Davos to Italy in winter. But I
can only tell the tale now, by arrangement with Einar Larssen,
because years have steeled Madame Larssen's nerves, and it will
not upset her for life if she comes across this account and rec-
ognizes, behind the substitute names, what she missed in the
Fasplana Inn.

A telegram summoned Mrs Walsh and Iris to the bedside of a
relative who was in extremis, for the tenth time in three years, in
a North Italian health resort. Iris and I had only been engaged a

week, so even strong-minded Mrs Walsh had to stretch a point and let me escort them. We set off from Davos comfortably enough, and it was a matter of carriages until late afternoon.

Twilight shut down on us negotiating an uncommonly trying pass of the Rhaetic Alps. Snowflakes big as one's joined thumbs coming down thick, the landscape blotted into unstarred greyness, only the ashy reflection of the nearer snow showing that we were on earth and not jolting over derelict worlds in an infinitude of blank space. At the Hospiz at the top of the pass we changed to a sledge and the driver removed all the horse bells before starting. The chime of them might start off some delicately poised mass of snow from the heights on top of us.

So, hushedly, we drove over a snow floor, coming at times on the top of a telegraph pole just over the surface, the wires making a slow Æolian harping level with our feet. The snow was falling its thickest when the accident occurred.

A bad spill over a buried obstruction. The women fell into the snow, I landed against a telegraph post and sustained all the casualties—a right wrist that began to swell and pain abominably and a left shoulder that appeared to be shrivelling and losing all feeling. The rest of the drive was nightmare, the wires playing the deuce's own melody, and myself almost light-headed before the flicker of lanterns came suddenly into view.

When my senses were really at my beck and call again we were in a big timber-built hall, a fire crackling in the chimney and an enormous number of Swiss of all ages and sizes acting sympathetic chorus while Iris and her mother attended to my injuries, aided by a slim young man with a mop of tow-coloured hair.

"Allow me to introduce myself, monsieur, and then you will perhaps fulfil the formality, so beloved in your country, by introducing me to the ladies with whom I have had the pleasure of working for some time." Thus the yellow-haired man, when I was propped in a chair. His French was good, but not of France. "I am your fellow guest, forced to stay for the night through the blocking of the farther road. My wife is here also, but at present she is resting in her own apartment. And my name—I have no card on my person—is Einar Larssen."

We three started in unison—"The violinist?" exclaimed Iris, and he bowed and pushed back a straggling lock self-consciously.

I made the necessary introductions. The landlord interposed nervously. "It is perhaps advisable to inform the ladies—" he began. Larssen interrupted. I distinctly saw him bestow a warning frown on the man, and the Switzer's face expressed the comprehension of one who receives secret orders. "Our host would impress on you that the 'Four Chamois' has but little accommodation to offer at the best of times, Madame Walsh," the violinist said smoothly. "I hear Madame coming, she will arrange with you for a fair division."

Madame Larssen appeared now, a frail, pretty little woman in the early twenties, and bustled Mrs Walsh and Iris off. I saw all the Swiss, the landlord and his wife, the several servants, and our driver exchange looks as the trio departed.

"It is most awkward, Monsieur Lambton," said Larssen, suddenly become businesslike. "Madame Larssen is of a nervous temperament, and for her sake we have been forced to a certain concealment and we might as well extend the concealment to Madame Walsh and mademoiselle; they will rest the easier for not knowing about it."

I could not imagine what the fellow was driving at. Infectious disease? Robbers? "It is behind that door they rest, monsieur," the landlord volunteered, indicating one at the side of the hall. "Three corpses."

"Most ladies are averse to such house-fellows," Larssen proceeded gently. "We will all be on our way in the morning; there is no need for them to know, eh?"

I agreed. "They will rest the easier for knowing nothing. Three corpses? Three at once?"

The landlord waxed voluble. They were the aftermath of an avalanche. There are several kinds of avalanche, and the nastiest is the dirt avalanche. It's like the tipping out of a titanic dust-cart; a filthy tide of mud and shingle, slabbed together with half-melted snow, packed with the trees, turves, rubbish heads, and corpses it has gathered in its course. The snow avalanche enfolds you dead in its chaste whiteness; the dirt variety pinches, chokes, and suffocates you slowly, then acts threshing-machine and steam-roller combined to the mortal part of you, until its force is spent and it settles with you interred somewhere in it.

Such an abomination had trickled its way down the valley hard by the inn of the Four Chamois early that winter, three men were lost in it, and that day diggers had found their remains. "Caspar Ragotli is entire," said mine host, with a nod at the door; "Melchoir Fischer—" He told us, detailedly, how this Melchoir was in pieces, most of them there, while of the third, Hans Buol, only one hand had been discovered, "But we know it for Buol's, by the open knife grasped in it," our entertainer proceeded, gloatingly. "A fine new knife from your Sheffield, Monsieur Lambton; and the hand being the right it sufficed for the whole, as the gentlemen will know—"

I felt thankful for Larssen's concealment when the ladies reappeared, prepared to make the best of things. We were merry enough over our mishap, now that food, fire, and four walls were our portion, with sounds of storm brushing up louder and louder without to add zest to enjoyment. The most awkward thing was that, with my injuries, I was limited to the stiff use of one hand alone and could scarcely lift that. I would stay up, if only to convince Iris there was nothing much the matter. If it had not been for my crocking I knew she would have been enjoying everything in this small adventure enormously, from the unexpected company to the robustious dog and severe cat who slipped in when a servant was sent to bring wood from the outhouse where they had been banished.

"But what makes them fidget round that door?" she asked innocently.

Larssen was behind her. Under fear of his eye the landlord answered composedly: "There is in that room a—a stock of meat, madame."

Now came the son of the house with the bag of an afternoon's hunt: a pair of marmots to be stuffed against the next tourist season. He placed them on a chest by the lethal door while his father took him aside for a word of caution. We made the three, host, hostess, and son, sup with us; and all was so comfortable that I forgot the other guests until Larssen whispered apologetically:

"It is not really disrespectful, Monsieur Lambton."

We kept shocking hours for a Swiss inn, the eight of us, after the tired servants had been packed off to their quarters.

"This is like home," said Larssen dreamily, when we were all basking round the fire. "I come from a farm—up in the wilds beyond Romsdal—and it was even so in the old hall. The big fire in the big fireplace—the cats and dogs going crackle, crackle, over the supper bones—the wind whistling—the clatter of voices—"

"The one thing missing is the scraping of thy violin, my Einar," his wife put in. "Come, thy fingers twitch; I know it; and our friends here would not, perhaps, object—eh?"

"A recital by Herr Larssen, free, and without the trouble of sitting still in a stuffy concert hall!" said Mrs Walsh, and the ensuing chorus of rapturous assent sent Madame Larssen running for her lord's instrument.

"You have heard of my Da Salo?" Larssen inquired, as he lifted the violin from its travelling case. "My *Cavalancti* Da Salo? It is said Cavalancti sold his eternal welfare for the power to make a certain number of instruments that should approach as near the God-given perfection of Stradivarius's work as devilry could accomplish."

He tilted the violin to show the play of light sinking in the amber lustre of it. "We will have no set pieces," he added, "but such old tunes as I played in our farm kitchen so far away and long ago!"

Tucking it under his chin, he swept us with the first notes right into the faery realm of sound. A realm of tingling frost that whipped the blood along the veins racingly, of icy wind that sang of the Elder Ice at the Back of Beyond: a very vocalization of the eternally young, eternally pure spirit of the Northland.

Ending with a queer suggestion of a lit farmhouse at night, the loneliness of stars and ice and snow crowding to it outside and inside fire and company, and the family spirit concentring round the holy hearth and stretching out invisible strands of love to absent ones far out in the frozen whaling fields, or at mean work in foreign cities, or dead and cherishing in the other world memory of home.

Then he plunged into another tune, and another; snatches all, all singing of the North, and the Northern chasteness that is fierce and passionate as the foulest vice of all other quarters of earth.

"You will not hear these at a paid-for concert—God forbid!" he observed, his dreamy voice filling a pause between two melodies. "You are hearing, my friends, what few but children of Norway ever hear, scraps of the Huldrasleet. The melodies of the Elf-Kind—the Huldra Folk we name them—no less. Snatches that bygone musicians overheard on chancey nights out in the loneliness of fiords and fells, and passed on down the ages. The Huldra Folk are the musicians of all time."

"You would like to hear them?" asked Mrs Walsh quizzically.

"I have heard them, dear madame. Five times have I heard the Elf-Kind, invisible but audible, holding revels out in the empty winter nights and summer early mornings on the heights of the Dovrefeld—I, Einar Larssen."

Mrs Walsh started a little; but the rest of us were not much surprised, if I can speak from analysis of my own feelings and a glance in the eyes of the others.

"There was one tune," Larssen went on meditatively. "It was a dark and windy night—like this one. I was searching for a strayed sheep. I found it in a field. Then, over a hedge, the melody began to flow. It *was* a tune! It got into my fingers and toes; I began to dance to it. There in the snow I danced, and my senses flowed out of my body in sheer ecstasy, while my emptied heart and head were filled with the tune."

His face queerly lit by firelight, his yellow mane tossing as he gesticulated illustratively, he carried us all on by the conviction of his voice over the monstrosity of his relation.

"Then the stark pines on the slope beyond the hedge bent and waved their branches—in time to the tune. The snow was swished about in powder, as the frozen grass-blades beneath waked and waved—to the tune. The stars began to glide about in the sky, and to bow themselves to and from the earth; growing bigger as they approached it and shrinking as they swirled back in the mazes of the dance—to the tune. Then, if you please, I woke. Woke, with the moon much farther across the heavens than she had been when the first note of the tune came to me, and the sheep I had come to find lying exhausted in a patch trampled flat and muddy by its hoofs. And I, also, lay in the middle of a bare trampled patch in surrounding snow. That is the truth."

He drew breath and proceeded:

"I did not remember the tune entirely, though I had heard it repeated many times. A short tune; very short. When the Huldra fiddler reached its end he began again, round and round in a circle of music. The middle part I remember, but of the end and beginning only certain detached notes. I tried often by playing what I recollect to make the forgotten parts slip into their places, but unavailingly—"

He went to the main door and opened it. The wind swept in steadily, but the snowfall had stopped and a big moon looked down on piled white mountains and glaring snowfields. "It was so; clear, windy, and white, when I heard the tune," he said thoughtfully.

"Similarity of outward circumstances will revive a train of emotion or thought experienced long ago," Mrs Walsh nodded.

He closed the door, and came back to the fire. Then his eyes lit and he drew the bow across the strings with a large gesture. Followed a few bars of melody. "The middle part," he explained.

Madame Larssen gave an abrupt little cry. "Einar, can it be you heard the Huldra King's Tune? Then thank heaven you cannot play it!"

"Why, my beloved?" he lifted his eyebrows gently.

"In my district there was a tradition that one man once played it through and something happened."

"What happened?"

"Nobody quite remembered. But it was dreadful."

"What *is* the Huldra King's Tune?" asked Iris.

"It is the crowning piece of Huldra music, and there is a spell attached to it. An enchantment, mademoiselle," Larssen elucidated.

"… As long as it is played in its entirety, all who are present must dance to it," he further informed her, after reflection.

"That does not sound very dreadful," she laughed.

"There's something further." He became thoughtful. "Ah; it is that the player cannot stop playing, whether he would or not. He can only stop if—let me consider—yes, if he plays it backwards or, failing that, if the strings of his violin are cut for him."

"You could safely play it now, monsieur," said the landlord. "So far as I am concerned. My rheumatics would stop my dancing, however magically you played."

"And we"—Mrs Walsh's gesture indicated the other ladies—"are resting to summon energy enough to crawl to bed. So, Herr Larssen, we are a safe audience if you can remember your wonderful tune."

"There was one more detail," he went on. "Ah, it is that if the tune is played often enough, inanimate things must dance, too."

"*That's* danger for us, as we are all nearly inanimate!" Mrs Walsh yawned frankly now.

He leant against the carved mantel and for a little while he played absently, his subconscious mind busy with reconstruction, fumbling amidst its orderly lumber, connecting, paring, arranging. Then he straightened himself and swept the bow purposefully across the strings.

Slowly at first, then with added lilt and swing, there rippled forth the complete, horrible tune.

I knew it, for between a chiming start and a clattering last bar the broken chords he had first remembered fitted in followingly. It was not very long, that tune; he reached the end, leapt, as it were, to the beginning, played it through again, and so to a third repetition.

Then the wonder began. During the second repetition a movement like the passing of a breeze had run round our little assembly. Sleepy eyes opened, heels beat time, figures stiffened. At the third we were on our feet.

It seemed perfectly natural. Though I was almost too tired and shaken to stand, the tune ran into my feet; I made a step towards Iris and almost fell, fetched up against the wall, and so fell to dancing. Dancing calmly and solemnly all by myself.

Iris made a step towards me, too; paused and shook her head. "Poor boy, you must sit and rest," she murmured, and paired off with the Swiss lad.

Somehow one knew the steps on first hearing the music. It was, perhaps, the Dance Primitive, holding in itself the potentialities of all saltatory art. Mainly it consisted of a mazy circling with a little crossing and up-and-down work, going on, over and over; monotonous yet tirelessly fascinating, like some Eastern music.

I repeat, it seemed perfectly natural. The landlord led off with his wife; they danced with decorous determination. Mrs Walsh and Madame Larssen were footing it with all the abandon two women paired together could be expected to indulge in. Larssen himself had begun to dance, playing conscientiously the while. I circled about, a little uncertain on my feet, my slinged arm for partner, and Iris and the lad sailed amongst us, light as thistledown.

Those clumsy-looking Swiss boys are amongst the best dancers in the world. Whenever she passed me, Iris smiled, her eyes full of faraway ecstasy.

The music quickened and took a richer tone; it rang back from the walls, it melted and echoed in the timber ceiling; the floor-boards hummed with it; every nerve in us was tingling, laughing, almost crying with too much rapture of sound and motion.

Time, weariness, place, all were not. The dead beyond the door were forgotten, there was no Earth, no more Time, nothing but a ringing emptiness of melody, a singing storm of tunefulness on which one could lean and be carried like an eagle down the wind.

Yet, through all the intoxication of it, I was dimly aware that we were in a homely Swiss inn-parlour, at the same time that we were in the Fourth Dimension of music. I was rapt out of my shaken body, yet saw my surroundings clearly; saw, presently, the cat and dog rise and, on their hind legs, join in, keeping time and threading the maze unerringly.

That appeared neither wonderful nor laughable, only natural; but my dazed senses half-awoke when the two dead marmots slith-ered off the chest, rose on their hind feet, and, with pluffed-out tails swaying in time to the tune, and a queer little pit-a-pat of tiny feet, that I seemed to hear through the other noises, set to one another and circled with the best of us. They swung past me, their heads level with my knees, and vanished amidst the other dancers. I noted their furry little faces, dropped jaws, frothy teeth, and glazed eyes. Dead, most undoubtedly dead, and dancing!

The cat and dog passed me again, and the marmots chanced to be near at the same time. The dog wrinkled his upper lip, disgusted at the deadness of them; the cat snapped at them in passing. The queerest thing was the others, with one exception, did not seem to notice the four small additions to the company. Only Larssen, figuring solemnly with his fiddle for a partner, saw. His eyes protruded as they squinted along the Da Salo at the quartette. "Dead," he gulped.

"Stop now, man!" I called. "This fooling—"

"I cannot," he cried back hoarsely, and began the melody over again for the fifteenth time at least. "The tradition is true—"

Then, as the opening movement rippled forth again, in the inner room three crashes sounded.

Two almost simultaneously, yet singularly distinct from one another, the third a few seconds later. Loud, resonant, wooden crashes. Then silence in that room, and in ours the swell and swing of the infernal melody and the pat of dancing feet.

The sound had been too pronounced for even enthralled senses to disregard. All looked at the door for a moment. The others forgot the interruption at once and danced on, eyes blank with ecstasy; only Larssen's face went white and the landlord's mottled grey. "Stop, monsieur!" the landlord cried.

"I cannot!" wailed Larssen, his voice shrill with horror. "I cannot! For heaven's sake, Monsieur Lambton, come and cut the strings!"

"My hands are useless—" I began, and stopped at a new sound.

You must understand that I had danced nearer to the door by that time. The new sound behind it was one of scuffling and scrambling, half a dozen sounds merged in one, then—pat, pat, patter, patter, pat—was a noise of steps keeping time to the tune.

Soft steps, you'll understand, not the click of shod feet, like ours. I went round, came in range again, and listened.

A fairly heavy thumping—like a man on stockinged feet—was approaching the door. "What's the matter, Cyril?" asked Iris, swaying by, still rapt, as the boy and the three other women were. She did not wait for an answer. The latch of the door rattled. The latch inside the other room, you understand.

"I'll play it backwards when I can!" gasped Larssen, as we crossed each other's track. The noises in the fatal room circled away from the door, then approached, and the latch was unhasped this time before the horrible soft-falling thumps retreated. You see how it was: as we were compelled to circle round our room so, whatever it was in the other room had to circle likewise, making an attempt whenever the door was in reach to open it and join us and the tune.

Larssen was fiddling desperately. "Backwards now!" I implored.

"I cannot—yet. But if I repeat it a few more times, I shall be able to reverse it," he called back.

A few more rounds would be too late. The inner room noises reached the door and it opened a crack. If—what was striving to come—joined us, would even ecstasy blind the women? And when the waking came—? I flung myself against the door in passing; it snapped to again. "A few more repetitions!" panted Larssen.

Inspiration came to me. The others, dancing in a hypnotized state, circled widely, but I could do the steps within a small compass: in front of the door.

I could do it. I did it. Larssen made an attempt to reverse the melody. He failed.

Two more repetitions. Iris and her partner, passing me, smiled at the quaint figure I must have cut, dancing by myself in narrow circles before the door. Larssen's ashen face was running with sweat that dripped from his chin and trickled, like the slack of a tide, over the amber glory of the Da Salo. The padding steps approached the door; it was jerked a little ajar. I drove it back with my sound shoulder; but a new danger arose. They—the dancers within—were imitating my tactics. They danced in a circumscribed space that grew smaller as the minutes passed.

If only we could have got the women out of the way! I gyrated, as well as I could, before the door all the time, driving it back with my shoulder as it was thrust ajar, again and again.

Picture it. See me, one arm in a sling and the other nearly powerless, prancing and twirling before the door, trying the while to keep a temperate expression on my sweat-drenched features for the benefit of the women. The landlord only kept from dropping with fear by the magic of the tune. Larssen stepping it absurdly, trickling features set like a Greek tragic mask, his long yellow tresses bobbing about, matted into rats'-tails, his eyes glaring down at the flooded, humming Da Salo. The women and the lad, unconscious of everything save the melody, dancing with the introspective gaze of the drugged.

The door was thrust ajar once more. I dashed it back, but not before a soft padding had pattered from the bottom of the opened crack into our room.

I almost collapsed. Cat and dog and dead marmots—oh, they were respectable beside the latest addition to our company!

The people circled on; the dog, the cat, the dead marmots, they all circled; and circling with them—but keeping ever a course that drew it nearer and nearer to Larssen all the while—was a little dark shadow with a long, thin, tarnished white gleam sticking from it. I beat back the door and what more was pressing against it, and fought with nausea.

Round and round Larssen's feet, nearer and nearer, the little shadow hopped, leapt, and pattered. Leaping and springing. It jumped higher and higher, always in time to the music—higher and higher—high as Larssen's elbow. In another minute I knew even the enraptured dancers could not fail to see it. The door was now beaten on, beaten with soft-falling, fierce thuds. I could not keep it shut much longer—

Up sprang the little shadow and the tarnished gleam, clear over Larssen's shoulder. A series of twangling, discordant snaps, that seemed to prick one's brain physically, and the tune stopped dead.

Thud! It sounded behind the door—very heavy. Then a succession of smaller thuds. I leant against the wall, panting. The dancers stopped, every face dazed and stupefied, and in an automatic way each dropped into the nearest seat.

Larssen dashed his handkerchief over his face. I contrived to throw my own on the floor behind him before he staggered to the fireplace. With my most usable hand I also managed to pick up my property again and place it on the seat, behind me, as I sat down on the chest by the door. The marmots were on the floor near my feet; I was enabled to hide my face for a few seconds, and to compose it, as I picked them up.

The eyes of the others cleared and became intelligent. "I really think I've been asleep," said Mrs Walsh.

"I believe I have," Iris rubbed her eyes.

"I think I have too," laughed Madame Larssen.

The landlord had made himself scarce at once, probably doubting his histrionic powers at such short notice. His wife followed him. The boy sat dazed.

"I had a dream, a ridiculous dream, too ridiculous to repeat," Mrs Walsh proceeded.

"I had a dream, likewise too absurd to relate," said Madame Larssen.

"I had—" Iris checked herself, and looked sudden apology at Larssen, who had arranged himself with the light at his back.

"Do not fear to hurt my feelings," he said blandly, his voice still a little unnatural. "You were all tired before I began. In brief, mademoiselle, I am not broken at the heart because my music had a soporific effect on you all."

"It wasn't as if you had been playing one of your own compositions," she apologized. "I am sleepy, Mother; I vote we make a move."

"Yes, we will tuck up our drowsiness in bed before it has a chance to insult anyone further," Madame Larssen chimed in gaily.

They trooped off; Larssen kept his face in shadow, I stood carefully before the chest, while bidding them good night. When they had gone, the landlord came back. For a little while we four men stared at one another. "Surely I have had a dream, gentlemen," said the landlord imploringly.

We said nothing. He hesitated, then, with the haste of dislike, snatched a candle and flung open the inner door. "Oh, Holy Virgin!" he cried.

Three coffins lay as they had tumbled from their trestles. About the room was spilt and tangled the coarse linen that charity had contributed—

The landlord reeled against one doorpost. Larssen clung, limp, to the other. "I'll burn the Da Salo before I'll play that tune again!" he whispered hoarsely.

I stepped back into the large room, brought my handkerchief, and from its folds replaced in one of the coffins a shrivelled hand grasping the tarnished knife that had cut the violin strings. The boy, most composed of us all, said stolidly:

"Ah, messieurs, it appears that the dead do not enjoy being disturbed!"

ISLAND OF THE HANDS

Margaret St Clair

Margaret St Clair (1911–1995) was one of the regular women contributors to the post-war science fiction and fantasy pulps, capable of producing enjoyable adventure fiction as well as more sophisticated stories, many under the alias Idris Seabright. She wrote steadily throughout the 1950s and early 1960s, turning more to novels in later years. These include The Sign of the Labrys *(1963), set underground after Earth has been devastated by a plague and* The Dancers of Noyo *(1973), her final novel, a weird post-hippie infused work where California has been devastated by a plague and the survivors return to a native American style culture. Only a few of her stories have been collected, in* The Best of Margaret St Clair *(1985) and, more recently,* The Hole in the Moon *(2019) compiled by Ramsey Campbell.*

E VER SINCE HE HAD BEGUN TO HAVE THE DREAMS ABOUT JOAN, there had been a compass in his head. He felt that he could go as directly to the spot from which she was calling him as a homing pigeon returns to its cote. He woke from those dreams—dreams in which she stood before him pale and dishevelled, weeping bitterly, imploring him, "Come, Oh, come,"—as surely oriented as an arrow in flight. Joan was the magnet, and he the steel. But Joan was dead.

They had hunted for her for nearly a week after her plane had crashed. Over and over the water, day after day, sectioning and resectioning the area where she must have gone down. There had never been any trace. How could there be? Garth was a water world, with its land areas confined to a few island chains where its scanty population lived. The best that could have happened was that she might have floated for a few hours, for a few days, before she drowned.

Dirk had been talking to her by rad when her plane had crashed. The flight had been going splendidly, rather monotonous really. She to see him in a few hours. And then her voice had soared up suddenly in a shocking scream, "The plane! What—Oh, my God!" Seconds later he had heard the final roaring crash.

Something had happened to Joan's plane in perfect weather, with visibility unlimited, with the engines purring silkenly. What? What had caused the crash?

Not long after the search for his wife was officially abandoned, Dirk began to have the dreams. Night after night with the compass in his brain pointing, nearly three months of nights, until he began to wonder whether grief for Joan—too soon lost, too well loved—was breaching the wall of sanity in him. And then his decision, no sooner reached than rejoiced in, the decision to abandon rationality and go to look for a woman who was certainly dead.

Dirk Huygens went to Larthi, the little settlement from which the official rescue planes had set out. He could pilot a plane himself, but in Larthi he hired a quadriga with two navigators to spell each other. He did not want the duties of piloting to distract him from the pointing of the needle in his head.

Sokeman was the name of the chief navigator, a lean nervous man who smoked and coughed continually. Ross, the second pilot, was of very different physical type—bullnecked and broad-shouldered, with a ready grin. They had good references.

"What were those coordinates again?" Sokeman asked suddenly. The three men were having a drink together in a waterfront bar in Larthi to bind the bargain they had made.

"63° 11′ west, 103° 01′ north," Huygens said. "Or thereabouts. As I told you, I can't be quite sure. I want the whole area searched."

"Um." Sokeman ordered another round of drinks.

"Why?" Huygens asked. He swallowed. "Is it—did you ever hear of land there?" Hope had begun a thin hammering in him.

"Land? Oh, no. Nothing out there but water. But it seems to me I've heard those coordinates before. Do you remember, Ross? Wasn't there a man a year or so ago asking about them?"

"I think so," Ross answered. "And a dame six months or so before that. A good looker." He grinned.

"What happened to them?" Huygens asked absently. The two pilots had told him it was too late to begin the search tonight.

Sokeman shrugged. "Don't know," he answered. "Maybe they hired boats. They didn't hire our rig."

The next day at dawn the search began. Hour after hour the quadriga beat back and forth across the water. Huygens, his hands pressed to his head, muttered directions. "To the west. Now, back. West again. South-south west. Steady as she goes. North. North through east. Back…" And hour after hour the quadriga obeyed him, hunting patiently, tirelessly, fruitlessly.

The day passed in a dazzle of empty waters. Then it was dark and time to go back to Larthi. So it was that day and the next day and the next and the next. Huygens saw that even the pilots, though they were being paid for the time spent in hunting, were growing impatient at the futility of their task.

On the fifth day he turned abruptly to Sokeman, who was piloting. "Go back," he ordered harshly. "Back to Larthi. It's no use."

Sokeman bit his lip. His eyes narrowed. Huygens thought he must be considering where he and the rig could claim to have earned a full day's pay. "It's almost sunset," he said. "Only an hour or two more. Let's finish out the day, eh, Mr Huygens? Then we'll go back."

"All right," Huygens said unemotionally. He sank back in his seat, his hands pressed over his eyes. Hope had made him sick. A thousand times in the last few days, it seemed to him, the voice in his brain had said "Here!" imperatively. And there had never been anything but the flat surface of the empty sea.

The quadriga wheeled and banked. Sokeman sent it back and forth in long sweeps above the water. Huygens endured the ship's motion impatiently. Now that he had come to a decision, he wanted to get it over with. He wanted to be back in the rooming house in Larthi, done with hope, getting ready to go back to Zavir. There was work waiting for him in the city. It would help him to forget.

The ship shook abruptly from stem to stern. Huygens had a sudden amazed conviction that it had rammed an invisible wall. Sokeman screamed shrilly, like a woman. It was as if a crushing weight pushed the quadriga down irresistibly toward the surface of the sea. Huygens heard a wild roaring in his ears. And then it was all black.

Huygens came back to consciousness to find he was vomiting. He levered himself up with one arm and looked around the quadriga's cabin. Sokeman was lying back in the pilot's seat, a huge lump swelling on his temple where it had struck against the side of the ship. Ross was stretched out in the aisle, but as Huygens watched he stirred and raised his head. The quadriga's stout frame was budded and pleated and crumpled in a hundred places. The ship must be completely wrecked.

Ross groaned. He sat up, holding on to the back of the pilot's seat. "Where are we?" he asked. "What happened to the ship?"

"I don't know," Huygens answered. Shakily he made his way to one of the ports and looked out. "We're on a little beach," he reported. "It's rocky and steep. I can't see much. There're trees and brush on three sides of us."

"It's land, anyway," Ross answered. He looked at Sokeman and whistled. Carefully he felt over the unconscious man's skull. "I don't think he's hurt bad," he said after a minute. "Anyhow, there's nothing we can do for him. Let's go outside and see what we can find."

The quadriga seemed to have crashed in a little cove. A dark mass of heavily-foliaged trees and brush came down almost to the edge of the water. "I don't think we can get through that," Huygens said, studying it. "Let's walk along the beach and see if we can find a trail."

They had gone crunching over the pebbles for perhaps a quarter of a mile when Ross said, "This is a funny place. Notice how misty the air is, and cold and still? It was a fine bright day, a little windy, when the ship crashed. And notice those trees. I never saw trees like that before, such a dark green, with little needles making up big fat leaves."

Huygens nodded. "I thought at first they were pseudoconifers," he said, "but—what's that at the edge of the water up ahead?"

The two men exchanged glances. "A motor boat," Ross said slowly. "There must be people here. A motor boat."

A little farther along they saw a cabin cruiser, drawn up carelessly on the shingle, and then another smaller boat. They might have been there a long time. A little beyond the last craft there was an opening in the heavy blackish brush. Overgrown as it was, it seemed to be a trail which led inward.

"Those motorboats are as queer as everything about this place," Ross said as the two men started back to the quadriga after Sokeman. "What are they doing here, so far from the nearest port? It reminds me of something..." He fell into a frowning abstraction.

Sokeman was standing outside the quadriga when they got back, though he looked white and sick. Huygens went into the ship for the aid kit, blankets, and other supplies. Then they started along the beach again, supporting Sokeman between them.

The trail was badly overgrown, and they had to stop frequently for Sokeman to rest. It was nearly dark when Ross said, "There's something off to the right, where the trees are sort of mashed down. Do you see it? Looks like it might be a wrecked plane."

They got up to it, and Ross was right. It was a wrecked plane, thoroughly wrecked. Huygens read the name on the fuselage—*Coma Berenices*—twice before he admitted to himself whose plane it was. *Coma Berenices* had been the name of Joan's plane.

He said something to the others. He dropped Sokeman's arm and ran crazily around the plane, looking for Joan. He found her under a bush to one side. She had been lying there for about three months, but there were things that made the identification unmistakable—a bracelet he had given her, her long bright hair, her wedding ring.

"Was that what you were... looking for?" Ross asked when he had gone back to where they were waiting for him.

"Yes," Huygens answered carefully. "It wasn't—quite what I wanted to find."

He took one of the blankets and spread it carefully over Joan. Ross said, "We'll come back tomorrow and, and fix things up." Huygens made no answer.

They went a good deal farther on before they made camp. Huygens, when he did sleep, slept soddenly. He did not dream. There was no reason for him to. Joan was dead.

Huygens woke early the next morning, before there was much light in the sky. Little streamers of mist floated in the still, heavy air. Sokeman and Ross were still asleep.

He was thirsty. They had found a tiny spring last night, welling up softly under a clump of blackish brush. He went over to the spring, scooped up the cold water in his hand, and began to drink.

He was just rising to his feet when he saw Joan coming toward him through the trees.

He ran toward her, his heart hammering insanely. When he was about ten feet from her he stopped suddenly, as if the impulse which had borne him on was exhausted. Foreknowledge was already in him. He could see, now, that the woman was not Joan; in a sense he had known that she was not Joan when he began to run. But this moment of realization was more cruel than any yet had been.

She was not Joan. She differed from her in a hundred, a thousand, tiny ways. Her face was a more perfect oval than Joan's, her hair brighter, her eyes hazel instead of grey. She was taller than Joan, and under her thin golden tunic her body was rounder and more lithe. She walked with a more deliberate grace than Joan had. But for all the differences the resemblance was uncanny, astonishing, incredible. Huygens stared at her, and belief and disbelief alternated in him like systole and diastole in the beating of the heart.

The woman smiled at him and held out her hands in welcome. "Hello, Dirk," she said.

"Are—you're not Joan."

"No."

After a minute Huygens said, "How did you know my name?"

She smiled at him again, but did not answer. A tatter of mist floated between them. Huygens would not have been surprised if she had dissolved in it. But when the mist cleared she was still there.

The sound of their voices had wakened the other two men. Ross came up, looking about alertly. When he saw the woman, he whistled softly. "Introduce me to your friend," he said in Huygens' ear.

"What's your name?" Huygens said to Joan-not-Joan.

He would have sworn the question was new to her. She looked troubled and disturbed. "Miranda," she answered, as if after thought.

Sokeman had been looking at the girl in silence, frowning. Now he said, "Our plane was wrecked. What's the name of this place?"

"This is the place of shaping. Its name is the Island of the Hands."

Sokeman's face remained blank, but Ross let out his low whistle again. He said stumblingly, "I think, I seem to remember, I believe I've heard…"

"Maybe," Miranda answered distantly. "The island is known to some people on Garth."

Ross's self-assurance was coming back. "Look here, Miranda," he said, "aren't there other people on the island? You know, people. A settlement, a town."

"Yes, there are people," Miranda replied. She had a low, musical voice, sweeter than Joan's had been. She moved closer to Dirk, smiling, and fingered the stuff of his sleeve. He saw that she was very beautiful. Without looking at Ross she said, "Shall I take you to them?"

Sokeman and Ross exchanged glances. "Yes," Ross said.

Miranda waited while the three men broke camp. Her eyes followed Dirk Huygens as he worked, and always she smiled. When they were ready she led them along the trail.

★

They walked for a long time, always slightly up, through the heavy, quiet air. Miranda said at last, "We turn to the right here. Do you see?" She indicated a barely perceptible track. "This is the way to the people, to those who have their desire. The other way leads to the Hands."

There were too many questions in Huygens' mind for him to ask any of them. He walked beside Miranda silently. Behind him the two men were talking in low tones. He heard Ross say something like "When I was a child... this place..." and then Sokeman's murmured, inaudible reply.

They came to the top of a slight rise. Below them, in a shallow valley, was a group of squat structures in a semicircle. They were small, almost huts, and there was about them an indefinable air of desolation and abandonment. "This is where the people live," Miranda said, turning to speak over her shoulder. "Shall we go down to them?"

Sokeman and Ross said "Yes" almost together. Ross was frowning and his lips were tight.

They had gone a few steps when a man came stumbling up the slope toward them. He collapsed almost at their feet. He was gaunt to the point of emaciation, with staring, bloodshot eyes, and his scanty clothing hung in tatters around him. Miranda walked around him with calm indifference. Huygens saw that the man was dead drunk. As they passed him, he tipped a phlomis bottle up with a shaking hand to get the last few drops from it. The bottle gave an unlikely gurgle as he lowered it.

There was a flash of movement ahead in the clear space where the houses were. Miranda led the three men toward it. When they had got close enough Huygens saw that it was a woman—surely an elderly woman, dressed in faded violet taffeta—who was moving in the measures of an intricate dance with a huge young man. The man moved with the precision of clockwork, as smoothly as if inaudible music were regulating him, but the woman stumbled from time to time. About and about they went in their fantastic dance against the background of the blackish trees, while streamers and tags of mist drifted slowly toward them.

As they moved closer to Huygens in their rhythmic circling, he saw that the woman was, as he had thought, wrinkled and old. Her partner, however, had the bland, impossible perfection of a dummy in a display of fashionable clothing. His empty face was bent down to the grey-haired woman in what was almost a caricature of admiring attentiveness.

Three other men, as alike him as peas, were waiting at the edge of the clear space. One of them stepped up to the dancing couple and tapped the huge young man on the shoulder. And docilely the dancing giant resigned the grey-haired woman to the second man. He moved off with her in the perfect and uncanny clockwork step.

"She dances," Miranda said as if in explanation. "Always she dances. It is her desire."

The elderly dancer stopped abruptly. "I'm tired," she whimpered. Instantly the man who had been dancing with her knelt before her and kissed her hand. It was a parody of adoration. Then he picked her up in his enormous arms and, holding her as if she were something infinitely precious and frail, carried her off to one of the huts. The other three men followed behind.

The grotesque spectacle had kept Huygens silent. Now he turned to Miranda. "What is it?" he demanded. "I don't understand. Are they all like this?"

"All? Oh, no." Miranda shook her bright head. "Their desires are different, you see." She hesitated. "They stay in the huts most of the time," she said. "If you want to see them, you must look in the windows. They will not care. They will not notice you."

Ross had already gone to the window of the nearest hut and was looking in. After an instant Huygens followed him.

The light was bad. At first all Huygens could see was a heap of something on the floor and, seemingly buried in it, the head and shoulders of a man. Then he perceived that the heap was a glinting mass of faceted jewels, sending out sparks of purple, red, green, topaz, and gold. A naked man, wizened and under-sized, was standing waist-deep in the pile. He was plunging his hands in it over and over, bringing up handfuls of coruscating jewels and letting them drop over his head and breast.

In the next hut a woman sat on a low bed. In her arms she held a young child. She talked to it, played with it, rocked it in her arms. And all the time the child was perfectly passive and mute.

Once only it moved its hands a little. There was something horrible in its inactivity.

"Have you seen enough?" Miranda asked as he turned from the window. "Are you ready to go to the place of shaping, to visit the Hands?"

Ross drew in his breath. Almost diffidently he asked, "Is it allowed? May anyone... shape with the Hands?"

"Oh, yes," Miranda answered with a grave smile. "This is the Island of the Hands."

She turned and began leading them around the semicircle of buildings. Huygens followed her automatically. His mind was in confusion. As they began to walk uphill again he said, "What is this place, Miranda? Ross and Sokeman seem to understand, but I don't."

"What do you want to know?" Miranda asked in her sweet voice.

"What the island is, what those people are doing here, what the Hands are—everything. How was it we didn't see the island? What made our plane crash?"

"I will tell you what I know," Miranda said. She put out her hand and touched his arm lightly, smiling. With a shock of surprise he saw that on her finger was a gem-set wedding ring.

"The Island of the Hands was made by a great, by a supreme, man of science long ago. He had lost his wife, and he felt he could not live without her. He made the place of shaping so he could bring her back. You will understand that part better when you see the Hands.

"After he died, the island remained. People began to come to it, one or two a year, people who had desires they could not bear to leave ungratified. They come to the islands, and with the Hands they make their desires. And they live in the huts—I don't know who built them—until they die.

"The island cannot be seen from above. Only a little of its coast is visible from the water's edge. There is a—a space around the Hands that bends the rays of light. And force goes up from the place of shaping. Your plane crashed against that force."

Some of Huygens' confusion was gone, but a mystery remained. "Who are you?" he said to the woman who looked so uncannily like Joan. "What are you doing here?"

"I am Miranda," she answered readily. "This is where I live."

"But—" Huygens bit his lip. He fell silent, his head lowered, as he tried to think.

Ross and Sokeman were talking behind him. He heard Sokeman say something about the rucksack of food Ross had left behind at the camping place, and then remark, "I'm not hungry. That's strange. We haven't had anything to eat today."

"I don't think we need to eat here," Ross answered. In a more intimate tone he said, "What are you going to make for yourself, Chet?" There was a pause. Then, for answer, came only Sokeman's nervous laugh.

The place of shaping surprised Dirk. He had been expecting he hardly knew what—an amphitheatre, a building like a temple, a huge cave. But Miranda merely led them to a level spot, clear of trees, where the white mists that floated over the island were almost chokingly thick. Then, as he peered and strained his eyes, he saw, very dimly through the mist, the outline of a huge, a gigantic, a cyclopean pair of hands. The fingers of one hand rested lightly on the back of the other, and though the hands were as quiet as if they had been hewn out of stone, it was as if they but rested from the labour of creation, and would again create.

"Go no nearer," Miranda said warningly. "Do you see the line?" She indicated a luminous mark, as slender as a thread, that ran off on both sides into the thick white mist. "You must not step over that. It is very dangerous.

"Now, this is the way that the shaping is done. The one who would create his desire for himself kneels in front of the line and stretches his hands over the line into the fog. And what he wants he thinks of with all his heart and his soul and his hope. And the Hands shape his desire for him.

"Dirk, I am not that Joan whom you lost. Will you be the first to use the Hands? Will you have the Hands shape her again for you?"

Huygens' heart gave a bound. He realized now that he had repressed awareness of the possibility of which Miranda spoke into the depths of his brain. It was impossible, it was wonderful, it was horrible. He thought of the child, inert as a dummy, he had seen on the woman's lap in the hut. He thought of the blank, fatuous faces of the men who had danced with the woman in the violet dress. "Would she—would she be really Joan?" he asked. "Would what I made be Joan the way she really was?"

Miranda raised her shoulders in a tiny shrug. "There are two things, I think, that determine what the hands shape. One is the force of the longing, the force of the desire. The other is the clearness of the image in the mind. But if the shaper does not like what the Hands have shaped for him, he can let the creation slip back into the mist.

"One thing more I must tell you. You may use the Hands for shaping but once. You may stay here as long as you like, having the Hands shape and reshape your desire for you, until it is as close as may be to what is in your heart. But once you have taken your hands from the fog, you can never put them in again. No one is strong enough. You would be lost."

"A radiation," the part of Huygens' brain which could still function was saying. "Perhaps a radiation to which a second exposure brings death... Joan, Joan, Joan! What shall I do?"

Miranda was studying him with her hazel eyes. "Let one of the others be first, then," she said. "Watch one of them use the Hands, Dirk."

Sokeman stepped forward. His greyish face was faintly flushed. He knelt down on the ground. Slowly he stretched out his hands over the line into the fog. They disappeared. And the gigantic Hands in the fog before him—were they a long way off, or were they close?—began to stir.

Sokeman's eyes were closed. He seemed to be barely breathing. The Hands hesitated, trembled. Then, working in the mist like a sculptor shaping plastic clay, they began to create.

An opalescent flask of xoanon floated phantasmagorically in the mist. It faded, was followed by a succession of bottles and flasks. Dirk recognized one or two liquors which had the reputation of being nerve poisons among them. A stack of currency flicked into being and out of it again. There followed more bottles and flasks.

"None of those is what he really wants," Miranda said softly in Dirk's ear. "Wait. He will get over being shy in a little while."

The Hands paused. Then they began to work again, but not as before. This time there was a purpose and intentness which had been lacking. The Hands worked in the fog, slowly and thoughtfully, for a long time. Sokeman's face had a dark, congested, look. But at last he drew his hands out of the fog. There was a golden phial in one of them.

"What is it?" Dirk said to Miranda.

"A drug, I think. Yes." Sokeman had gone a few steps with the phial in his hand. Now he halted, half-turned away from them, and tipped something from the phial on the back of his wrist. He raised the wrist to his lips and touched it with the tip of his tongue.

"Will you be next, Dirk?" Miranda said.

"I—" He saw that her whole body was trembling. Her hands were clenched until the knuckles were white. "Why do you want me to try?" he asked.

She looked so exactly like Joan as she answered, "Because, because I have to know," that a wave of longing swept over him. Without a word he knelt down by the shining line and thrust his hands into the mist.

It was as if he had plunged them into a swift cold stream. The force seemed to tug and wrench at his body. And along with the sensation of coldness and swift motion there was a peculiar languor and fatigue, as if his will were being sucked away from him.

Huygens bit his lip. The Hands were stirring. With all his force he brought Joan before his mind, Joan as she had been one day late in spring when they had gone cruising among the islands. She had stood by the prow of the cruiser, leaning forward into the wind and laughing, and her youth had been like the flash of the sun on the ripple of the water.

He could not live without her. He would bring her back.

The Hands paused in their labour. Joan moved toward him through the mist, smiling, her head held high: and if there was a blankness in her eyes, he could ignore it, he needed her so. But when she was almost up to him she wavered like a reflection in disturbed water. For all his desperate trying she grew dimmer and at last dissolved. There was nothing there in the mist.

Another phantasm of Joan came toward him. She faded, was replaced by another image and another one. Always they had that curious blankness in the eyes. Dirk felt that his life was going out into the images his desperation created. And yet they would not live.

His mind caught at other aspects of Joan. A wave of perfume— the perfume she had used—came toward him from the mist. It was fresh and mysterious and exciting all at once; it made his heart pound with longing for her. For a moment, before the perfume floated away, Huygens felt the warmth and enveloping tenderness of Joan so clearly that he was certain she must be standing beside him. Then the perfume faded and a second later the sense of Joan's physical presence went too. Huygens, his hands tingling with that cold languor, strove desperately to bring her image before his mind once more. But something always eluded him in her—the look in the eyes, the lift of the chin, the shape of the face.

He kept on trying long after he knew its hopelessness. Time after time he created, while Miranda waited patiently. The Joans he made had grown as frail as candle-smoke, before he gave up at last. He turned to Miranda and said, "I loved her, though."

"Yes." Miranda's face was expressionless, but she seemed taller than she had been, and her eyes glowed. After a moment she said, "I think that is why you could not make her, Dirk. When a man loves a woman, he cannot detach her enough from him to see her clearly. His love for her makes a mist. Joan was not a woman for you, but a climate within which you could feel and think. *He*—" she motioned to Ross, who had knelt down by the line as soon as Huygens had risen—"will have no such difficulty in shaping a woman for himself."

It was true, the Hands were shaping a voluptuous, full-bodied woman for the other pilot. He was grinning and his eyes were hard. Huygens watched unseeingly for a moment. Then he turned away.

"Where are you going?" Miranda asked quickly.

"Back to the wreck of Joan's plane. To bury her."

He had buried her, and night had come on. Now he sat sleepless under one of the black trees and listened to the hiss… hiss… hiss… of the waves as they rolled on the beach. His mind was full of loss and pain.

A shadow moved. Miranda came toward him. She sat down beside him. For a time there was silence. Then Miranda said in her sweet voice, "Do not grieve so, Dirk."

He turned on her savagely. "Don't grieve! When I've lost her! When—" He could not go on.

"Poor Dirk."

"Who are you, Miranda? I know you're not Joan. But you're so like her... I keep thinking that you'll say to me, 'Yes, I'm Joan. It was only a joke, I was only teasing you. I won't tease you any more. I'm Joan, your wife.'"

Miranda laid her hand over his and he felt such a warmth of tenderness flow out from her that it dizzied him. He caught at her, not in desire, but in loneliness and despair. "Whoever you are—Oh, be Joan! Be Joan!" he said.

She put her arms around him tenderly. "Dirk, sweetheart. Darling. Oh, yes. I'm whoever you want me to be."

When the grey day had come and it was light, he said to her, "Why do you look at me so much, Miranda? Whenever I look at you, you are watching me."

She scooped up sand and let it trickle through her fingers. "Because I love you, Dirk," she answered. "I love to look at you."

"But—don't you ever think about anything except me? Is love all you ever think about?"

She raised her eyebrows a little, as if she were surprised. "Why, yes. What else should I think of? What else is there in life but love?"

"You're a strange woman, Miranda."

She took his hand and put it against her breast so he could feel the beating of her heart. "I'm not strange." she said earnestly. "Do you feel my heart beating? It beats because I love you. I'm a woman who… who was made to give and receive love."

Huygens looked at her and nodded. "Yes," he answered sombrely.

The next night was nearly over when Huygens woke abruptly from sleep. He had been dreaming of Joan. For a moment he lay listening to Miranda's quiet breathing. Then he put out his hand to wake her. He had buried Joan two days ago. But in this moment he knew, with perfect and unshakable conviction, that Joan was not dead.

Miranda roused at his touch. She sat up, and even in the darkness he knew that she was smiling. "What is it, Dirk?"

"Where is Joan?"

She drew away from him. "She is dead. You… buried her yourself."

"She is not dead." He caught her wrist in a savage grip. "You know where she is. Tell me. If you won't, I'll make you tell."

"You're hurting me," Miranda said sadly. "… It wasn't enough, was it? I might have known. But you can't get her back, Dirk."

"Where is she?"

"In the place of shaping. Inside the mist."

He got to his feet. Miranda sprang up after him, in quick alarm. "You can't go after her. If you do, you will never come out."

"Even if that was true," he said quietly, "do you think I'd stay here? When Joan is still alive?"

Miranda said nothing more. She watched and followed him to the place of shaping. He felt a moment of pity for her as she stood there, so quiet and lonely. "Goodbye," he said. Then he stepped over the line into the mist.

It was as if he had stepped into a roaring world of greenish glass. A current caught at him fiercely, and he felt himself toppling. He struggled against it, and it noosed itself treacherously about his knees and sent him sideways, up, about, down, and up again. His muscles flexed to fight it; then he remembered that Joan, somewhere within this glassy flux, must have been gripped by the current as he was. Wisely he ceased to resist.

Time passed, if there time had meaning. There were desperate eddies, whirlpools, watery precipices. Sometimes he seemed to be climbing shuddering crystal alps or leaping incredible crevices. He toiled onward over a plain of vitreous volcanic rock. And always, mingled with his exertions, real or unreal, came the awareness that will and intelligence were leaving him.

The motion slackened at last. He was borne almost gently on. He floated to a halt and stranded, as if whatever had carried him hither had abandoned him. Torpidly he felt that he had come to the dead centre of things. Everything ended here, in sleep and uncreation, in the ambiguous twilight haze.

Joan was somewhere, needed him. He would not sleep. Desperately he roused himself and stared around the sad, dull-coloured expanse. Fragments of creation floated by him—wraith-like faces, dim jewels, disarticulated limbs. And with these were stranger shapes and constructions, contours of which he could find no analogue and no name. Neither at this nor any other time did he see any sign of the Hands.

Joan came toward him, smiling, and another Joan after her and another. There were ten, twenty, a hundred. And still they seemed to form from the haze like bubbles and break as bubbles break. They stood about him smiling dimly, and he saw with dull eyes that for every Joan a phantom Dirk Huygens had sprung up and stood holding out his vague arms to her.

Lethargy weighed on him always more heavily. He tried to walk toward the wavering phantoms and found that his limbs were remote and disobedient as if a dream. He sank to his knees and crawled a little way. Then he fell over on his side and sleep claimed him utterly.

At the centre of him something was groaning and crying out and striving to waken him, as a man might beat on a stone wall with ineffectual hands. He roused a little at last, and then more, as fear grew in him. The unsleeping sentinel in the depths of the mind told him clearly that if he slept again he would not wake. This was his last chance. He must find Joan now or lie sleeping on the dun-coloured plain until time had come to an end. But his torpor was dreadful, like a crushing burden. He could scarcely breathe under it.

He sank his teeth into his lower lip with all his strength. The flesh broke. As the blood began to trickle his head cleared.

Where could Joan be? Had the myriad phantom Joans come from her? If the current that had floated him here had brought her too, she could not be far. But near and far, in this ambiguous place, were all one. He looked around and thought he saw a low mound disturb the plain ahead. He plodded toward it. But when he reached it it was the body of a man, flattened by slumber, who might have been lying there for centuries while sleep silted over him. And Huygens' heavy eyes could make out no other mound against the dead level of the plain.

A leaden hopelessness came over him. He wanted to lie down beside the unknown man and let sleep drown him. To fight the desire, he ground his teeth into his already wounded lip. And as pain burned along his nerves he felt, for a moment only, the pointing of the compass in his head.

He gasped with relief. At a stumbling run he started toward the point to which it had directed him. And though he moved more and more slowly—it was as though the spot toward which he struggled was the source of the vast choking lethargy which lay on everything—he never stopped moving. He toiled through thickening cob-webs for a time that might have been centuries. And he came to Joan at last.

It was real Joan. She lay in a shallow depression into which she had drifted, and she was as wan and bloodless as the twilight around her. There was a jagged scar under her left breast, as if whatever wound she had received had healed distortedly. But she was alive.

He gathered her in his arms and kissed her. She stirred and opened drowned eyes to him. "Oh… Dirk… How alive you are! I dreamed of you. Have I been dead?"

"Get up, Joan," he said thickly. "We have to—to—" He could not remember the word.

"Go to sleep," she said, as if to a child. "This place hates us awake. We are too alive for it. Go back to sleep." She was sinking away from his embrace.

He dug his nails into her wrist. She gave a tiny cry, and he pulled her to her feet. "Wake up!" he said desperately.

"Ah, why? We can never leave."

It was true, he saw. How could he push his way alone, much less cumbered with Joan, through the glassy torrent that had floated him here? Awake, Joan and he vexed this sad, dun-coloured world;

and it would cover them with layer upon layer of lethargy. They could never escape.

It did not much matter. But he had wanted her when he was awake. He would kiss her once more before sleep covered them.

He tipped her head up and put his lips to hers. And because it was Joan's mouth he touched, the contact was sweet to him.

She stirred and put her arms around his shoulders. "When you touch me," she said laboriously, "I feel more awake." She managed to smile at him.

More awake. Yes, it was as if between their two bodies they sheltered a tiny warmth of consciousness from the chill lethargy of this dead place. He kissed her again, embracing her tenderly, and before he had taken his lips from hers he felt a weak current fretting at his heels.

The current which had seized him when he stepped over the shining line into the place of shaping had been glassy and smooth, for all its violence. But even in its infancy this new force was as jagged and rough as if it flowed flint knives. Cross currents jarred and warred within it, and as its strength increased he felt his flesh wounded by it a thousand times.

The noise it made was a confused, painful screaming. Joan said almost inaudibly, "… to get rid of us." The sound of the flow rose to a rattling hysteria. Then Huygens clasped his wife in a rigid grip and the jagged torrent closed over them.

They were hurled head over heels with crazy violence. Dirk had hallucinated moments when he felt they were standing motionless on a broad plain while rocks beat up at them. He forced Joan's head down against his shoulder to protect her face, and as well as he could he sheltered her with his body and his limbs. There were times when the current would run smooth as glass, and he dreaded these times most, for then the numbing lethargy would come over him again. He knew that if his grip on Joan relaxed now she would be lost utterly, hopelessly.

They were dropping through jagged stars from a high, high cliff. The stars burned his flesh like fire, and he held Joan in a tighter grasp. They rose through a mesh of stinging fireflies, they sank into a pit whose stone sides rustled cruelly at them. No, they were still standing in the autumnal haze, embracing benumbedly. The current was beating against them bitterly, like hail. And suddenly Dirk knew that its tormented force had brought them to the edge of its world, to the shining line.

There was some reason, Dirk knew, why he and Joan must get over it. Some reason... But he could not remember what the reason was. And who was Joan? Who was Dirk?

The current welled up in a glassy crescendo. Joan was half torn from his arms. He struggled after her wildly, caught her by one wrist. Still holding her, he fought upward through an excoriating rain. Though he had forgotten who he was, he knew that it was laid on him as a law to battle upward, never to let Joan go.

The moment tautened like a bow string. Dirk made a last, consuming effort. And then he and Joan were over the line.

They lay exhausted on the ground for many minutes, like people half-drowned. When Dirk's strength had come back a little, he went to the place where he and the others had camped on the first night, and brought back blankets and the aid kit. He smoothed ointment over Joan's bleeding limbs and covered her with the blankets. He looked toward the Hands, wondering at the difference between what seemed to be reality on this side of the line and on that. Then he lay down beside her and fell instantly into deep natural sleep.

It was nearly a day later when he awoke. Miranda was standing near him.

She looked at him and Joan. Her face was white. Slowly she said, "You brought her back, then, Dirk." Her voice was sweet as she said it, and for all her pallor Dirk thought he had never seen a woman as beautiful.

Joan stirred and sat up. She looked at Miranda and her eyes widened. She got to her feet. "You lived, then," she said.

Miranda laughed. "Sister—mother—" she answered, "why should I not live?"

Dirk drew in his breath. He stared at their two faces, so uncannily alike. "What does she mean?" he asked his wife.

"That I made her," Joan said.

There was an instant's silence. The words he had just heard echoed meaninglessly in Dirk Huygens' brain. Then Joan said, "I made her, you see. When my plane crashed on the island, I was badly hurt. I knew I had not long to live, and I knew what island this was. I didn't want to die.

"I went to the place of shaping. It was a hard trip for me. When I got there I knelt by the line and put my hands into the mist. And I had the Hands shape Joan, shape my own self, for me.

"I didn't want to die, you see, Dirk, and I thought that if another Joan, a Joan just like me, lived on, I would not be really dead. But when Joan came out of the mist to me I knew that I had not made her well. Her face was vacant and strange, and she moved weakly, as if she was barely alive." Dirk started. He looked at Miranda and knew by her expression that his surmise was right. "She did not live," he said to Joan. "She went back to the wreck of the plane and died there. I buried her."

Joan nodded. "It was wrong," she said, twisting her fingers. "I should not have done it. It was wrong.

"When I saw that the second Joan would not go on living, I tried again. I put my hands back into the mist—Oh, how strong the current was, it pulled like death!—and had the Hands shape for me once more. And this time they shaped Miranda.

"Miranda, Dirk, is Joan as I always wanted her to be. When I made her I made myself after the pattern of a secret dream I had. She is more beautiful than I, taller, she has a sweeter voice. Even her name is different from mine. I never liked my name."

Comprehension was coming to Huygens. Miranda, then, was Joan's idealized picture of herself. Even the gem-set wedding ring on Miranda's hand—Joan had said once that she preferred gem-set bands to plain.

"I made her with all the strength and longing that were in me. I made her loving you, Dirk, because I was dying and was sick for you. And when she came out of the mist toward me I saw that she was well made and would live.

"I fainted then. The current swept me away with it. And after that there was nothing except sleep and heavy dreams, Dirk, until you came and woke me up. You brought me back to life." She turned to her husband. Dirk drew her to him and held her for a moment, embraced.

"You have won, real woman," Miranda said bitterly. "You have taken the real man from me, who am not quite real. Take him and have your desire of him, then. But I had him once." She put her hands over her eyes.

Joan took a step toward her. "Forgive me, Miranda," she said humbly. "I should never have shaped you. Forgive me for it." There were tears on her cheeks.

Miranda uncovered her face. She was as pale as death, but Dirk saw that she was dry-eyed. "You have done me no wrong," she said proudly. "Take your man and go. There are boats on the beach. I wish you joy of him. Goodbye." She turned away.

"What will you do, Miranda?" Joan asked, weeping. "What will become of you?"

"Oh, I?" Miranda said. She laughed. "I will go to the place of shaping and make Dirk for myself. I will shape him with all the love that is in me, and he will love me and be my desire. And if he is not quite real, why, neither am I quite real." She started through the trees.

Joan cried out in pity. She would have gone after Miranda, but Dirk held her back. "Let her go," he said, though he was deeply troubled. "We cannot help her. This is best for her."

For a moment he and Joan looked at Miranda as she walked away, her head high. Dirk knew that he would remember Miranda, her beauty and the love she had given him, to the end of his days. Then he and Joan started down to the beach, toward the clean, effacing sea and the boats which would take them away.

THE UNWANTED

Mary Elizabeth Counselman

Mary Elizabeth Counselman (1911–1995) was a poet and short-story writer who became known as "The Queen of Weird Tales*" because of the popularity of her thirty stories in that magazine. She contributed to many periodicals, including* Collier's Weekly, Saturday Evening Post *and* Jungle Stories *but it was her appearances in* Weird Tales *that were the most memorable. Her first story was "The House of Shadows" (1933), and several others, including "The Shot-Tower Ghost" (1949) and "The Green Window" (1949), were inspired by her own direct experiences. Her best-known story, "The Three Marked Pennies", was regarded as one of the most popular the magazine published. Several of her strange stories were collected in* Half in Shadow *(1964; reprinted with several different stories in 1978) whilst* African Yesterdays *(1975) brought together her stories based on native African folklore. The following is perhaps the most poignant story* Weird Tales *published.*

TRUDGING UP THE STONY MOUNTAIN ROAD, WITH THE relentless Alabama sun beating down on my head, I began to wish two things, in order of their intensity: I wished I had a big, cold, frosted-over glass of something—iced tea, lemonade, water, anything wet. And I wished I had never applied to my prolific Uncle Sam for this job as census-taker!

I sat down under a gnarled old tree, glaring up at the steep incline ahead of me, and decided that there are entirely too many citizens of the United States, and that they live too far apart. The district I was supposed to cover was a section of the Blue Ridge foothills, in which all the inhabitants were said to have one leg shorter than the other—from living on that sheer cliff of a mountain! Already I had covered the few scattered farms along this winding road that seemed determined to end at the gates of Heaven. Suspicious mountain-eyes had peeked at me from every cranny of wind-worn little shacks, built of slab pine. Lean old hound dogs had run out at me, roaring annihilation, then leaping up to lick me all over the face. Small tow-headed children in flour-sack dresses scattered before me like chickens before a hawk.

But they had to be counted, every blessed one of them. Uncle Sam loved them all, and most of them were on his personal relief-list, up here on Bent Mountain where nothing but honeysuckle and dogwood could be made to grow without a maximum of effort.

I sat for a minute, panting and mopping the perspiration—no, sweat! This was nothing to Emily Post! Then I shifted my big leather folder to the other aching arm and started up the mountain once more. Just ahead, over the tops of scrub pine and oak, I could see a thin curl of smoke—indicating that I had either come to another cabin, or had unfortunately stumbled on somebody's still. Pausing only to examine a blister on my heel, I climbed the hill towards that beckoning smoke-puff. If it was a farm, they would have water of sorts; if it was a still, I would take a drink of "white lightning", and nothing else would matter after that!

Rounding a turn in the snake-like road, I came upon a typical mountain cabin, like any of a score of others I had stopped at this morning. Bright red peppers were hanging in strings from the rafters of a low front stoop, built on to the front of a slab-pine shack. There was the usual gourdpole standing, gaunt and skeletal, in the yard. Martins darted in and out of the hanging gourd bird-houses, those professional hawk-warners for the chickens that clucked and scratched about the yard. Then, bubbling up clear and sweet as the one Moses struck from a rock, I saw a mountain spring just beyond the house. A gourd-dipper hung beside it, and a large water-melon lay chilling in its depths beside two brown crocks of milk or butter. With a faint moan I headed for this oasis—

And stopped short.

A tall, spare mountaineer with a bushy red beard and a missing right arm had appeared, as though the rocky ground had sprouted him. His narrow blue eyes held an expression almost identical to the look of the rifle bore he held cradled in his left arm. It was pointed directly at my heart, which was pounding against my ribs like a trapped rabbit.

But I managed to smile. "Good morning, sir. I'm here to take the census... Are you the head of the house?"

The blue eyes narrowed a fraction. Their owner spat. I heard the click of a cocked rifle as he frowned, as though puzzled at the word "census"; then, in a deep rusty drawl:

"You ain't takin' nothin' around here, Ma'm. Git! Besides," he added with simple dignity, "we ain't got nary'ne. We're pore folks…"

I stifled a giggle, managing to keep my face straight with an effort—in spite of that deadly-looking weapon levelled at my chest.

"No, no. I mean… The Government sent me to…"

At the word, my unwilling host stiffened a bit more. His cold eyes flicked a look at my official folder, and he snorted.

"We don't want no re-lief!" he snapped. "Them as can't do for theirselves—like them shif'less Hambys down the road!—you give them your relief! Me and Marthy can keep keer of one 'nother!"

A grin of admiration crept over my face at sight of this one-armed, undernourished old hellion, standing here on his little piece of unfertile land and defying the whole world to help or hinder him. This, I thought, is our American heritage. Pioneers like these hill-people had made our nation what it is today. But some of them, like this old farmer, were still pioneering, still fighting to carve a living out of wilderness and weather. He didn't think of himself as a "citizen", didn't trade on it, and had probably never voted or paid taxes in his life. But he was an American, all right!

"Look," I said gently. "All I'm supposed to do is take your name, and the names of all your family. For the files in Washington. They have to know how many people there are in the country. Every ten years, we…"

"How-come?" he asked simply. "How-come they want to know about us? Me and Marthy don't bother nobody. Don't ask favours.

Don't aim fer nobody to push us around. We jest want to be let alone. Was anybody down in the bed, I reckon we'd help 'em. Rest o' the time—leave us be!"

I gulped, telling myself that here, again, was a typical American. It was obvious that my "basic questions" would be roundly resented by this two-fisted individualist, and certainly not answered unless I resorted to a sneak-approach.

I shrugged, and laid my folder down on a sawed-off stump.

"All right, Mr... er? I didn't catch the name?"

"I don't aim to drop it," the old hellion answered dryly, but a twinkle of humour came into those rifle-eyes of his. The muzzle of his weapon lowered only a fraction. He jerked his thumb towards the spring. "You dry? Git ye a drink, if you're a mind to. Then," he added politely but firmly, "I reckon you'll be on your way? Got a tin lizzie someplace?"

"Parked down at Stoots General Store. I had to walk the rest of the way," I let my voice fall an octave, forlornly, hoping to play on his sympathy. After all, he was a citizen, and I was being paid, not to hike up and down these mountains, but to list the people living on them. "Think your... er, wife?... would mind if I sat down on that cool-looking porch for a minute and caught my breath? Folks who live in town," I added, grinning at him and trying flattery, "live from side to side. Not up and down, like you-all around these parts! I wouldn't last a week!"

That drew a chuckle from him. But the rifle was still pointed in my general direction. Then I saw him stiffen, looking past my shoulder at someone. He frowned; shook his head slightly. But I turned too quickly—in time to see a frail, quiet-looking, little woman with greying hair and soft luminous dark eyes peeking out at me from the cabin doorway. She started to duck back out of sight, in obedience to the man's headshake. Then she seemed to think better of it, and stepped out into full view. There was a kind of glow about her face, a warm happy look, that drew me at once.

"Why, Jared!" she scolded in a mild sweet drawl. "Didn' you ask the lady to come in and set? Shame on you!" She winked at me cheerfully, a woman's wink, sharing the eccentricities of menfolk as our mutual cross. "I reckon you're jest plumb tuckered out, ain't you, ma'm? Why, come in! I'll send one o' the childurn to the sprang to fetch ye a cold drink o' buttermilk. Don't nothin' cool me off like buttermilk, of a hot day!" she chattered on hospitably, then raised her voice. "Tommee! Cleavydel!... Now, where'd them young 'uns git off to? Berry-pickin', I'll be bound... Raynell! Woodrow!" she shouted again, then gave up, shaking her head and smiling.

I hesitated, glancing back at the man with the rifle... and caught a peculiar look of alarm on his bearded face. He opened his mouth once as though about to protest, then sighed, and turned away to the spring.

"I'll fetch the buttermilk," he offered gruffly. "I... I reckon Marthy would like a mite o' company now and then, at that. Man-person don't take no stock in visitin'!"

"Well," I hesitated, as he strode out of earshot. "I'm not exactly here for a visit—" I eyed the little woman, whose bright eyes instantly took on a look of sensitive withdrawal.

"Oh—! You... you ain't from County Welfare?" she faltered. "Jared, he's not agin any kind of charity. Even the soldier kind. He lost that—'ere arm of his'n in the German war. Come back here to his pa's place and found it growed up in weeds, all his folks died off. Typhoid. I... I..." She flushed, and lowered her eyes. "I was only a girl-baby when I first seen him, a-huntin' rabbits with that one arm. Took a shine to one another first sight, and I run off from my daddy to marry him..."

She stopped, as if shocked at the flood of pent-up conversation that burst from her at sight of another woman. From what the old man had said, I sensed that she did not have the pleasure of much company, up here off the beaten trail. Church-going was about the only recreation most of these mountain women had, anyway; and there was something withdrawn about this household. I had sensed it before, though there was nothing I could put my finger on and call it "unusual". This middle-aged couple seemed a cross-section of the mountaineer families I had encountered today and yesterday, on my census-taking trek over the district assigned me. All were poor. All were suspicious, more or less, of the personal questions I had to ask. All had large families of children.

I sat down on the porch and opened my folder, smiling. "No, no," I answered her question. "The Government makes a... a list of all the folks living in this country, and I'm here to ask you a few questions. About your family and your farm... Your name is—?" I waited, pencil poised.

The little grey woman's face cleared. "Oh!" She beamed "I... I catch on now to what you...! Our oldest boy told me about it, just yesterday. Said a lady was over to Baldy Gap, askin' questions for the Gover'mint. Likely 't'was you, yourself?" I nodded, beaming back at her.

"Well, then!" she said eagerly. "I'll be happy and glad to answer ye. Jared," she lowered her voice apologetically, "he's a mite ill at strangers. Don't you take hurt by nothin' he says!"

I sat back in the split-bottom rocker, thankful to get the business over with so smoothly. Their name, I learned, was Forney. Jared C. The "C." was just an initial; it didn't stand for anything. Jared's mother had simply thought it sounded well. Martha Ann was her name, aged forty-eight to her husband's sixty-seven. They had, she said brightly, eleven children. Woodrow was the oldest. The youngest, a baby in arms, was not yet named. He was simply called "the least one".

Smiling, I jotted down the names in my book, then asked Martha Forney to supply their birth dates. Rocking gently, she ticked them off with the fond memory of any mother. I stopped, frowning slightly at one apparent error in my figures...

"Oh—I'm sorry! I must have got the names mixed." I laughed gaily. "I have the birthday of your youngest child listed as second! 1934..."

Martha Forney turned towards me, her great luminous eyes glowing with matter-of-fact pride at having mothered this large brood.

"10th May... 1934?" She corroborated the figures I had set down, then nodded happily. "Yes, that's right. That's when the least'ne come to us. Woodrow, he was the first. I reckon on account of Jared's arm and us needing a half-growed boy to help us around the place. But then," she burst out shyly, "I... I got to honin' for a little'ne. One I could hold in my arms... And the next mornin', why, there he was! Nestled down in the bed on my side, a -kickin' the covers and cooin' like a turtledove...!"

My jaws dropped. I blinked, peering at my cheery-voiced hostess with a look of shock. Then, I jumped. Jared Forney was looming over me, with a crock of buttermilk held in the crook of his one arm. His bearded face was like a thundercloud of anger, with flashes of lethal lightning darting from those cold blue eyes.

With an ominous thump he set down the crock and towered above me, single fist clenched as though he seriously debated smashing it into my startled face.

"Marthy!" he snapped. "Git on into the house!... And you," he glared at me. "You jest git! You got no call to come sneakin' around our place, a-progin' into things that don't consarn you... and a-pokin' fun at them that's afficted!"

Afficted? I glanced at that stump of an arm, wondering if that was what he referred to. But the gentle, protective look he threw after his wife's meekly retreating figure made me wonder. Then suddenly I remembered those weirdly garbled figures on my census sheet, and thought I understood.

"Oh, I... I'm terribly sorry," I murmured. "I... just didn't understand. She... she was telling me about the children, their names, and when they were born..."

"We got no young'nes," the old man cut me off, very quietly. "You mustn't mind Marthy. She's... not right in her head. And you oughtn't to been pesterin' her, upsettin' her with all them questions...!" he fired at me fiercely. "Ma'm, if there's anything important you want to ask, ask me! And then, I'll thank ye to git off'n my property and back where you belong!"

"Yes. Yes, of course," I nodded humbly, and managed to stammer out the last few questions about crops, acreage, and the rest, which the old fellow answered in a flat gruff voice. I scribbled down the information hurriedly, and was about to get to hell out of there, when I happened to glance back at the cabin door.

The little grey-haired woman was standing just inside, half in shadow, half in clear mountain sunlight that slanted through the pines overhead. Her arms cuddled a wad of clothing close to her breast, and as she bent over it, crooning, I thought I saw a baby's small chubby hand wave from the folds of the cloth, playfully patting at her cheek.

I whirled to face the old man, frowning. "I thought you had no children," I called his hand rather coolly; then decided that their offspring must be illegitimate, to account for his queer attitude. My face softened. "Everybody," I said kindly, "is entitled to his status as a citizen of this country, Mr Forney. Your baby is, too. He's entitled to free education, the right to vote when he's twenty-one, the right to apply for certain benefits..."

My words broke off, like glass. Jared Forney was staring at me as if I had taken leave of my senses. His blue eyes darted towards his wife, then back to me with a shocked, amazed expression I shall never forget.

"You... you see it?" he whispered sharply. "You see ary baby...?"

I gaped at him, then glanced back at the woman, at the cooing child in her arms. A soft rounded little cheek peeped out from the folds of the old dress, which she held lightly in her embrace, rocking it. I saw a tendril of curly blond hair, a flash of big innocent baby-eyes. I turned back to Jared Forney, deciding that he, and not his quiet gentle little wife, was the mental case. Anyone could mix the birth dates of eleven children, especially a vague, unlettered mountain woman like Mrs Forney.

"See it?" I echoed, puzzled. "See what, the baby? Of course I do! You weren't trying to hide it? Surely," I said softly, "you are not ashamed of a sweet little cherub like that?... And I've got to take his name and birth date," I added firmly. "That's the law, Mr Forney. You could be fined and put in jail for withholding information from a census-taker."

The mild threat went right over his head. Jared Forney continued to stare at me, then back at his wife. He shook his head, muttering, then sat down weakly in a chair, mopping his forehead with a great red bandana, pulled from his overall pocket.

"Well, I swannee!" he whispered in a shaken voice. "Well, the Lord holp my time! Well... I... swannee!"

I frowned at him impatiently, pencil raised. "Please, Mr Forney," I pursued the advantage I seemed to have gained, for some reason I could not fathom. "If you have other children, you must tell me their names—or let your wife tell me. It doesn't matter... er... whether they are legally yours..." I began.

Her jerked up his head, glaring at me. "Don't you say nothin' like that about Marthy!" he cut me short. "There ain't a finer, better woman in these hills than my old 'oman! Even if... even if she is a mite..." He gulped, casting another wary glance at the quiet figure with that baby in her arms. Then, swallowing twice, he called uncertainly: "Woodrow? where are ye at, son? Cleavydel? Tom? Raynell...?"

Instantly, at his call, a group of children appeared from the shadowy pine coppice at our left. Sunlight, slanting golden through the quill-like leaves, made my eyes burn and smart, so that I could not see their faces clearly. But as they moved forward, in a smiling group, I made out the features of two young girls in their teens, a small boy of perhaps eleven, and a tall youth in his early twenties. They were all strong, healthy-looking children, in spite of a pronounced pallor that was unusual among these sun-tanned mountaineers. They were dressed in neat flour-sack shifts, or cut-down overalls, obviously having belonged to their father. All four were bare-footed, and swinging lard-cans brimful of blackberries. I remember thinking it odd at the time that none of their faces and hands were stained with the dark purple juice... but perhaps they had removed these berry stains at the spring on their way to the cabin. What struck me as especially odd was their colouring.

The two girls were completely unalike, and would never have been taken for sisters. One was sturdy and dark, the other slim and blonde. The boys were as unlike each other as they were unlike the girls. One, the younger, had a pronounced Eurasian cast to his features, with small black slanted eyes. The older was a redhead, lanky, freckled, and grinning. All of them seemed in high spirits, with a glow of such pure happiness in each face that I could not help glowing back at them.

"What a fine bunch of kids!" I commented to Mrs Forney, with a faint look of reproach for her dour spouse.

Jared Forney gaped at me again, his face paling. He followed my gaze, squinting and shading his eyes against the sun, then shook his head.

"I swannee!" he gulped. "I... I... Ain't nobody but her ever really seen..."

He broke off again, mopping his forehead once more and glancing sheepishly back at his wife.

"Well," I said briskly, "I'm sorry, but I've got to be getting along." I turned back to Mrs Forney again, to ask pleasantly, "Do you have the children's birthdays listed in your family Bible? If you could get it for me, let me copy them..."

Martha Forney glanced past me at her husband, a mild look of accusation.

"I... did have 'em wrote down," she said gently. "Hit was a peddler come by here, and I ast him if he'd write 'em for me. I never learned to read or write..." She confessed timidly. "But I had all the dates in my head, and he wrote down what I told him. Then Jared," again she glanced at the hunched muttering figure, "he seen 'em and tore out the page. Said hit was a sin and a 'bomination to the Lord to write a lie in His Book... But it was Him sent 'em! Every one! I... I know I never birthed ary one of 'em my own self, not like other women have kids. But... I..." She floundered, a vague bewildered look coming into her face as though she puzzled over an old familiar problem, still unsolved to her satisfaction. "I'm their maw..."

Then, suddenly, she turned to me. Those luminous dark eyes, alight with an innocent happiness and devotion, seemed to blot out the poverty and squalor of that small mountain farm, bathing it in a soft golden glow like the sunlight sifting through the trees overhead.

"Ma'm," she said abruptly, in a quiet voice like the murmur of a mountain brook, "Ma'm... You love kids, too, don't ye? You got any young'nes of your own?"

I said I had a little boy, aged six, whom I loved dearly... and added, politely, that I should be getting back to him before suppertime. Martha Forney nodded, beaming. She shot a look of triumph at the old man, who was still muttering under his breath.

"There, Jared!" she said happily. "You see? That's all there is to it. There's some as don't want young'nes," she added sadly. "For one reason or another, they don't want to bring a baby into the world. There's some as destroy... But once they've started, once they've come just so far towards bein' borned, they can't go back—poor mites! All they ever want is... just to be wanted and loved, and mebbe needed, like Woodrow. Why, there must be thousands," she said softly, "a-pushin' and crowdin' outside some place, in hopes somebody'll let 'em come on ahead and be somebody's young'ne. Now, Woodrow, I reckon he waited for years out there, wherever it is they have to wait. He was a real big boy when I... I wanted a son. And," she sighed, happily, "that very evening, I heard somebody choppin' firewood out back o' the cabin. Thought it was Jared... but he was off a-huntin' possum! When he come back and found all that stovewood, he thought I done it—or some neighbour who was wantin' to shame him for leavin' me alone, without ary man-person to do for me. But... it was Woodrow! Jared, he ain't never been able to see his boy a-holpin' him around the place—just sees what he does. He's learned," the little old woman chuckled, "to tell him and then go off some place. When he gits back, the chores is done. Woodrow," she spoke proudly with a note of deep fondness, "he's a right handy boy around a farm. Ain't hardly nothin' he can't turn his hand to!... and," her eyes saddened, "why there was somebody once that didn't want a son like him, I jest can't understand!"

I had sat in wordless amazement, listening to all this. Now it was my turn to gape at Jared Forney, wracking my brain to figure out which of these two old mountain people was the insane one... or whether I was! Out of sheer desire to get my feet on solid earth again, I scribbled some figures on my census sheet, cleared my throat, and asked little Mrs Forney point-blank:

"And… the baby's birthday? He's about… eight months old, isn't he? Some… er… some neighbour left them on your doorstep? They're foster-children, is that it?"

"No ma'm," Martha Forney said clearly. "They're mine! I… I caused 'em to git borned, jest by wishin'… and lovin'. Like an old hen settin' on another hen's eggs!" she chuckled with a matter-of-fact humour that made my scalp stir. "Of course they ain't… ain't regular young'nes. Jared, now, he ain't never seen 'em… exceptin' once when he was likkered up," she said in a tone of mild reproof for past sins. "Fell in a ditch full o' rain water, and liked to drownded! Hit was Cleavydel holped him out… and he was that ashamed before his own daughter, he never has drunk another jugful! Oh! mabbe a nip now and then," she added with a tender tolerant grimace at her errant spouse. "But not, you know, drinkin'. Them kids has been the makin' of Jared," she said complacently. "Time was he'd beat me and go off to town for a week or more," she confided. "But now he knows the young'nes is lookin' up to him… even if he can't see them!… and he's as good a man as you'd find in these hills!"

I almost snickered, noting the sheepish, subdued, and even proud look on the old man's face. Here, indeed, was a fine and loving father… But I still could not understand the origin of that smiling group of children before me, and of the baby in the woman's arms—the baby she said was born before those other three half-grown children!

"Er…" I tried again, helplessly. "Mrs Forney… You mean they're adopted? I mean, not legally adopted, but… You say they were given to you by somebody who didn't want them', as you call it? I… I'm afraid I don't quite…"

"They wasn't give to me," Martha Forney interrupted stoutly, with a fond smile from the baby to the group near the pine coppice. "I taken 'em! They was supposed to be born to some other woman, every last one of 'em! Some woman who didn't want 'em to be born... But I did! You can do anything, if you're a mind to... and the Lord thinks it's right. So," she finished matter-of-factly, "Jared and me have got eleven young'nes. Nary one of 'em looks like us, except Woodrow's a redhead like Jared. But that's accidental, o'course. They look like their real ma and pa... John Henry!" she raised her voice abruptly. "Where are you, son?... John Henry," she explained to me in a half-whisper, "he's kind of timid. Ressie May!" she called again, then sighed: "Folks can think up more reasons for not wantin' young'nes, seems like!"

I rubbed my eyes, staring at the group of children beside the cabin, waiting in a silent, good-humoured group for whatever fond command their parents might issue next. As I looked, two more dim figures—for they all seemed dim, all at once, like figures in an old snapshot, faded by time—joined the others. One, a thin sad-eyed boy of seven, with a markedly Jewish cast to his features, smiled at me and ducked his head shyly, playing with a flower in his hand—a mountain daisy that, oddly enough looked clumsy and solid in the misty fingers that held it. The second new figure—I started—was a little coloured girl. She giggled silently as my gaze fell on her, digging one bare black toe into the dust. On her face, too, was that blissful glow of complete happiness and security from all hurt.

"Ressie May's coloured," Mrs Forney whispered. "But she don't know it! To me, she's jest like all the rest o' my young'nes..."

Suddenly Jared Forney leaped to his feet, glowering down at me.

"I ain't gonna have no more of this!" he thundered nervously. "They... they ain't there, and you both know it! You don't see nary young'ne, and neither does Marthy! I tell her over and over, it's all in her mind—from wantin' a passel o' kids we never could have! She's... sickly, Marthy is. She... Her paw alluz allowed she was a wood's colt, her ownself, and he tuck it out in beatin' her till she run off from him! All that's mixed up in her head, and now... well, she's a mite teched, as folks around here know. Her with her make-like young'nes named Woodrow, and Cleavydel, and... and some of 'em not even of our faith or colour! I... I don't know where she gits all them berries she says the children pick, or how she does all them chores behindst my back—that she makes out like Woodrow done! But... if it made her any happier," he lowered his voice, speaking fiercely for my ears only, "I'd pretend the Devil was takin' the night with us!"

My eyes misted, and I was about to nod in complete sympathy. But he wasn't having any. To this hard-bitten old rascal, I was against him, like the rest of the world, just another menace to his wife's peace of mind.

"And now," he snarled, "you git! You got no call to set there, makin' a mock of them as cain't help theirselves. And laughin', makin' out like you see them young'nes same as she...!"

"But... but I do see..."

I broke off hastily. Jared Forney's rifle had appeared again as if by magic, cradled in that good arm of his... and pointed unwaveringly at my forehead. His left eye sighted along the barrel, drawing a bead on a spot just between my startled eyes... and I didn't stop to protest any longer. There was cold-blooded murder in that squinting blue eye, and a fierce proud protectiveness for that vague little wife of his that brooked no argument.

I turned and ran, hugging my census-folder under my arm and not stopping to pick up a pencil that bounced from behind my ear. I ran, praying. Then I heard the click of a cocked rifle and just ran.

Only once did I so much as glance back over my shoulder at the humble little mountain cabin. When I did... well, it was only a bundle of old clothes that crooning woman was cuddling in her empty arms. There were four lard-buckets brimful of blackberries someone had picked and set down just beyond the pine coppice. But the group of smiling, ill-assorted children had disappeared.

For me, that is, they had disappeared—perhaps because... I don't know. Because I didn't care enough, and it took that to make them live and to keep them alive. Perhaps it was only my devotion to my own little boy that made me see them at all, as Jared Forney's childless wife saw them. Rather sadly, I took out my census sheet, a few yards down the road, and scratched out the names of eleven children that no one—no one but Martha Forney—had wanted to live. Uncle Sam, I realized with a wry smile, might take a dim view of statistics such as those. Dream-children. Wish-children, born only of will and need... and love. The unwanted. The unborn...

But for little old Mrs Forney, their "mother" with the heart as big as all outdoors, I am quite certain that they are very much alive. And the Bureau of Vital Statistics could be wrong!

THE SEVENTH HORSE

Leonora Carrington

Leonora Carrington (1917–2011) was a born rebel, perhaps because her father, a rich businessman in the textile business, was strict. She was expelled from two schools and only settled down when she attended the art school in Florence. She became fascinated with the surrealist art movement and was soon living with the artist Max Ernst, whom she had met in 1937. During the War Ernst was arrested first by the French for being an alien, and then by the Germans, who saw his work as degenerate. He was smuggled out of France to live in the United States, but left Carrington behind. She fled to Spain and then Portugal where, thanks to the Mexican diplomat, she was able to travel to Mexico, where she lived for most of the rest of her life. She had many exhibitions of her art and paintings—she had a special fascination for horses, as evident in the following story. Her writings are every bit as surreal as her art, rather more fantasy than supernatural, but because you never know which way the story will twist, they are always a surprise. Few of her stories were collected at the time they were written and were only generally available in her later life, with The Oval Lady *(1975) and* The Seventh Horse *(1988). Thankfully there has been a recent volume* The Complete Stories of Leonora Carrington *(2017) which showcases her mischievous diversity and imagination.*

A STRANGE-LOOKING CREATURE WAS HOPPING ABOUT IN THE midst of a bramble bush. She was caught by her long hair, which was so closely entwined in the brambles that she could move neither backwards nor forwards. She was cursing and hopping till the blood flowed down her body.

"I do not like the look of it," said one of the two ladies who intended to visit the rose garden.

"It might be a young woman... and yet..."

"This is my garden," replied the other, who was as thin and dry as a stick. "And I strongly object to trespassers. I expect it is my poor silly little husband who has let her in. He is such a child you know."

"I've been here for years," shrieked the creature angrily. "But you are too stupid to have seen me."

"Impertinent as well," remarked the first lady, who was called Miss Myrtle. "I think you had better call the gardener, Mildred. I don't think it is quite safe to go so near. The creature seems to have no modesty."

Hevalino tugged angrily at her hair as if she would like to get at Mildred and her companion. The two ladies turned to go, not before they had exchanged a long look of hate with Hevalino.

The spring evening was lengthening before the gardener came to set Hevalino free.

"John," said Hevalino, lying down on the grass, "can you count up to seven? Do you know that I can hate for seventy-seven million years without stopping for rest. Tell those miserable people that they are doomed." She trailed off towards the stable where she lived, muttering as she went: "Seventy-seven, seventy-seven."

There were certain parts of the garden where all the flowers, trees, and plants grew tangled together. Even on the hottest days these places were in blue shadow. There were deserted figures overgrown with moss, still fountains, and old toys, decapitated and destitute. Nobody went there except Hevalino; she would kneel and eat the short grass and watch a fascinating bird who never moved away from his shadow. He let his shadow glide around him as the day went by and over him when there was a moon. He always sat with his hairy mouth wide open, and moths and little insects would fly in and out.

Hevalino went to see the bird dining the night after she was caught in the brambles. A retinue of six horses accompanied her. They walked seven times around the fat bird in silence.

"Who's there?" said the bird eventually, in a whistling voice.

"It is I, Hevalino, with my six horses."

"You are keeping me awake with your stumping and snorting," came the plaintive reply. "If I cannot sleep I can see neither the past nor the future. I shall waste away if you won't go away and let me sleep."

"They are going to come and kill you," said Hevalino. "You had better keep awake. I heard somebody say you would be roasted in hot fat, stuffed with parsley and onions, and then eaten."

The corpulent bird cast an apprehensive eye on Hevalino, who was watching him closely.

"How do you know?" breathed the bird. "Just tell me that."

"You are much too fat to fly," continued Hevalino relentlessly. "If you tried to fly you'd be like a fat toad doing his death dance."

"How do you know this?" screamed the bird. "They can't know where I am. I've been here for seventy-seven years."

"They don't know yet... not yet." Hevalino had her face close to his open beak; her lips were drawn back and the bird could see her long wolves' teeth.

His fat little body quivered like a jelly.

"What do you want of me?"

Hevalino gave a sort of crooked smile. "Ah, that's better." She and the six horses made a circle around the bird and watched him with their prominent and relentless eyes.

"I want to know exactly what is going on in the house," said she. "And be quick about it." The bird cast a frightened look around him, but the horses had sat down. There was no escape. He became wet with sweat and the feathers clung, draggled, to his fat stomach.

"I cannot say," he said at last in a strangled voice. "Something terrible will befall us if I say what I can see."

"Roasted in hot fat and eaten," said Hevalino.

"You are mad to want to know things that do not concern you...!"

"I am waiting," said Hevalino. The bird gave a long convulsive shudder and turned his eyes, which had become bulging and sightless, to the east.

"They are at dinner," he said eventually, and a great black moth flew out of his mouth.

"The table is laid for three people. Mildred and her husband have begun to eat their soup. She is watching him suspiciously. 'I found something unpleasant in the garden today,' she says, laying down her spoon; I doubt if she will eat any more now.

"'What was that?' asks he. 'Why do you look so angry?'

"Miss Myrtle has now come into the room. She looks from one to the other. She seems to guess what they are discussing, for she says, 'Yes, really, Philip, I think you ought to be more careful whom you let into the garden.'

"'What are you talking about?' he says angrily. 'How do you expect me to stop anything if I don't know what I am stopping?'

"'It was an unpleasant-looking creature half naked and caught in a bramble bush. I had to turn my eyes away.'

"'You let this creature free, of course?'

"'Indeed I did not. I consider it just as well that she was trapped as she was. By the cruel look on her face I should judge she would have done us serious harm.'

"'What! You left this poor creature trapped in the brambles? Mildred, there are times when you revolt me. I am sick of you pottering around the village and annoying the poor with your religious preamble, and now when you see a poor thing in your own garden you do nothing but shudder with false modesty.'

"Mildred gives a shocked cry and covers her face with a slightly soiled handkerchief. 'Philip, why do you say such cruel things to me, your wife?'

"Philip, with an expression of resigned annoyance, asks, 'Try and describe this creature. Is it an animal or a woman?'

"'I can say no more,' sobs the wife. 'After what you have said to me I feel faint.'

"'You should be more careful,' whispers Miss Myrtle. 'In her delicate condition!'

"'What do you mean "delicate condition"?' asks Philip irritably. 'I do wish people would say what they mean.'

"'Why surely you must know,' Miss Myrtle simpers. 'You are going to become a daddy in a short time…' Philip goes white with rage. 'I won't stand these fatuous lies. It is quite impossible that Mildred is pregnant. She has not graced my bed for five whole years, and unless the Holy Ghost is in the house I don't see how it came about. For Mildred is unpleasantly virtuous, and I cannot imagine her abandoning herself to anybody.'

"'Mildred, is this true?' says Miss Myrtle, trembling with delicious expectation. Mildred shrieks and sobs: 'He is a liar. I am going to have a darling little baby in three months.'

"Philip flings down his spoon and serviette and gets to his feet. 'For the seventh time in seven days I shall finish my dinner upstairs,' says he, and stops for an instant as if his words have awakened some memory. He puts it away from him and shakes his head. 'All I ask is that you don't come whining after me,' he says to his wife and quits the room. She shrieks: 'Philip, my darling little husband; come back and eat your soup, I promise I won't be naughty anymore.'

"'Too late,' comes the voice of Philip from the staircase, 'too late now.'

"He goes slowly up to the top of the house with his eyes looking a long way ahead of him. His face is strained as if in the effort of listening to faraway voices chattering between nightmares and dead reality. He reaches the attic at the top of the house, where he seats himself on an old trunk. I believe the trunk is filled with ancient laces, frilly knickers, and dresses. But they are old and torn; there is a black moth making his dinner on them as Philip sits staring at the window. He considers a stuffed hedgepig on the mantel piece, who looks worn out with suffering. Philip seems to be smothered with the atmosphere of this attic; he flings open the window and gives a long..."

Here the bird paused, and a long sickening neigh rent the night. The six horses leapt to their feet and replied in their piercing voices. Hevalino stood stock-still, with her lips drawn back and her nostrils quivering. "Philip, the friend of the horses..." The six horses thundered off towards the stable, as if obeying an age-old summons. Hevalino, with a shuddering sigh, followed, her hair streaming behind her.

Philip was at the stable door as they arrived. His face was luminous and as white as snow. He counted seven horses as they galloped by. He caught the seventh by the mane, and leapt onto her back. The mare galloped as if her heart would burst. And all the time Philip was in a great ecstasy of love; he felt he had grown onto the back of this beautiful black mare, and that they were one creature.

At the crack of dawn all the horses were back in their places. And the little wrinkled groom was rubbing off the caked sweat and mud of the night. His creased face smiled wisely as he rubbed his charges with infinite care. He appeared not to notice the master, who stood alone in an empty stall. But he knew he was there.

"How many horses have I?" said Philip at last.

"Six, sir," said the little groom, without ceasing to smile.

That night the corpse of Mildred was found near the stable. One would believe that she had been trampled to death... and yet "They are all as gentle as lambs," said the little groom. If Mildred had been pregnant there was no sign of it as she was stuffed into a respectable black coffin. However nobody could explain the presence of a small misshapen foal that had found its way into the seventh empty stall.

STORY SOURCES

The following gives the first publication details for each story and the sources used. They are listed in alphabetical order of author.

"The Bishop of Hell" by Marjorie Bowen, first published in *The Blue Magazine*, September 1925 and collected in *The Gorgeous Lovers and Other Stories* (London: Bodley Head, 1929).

"A Revelation" by Mary E. Braddon, first published in *The Misletoe Bough*, Christmas 1888 and collected in *The Cold Embrace and Other Uncollected Ghost Stories* edited by Richard Dalby (Ashcroft, Canada: Ash-Tree Press, 2000).

"The Christmas in the Fog" by Frances Hodgson Burnett, first published in *Good Housekeeping*, December 1914.

"The Seventh Horse" by Leonora Carrington, first published in *VVV* #2–3, 1943 and collected in *The Seventh Horse and Other Tales* (New York: E.P. Dutton, 1988).

"The Sculptor's Angel" by Marie Corelli, first published in *Nash's Magazine*, December 1913 and collected in *The Love of Long Ago and Other Stories* (London: Methuen, 1920).

"The Unwanted" by Mary Elizabeth Counselman, first published in *Weird Tales*, January 1951.

"White Lady" by Sophie Wenzel Ellis, first published in *Strange Tales*, January 1933.

"The Wonderful Tune" by Jessie Douglas Kerruish, first published in *At Dead of Night*, edited by Christine Campbell Thomson (London: Selwyn & Blount, 1931).

"The Antimacassar" by Greye La Spina, first published in *Weird Tales*, May 1949.

"The Haunted Flat" by Marie Belloc Lowndes, first published in *The Grand Magazine*, August 1920.

"From the Dead" by Edith Nesbit, first published in *Illustrated London News*, 8 September 1892 and collected in *Grim Tales* (London: A.D. Innes, 1893).

"The Laughing Thing" by G. G. Pendarves, first published in *Weird Tales*, May 1929.

"A Modern Circe" by Alicia Ramsey, first published in *The Novel Magazine*, December 1919.

"Island of the Hands" by Margaret St Clair, first published in *Weird Tales*, September 1952 and collected in *Three Worlds of Futurity* (New York: Ace Books, 1964).

"The Nature of the Evidence" by May Sinclair, first published in *Fortune*, May 1923 and collected in *Uncanny Stories* (London: Hutchinson, 1923).

"Candlelight" by Lady Eleanor Smith, first published in *The Story-teller*, March 1931 and collected in *Satan's Circus and Other Stories* (London: Gollancz, 1932).

ALSO AVAILABLE

A young girl whose love for her fiancé continues even after her death; a sinister old lady with claw-like hands who cares little for the qualities of her companions provided they are young and full of life; and a haunted mirror that foretells of approaching death for those who gaze into its depths. These are just some of the haunting tales gathered in this classic collection of macabre short stories.

The Face in the Glass is the first selection of Mary Elizabeth Braddon's supernatural short stories to be widely available in more than 100 years. By turns curious, sinister, haunting and terrifying, each tale explores the dark shadows that exist beyond the rational world.

British Library Tales of the Weird collects a thrilling array of uncanny storytelling, from the realms of gothic, supernatural and horror fiction. With stories ranging from the nineteenth century to the present day, this series revives long-lost material from the Library's vaults to thrill again alongside beloved classics of the weird fiction genre.

We welcome any suggestions, corrections or feedback you may have, and will aim to respond to all items addressed to the following:

The Editor (Tales of the Weird), British Library Publishing,
The British Library, 96 Euston Road, London NW1 2DB

We also welcome enquiries through our Twitter account, @BL_Publishing.